The Best of
CARNAGE
House
Year One

Edited by
Josh Darling and Jacque Day

Carnage House, LLC
This is Your Trigger Warning

www.carnagehouse.com

A very special thanks to

Mandy Schonzeit
Art Pallone
Simon Barrett
Jim Darling
Frances Lu-Pai Ippolito
Moaner T. Lawrence
Chris McAuley
Frank Swaim
Mandy Swaim
Jesse Vogelaar
Ary Rae Vogelaar

We couldn't have done this without you.

And to

Clive Barker
Granddaddy of us all

Contents

Introductions

I hate writing intros, so this will be short and sweet and flavored with putrid entrails.

Carnage House started on a whim after I saw multiple writers in the splatterpunk and extreme horror subgenres make social media posts about limited opportunities for short story publishing. It took me months to work up the courage to slap together a website —it was hand coded at the last minute when I couldn't get WordPress to work. Jacque Day, who I think must have been crazy, offered to help, and I realized this would be impossible to do without her.

Since then it's grown.

A lot.

That has nothing to do with me.

No one sees a band and says, "Yo, that was such a kick-ass stage they played on."

"And it was made of wood —those are my favorite."

Carnage House is a stage for celebrating the hard work of storytellers with transgressive voices, the dark, the weird, the gross, the political horror, and the outsider's outsider. We don't do cozy. If there's a shot AI could write it, it probably doesn't meet our community standards.

I could get into how much I've grown because of this e-zine, how I've learned to allow people to help me, how I've become more resilient to adversity, and how I've mastered the art of writing sentences that read like heartfelt platitudes. But my journey doesn't matter. What matters are the stories in this book. It is one of the crowning achievements of my life to work with and publish the authors herein.

No amount of hype will live up to what they've written. That said, I take great pride in presenting to you *The Best of Carnage House: Year One*.

–Josh Darling

Someone wake me up. Or pinch me.

Yeah.

Like that.

Everything Josh said, and this —After he explained the concept for Carnage House to me, I instantly fused with the idea. He envisioned a web publication with no hierarchy, no headliners, saying, "Here, everyone is a star." The platform he labored over for months delivers on that promise. Every time the website is refreshed, the stories appear in a different order. The same with the authors page. Go test it. See for yourself. He also envisioned Carnage House as a space to lift up writers, not only to showcase their work, but also to help writers improve their craft. This was a concept I could get behind, commit to.

This "random" hierarchy is a little harder to bring to a book. (We toyed with the idea of randomizing the running order in every printed copy, but the technology eludes us.) Still, we've clung to the spirit of it, so the stories in this volume appear in no particular hierarchical order. In fact, we didn't choose the order at all —the website, with its randomized code, did. Somewhere there exists video of Josh Darling refreshing the website over and over again and rattling off the list.

All this, we must balance with our work as editors. We took seriously the task of narrowing down a year's worth of contributions into the selections within, which we did with the help of Michael Errol Swaim and Holly Nicholls.

But to echo Josh, it's not about us —it's about the voices that follow. We know they will enthrall you as they have us.

– Jacque Day

A NOTE ON LANGUAGE

No, this isn't a disclaimer about profanity. (Though if you're squeamish about bad swears, buckle up.) This is about our decision to honor the diverse representations of the English language in this volume. Our contributors hail from all over the world, and to standardize the anthology strictly to U.S. English would undermine the voices of our authors across hemispheres and in some cases completely alter the vibe of a story. So we ask you to accept that sometimes local color is local colour, sometimes a neighbor is a neighbour, and sometimes, an ass is an arse.

ZACKARY L. STILLINGS

Lily (Collage)

HE OUTSTRETCHED HIS ARM, holding the sepia-toned photograph *just so*, squinting his right eye just slightly to ensure his vision could capture both the photograph and his canvas. *To create this,* he thought, *on that.*

In the pale sulfuric light, he envisioned what it could be, if only he had the skill. A perfect recreation of the perfect night, a perfect recreation of the perfect *person,* a perfect simulacrum of beauty itself. He lowered the photograph as he adjusted the wick of his oil lamp, so that the canvas was just slightly more illuminated, its pale surface ready for his art, his genius, her radiance.

The photograph had been taken right here, right where his canvas now sat, under the unevenly distributed light of the lamps he used to illuminate his home. One could almost sense the room's color from the photograph, despite its monochromatic tones. A fiery light burned on either side of her, brightening her already porcelain face in contrast to the dark brown of the basement room in which he worked. In the picture she smiled, coquettish, the look of one with a secret she would never tell.

He gazed at her half-smile, angelic and innocent, kissed by torchlight, then muted by the photograph's development, as though her true nature could not be revealed by anything so crude as a camera. He scoffed at his own hubris. An artist, he could be. But to capture the radiance of such a creature required a god.

And yet he had tried. That night, the night he took the photograph, he had *tried,* hunched behind a lens on a tripod, its back end draped like a cape behind him, looking through the camera at her. At her *perfection.* He had held the trigger in his hand outside of the cape. *Just like that, beautiful,* he told her, clicking the mechanism that would illuminate his entire basement in a flood of momentary sunlight. *You're doing great.*

He studied the photograph again, closing his eyes, remembering the first time he glimpsed her. The night had been cold, frightfully so. The kind of cold that turns breath into smoke, makes pedestrians mimic the innumerable stacks dotting the city's soot-covered skyline. The type of cold that stops the carriages from running, that freezes the pipes, that kills the strays.

The tavern had been crowded and humid, pungent with the smells of cheap perfume over body odor, the sweat of men caked with the sediments of factory exhaust. Smoke filled the place, making the lamplight wax and wane in unpredictable patterns as the men of the tavern drew in and exhaled their tobacco. He had taken a seat to the side of the cramped room, within view of the central pedestal where the ladies would dance, yet far enough from them that he would not be expected to pay for the view.

Because it was not the ladies' company he wanted. No, nothing so brutish. He had tried, once before, years ago, but quickly found that the ladies of the tavern were not to his taste. No, he was there to experience them, experience their art, experience *this*, experience *life* —experience something other than the dingy, muddy streets and exhaust-filled skies that characterized his day-to-day existence.

A woman approached. *Greta*, she had said on his first visit. *Sarah*, she had said the next time. *Alice*, a third. When he confronted her about the various names, she simply said, *whatever, darlin', what can I get for 'ya?*, and then grabbed him his glass of whiskey like each time before. Her face was hard and gaunt, and she reeked of booze and tobacco and regret. She placed a glass of whiskey in front of him, and he placed a few coins in her outstretched hand.

One of the ladies climbed up onto the stage in a large flowing dress, blowing kisses at the men leering at her. She slowly undressed, until she lay in a corset, moving her body to accentuate her breasts and her derriere for those holding out bills near the dais. But even though she was showing off for them, her gaze was elsewhere, off into the smoke, closer to the door.

A man strode forward, then, in a pristine black suit, cane and top hat in hand. He breezed past the wolves, walking directly to their prey.

To *his* prey. The man opened his jacket, certainly showing something valuable, before gesturing toward the back door of the room. The lady smiled, now ignoring the other patrons, before leading the gentleman to his dance. The next lady walked to the stage, and began a show of her own. He looked away. He'd seen it all before.

That is, until he looked in the corner, where she sat, eyes transfixed on the lady now dancing. Her face was pale, and round, and soft, and beautiful. She shone with some inner light, it seemed, a flower amongst the ash and smoke and darkness of this place. She was young, a trainee, perhaps, taking lessons in how to survive in this world from the grizzled women who had come before her.

She was beautiful. No. *No*. She was *beauty itself*.

It was then he did something he did not expect, something that eluded even his control. He drank his whiskey deep, his eyes not leaving her countenance until the glass had been drained. And then he waited, waited until her eyes roved to his corner of the room, until he could ensure that his gaze met hers through the tavern's amber haze.

When it finally happened, he smiled, friendly, kindly. *I don't want to hurt you*, he wanted to convey. *I just want to experience you.* She looked away quickly, the faintest traces of a smile playing at the corner of her mouth, her eyes occasionally flitting back to him. And soon his eyes saw her perfection change. In the lamplight, the faintest hue of pink began to color her ivory cheeks.

When she looked again, he gestured to her, two outstretched fingers extended toward her, bending slowly back to him. *Come.*

And she had. It had taken a few minutes, but eventually she crept over, furtive, not taking attention away from the ladies performing. He ordered her a glass of wine, and then finished another two whiskeys.

An hour passed. *I just want to photograph you*, he said. *You are the most beautiful creature I have ever seen*, he repeated. *You're simply radiant.* She continued to laugh, cutely, flirtatiously. *Please come*, he said. *I will pay whatever rate you wish.*

She had gotten up and spoken with another woman, who handed her a threadbare coat. When she returned, she told him her price.

Gladly, he replied.

And then, he photographed her. Right here in this basement, where his canvas now sat. He had captured her face, the most exquisite thing he had ever seen. Beauty itself. She'd looked fragile, in those pictures, vulnerable. But it was not enough. He needed more.

That price you gave, he told her, *I will double it if you undress.* She had hesitated then, her face apprehensive about the step before the precipice. *I will triple it*, he followed, pleading. And it was then that she slipped off her dress, her arms covering her body, and then, finally falling limp to her sides.

In the nude, she looked even more helpless, even more beautiful. She was something to be guarded, desired, loved, appreciated. It was not only her face that was radiant —her very essence radiated, down to her proportions, to the way her hips curved into her midsection, curving again toward her small breasts, curving again toward her angelic face, crowned with auburn hair cascading back down over her shoulders and shining like silk in the moonlight, even here, even in this cave. When he'd finished, she got dressed to leave.

What's your name? he'd asked.

Agnes, she responded.

But that won't do, he said. *You should be Rose, or Violet, or Lily. You're too beautiful to be an Agnes.* He contorted his face into a grin, then, conveying his sincerity, conveying his wonder.

Then you can call me Lily, she'd answered, before walking out the door, never to be seen again.

He smiled, looking back on that night, looking at the photograph, remembering those scant hours with the perfect being, remembering how finally seeing true beauty in this grotesque world had changed him.

An abrupt noise interrupted his reverie. His canvas coughed, and then groaned. *Confound it,* he thought, *the drugs should have lasted longer than this.*

But this world needed to see Lily's beauty, even after her death. And it was now that he would give it to them.

⚔

He had begun collecting his materials months earlier, once he knew he would never see the real Lily again. The night after he first met her, he had returned to the tavern, hoping to see her again, taking notes from the experienced ladies on how best to separate the factory workers from their coin. He had practiced his speech that entire day. *I'll help you,* he'd wanted to say. *You deserve so much more than this,* he'd wanted to promise. *The world should see you.*

But she was not there. Nor was she there the next night, or the night after that, or the night after that. His anxiety grew like a tumor. He stopped sleeping. One drink a night became two, before becoming three, until he was lost in his cups more often than not. Night after night, the ladies danced, men came, people drank, and he waited and waited for a girl who never again entered the tavern.

Eventually, he steeled himself to ask. *Greta,* he'd entreated, trying to flag down the waitress. *The girl. Lily, where is she?* It had been several weeks by this point, and he'd been to the tavern every day, hoping to catch just a glimpse of her.

Lily? she'd replied, her voice smoky, sandpaper-rough. *Who the fuck's Lily?*

He jolted then. In the weeks since he'd seen her, his mind had been filled with images and scenes and dreams and desires of what he would do for Lily. How he had been blessed to have been the person to see her, to truly see her, and how it was his divine providence to show her to the world. *I will take Lily to meet the mayor,* he thought, *and I will take her to museums, because she belongs in one,* he told himself, *and she will be the most famous woman on earth, because I will show this dark world that it cannot exist without her light.*

But the waitress's words reminded him that, for all of his grandiose plans, he was the first to call Lily by that name —her prophet, of sorts, certain to be revered only when history realized her importance. He looked down at his glass, embarrassed, forgetting that no one had yet seen her as he had. *Agnes,* he said. *I meant Agnes.*

The sides of her mouth dropped, and a momentary shade passed over her face as her composure faltered.

Agnes, she'd said, her voice catching. *Agnes ain't comin' back.*

His brow furrowed, puzzlement taking over.

'Er dad found out she was 'ere, the waitress went on. *Bashed 'er over the 'ead a few times, ain't no daughter 'uv 'is gonna' be no slut, I guess. Except the ole' man 'it 'er too good, and she never woke up. A friend 'uv 'ers came and told us a day or two ago. Its 'orrible, pretty thing like that. Maybe it was a blessing to 'er. Not to 'ave to live like t his.* She looked down at him, shaking her head.

He looked up at her big gray eyes, glazed over with the sheen of repressed tears, hidden behind a fake half-smile of crooked, decaying teeth. And then he screamed. Raged. *Broke.* He threw his glass at the wall, shattering it into a thousand glittering shards, the tiny explosion raining crystal down on nearby tables.

Men stood to confront him. Ladies gasped. The waitress recoiled in horror.

And he ran. Ran out of the tavern, down the street, by tenement blocks and factory homes and motor carriages and beggars and straight into his home, where he broke down as though the only spark of light in his life had been blown out before it could catch fire.

He awoke with Lily's face emblazoned in his memory, an iron-hot brand that marked him forever. He turned the image in his mind, recalling her from every angle, conjuring the tactile sense of the memory of caressing her cheek, imagining her soft reaction. He recalled her breasts, the slight curve of her stomach as it widened to her hips, and it struck him that his thoughts of her were not sexual. Indeed, the moment he envisioned sex in the context of Lily he felt embarrassed, ashamed even. No, he did not view Lily as a *her* at all. Rather, he remembered her as one remembers an impossible sky, a natural wonder, an artistic masterpiece.

The world needed to see her light, but its darkness had destroyed her before she could save it. Before he could help her save it. He cried for weeks, his melancholy at the loss of true beauty almost too much to bear. Nights on end he clutched her photograph, lamenting her loss, before realizing the only thing he could do, for himself, for his sanity, for this wretched world that had destroyed her, was to bring her back.

In his mind he combed through her features, comparing his memory with his photographs of her, determining which aspects of her would be the most striking, the most difficult to recreate. Her eyes, of course —it would be difficult to find a match for the deep, emerald green that providence had blessed her with. Her nose, as well, could prove difficult. While on the smaller side, the way it fit onto the frame of her round face was, itself, a thing of beauty. The thought of her face, of course, also reminded him that his canvas would need to have unobtrusive cheekbones, to ensure he could replicate her softness. Her hair was wavy, shoulder length, a deep brown kissed with red. That should be one of his easier tasks to find, but keeping it fresh and intact could be an issue. And then the breasts. It would not do for them to be inaccurate. Too small, and they would not demonstrate her femininity, too large and they would be obscene.

His search began in the opium cellars. There were dozens across the city, the last stop before the grave for the poor souls chewed up and spit out by the city and its industry. From the westernmost bridge to the muddy boundary where the river met the sea, the cellars were littered with women maimed by accidents with industrial sewing machines, men with faces melted from exhaust explosions, and children orphaned by a parent's premature death. They were dark, rotting places, where needles substituted for glasses, small lighters momentarily took the place of bright oil lamps, and despair of an entirely unique character held court.

The door to the first cellar he visited was wooden and built so that one had to descend directly into it from street level. A bespectacled old man with spindly fingers and graying skin staffed its entrance. *Ten pence to enter, son,* he'd said.

He looked at the old man with the most plaintive expression he could muster, holding his hat in his hands at his chest, already appearing misplaced here. *I don't mean to be a bother, sir, I'm simply looking for my cousin... we can't find 'em, you see, and this is our last hope. Please, just a look.* The man nodded, and gestured at the door leading to the cellar's interior.

The entrance was naught but a foyer, of sorts. The light had spilled into it when he opened the cellar hatch, but that was the extent that daylight could penetrate this place. The doors closed, and darkness closed in, even more so when he opened the entrance into the main room. He could tell a difference in his environment immediately; the smell alone nearly stopped him, a wall of body odor and sex and piss and vomit. He suppressed a gag and held his sleeve to his nose, hoping that the scent of his coat could mask the smell of their addiction.

It was not only the odor that hit him; noteworthy, too, was the darkness. A solitary candle rested in a sconce on the left side of the room from which emanated a low, flickering light, momentarily illuminating the shapes lying haphazardly along the floor. The cellar room was large. So large, in fact, that the back corners received almost no light at all.

He began searching, walking to each of the prostrate shapes, examining their features. The first barely reacted, with only her blank eyes following his movements as he shook her shoulder. *This one will not do,* he thought. Nor would the next, or the next, or the next, until he found himself beside the candle. He turned his head at a new noise; in the back corner, the faint sounds of two men partaking, the sounds of fingers slapping arms, hushed voices pregnant with risk.

And then he felt it. A young woman, arms outstretched, fingers now barely touching the laces of his boot, as though reaching him had been the objective of some obscene race. He recoiled from the touch, surprise rushing over him followed almost immediately by disdain, and eventually, pity. He looked at her, and she looked at him, her face sharp, her skin pale, her eyes sad, and her nose...*perfect.* He reached down, grabbed her hand. *Let's get you out of here,* he said. She said nothing, seemed barely to register her existence at all —let alone his.

He carried her out, thanking the man on the way before loading her into his carriage and taking her home, taking her straight to the basement. There, he placed chloroform over her mouth to ensure she would not wake up, and strapped her to the chair where Lily had once posed for him.

One final time, he examined her nose, holding Lily's photograph up to her face. He had been right. It was perfect. He pulled out his scalpel, carefully extracting the skin and cartilaginous tissue of her nose, taking every care to preserve the delicate curves of the nostrils, the slight dimples where they would meet the nose's central ridge, placing cotton bandages between where he was working and the skin to diminish the amount of blood spilled during the operation.

His work took just half an hour. He fondled the liberated nose like a religious icon, looking incessantly from it to Lily's photograph, yearning for the day it could be placed onto his masterpiece.

Do you know how important you are? he asked her, caressing her face, receiving no response. *Of course you don't. But it is a kindness, this. To spare you from this wretched existence and make you part of something perfect, to make you perfect.* He smiled at the girl's unmoving, bloody, comatose body, knowing that his Lily was worth a thousand of her. Then, he snapped her neck.

In this same manner he collected all the parts he needed for his work. The nose he had found on his first endeavor. That, he learned, was luck. In the following months, he made slow progress. It took another four visits to the opium cellars before he located ears sufficiently like Lily's, and another six after that before finding the perfect breasts to add to his canvas. While he was able to find a human-hair wig to match Lily's, he was not so fortunate in locating her eyes, the emerald green proving nearly impossible to match.

But he had done it, eventually, placing a man's two orbs in the same preservation liquids as the other parts, the donors' bodies left by the river, or in the street, or wherever convenient, always with a needle in the arm, always a reminder of what the world had made them, a reminder of what he had saved them from.

But the canvas, the template on which he would bring Lily back into this world, long eluded him. Until, one day, he found her.

She was stepping out of a motor carriage, dropped off by a driver no doubt searching for a safe place to park the expensive vehicle among the impoverished masses. She'd acted lost —and indeed, looked it. She wore a frilly robin's-egg dress, fitted, but not obscenely so. On her head sat a matching bonnet, which accentuated her face's shape with lacy white frills. Her clothing screamed of privilege, even more so when juxtaposed against the blacks and browns and grays of the working classes. She looked around nervously, her unease growing more palpable by the second.

He knew, there and then, that she was the one.

May I help you, m'lady, he'd said. *It appears you are looking for something.*

Oh yes, that would be lovely, she'd said, the education apparent in her voice. *I am hoping to be fitted for a new dress and my seamstress is supposed to be here and I have just never been here before. My driver is coming to walk me soon once he is able to find a garage, but if you know where Wilhelmina's is, I would be much obliged.* She'd smiled at him then, her gratitude plain.

Wilhelmina's! he'd exclaimed. *Why it is just this way! I can show you where it is, if you have thirty seconds to walk. Surely your driver will not be back by then.*

She giggled as if out of practice. *Well, that would be splendid! How silly of us to be this close and not even know it.*

After me, he had replied, marshalling a cheery voice to convince her of her safety. *Right this way!* They went into an isolated side street, and after a block, turned into an empty alleyway.

Are we almost there? she'd asked, her voice betraying the first traces of unease.

He turned toward her, pointing to a door just ahead. *We're here! Just go up there and let them know you've arrived. I can send your driver over.* He then stepped back toward the wall, gesturing with his arm to the door.

She hesitated, perhaps realizing in the deepest recesses of her mind that something was wrong. But manners and politesse won out. *Thank you, good sir,* she'd said, gathering up the dirty hem of her dress before turning her back toward him.

He struck her as hard as he could on the back of the skull. She collapsed, motionless. Thirty seconds later, he had dragged her body into his home.

"You're probably right," he said to its unhearing ears. "It won't do to have you waking up during this." He prepared another vial of a strong anesthetic combined with a certain coagulant, and injected it between its toes.

He began with the hair. That part was easy; he took his scissors and cut it as short as he could. Those who would eventually see his work would never know that the hair they were seeing was a wig, and so he needed only to ensure that the canvas's real hair did not show.

From there, his task became monumentally more difficult, requiring his artistry, and *her* perfection. Taking one last look at Lily's photograph, he pulled out the new nose, eyes, and ears from the preservation liquid, admiring them one last time before they achieved their ultimate purpose.

He first dug a small teaspoon into the canvas's eye sockets, the spoon caressing the curves of its eyes before hitting the tougher musculature that housed the nerves connecting eye to brain. With some additional effort, he pushed through, popping out each eye with a satisfying *squelch.* He placed cotton swabs in the sockets to soak up the tiny pools of blood that were developing where its eyes had been.

The nose proved more difficult. His scalpel hit its first mark on the right side of its bony ridge, and immediately, a ruby droplet appeared on the canvas's face, a jewel on a necklace. He paused to admire it for a second, the yellow lamplight reflecting off the liquid, itself a form of art, and he smiled. *Beauty,* he thought.

His scalpel continued, removing all traces of its former imperfection down to the bone. As he'd done with the eyes, he covered the wound in cotton swabs. He then turned to the ears, cutting the canvas's cartilage until its imperfections were gone, to be replaced by Lily's radiance.

An hour later, the canvas had been stripped of its facial imperfections, prepared to be made *whole* again, prepared to be made *perfect.* He looked to the two eyes he had collected, small pieces of Lily that the gods had seen fit to retain in this world, for his art, his masterpiece. Even now in the flickering lamplight they shone with the same jeweled radiance that Lily's had in life. He removed the blood-soaked cotton swabs from the eye sockets, inserting each eye into its proper place, marveling at the result.

"*Amazing,*" he said to himself, lost in the moment of his vision turning into reality, a tear slowly trailing down his cheek.

But there was more work to do. He pulled out his needle and thread and began to attach the nose to the canvas, ensuring that it fit *just so* before applying the stitches that would bring back Lily's beauty. He performed the same task with her ears, reattaching the perfect part where the imperfection had been, making the canvas more than the mere sum of its replacement parts.

From there, he moved to its breasts, which were large and all too unbefitting Lily's frame. He brought out the small handsaw he had found for this purpose and removed the first of them. The blood surprised him, creating a flood he did not expect. While the face bled, it had not bled mortally, and the canvas, he knew, would still survive. With the breast, however, the significance of the bleeding indicated a mortal wound.

He began to panic. What, then, would all his work have been for? The profusely bleeding chest threatened the canvas, threatened Lily's legacy. He took all of the remaining cotton he had, all of the remaining fabric, and attempted to bind the gushing area where the breast had been. It kept bleeding.

His breathing quickened. *No, this will not do,* he thought, and quickly began fretting throughout his basement. "Stop," he said, commanding himself. "All you need are the pictures. Get the pictures." The thought of Lily's photos instantly calmed him, his frenetic pace slowing. Now, he could think, finally, once more. *The makeup. Hide the sutures.*

Yes, that was the first task. Hiding the surgery, making the canvas look as natural as possible, as beautiful as Lily had been. He placed heavy powder on its face before adding additional layers of concealment, paying special attention to the suture lines around the nose, making sure to highlight the eyes and the radiant green they now emanated. Once he was convinced of its beauty, the most beautiful the canvas had ever looked, he removed the bandages from the exposed breast and the gash where its twin had been, and then draped a dress over it. Finally, after ensuring that the eyes were open, he placed the wig on its head, arranging the locks so that they fell just like Lily's had in the perfect photograph taken so many months ago.

Quickly, so quickly, he ran behind his camera, which he had prepared for this precise moment, again climbed under its black shroud, again held his hand outside to activate the flash, and again, marveled at the beauty he beheld through his lens.

When he emerged from behind the camera, he was weeping. "Lily," he said, sobbing. "Lily, I am so close to bringing your light back." He sniffled, before fully breaking down in front of his canvas. "One day soon, I'll perfect it. *Perfect you.* But until then, I can begin to show the world what it destroyed."

Early that morning, in the smallest, darkest hours when the world slept a deep sleep, he placed his canvas outside City Hall as a public display of his art, of Lily's brilliance. He smiled at it, seated next to a gigantic stone fountain. Art framing art.

And now, seeing what he created, this new Lily, this Second Lily, knowing his power to bring her light back into this city, into this land, he prepared to perfect his work, to keep sharing her radiance with the world.

PAUL O'NEILL

Just a Little Nibble

REGRET WORMS MY GUT as we stroll under the midnight trees. Gail finally agreed to a third date, but it's all going to end in disaster. I can feel the doom of it in my blood.

I've gone too far this time.

Gail's sleek form glides ahead of me. The moon is so strong tonight. It beams its silver blessing down upon us.

I'm just a girl following another girl, praying she'll kiss me under the stars.

Gail turns, graceful as a dancer. The look she gives me makes my foot forget how to do the walky thing. I feel all jellied inside, like my soul has curdled. In a good way. In a warm, liquid way.

It's those eyes. Greener than any eyes have the right to be. Something straight out of a midnight faery tale. How did I get so lucky?

The innocent smell of sugar and sweet things rises from my skin. It's a scent I can't seem to get rid of no matter how hard I scrub. The candy floss of it marries with the humid summer air and the spongy earth beneath us.

I stare down at my hands. There's dirt all up in my fingernails. Damn it.

Everything has to be perfect.

Tonight is the night.

If I have to wait any longer to taste her, I might just die.

"Where you taking me, Emmeline?" Gail asks in her playful kitten voice.

Can I make English things come out my mouth? Make the words? Come on, Emmeline, you can do it. Breathe. Try to think of calming things. Kneading dough. Flooffy cats. Gail running her tongue over that spot just behind my ear where it tingles and —

"Told you," I manage to force out. God, I sound like a squeaky, oily-faced teenager. "It's a surprise."

Gail was made for the moon. I can feel my whole stupid body swooning forward as if magnetised. My Gail with the dream eyes and those slick lips.

Looking at her with my eyes so wide I can almost imagine them drooling, I can't recall ever having seen her in the daytime. She's a proper night owl, her skin so fair, so blemishless. Oh, to trace my fingers over her shoulders, that hollow in her neck.

She's been my dream since we were at school together —I just hadn't realised it. Hadn't realised a lot of things about myself until I hit my twenties. Those butterflies I lied to myself about for so many long years.

Everyone picked on Gail. Gail the Pale, is what they called her. What I called her. They'd pull her hood down to annoy her and she'd hurry it back up like her skin burned.

My poor Gail. You're okay, now. You're with me. You'll always be with me, won't you? Say you'll be my forever girl.

I let my small rucksack fall to the grass. Beyond this spot, gravestones jut out the ground like crumbling fingertips.

"Was gonna leave this until afterwards, but I could use a drink." I take out a bottle of white zinfandel and two plastic cups.

Gail slinks her way over to me, takes the bottle, unscrews it. The way her throat moves as she glugs straight from the bottle captivates me. I want to kiss that neck. Place my hand around it.

I take the bottle when she offers it. "Your eyes are green emeralds. A-Anybody ever tell you that before? It's like looking at a dragon, or something."

"A dragon? No one's said that to me before. You're really something."

"You're something more. Cheers."

I raise the bottle, chug it down, praying the wine will stop my heart and other things from fluttering about so much. I can't think straight with her looking at me like that.

"Can I..." Gail moves towards me, places a hand on my cheek, draws me near.

You can do anything you want, I almost say, melting on the spot.

The kiss is soft. The kiss is everything. I lean in, begging for more. The bottle hits the ground. The wine flows out and I do not care. Nothing else matters but Gail's lips on mine.

Take me under the light of the moon. Do with me as you will. Kill me now and do it again and again.

Gail pulls away, looks me in the eyes, moves down to my neck. Her gentle kisses flush me all over with fire, curling my toes.

"No, not yet," I say, remembering why I brought her here, pushing gently at her bony shoulders. "Calm down there, puddle maker."

"I want a taste. Just a little nibble."

She leans in again and I offer my neck, stare at the moon and the fluff of wispy cloud moving across it. I've never been so electrically happy.

"I need to show you something." I step back, bite my lip. "Before someone finds what I've done. Ruins it."

"You're full of surprises."

"Right back at you."

I focus on my hands. Stupid dirt under my nails. I scratch them against the roughness of my jeans, hating the ear-twitching sound that breaks the perfect scene. Even the wind stops sighing through the trees as if waiting for me to stop ruining everything.

"This way," I say, "my lovely...flowerness thing."

Flowerness? The cringe ices away the heat I felt two seconds ago. Stupid, awkward muppet. Why you gotta be like this, Emmeline? Get it together.

"You seem to have lost your tongue," Gail says. "Need to borrow mine's?"

When she runs her tongue over her moist lips, my thighs quiver, almost collapse me onto the grass.

The laugh that puffs out of me is all nerves as I walk by her, imploring my nose not to sniff her, doing it anyway. I'm high on this girl. She's got me good.

"Come on," I say. "Follow me."

The ground is uneven and bouncy under my mud-caked Reeboks. I can feel the trees sighing in the breeze, the stone dust smell of the tombstones as we get into the cemetery proper.

You've gone too far, Emmeline. What was I thinking, doing all this?

Gail had always been into dark things. Back in school, I remember sitting near her, something inside screaming at me to lean closer, smell her earthy aroma, place my hand on hers. What I'd done instead was join the others in recoiling from the weird girl, hurl names at her. Gail the Pale.

With her fair skin and hair so blond it was almost silver, she didn't exactly help herself by filling her notebooks with weird symbols, scribbles of sacrifices, demon chants, crosses.

I glance over my shoulder. Her eyes twinkle with sly promise. Beneath those lacy black clothes, I know one entire arm is tattooed with the same symbols and scribbles.

We're at the spot. The spot where I'd spent far too much time earlier today. My shoulders still ache. I wonder what they'd say if they found out what I'd been up to. *Emmeline, you've gone too far. There's something wrong with you, Emmeline.*

Gail places an icy hand on the small of my back, instantly making my lips part, my body turn.

"What is all this?" she says.

She isn't doing a runner, screaming for help. Not yet.

I move closer to the shallow, rectangular hole with its fresh, chocolaty soil.

"I know you're into certain things," I say. "Darkish things. So, I made this for you, for us, to enjoy together. Promise you won't ever tell anyone what I've done?"

This is the moment she leaves me.

The moment she turns her green, green eyes on me like I'm a sticky piece of chewing gum caught on the sole of her Doc Martens.

She stares down at the disturbed, crumbly dirt, a smile rising up one side of her face. The moonlight makes a shadow of her dimple. What a perfect night. Kiss me under a moonlight sky and say you'll never leave. That I'm always yours.

"You're something else," Gail says, coming nearer. "How did you know —" She shakes her head, looks back down at the ground. "I want to nibble on that creamy skin of yours. Taste you. Throw you down right here. Show you...things."

"You promise?"

"Wanna see?"

"Later." I breathe out a sigh that feels like I've betrayed my own soul. "Why don't you dig up your present?"

"Present? Starting to feel like Christmas."

She's not running. She's taking a shovel, stabbing it into the ground, throwing dirt into a growing mound. She's getting into it. Really into it, in fact. Racing, trying to find what a silly girl like me has buried for her in a shallow grave on a moonlit night.

I cast a look at the grave marker. It looks as if it would flake and crumble away at the slightest suggestion of a spade.

Here lies Mary Hollywood. We'll never forget your gifts.

I can't help the laugh that trickles out.

The spade *thunks* wood.

Gail stops, looks down.

"Is that an actual coffin? Emmeline, what did you do here?"

"Why don't you open it up?"

This is it. You've gone too far, Emmeline. She's gonna throw the spade at me, leaving only the dream of her lips on my neck as I touch myself in the bathtub the rest of my lonely days.

But Gail's eyes are green fire. Shiny in the dark. Elated. Hungry.

She leans over the hole, sniffs, closes her eyes. "Is this real?"

Without waiting for an answer, she's down on her hands and knees, prying off the coffin lid. It comes away in splinters as she claws, revealing the shape inside.

"He's as fresh as I could make him," I say.

Looking down at the thing I'd spent so long creating, I can see the way the moon plays over the eyes, the mouth, the stringy hair.

Gail's on her knees, jeans dampened from the soil. "You know what I...what I am?"

The question hisses out those beautiful lips with an ache I'd never before heard from her. My heart flutters at the lonely sound.

Take me, I call out silently, with everything in me. *Take me now, under the bed of stars and the watching trees.*

"You take the first bite," I say. "If you want to show me how much I mean to you, how far you're willing to go, bite him."

"What?"

"Go on. Bite him. You won't regret it."

This is the moment, my big idea seen to fruition in the graveyard. My test. Had anyone done this in the history of humankind? Was I the first true weirdo to think this a good idea? Always too far, Emmeline. Always taking it too far.

"Listen," I start. "It's just a jo —"

Gail opens her mouth wide, stretching the muscles in her neck. Her head is a blur as she sinks her teeth into the man's head.

There's the sound of gnashing, something crumbling.

Gail straightens. Her hands are trembling as she spits and paws at her mouth. Pieces of the man slide down her chest, land by her boots.

"That's not..." she says, hand over her mouth, gagging, eyes wide.

I look into the hole I'd dug hours earlier, into the small box I'd placed in the fake grave as a makeshift coffin. The man's face I'd moulded was smooshed in. At its neck, where Gail had sunk her teeth, were layers of red jam and sponge cake. Its vanilla, candy floss scent touches my nose. It's the same smell that's lived in my skin these last few years, ever since I opened my cake shop. I'd challenge myself to bake bigger and cooler cakes, getting quite the following on Instagram for my "super realistic" works.

This had been the biggest challenge yet.

And it had paid off.

The thing actually looked like a corpse. Even the headstone was cake.

"My cake's not that bad, is it?" I ask. "W-what do you think? Do you like it?"

Gail claws at her tongue like it burns. "That's not...I..."

"Hold on. Did you actually think I would ask you to eat a dead person?"

"Well, you did bring me to a graveyard in the middle of the night."

"But you...wait. You thought I was serving you a real corpse, and you actually ate it? You'd do that for me?"

She loves me. She's going to look me in the eye with those green butterfly makers and set her lips on my lips. We'll move in together and smooch it up on the couch the rest of our days. She'll be my forever queen and I'll make her all the cake she can handle.

But she's not looking at me. The sleekness of her movements is gone as she stands, runs her trembling hands up and down her thighs. She stares at the moon as if in prayer, bites her lip, turns away from me.

"Gail, I'm sorry I went too far. It was stupid. Let's forget about it. I always go too far."

Her back quivers. She groans, places her hands over her eyes, shakes out a breath like she's struggling to keep hold of herself.

"It was just supposed to be a joke. I remembered how much you like dark, weird things, so I thought of the darkest, weirdest trick I could try and, I don't know...I guess I wanted to show you that I see you. See you for who you really are."

"Who I am? Who I am? You've no idea. You should never have done this. Now I'm —" She drives her nails into the back of her neck so hard that blood trickles down her skin. "You've no idea who I am. What I am. How hard it is to stay in control. And you tempt me with this."

"Would you look at me? Please? I'm sorry. I'll do anything to make it right."

"Anything?"

"Anything." I try to be all sexy, but I sound more like an injured cat. "Just let me look at you. Let's forget about this, okay? It was stupid of me."

Gail turns.

The moonlight shines its colours over her lovely, pale face.

Something catches my eye like diamonds twinkling.

I take a step back, stumble over the spade, barely keep myself from landing on my arse.

Two fangs glint out of each side of Gail's luscious mouth. They grow larger, sharper as she smiles.

"Gail? What are you doing?"

She steps forward, her movements slick as liquid, predatory. "Let me kiss that neck again."

Shame wheedles its hot way up my neck as I consider proffering it to my love, letting those fangs sink into me, giving her everything.

I back away, palms up. "What are you? Get away. No. Don't!"

"Just a little nibble is all I need. Just a little nibble."

REBECCA CUTHBERT

Plea from the Ghost Haunting Your One-Bedroom Queens Apartment That You Clean This Place the Fuck Up

Hey.

It's me.

The ghost haunting your one-bedroom Queens apartment.

Yeah, so, I know I usually keep to the hall closet where you store the vacuum you don't use enough; or to the inside of the walls, where I bang on rusty pipes and make sighing noises; or, that one time, to the medicine cabinet, so that you saw me in the mirror when you got out of the shower and wiped the steam away and screamed and then almost fainted. But I've materialized in front of you today for something much more important than parlor tricks, Patricia.

That's right. Your utter lack of anything close to housekeeping. And I mean like *utter lack*.

This is a goddamn intervention.

This place smells like someone swallowed a fart, let it ferment for a month, then burped it back up. I know you're still all excited about finally getting better after weeks of long Covid —you're joining friends for brunch, you met that one guy on Tinder and brought him home and then just as you two got naked in the stained sheets you haven't washed since last fall I whispered his name in his ear but he was looking at your face and clearly *you* didn't say it so he freaked out hard and then left —you were cooped up so long, here, with me, and now you want to enjoy living la vida loca again.

Oh, is that a dated reference?

Sorry.

It's hard to keep up with cultural trends when you're a ghost haunting a one-bedroom Queens apartment that could really use a Febreze hose-down.

Actually, you know what? Skip the Febreze. That would be like pissing on a house fire. Throw everything that can't be dunked in bleach out by the curb. Let the rats raise their young in your heap of offal until the city workers show up to haul it away, holding their noses and saying, *Jesus Christ is there a goddamn dead body somewhere in here holy fuck I need a new job.*

Anywho. Patricia. You don't even shut the kitchen cabinets. You don't even try. Like, who's the ghost here? Who's supposed to be opening cabinet doors? And then slamming them? And then opening them again? I'll give you a hint, Patricia: Not you.

And I didn't want to bring this up, because really, I didn't want to embarrass you. But. *But.* I know the underwear you're wearing *right now* are three days' dirty. THREE. Because three days ago you ran out of clean laundry, and what did you do when faced with that domestic dilemma, Patricia? Did you fill your coat pocket with quarters and head down to the laundromat with your bulging hamper, like a fucking normal person?

No.

You just shrugged and recycled a pair of crusty granny panties from the hamper. And Patricia? You're a little ripe.

Like, portable-toilet-on-a-hot-day-full-of-drunk-concertgoers'-puke ripe.

Listen to me, though, going on and on. But this isn't about me, Patricia. It's not about you, even —not really. It's about *us*. Us, here. Your life. My afterlife. Together, in this one-bedroom Queens apartment that has become nothing more than a cockroach fuckshack.

Because while you can go out and party like it's 1999 —and I was there in '99, Patricia, and it *was* a party —I can't. I can't leave this apartment, and I think you know that, or you *should* know that; it's a pretty standard ghost fact. Like it's basically common knowledge, but then again you apparently don't know how to operate the dollar-store toilet brush that I guess you bought when you were in an optimistic mood, so. Who knows.

Anyway.

If you don't spend at least a *little* time cleaning up this weekend, I swear to God, Patricia, I will double down on the haunting. My handsome-but-transparent face will be the first thing you see in the morning and the last thing you see at night. I'll be all over you like stink on —well, like the stink that's already on *you*, but we don't need to go over that again, do we?

Being stuck in this cesspit makes me want to kill myself.

But Patricia, as a ghost haunting your one-bedroom Queens apartment, I can't do that, since I'm already dead. So you can see how my only choice was to concentrate my energy enough to become at least partially solid and confront you, here, today, in your living room. In *our* living room, where —*Jesus*, Patricia, is that a *human dump* in the corner?

This is just too much.

Neither life nor death prepared me for this.

Because —and admitting this doesn't feel good, but it's important for me to be vulnerable with you so you know you can *talk* to me, though since I started sharing my thoughts with you about all of this, you've stayed pretty quiet, maybe because I'm the ghost haunting your one-bedroom Queens apartment and you're scared shitless, which would be understandable —ghosts have fears, too.

And do you know what mine is? My biggest one? The one that keeps me up at night, and the fact that I don't sleep isn't important right now?

It's you having a terrible accident in this shit-heap, like slipping on one of the sixteen fast-food wrappers on your bedroom floor, banana-peel style, smashing your head open, and *dying*. Because if you die in this apartment, here, with me, and if you do not move on to whatever world comes next —one where dumbass angels play dumbass harps or hellfire burns the short-hairs off people's ballsacks, but how should I know, because I didn't get a ticket to either fucking one —then this cursed afterlife becomes eternal for us both, *Patricia*. Long. Endlessly long. Like the rope of Yeti hair that you could pull out of the bathroom sink if it ever occurred to you to do so.

Alrighty. I think that about covers it. And I feel better. Do you feel better?

It's fine. Take your time. When you want to talk, I'll be here.

Since, you know, I can't leave.

Like, ever.

Patricia?

PHIL KEELING

The Beguiler of Swarms

DR. PAYTON BOYD SPENT most of his life correcting people. He supposed it was his fault. It was part of the hazard of studying insects and arachnids. Like most subjects in the modern age, people made up their minds about everything, and it went double for bugs. It didn't matter what tone of voice he used or credentials he flashed. Nothing was good enough.

No, that mark on your arm isn't from a Brown Recluse.

No, you can't tell a ladybug's age by counting its spots.

No, you weren't bitten by a cockroach. Cockroaches almost never bite.

Of course, there were exceptions to every rule. Payton always left these conversations with a satisfied feeling, as if his niche focus of study helped clarify yet another invertebrate myth.

Then the attacks began.

There was no grand moment that spurred them. No recurring town curse or hidden cache of steadily leaking nuclear waste. One day the coastal town of Spoil, Georgia, had been its usual self, and the next day, everything changed.

There were hints. Clues that a hideous shift was on the horizon. Boyd was one of the unlucky few who'd seen such a hint. The week before, the color of the sky changed to a shining brown, the shade of shoe polish. He'd been called in by the local police to provide assistance on a murder. Despite his otherwise milquetoast career as a professor of entomology at the local university, this wasn't an unusual event.

Spoil wasn't a huge town, and its police department didn't have the money or need for a full-time forensic entomologist. Determining time of death based on the life cycle of fly larvae was more of a parlor trick to local detectives. But Boyd had offered his assistance on more than one occasion, and it wasn't long before he was asked to take a look at any decomposing creature the cops found, whether it was a person or suspicious roadkill. Rotting corpses hadn't become a standard feature on the streets of Spoil.

The day began with the sober tone of a detective asking for Boyd's opinion on a home invasion in Spanish Creek, a well-heeled neighborhood out near the salt marshes. He was led into the McMansion by a policeman with an ash-colored face. The cop wouldn't look at anything but the floor. When they entered the nursery, Boyd saw why.

Something had come in the night and turned the crib into a cage of gore and gristle. Unspeakable stains smeared the white carpet beneath. As Boyd approached, the greasy faces of several dozen cockroaches peered curiously over the linen sheets. More still skittered gently near the silent air conditioning vents. He realized the air in the room was the humid soup of the low country outside.

"They turned off the AC," an investigator told him, gesturing toward the hordes of roaches gathering in the corners of the room. "They kept getting in."

Boyd found himself shaking at the sight of the unidentifiable mass in the bassinet. He swatted at the roaches, each the size of a wine cork, and was disturbed to find they wouldn't scatter from the crib. It was as if they'd claimed the quarry inside, and refused to be intimidated. Beyond their shining bodies, Boyd couldn't find any evidence of flies or larvae to investigate.

There was nothing left for maggots to feed on.

Boyd didn't know what to tell the police. By the time he made it to his car, his guts were filled with equal parts acid and pity. Pity for the shattered people inside the house. Acid for him and him alone. He left before he had the chance to see the parents, and no one stopped him. He didn't want to see their faces. The sickened and confused faces of the police had done enough. He didn't want to see the ache and torment of the parents in Spanish Creek, who had spent their lives dedicated to buying themselves a tangible level of security that was completely ignored by the forces of nature.

Some seven days later, Boyd mused, the swarm had begun on the outskirts of town. Denizens of Spanish Creek, and the surrounding golf communities, had overwhelmed the police and animal control with reports of swarms. Hundreds of thousands of glistening roaches lumbered through the air on clumsy wings, clogging exhaust pipes and splattering themselves in suicidal handfuls against windows. The police reported the revolted phone calls, which were a constant for a full hour until they suddenly stopped. Shocked voices over the police radio chatter explained why. The tidy, wealthy communities were silent, gore encrusting their streets like bubble gum scraped from the bottom of a shoe.

Things only got worse.

The perimeter of roaches closed in on Spoil, getting tighter and tighter as confusion turned to chaos and an entire city fell beneath the ruthlessly efficient hunger of the swarm. In days, militias of men and women armed with everything from shotguns to industrial-sized cans of bug spray rose and fell. There was nothing supernatural in how the roaches kept coming. They were bred for this over millions of years —born survivors. Boyd knew he might have been the only person in the city whose fear of the creatures was adulterated with at least a drop of fascination and even respect.

A cockroach could live for a week without its head. Humans? Not so much. He'd seen enough examples of both in the previous week to know for certain how true those facts were. He'd watched police cruisers crumple beneath the weight of the scuttling horde. He'd listened to death rattles interrupted by tiny bodies erupting through flesh and skin. He'd seen the sun blotted out by millions of copper-colored creatures bulldozing their way through the summer sky. Fuel lines burst with the corpses of dead roaches. One by one, the main routes out of the city became flooded with the swarm, completely inaccessible, even if they could be reached somehow.

Boyd knew they had always had the numbers. Something had shifted. Something in the world made the creatures decide their place in the food chain was insufficient. From where Boyd stood, it looked like the fight was over. He was far from the only one who felt that way. If more of the bodies had been left behind, he might have an easier go of guessing how many were dead. The roaches left little behind but the bones, which attracted other creatures from the surrounding marshes to finish the job. The situation was desperate, which is how they'd ended up with Whistle.

He sat in one of the elementary school's chairs, one designed specifically for children. He was a smaller framed man, but still seemed ridiculously large in the plastic seat. He had one knee crossed casually over the other. He spoke, bent over a chicken wing, muttering and smacking around the bone. No one knew where he'd found it, and though many of the survivors surrounding him in the gymnasium were hungry, nobody asked. No one was sure where Whistle had come from.

"The kids," he said between bites. "What's most important is keeping them safe, am I right?"

No one answered.

No one needed to.

Whatever disagreements the people of Spoil had in the past, protecting their children was never in question. Of the hundred survivors crowding the school's gym, two-thirds of them were children. As people scrambled for shelter, they pushed the kids ahead, in the hope they would find safety before their elders did. Sometimes this worked out. Sometimes it meant the younger ones were the first victims of the swarm.

The road to hell is paved with good intentions, Boyd thought.

"People come running in times like these," Whistle said. "They go looking for someone with a solution. Right solution, wrong solution, it doesn't matter to them. Mostly they just want someone to lead."

Whistle tossed his spent chicken bone across the gym. It whizzed lazily over several people's heads landing with a muted thump on the polished wood floor. Some of the kids watched it sail and laughed, forgetting for a moment the hell their lives had devolved into.

"Well, I'm always happy to lead," Whistle said, standing to a full height that barely reached many of the children present. "But I don't work for free."

If there was anyone with the energy to scold the strange man for thinking about payment at a time like this, no one did. It might have been pure exhaustion and fear that kept everyone quiet. He was right. People didn't want to lead. Not now. They wanted to be instructed. Even Boyd couldn't bring himself to do anything and he was in a better position than anyone else in the room to understand the creatures that hunted them. He wanted to help, just like everyone else. He couldn't begin to guess how to start. Instead, he found himself watching constantly from the sidelines. It might have been the exhaustion that left them mute. Boyd guessed it had more to do with Whistle himself.

Spoil was well known for its population of odd characters. Bohemians, artists, and general eccentrics flooded the city limits for as long as anyone could remember. They made a name for themselves as local celebrities and added color to the town. Most people liked having them around, but no one had ever seen Whistle before. No one knew where he'd come from. Dressed in scraps of clashing animal print, he would have been hard to miss. Zebra stitched with lion stitched with leopard stitched with snake: The combination was a dull roar against the eyes. His shirt and pants were sewn and stapled together. His small frame floated inside the cloud of baggy fabric. He was otherwise unimpressive. Without his eccentric clothing, he would have blended anywhere in the world. Still, Whistle frightened Boyd. His eyes twinkled like glass at the bottom of a sewer pipe, nothing but emptiness and trouble deep down.

"How can you help?" asked Bob Chambers, perhaps the only person left who would have felt comfortable in a leadership role. He'd been a local alderman for years before retiring and spending the past few years watching the boats come and go from his historic home on the harbor. Old, drafty houses like his had been some of the quickest for the roaches to clear out. Though he'd survived admirably for his age, no one asked where his wife was.

"I have abilities that, perhaps, others lack," Whistle said, bouncing back and forth on the balls of his feet. "Specialized skills, to be sure, but useful." His dark eyes twinkled again. "And I'll use them."

The crowd murmured. They'd maybe expected a getaway plan or directions to a safe haven. An actual method of removing the swarms of roaches from Spoil? It seemed impossible.

"How?" Boyd asked, surprising himself with the question.

"Niche skills!" Whistle said, pulling a recorder from the folds of his many-printed shirt. The instrument was made of the same cheap plastic as a child's recorder. It was yellowed with age and didn't look like a tool to save lives. It barely looked like it could squeak out "Hot Cross Buns." Whistle blew into the instrument. It didn't produce any sound. He cackled.

"What?" Whistle asked when no one reacted. "You've never heard of a dog whistle? Well, this is a roach whistle!"

Chambers frowned, not even pretending to understand how this was meant to work.

"And if your plan and your...eh..." The old politician grumbled over the word. "...*Skills* do the trick? What do you want?"

"I want a house and a place to live, Alderman," Whistle said, his fingers dancing absently across the recorder's tone holes. "I've been on the road for a long, long time." Whistle's eyes gleamed in a way that was difficult for Boyd to parse. They seemed...covetous. "And this seems like a real nice community. Not that I know much about nice communities."

Boyd sighed. This was getting insane. Did they have time for this? He searched the room to see if other faces conveyed the same lack of hope he felt. What he saw instead was movement in the corners of the gym. Slow, familiar movement.

"You want a house?" Chambers asked. "Any house?"

Boyd opened his mouth to say something, anything, to alert the room of the danger he knew was coming.

"No, not just any house," Whistle said, then laughed. His eyes were wide and manic. "I want your house. The house where your wife died."

Chambers sputtered, and for one wild moment it looked to Boyd as if the old alderman would attack the smaller man. But the confrontation was interrupted by the low drone of heavy wings. The roaches had found a way in, and the only sound to drown out their awful descent were the screams of the people in the gymnasium. Boyd and Chambers dropped at the same time. While Boyd threw his arms up to defend himself from incoming creatures, the older man fell forward, hitting the gymnasium floor with a heavy thump. The roaches swarmed through his hair and into his ears, crawling their way in and out of orifices. They worked with a speed that left Boyd breathless, and as their glistening bodies worked their way out of the dead alderman's nostrils and mouth and crept toward Boyd, he found himself muttering pleading cries. It didn't sound like him. There was no dignity here.

Boyd squeezed his eyes shut and pressed his face into the smooth surface of the gym floor, smelling rubber and bare feet. As he waited for death, he heard the sound of shuddering wings, like every insect in existence had entered the gym. There was a series of faint pops, like a gentle chorus of burping frogs. The room was silent.

He rolled over.

Chambers was dead, his body picked clean like every other corpse Boyd had seen in the past week. Blood spatters dotted the walls and the floor, and Boyd lifted himself to his feet, taking in the sight. Whistle leaned against a nearby wall, a wan smile playing across his lips as he observed the silent shock around him.

Piles of roaches lined every surface of the gym. They gathered in corners and made hills around those, like Boyd, who had dropped to the floor to avoid them.

They were everywhere.

Whistle brought his recorder to his lips and began to play. The cockroaches swirled in formation, and as Whistle played his silent song he danced out of the gym. The roaches, millions of them, followed.

In three blocks, the march from the elementary school turned into a victory parade. Like the pied piper, Whistle danced down the street, his fingers flying in a ghastly, silent symphony, driving millions of cockroaches to suicide. In waves, they hurled themselves into buildings with sickening ferocity. Others simply flew straight up, escaping the sound, before popping from the inside out, showering laughing survivors with chitin and foul-smelling viscera. When the survivors made it to the harbor, Whistle played an elaborate glissando of notes. The music spun the final swarms of roaches into tornadoes and funnels of glistening copper that gave way to a rainfall of invertebrates, falling steadily into the river where they drowned. The corpses of the murderous creatures lined the surface of the river as far as the eye could see. Whistle was lost in a sea of cheering citizens, who carried him away on their backs.

Boyd would see Whistle only once more.

It was a week later outside the courthouse. The governor arrived in the wake of the citywide massacre to assess future plans. There was talk of a marketing campaign, something dedicated to the suddenly devalued property and quiet community that might bring in new residents. In a matter of a week, roaches had devoured a third of the town. Another third was poised to move out. Despite its ultimate triumph over the bugs, Spoil was becoming a ghost town.

Later on, Boyd would hear how this was used as an excuse not to pay Whistle. Even after everything that happened, he understood. A strange vagrant had saved the city by hypnotizing millions of insects into suicide. It was a hard sell for a politician.

Boyd was on his way into the courthouse when he passed Whistle, who offered that mysterious grin before stopping at the threshold of the front door.

"You're the bug doctor," the odd man muttered.

"Yes," Boyd said.

A grin crossed Whistle's face. He patted Boyd on the shoulder like a man offering condolences on a football loss.

"Well," Whistle said, straightening his garish, leopard-print shirt. "Sorry for killing all of your kids."

Boyd chuckled. It was an odd thing to say, even for the little man who'd saved the town. Whistle wasn't the first person to assume Boyd had a paternal affection for insects. Whistle wandered around the corner of the courthouse, heading toward the harbor. Boyd watched him go. As he entered the courthouse, Boyd thought he could hear Whistle's recorder —but this time it wasn't the frantic, staccato tune that he'd imagined as the piper had mimed the little creatures to their deaths. Instead, the song Boyd thought he heard was slow and sad.

But had he heard it at all?

He couldn't say for sure, but whether real or imagined, Whistle's farewell tune haunted Boyd's memory for years to come, particularly as the children of Spoil began to disappear. The vanishings happened slowly over weeks. When their bodies began turning up beneath the shells of dead roaches that floated on the river, Whistle was long gone, and the town of Spoil with him.

J.N.C

Good Boy, Sabnock

AFTER YAWNING, SERAFINA DIABLO stretched and opened her eyes. She leaned up in the driver's seat of the 1946 rat-rod Dodge Ram but didn't bother touching the wheel or gear shift.

Why the Holy Hell is Sabnock going under eighty?

Smiling, she hiked her neon-green miniskirt up and slid her red-laced thong down. After spreading her legs wide, she extended her right foot out the window and rested the other on the cherry-red dash. The hot summer wind blew her ebony curls back as her hips gyrated. She pressed her wet labia into the steering wheel.

"You like that Sabnock?" she purred.

The vehicle rumbled in horny desire. Serafina knew under the chassis, Sabnock's steel phallus was extending from the carburetor. Abruptly, she brought her legs back in. She pulled her skirt down. Reaching into the glovebox, she removed a tissue. She wiped her glistening fluids from the wheel.

"If you're a good boy, I might give you more."

In response, the engine revved and the tires squealed. Sabnock sped up. Rounding a bend, he caused speckled grouse to flap up from the tall grass lining the highway. A single, especially fat bird flew toward the tarmac —Sabnock's front tires jumped, his hood popped open and slammed down in a burst of blood and feathers. The front tires bounced down with a squeal. Red droplets splattered the windshield.

"Is that why you were going so slow, baby? You're hungry? Wanna go looking for a man?"

The engine emitted an animalistic growl.

"Good boy, get to work and catch one."

Cynthia Walsh screamed.

In the back seat of Brad MacIntosh's Camaro, she was pinned under him as he fought to rip her panties off. His first strike brought the taste of blood to her lips. When he cuffed her open-handed on the side of her head, she almost lost consciousness.

Everything shook violently for a few minutes as a ringing pierced her skull.

Brad's face paled. "Babe, I'm sorry. I just got mad. Are you okay?"

Without warning, yellow lights flooded the back windows and lit up the car. A powerful engine rumbled, shaking the ash-covered pennies in the cup holder.

"What the fuck?" Brad yelled. "Someone found us. Don't make a peep. I'll bust your ass good if you do."

He pulled his jeans up. After grabbing his baseball bat from the floor, he leaped shirtless out of the car.

Chrome gleamed under a blue moonbeam cutting through the canopy. A rat-rod pickup truck faced them from twenty yards away. The driver, a woman, exited and walked toward him. Tight clothes hugged her shapely form. Her lipstick was bright red.

Brad ran toward her with the bat raised.

"Bitch, this is private property."

The woman moved fast —diving in a roll to the right.

As Brad turned toward her, the truck lurched forward. Cynthia sat up to see it pounce. The hood raised high, revealing an engine with hundreds of gleaming blades like shark teeth rotated around the fan belt. The engine revved as the truck swallowed Brad in gulps, his feet kicking.

Cynthia cringed at the sound of meat and bone grinding into the fan blades. Blood sprayed from the rat rod's grill as a pink mist billowed upward. Bits of flesh and tattered strips of clothing fell to the ground.

"Good boy, Sabnock," the woman said over her shoulder as she walked toward the Camaro.

The woman opened the door.

"You okay in there?"

"You just saved me," Cynthia said, pulling her clothes on. "How did you know?"

"I didn't, my truck knew. Don't worry —he only eats men."

Cynthia glanced at the gore-splattered vehicle, then back at the woman.

"Brad?"

"He was chewed up, his soul swallowed and sent straight to hell."

"What's your name?"

"I'm Serafina." The woman extended a hand to help Cynthia from the car. "I'm Satan's favorite daughter, and he gave me Sabnock on my sixteenth birthday."

"Sabnock?"

"He's a demon lord, a Grand Marquis of Hell. He ate Dad's favorite imp. Now he's bound to that car. I'll drop you off in the next town. You must promise to never, ever tell anyone my name or reveal what happened here."

"I promise."

Serafina brought Cynthia in for a hug and brushed her blonde bangs away. She placed a gentle kiss on Cynthia's cheek, leaving a tiny, red smear. "On your soul?"

"On my soul."

Sabnock growled and jumped forward a few inches. Cynthia cringed. Serafina hugged her tighter, turning to the vehicle.

"Bad boy! Don't be so jealous."

The sergeant took a bite of his sausage roll then tossed the rest out his open window. After a few chews, he washed it down with a long sip of syrupy diet cola. After chucking the empty cup out the window, he let out a long, rumbling belch.

He kissed the rosary around his neck, tilted his Smokey Bear hat back, and leaned into a nap.

The radio beeped. Static buzzed for a few seconds, and the voice of his childhood friend echoed over the band.

"You out there Hunter?" Sgt. Dell Smith asked.

"Roger that, Dell, and fuck you. I was about to catch some shut-eye. Don't you have some paperwork to fill out? Or a chicken to fuck?"

"Goddamn, boy, you should've seen this new piece of ass that came through town in a hot rod and dropped off little Cynthia Walsh at the post office. Cynthia told Pat Greene that she was hitchhiking, and the lady gave her a ride."

"What'd the stranger do next?"

"She went to the café long enough to get a bite to eat and then leave."

"You think she was from the city?"

"Had to be. The slut wasn't wearing a bra, and her nips were like tater tots. She had a nice fat ass just like you like them."

Hunter sat up and reached under the overhang of his stomach roll and rubbed his crotch. "Damn, I always miss the good shit. What was she wearing?"

"Of all things, a fucking-ugly green miniskirt and a black tube top. She had brunette curls and the reddest lipstick I've ever seen, and my God, you should've seen her hot rod."

"What kind?"

"An old, souped-up Dodge Ram, 1940s, I think. Looked like something a real greaser would drive. They call 'em rat rods, right? Fifteen-by-fourteen treads in the back, and the paint job was sparkling rust with flecks of darker crimson. Never seen anything like it. I walked by and got a close look. A supercharged V8 stuck out of the hood, all chrome and shiny. And it had large white eagle's wings painted behind each front fender."

"Beauty and the beast, huh?"

"Yep, exactly, and guess what?"

"What?"

"She's a dyke. She flirted with Lou Ann at the counter and told her as much. She even got Lou Ann's number before she left."

Hunter quit touching his cock. His vision began to redden as his temples pounded harder. He adjusted his seat belt then started the vehicle.

"My Lou Ann?" he asked.

"Like I said, she got her number."

"When did the little bitch leave?"

"About ten minutes ago. Heading south on I-44, your way. I'll send you the license and registration, but you'll know it by the hood ornament."

"Let me guess —a ram's head?"

"No, a wicked-looking gold lion's head. You owe me a pitcher at the Roadhouse. You owe me a pitcher"

"Fuck you."

"Over and out."

He started the Mustang and straightened his hat. He looked into the rearview mirror, and an infinity loop of stern, white faces in mirrored sunglasses gazed back.

"Dear Father in Heaven, give me the strength to teach that fucking-lesbo-whore-sinner a lesson today. Amen."

The woman sat on the pickup's hood, straddling the lion's head. She spread her legs and gyrated, rubbing her crotch into the ornament.

Hunter flicked the sirens on and stopped fifty yards away. After the dust cleared, he was surprised she still sat on the hood. She gyrated harder, arching her back. Her red lips parted. She moaned.

What in the Hell? Hunter thought, shifting into the park. He deactivated the sirens, exited the car, and drew his .38 revolver.

"What the fuck are you doing?" he shouted.

The woman slid down to the front of the truck. She turned around, bending, and put her hands on the hood. She pushed her rear toward him and swayed from side to side.

"Come and frisk me, Mr. Policeman," her husky voice called. "I'm ready for you."

As she swayed, the neon-green skirt teased up inch by inch. A black thong divided her plump heart-shaped ass.

His pulse quickened as she slid the thong down.

My lucky day. The bitch is as crazy as she is horny.

"Come take me from behind, Daddy," she cooed. Her red nails grasped her buttocks and spread them.

Hunter smiled at what she'd revealed and eased his gun back into the holster.

"Right here?" he asked, looking around. No one was approaching from either end of the highway.

"Right here, big daddy. Give it to me raw."

He stopped a yard away from her and unbuckled his gun belt, lowering it with his pants. When he dropped his boxers, a semi-flaccid erection flopped out. He stroked it to hardness as he shuffled forward.

In a blur of movement, the woman ducked and rolled to Hunter's right. She scurried away from the truck.

"You cunt!" Hunter strained to reach the gun belt around his ankles.

A thunderous roar startled him —a sound similar to a big cat on the Discovery Channel.

He froze.

Was that from the truck?

Another roar came from behind the vehicle's chrome grill. The truck rolled forward a few inches.

"Jesus Christ." Hunter screamed as he tripped and fell backward. He landed hard on his ass. The hood popped up. The vehicle bent down toward him. The giant maw of the engine bay opened. Blades around the fan whistled in movement.

Again, he strained for the revolver, but his girth impeded the action.

"Looks like you should've laid off the jelly donuts." The woman giggled.

"Fuck you, you goddamn dyke."

"Fuck me? No, fuck you, sic 'em, boy."

The truck lurched forward. Hunter was sucked toward it by an invisible force. He grabbed the top of the hood to no avail. First, his fingers and then his hands were ground into the fan blades. His flesh and blood splattered on his face, filling his screaming mouth and wide eyes. The hood slammed down, shattering his spine.

The truck tilted upward and gulped the man down.

Still alive, he fell headfirst down a long, chrome tunnel and toward a bright, reddish-orange light. Hunter's hands and body were intact but were wispy as if made of smoke. As he fell deeper and deeper, the heat intensified and the sides of the tunnel glowed white-hot.

Are those flames?

Serafina scratched the truck behind an ear. "Good boy, Sabnock. Let's get the fuck out of here. Texas sucks."

DREW NICKS

Frottage

HE SPOTTED HER EARLIER and now followed close behind, squeezing through throngs of people assembled for the midday train.

It was her hair and figure that got his attention. He'd been milling about in the subway station since 9 a.m., waiting and biding his time for just the right specimen. He'd nearly given up hope when he spotted her platinum blonde hair through the crowd. He eyed her round Elizabeth Taylor sunglasses and began to salivate.

She stopped at the Market Street platform. The train was to depart at 1:35 p.m. He looked to the ornate clock on the wall. 1:25 p.m. *Ten minutes, I can wait.* He sat down on a crowded bench between two elderly ladies. He seemed to have interrupted their conversation, but he didn't care. He kept his eagle eyes on his prey.

She stood near the edge of the platform glancing into the tunnel. He admired her. Stared at her body. Supple breasts. A heart-shaped butt beneath yoga pants. This will be grand.

The tunnel rumbled and shook as the graffiti-covered behemoth rolled to the platform. She was the first to step on the aged beast. He stood from the bench as did the old ladies. He sped across the floor to the open door and stepped in. She sat on one of the bench seats, not removing her sunglasses. He sat a seat away. Her purse occupied the seat between.

The train filled quickly. Soon, the entire car smelled of body odor and flatulence. The two elderly ladies, whom he interrupted earlier, became what he needed. When they hobbled onto the car, she gave up her seat for them. He followed suit and stood so close to her he could smell her sweat.

It was sweet.

The train lurched to life and opportunity knocked as soon as the lights dimmed. He stepped close to her and began his deed. He rubbed his body close against her, feigning that others behind him had forced him into this, like sardines packed into a can. His dick was instantly rock hard.

For several moments, it appeared she didn't notice or was so used to these things occurring, that she didn't see his ulterior motive.

He rocked back and forth with the natural flow of the train, feeling his dick rubbing through the material of his pants against the curves of her ass. It felt so good. He felt pressure building in his lower body. He wanted to touch. To feel. To experience the discomfort wriggling through her flesh.

He put his hands on her hips and felt the ejaculate running along the inside of his pants. He felt something wriggle on her hips, but not wriggles of discomfort or gooseflesh. He pulled his hands away.

The car jostled and the lights flickered. He looked about in confusion, nearly losing his cool.

She turned sharply and stared at him through dark lenses. Her petite mouth tightened into an angry grimace.

"Eww, you fucking pervert! What the fuck are you doing?"

He stumbled in his thought process for a moment, trying to figure out what the hell he'd felt along this woman's body.

His meticulously practiced response crept out. "I'm sorry!" he said with what sounded like genuine assurance. "The train is so crowded and that asshole behind me...!" He gestured at a confused looking man standing behind him. "...pushed me into you. I didn't mean anything by it."

He held up his hands in supplication and forced a puppy-dog look across his sharp face.

"Ok," she said. "It's fine, just go somewhere else."

She turned away, and he, in turn, slunk away in mock shame. He didn't go far. He needed to keep a close eye on her. This was a different kind of woman. One, he was sure, he'd never find again.

The train pulled into Market Street at precisely one minute after two, and he watched her, five rows of seats separating them the whole way. He couldn't get her out of his mind. She was unlike any other woman he'd ever groped on the subway. He had to know more about her. Had to see, at least, a small portion of her daily life. He thought he may be in love. True love, as far as he could tell. If only he could identify what was so different about her hips.

When the doors slid open, he watched her step out. He scrambled out the nearest door.

The platform was crowded and filled with a mélange of scents. Stale soft drinks, baby feces, body odor, and a sharp stinging smell that was hard to identify. He never lost sight of her. Her platinum hair bobbed up and down in a sea of darker shades.

He muscled his way through the crowd, his eyes on the crown of gold. She reached the staircase leading to the street and glanced back. He hunched low, hiding himself in an ocean of indiscriminate faces, though his eyes tracked her every movement.

She turned back to the stairs and he followed suit. Perhaps she'd lead him to where she lived. His mind kicked into overdrive with hope.

Above ground, the day was as gray as the interior of a well done steak. Clouds hung low in the sky forming a row of huge bubbles. Somewhere, in the distance, thunder rumbled.

She was perhaps twenty feet ahead of him. He bobbed and weaved in and out of alley entrances, behind phone booths, and behind as many people as he could. The wind picked up, blowing newspapers, soda cups, beer cans, and other refuse down the street in unfocused arcs. Blowing in that wind, he was certain was the scent of her perfume, sweet and floral mixed with something else. He thought it smelled a bit like almonds. Strange.

For three blocks he followed her, even as the surrounding crowds thinned and the environment grew more derelict the farther they went. Aged brick and stucco buildings lay as shells of their former selves. Broken windows high above gazed down on the street from blackened apertures. At street level, most of the windows had been replaced by graffiti-covered plywood. Each piece advertised allegiance to one gang or another.

She kept walking.

Where is she taking me?

She stopped in front of a tall brick building with shadows of a former sign. The building, he guessed, had been a hotel in its glory days. Those days were long past. The dilapidated wreck looked abandoned. The roof leaned precariously to the west side. In a flash, she mounted the steps and disappeared into the yawning black void where a door once stood.

He raced up the steps and stood before the empty doorway. The thick scent of mildew, rot, fire, and feces hung stagnant in the air. He peered into the darkness. Dust danced in the air, illuminated through cracks in the plywood and brickwork. The remains of the lobby had decayed extensively, the reception desk had been attacked with a sharp implement at some point in its life, and the staircase to the second floor had collapsed, lying in heaps of detritus on the old hardwood floor.

So she doesn't live upstairs. But where did she go so fast?

He nearly crossed the threshold before he thought better of himself. *Best not push my luck.* Turning, he climbed back down the steps and walked back into the dreary day.

Later that night, he couldn't get his mind off that rare and radiant maiden. Her smell. Her body. Most of all, he couldn't stop thinking about what lay beneath her clothes and what enticed him about her hips.

In his dank apartment, fruit flies swarmed in the kitchen and the living room. Vast mounds of uneaten food and discarded takeout containers littered much of the available space. Errant fly strips hung ineffectively from the ceiling. Posters of extreme close-ups of female genitalia hung along the living room walls.

He sat in the bathroom, on the lid of the toilet, cock in hand, masturbating like a teenager who'd just discovered the act. His eyes were closed, sweat streamed down his face, and he licked his parched lips while visions of her raced through his head.

She danced before him in a blackened void, sensually removing one piece of clothing at a time. First went her sweater and next came the socks. He was in ecstasy watching this lovely creature dance just for him.

His jerking motions became more rapid when her shirt came off. Her bright blonde hair fell in playful curls along her small, well formed breasts. When her hands reached down to her restricting pants, he could hold back no longer. His cock shuddered and spat forth ropey white strands upon the bathroom floor. Her image faded from his mind's eye.

He was back in the bathroom, disappointed that his vision had been just that. The musty, gray-hued bath mat seemed to wriggle along the cold tile. The puddle of jizz rapidly congealed on the floor. He stared at it with glazed eyes.

This woman has all of me, he thought. *I can't let her go. Never again. She is the only one for me. My everything.*

At 9 a.m., from the confines of a trash-filled bush, he watched her step down the crumbling stone steps and into the bright sunshine. He waited a few additional minutes before he edged out from his hiding place. Stretching aching limbs, he stood before the decrepit structure. The strong scent of decay emanated from the building itself. He pushed strange inklings aside and climbed the steps. He took a deep breath, crossed the threshold, and exhaled.

The lobby was dimmer than he'd remembered. Roaches scuttled between concrete chunks and broken timbers. He wished he'd brought a flashlight but that would take too long to acquire now. He advanced down a long, lightless hallway, weary and listening for signs of life. The building seemed silent except for the sounds of rats in the walls.

The hall received intermittent light through shattered shutters and broken plywood. Mice scurried between his feet. The farther along he went, a strange odor built. A scent akin to vinegar mixed with human sweat. It was intoxicating. There were rooms on both sides of the corridor. None showed signs of habitation. Well, no human habitation anyway. Vermin signs were everywhere. Gaping holes in the plaster showed evidence of raccoon and possum life.

After ten minutes, he found her room. It was not what he expected. The sparse furnishings were original to the building. A heavily stained mattress sat beneath a partially open window. A rat-gnawed wooden chair sat in the center of the room, and a dresser, coated in dust, was pressed tightly against the far wall.

Here, the sweat/vinegar smell was the strongest.

He felt like he was in heaven. He crossed to the dresser and opened the top drawer. *Gold mine!* He'd found her panties. He grabbed the top pair, held them to his face, and inhaled deeply. They were moist and sticky. Reaching down, he unzipped his fly and began his deed.

Euphoria coursed through his frame. An unusual warmth filled his loins. Soon, he could not hold back his urges. Semen shot forth with the power of a fire hose. He collapsed onto the mattress, spent. It was then he heard the approaching footsteps. His body froze.

"What are you doing in my room?"

There she stood in all her feminine glory wearing the Liz Taylor sunglasses. Dirty light through broken slats highlighted her blonde hair. In addition to the yoga pants he'd fallen for, she wore a perplexed look.

"I...I..." he stammered through post-orgasmic shudders.

"Is this what you want?" she asked, cupping her breasts in her hands.

He couldn't believe it. His dream was coming true. The limp sausage in his hand began to grow stiff.

She moved to his position, removing her shirt and bra in the process. She straddled him. Their bodies moved in unison with passion.

He couldn't believe it was happening. *Maybe the big man is looking out for me.* His hands moved to her taut waist and legs. He slipped his hands beneath her waistband, and his body shuddered. He hadn't noticed the sunglasses fall away.

When her pants slipped off, he screamed. Tentacles wriggled from her hips and latched onto his dick.

"Isn't this what you wanted?"

She stared down at him with gangrenous eyes.

He struggled to get away. He could feel sharpened barbs digging into sensitive tissue. In a moment, his organ was wrenched from his filthy body. His screech reached ear-piercing volume before he was silenced by another tentacle.

The last thing he saw was the animalistic pleasure upon his obsession's face.

CHRISTOPHER MICHAEL BLAKE

The Ugly

"Through the window, I saw the Ugly, and the Ugly was inside you."

"Lynn, it's Dr. Lawrence. Can you open up? Please?" the psychiatrist asked, knocking on the apartment door.

"Dr. Lawrence, I can't believe the police called you. You shouldn't have come," Lynn stressed.

"Lynn, it would make everyone out here —myself, Roger, and the police —feel better if you opened the door."

"I'm afraid I can't do that. You of all people should understand why."

"Does this have to do with that infection you claim to have? Lynn, I warned you against coming off your medication. I told you your symptoms manifest an underlying mania brought on by the realization of past trauma. There is nothing wrong with your skin. Why don't you come out of there, and we can discuss this?"

"If you think she's going to hurt herself or if she is a threat to others, I have to send the team inside," the tactical police officer at the end of the hallway said into Dr. Lawrence's earpiece.

"Give me a few more minutes to talk her down from this."

"How is Roger?" Lynn sniffled from behind the apartment door.

"He's fine, Lynn. The paramedics are treating him now," Dr. Lawrence said, implying there was no permanent damage to her fiancé. The bloody wound across Roger's cheek and the head dressing applied by the paramedics told a different story.

"Tell Roger I never meant to hurt him. Really, I didn't, but *the Ugly* was smeared all over him. I had to... I just had to." Lynn sobbed.

"Then why did you? Answer me, Lynn. Let me help you. The situation out here is escalating, and once I'm gone, the police will have no alternative but to storm their way inside and take you by force."

"You already know why I hurt Roger. I can't let *the Ugly* spread to anyone else. It needs to be cut away."

"Are you suggesting your disease is infectious?" Dr. Lawrence remembered what Lynn told him during therapy about a cyst protruding up her back and spreading throughout her skin. He recalled Lynn swearing she felt *the Ugly* crawling through-out her body.

"I told you, doctor, only you wouldn't listen to me. This isn't imaginary. This is more than cancer, a blight, or a disease. It's *the Ugly,* and it's spreading. I can feel it," Lynn blubbered.

"Lynn, you know that's not true. If this skin disease is spreading, wouldn't I be infected? I've been treating you for months, and I'm perfectly fine. Let me in, and we can discuss this. I promise I can help see you through this mess, but it starts with you opening the door."

"I'm sorry, Dr. Lawrence. I saw it through the window when you approached. It's too late for both of us."

"Lynn!" Dr. Lawrence yelled, pounding on the door. In his earpiece, Dr. Lawrence heard the order for a tactical breach. The special operations team flooded the corridor and knocked down Lynn's door as Dr. Lawrence was ushered out of the way.

After the police breached the apartment, the team leader, whose uniform name tag read Reynolds, met with Dr. Lawrence.

"I haven't seen Lynn come out yet. Can I go in?" Dr. Lawrence asked.

"That is what I wanted to talk to you about, doc. Lynn's dead."

"What? My Lord in heaven. I shouldn't have waited. I should have let your team go inside immediately."

"I don't think it would have mattered. Are you sure that person was Lynn on the other side of the door?"

"Of course, I'm sure. I've been treating Lynn for months."

"I was afraid you'd say that," Reynolds said.

"What do you mean? Can I go in there and see her?"

"I don't think that's such a good idea, doc. The sole occupant of that room, there's just no way... What I mean is, it's likely Lynn's been dead for hours."

"This must be some mistake. You're mistaken," Dr. Lawrence said.

"Lynn used an electric saw to split open her skull and remove pieces of her brain. Then she pulled the skin from her face with a filleting knife. Chunks of her organs were removed by her own hand. Everything was put on display in jars in her living room on the mantel. There's no way she survived all the blood loss while operating on herself," Reynolds said.

"You heard Lynn on the other side of the door speaking to me through your earpiece," Dr. Lawrence said. "She was alive a short while ago, I'm certain. I'm not crazy."

"I didn't say you were crazy. I thought I heard her too, but I'm open to the possibility it wasn't Lynn we heard on the other end of the door."

"Your men inside must be mistaken about her time of death. What makes you so certain about when she passed?"

"We found her tongue in one of the jars. It's been there for hours. I'm sorry, Dr. Lawrence."

Dr. Lawrence stood outside the apartment and placed his hands on his waist. As he moved away from the door, Dr. Lawrence felt something push against his midsection. He lifted his shirt. A small, white, egg-like cyst was protruding beneath the skin. He could feel *the Ugly* crawling inside him.

MICHAEL FOWLER

The Critch

WHEN THE SUN BEGAN setting, his top four coworkers had concluded their af-
ter-dinner swim and returned to their cabins. Dugan stood alone in the pool. He lowered
the handgun from his temple and laid it on the tiled edge. Using his freed-up hand, he
lifted a glass of red to his parched, chlorinated lips.

He had to admit, the first evening of the morale-boosting and team-building trip
hadn't broken much ice, except the stuff that chilled drinks. After grilled food and
cocktails in the cabin he shared with the men, his folks had gone on drinking at the
poolside —none getting rowdy, not even red-faced Neil —but despite being socially
lubricated by alcohol they remained on edge. They kept looking warily at him and at each
other, meanwhile drinking and smoking and holding guns to the sides of their heads as if
about to commit suicide at any moment: a typical work party. In his mind's eye, he saw
Marjorie's well-manicured red nails gripping her .22, its muzzle lost in her lush red locks.
Tom's thick fingers and chunky gold class ring on the handle of his 9mm. Nervous Neil
steadying his revolver in one hand and twirling a glass in the other, a cigarette clenched in
his mouth.

Were the guns loaded? Maybe. His, within easy reach beside him, was not, but the
ammo was a few steps away, by his bed in the men's cabin. It had to be nearby and readily
available if he was to obtain that voluptuous feel of release, that liberation from life's woes,
that a gun can give. Such comfort was stronger than booze, more powerful than nicotine,
and like those substances, it delivered a buzz. A compact gun was as easy on the hand
as a cig or a glass. What's more, thanks to the passage of House Bill 7983 decades ago,
self-directed firearms were perfectly legal. A lot of people had come to enjoy this right.

The pistols bothered Dugan: They were indicators of low morale. To see his most
productive people, himself included, comforting themselves by pressing a solid .22 or
9mm against their throbbing temples, or keeping one close to hand, was distressing.
Worse, everyone carried guns now: students in class as young as eighteen and the elderly in
retirement homes, doctors and lawyers in offices, and truck drivers and sanitation workers
on the street. All went about with a means of self-destruction within reach, filling a strong
emotional need. He considered gun-grasping to be a sign of widespread sickness and of a
less than fully productive workforce. But only Dugan and a few psychologists who posted
warnings online seemed to notice or care.

Dugan held the snout of his 9mm, a nickel-plated Rogers, to his sideburn, for sensual comfort, and to delay joining the others in the cabin. After toweling off in their individual rooms they would return to the pool in casual evening garb, guns in hand of course —except perhaps alcoholic Linda who was trying to kick the hardware habit if not the booze —to socialize for another hour or two before turning in.

Tomorrow, after breakfast at the hotel restaurant, he would lead his guests along a hiking trail through caverns and woods to a scenic lake for boating or fishing, but how to fill the rest of this evening? He had brought along poker chips and cards, a few classic movies, and even a pair of bongos to tap on and pass back and forth —yes bongos, what had he been thinking? This was no hootenanny, and he was chief morale officer, not a bandleader. Well, let his people entertain themselves for a bit, while he enjoyed the full moon coming into view overhead, and the now peaceful pool within its rectangle of electric lights. There was also his wine to be sipped. Who knows, maybe his absence would boost everyone's morale.

Someone or something jumped in the water beside him, splashing his face, his glass, and dousing the gun beside him. The submerged creature surfaced revealing an almost human face with a crooked grin and oddly sleek head, calling to mind a great eel. Dugan knew it was one of the Evolving Ones recently welcomed into society. He noticed a family of three Evolving Ones occupying a cabin nearby. With the exception of the small piglike animal they led around on a leash, all three Evolving Ones appeared to be two-armed, two-legged hominids attired in the same style of clothes Dugan and his party wore. Up close, in the growing darkness, this adult male in swim trunks resembled an upright eel —a friendly, toothless eel.

"Eli," said the Evolving One, offering a humanoid hand with a trace webbing linking its four fingers. Was the webbing coming or going? Dugan wondered. He'd heard the Evolving Ones could change their appearance like *that*.

"Dugan," he replied, placing his glass at poolside beside the gun and taking the webbed hand in his. It felt like a living fish, cold, slimy, and prickly. This was his first face-to-face with an Evolving One. He didn't know what to expect.

"Lovely evening," said the Evolving One. The warm water came up to their chests. He cast a glance at Dugan's damp gun an arm's length away. "Thinking of shooting yourself this fine night?"

"Yes, I always am. Suicide goes well with eerie moonlight. I wish I could stop lugging that thing around, it's a nasty habit." Dugan regretted the men had carried the cooler inside with them, or he would have offered the Evolving One, whom he saw eyeing his nearly empty glass, a beer. He wondered what Evolving Ones drank. "Does my little gun there offend you?"

"I find the pistol a bit retrograde," said Eli. "My people once held weapons to their heads too, for the relief in it. Centuries ago we used the same old-fashioned firearms you still employ, but recently those gave way to modern electronic and laser devices that are less bulky and intrusive. They could be clipped to one's hair or collar and activated with a button, destroying only the owner. The consolation that wearing one gave was immeasurable. I may still have one or two of them at home."

"Self-detonators, the new wave of potential suicide implementation," Dugan said with mock approval. "I'm sure such items are in the works here, sad to say. Where does it end? My theory is that available suicide promotes actual suicide. Suicides are up all across society, mass shootings too. Life is cheap."

"With luck, you'll evolve beyond all that despair and slaughter, as we Evolving Ones are beginning to do. We're almost there. Meanwhile, I know of a nice alternative to guns and personal detonators."

Dugan was certain he saw an instantaneous change in Eli's physiognomy, the eel-like face elongating and roughening into a toothier alligator-mien. He watched as the smoother and more blunted eel returned to the fore, the harmless fish replacing the fierce reptile in an instant. Beneath those fleeting shifts, the almost human face remained visible.

"Let me show you something," Eli said. "It's what got me through each day until I became reconciled to life, as I am now, and as many of us Evolving Ones are now. It's much more satisfactory than a gun or a detonator."

Opening his left hand, Eli exposed a curled up creature of some sort covering his palm. Its segments of off white rings stretched out, and its many hairy legs writhed sluggishly. "Say hello to Jiggs, my critch."

"That's hideous," Dugan said, recalling the leashed pig-like creature he'd glimpsed earlier. No telling what sort of beasts the Evolving Ones consorted with. "And you carry that on you?"

"Oh yes, everywhere I go —that is until recently, and now just on occasion, as you can see. Don't worry, critches are perfectly harmless unless you pinch or slap them, and I'm sure you won't do that to Jiggs. Even if you abused him, you would only receive a slight nip or scratch in retaliation. Here, wildlife experts have found them free of disease and no threat to the ecosystem. Critches secrete nothing and inject nothing, are free of bacteria and viruses, and subsist mainly on water, even chlorinated water. Jiggs is having a grand time in the pool. Add a few scraps of leftovers to his water —garbage, that is, but nothing too spicy —and Jiggs is perfectly content. Critches are approved by your Department of Health, too, for the reasons I mentioned."

"Are they now?" Dugan asked, controlling his repulsion.

"Here, take him in your hand. Better, put him on your shoulder. He likes shoulders, a high roost gives him a more comprehensive view."

Dugan, still reluctant to join his coworkers, did just that, and placed the calmly writhing critch on his left shoulder, where he sometimes rested his gun. He felt the animal's tentacles secure a soft grip on him, and tried hard to rein in his disgust. Eli hadn't mentioned it, but Jiggs smelled rancid, like raising the lid off a dumpster.

"Relax. Jiggs likes you already," Eli said. "He's a receptive parasite, or better say a pet, and will adjust to your lifestyle and devote himself to your welfare in a heartbeat, though he's never encountered you or any human before. Understand, though, that he won't evolve with you, should you change form as we Evolving Ones do. Critches are lower life-forms that haven't altered over millennia, and may never alter, but they're adept at attuning themselves to intelligent hosts or owners." Dugan shivered in discomfort. Eli continued. "A few seconds more and you'll feel the incredible relief of a critch, much more soothing than a gun to the head."

"I don't see how," Dugan said, still wanting to brush the critch off him to suppress his disgust-induced quivering. He didn't want Jiggs to sting or bite him or whatever it did when offended, so he remained motionless. "The whole comfort of a gun is it can remove one from this...vale of despair...any time one chooses. How can Jiggs be a substitute for that, if, as you say, he's harmless?"

"That's the magic of a critch," Eli said. "The pure revulsion one derives from his loathsome presence does the trick. You accept ugly Jiggs, you accept ugly life: simple as that. If that sounds impossible to you —and I'm sure it does —remember that Jiggs is impossibly ugly. Now, stand still and let Jiggs do his work. You're shaking too much. You'll find he's much better consolation than a gun —and more intoxicating too, headier than any drug, or the wine I see you're enjoying."

Dugan tried to remain calm as the whitish segmented thing gripped his shoulder. But where he initially felt revulsion, a spreading euphoria took its place as if he were working on a bottle of pricey merlot.

"I've been addicted to Jiggs for some years now," Eli went on, "and have put away all my firearms and explosives thanks to his beneficent morale-boosting, I suppose you might call it. I'm certain without Jiggs by my side, I would have died of despair or actually blown my head off long before this moonlit evening." He reached out and gave Jiggs an affectionate stroke with his fingertip. Jiggs responded by flexing his revolting tentacles.

"Jiggs's ugliness saved you?"

"You said it," Eli said. "Such ugliness as Jiggs's is truly life-preserving." Eli's features underwent another transformation. His face turned shark-like, massive and unreasoning, and his body became an aquatic missile. The change lasted a second, and again the milder Eli stood before him, up to his hominid chest in water, his plump eely lips curved in a smile.

"I want you to have Jiggs as your own. Take him off my hands, won't you?" Eli entreated.

This was too much, and something in the Evolving One's jelly-lipped smile suggested deception.

"You're joking," Dugan said.

"Not at all, I'm evolving past my need of him. You humans won't for hundreds of years to come —if you follow the path of us Evolving Ones. You need Jiggs more than I do now. Don't worry. He's used to changing owners. I inherited him from an elderly female librarian of my acquaintance who lived alone. Jiggs sat in her lap as she read through the night. She claimed he turned the pages of her book for her. She's the one who named him, I suppose taking the name from some old novel, and he was her critch for years

—her only one, though some Evolving Ones keep colonies of the critters, as we used to before our latest and perhaps final evolutionary phase. Thanks to Jiggs, she put aside the head-vaporizing laser adornment that was such a consolation to her, until she got so old she no longer feared or resented life. Then she gave Jiggs to me. She lived comfortably for another year after that, no longer tormented by life."

"And you are no longer tormented by life?"

"Correct, but not because I'm elderly and prepared to die. I'm no doddering librarian." He gave a low chuckle that sounded like water gurgling in a drain. "But I'm reaching a state of development, more so each day, where life no longer distresses me. On the contrary, I act more and more out of a blind will or compulsion to satisfy myself and perform what I used to consider questionable and even objectionable deeds, without a care about how I may affect others. I act for my own gain, and that's all. Life now pleases me."

Jiggs had left Dugan's shoulder and crawled along the poolside. It caressed his gun with loathsome feelers, and knocked over his wineglass, which broke against the tiles, staining them red.

"Let me think on it." Dugan enjoyed the contact with Jiggs and felt stronger with it on his shoulder. The situation was unheard of... "I'm terrible with pets, the ones I've kept ended up getting on my nerves. In fact, I should get back to my cabin. I'm having a get-together with some coworkers, and I've been out here soaking myself long enough."

"I'd like you to stay a while longer."

Eli reached into the water and grabbed Dugan's left thigh, lifting it so Dugan's bent knee rose above the surface. Dugan stood unsteadily on one leg, trapped in the Evolving One's humiliating embrace. Then, as he stared dumbly at the Evolving One's benign eel-like face, the shark-visage took command. He beheld a predatory life-form that thrived without compunction or compassion. A moment later the humanoid-eel returned, then the shark came again with rows of eager teeth. Eli's appearance wavered back and forth between the two forms, as if he couldn't decide which to claim.

Jiggs climbed back onto Dugan's shoulder, distracting him. The critch extended its tentacles and feelers as if for flight, in a hideous ball of hairy, scaly projections that looked like an exploded star. As the drug-like embrace of the creature seeped through him, Dugan found his gun within the critch's many folds and grasped the handle. The shark-Eli lunged at him, and he pointed the weapon and fired. The gun had been loaded and a dead humanoid fell back and floated in the water, his evolution halted.

The shot brought Dugan's coworkers rushing from their cabins and over to the pool. He greeted them with a laugh.

"Have I got a story for you," he said as the critch reduced to its normal size on his shoulder. A lively, happy Dugan began to tell it.

CHRIS W. MCGUINNESS
Pieces of Victor

MY HUNCH ABOUT DEATH was right.

A whole lot of nothing like falling into a sleep so deep you don't even dream.

Just blackness.

Nothing and nothing and more nothing.

Disappointing as hell, but damn peaceful.

I was enjoying total obliteration when I was rudely awakened. The taste of frigid water, gritty silt, and industrial sludge filled my mouth. I wanted to gag but somehow avoided spewing up whatever was in my guts. I opened my eyes to a disorienting Dutch angle of my surroundings. A crooked night sky occupied half of my vision, and a dark swath of rocky shoreline dominated the other. I heard the roar of rushing water and felt muddy sand sticking to my cheek. I smelled the wet, fecal reek of the big river.

This is where they dumped me.

Just like the others.

I tried to scream. No dice. The freezing air whistled through my windpipe and out the ragged hole below my neck. That's when I knew, I'd bought it. I hadn't survived the half-assed trap they laid for me. I was nothing more than a bloated head washed up on a riverbank. The stars above me shone bright and white, like cruel and terrible diamonds.

Fuck.

I wanted more than anything to mutter the word out loud. Watch it rise from my lips in a thick cloud of white steam. But nothing happened. My jaw moved, but the parts of me that made sound were gone.

It made sense if you knew how things went in my line of work.

I was an "associate," not a true member of the outfit because I was Irish, not Sicilian, thus forever a bridesmaid in the eyes of the old greaseballs running things. Despite this handicap, I'd made myself useful as hell, earning a living as muscle for hire. A professional leg-breaker. The kind of guy you send to put fear into the deadbeats who owed you money. I put the hurt on a lot of people in my time. Never put someone in the ground, but I put a lot of bastards in wheelchairs. Brute force was my trade, and I was good at it. Hell, I loved it. But something had gone wrong. Someone decided I wasn't as indispensable as I thought I was.

The last thing I remember was stumbling out of Marv's Tavern after a long day of brutalizing degenerate assholes who couldn't pay their debts. I'd drunk most of my pay and was on my way to call on my girl. There was a shape. An amorphous shadow in the corner of my eye. Someone stepped out of the darkened doorway to my left.

They raised their hands. There was a flash of cold, blue metal. A thunderous sound.

Then the darkness.

Wind whipped over the barren shore. Freezing air whistled through a dime-sized hole in my left temple. No doubt there were two or three more similar holes in my torso, which was likely wrapped in garbage bags and weighed down with chains, sinking into the muck at the bottom of the Cuyahoga River. I blinked my eyes, trying to figure out if all this was real. A fly landed on my nose. I reached up to scratch it out of instinct. I felt my hand, the left one, twitch. Wherever it was, it seemed to be trapped under something jagged and heavy. I put a little more *oomph* into it and felt the weight start to tumble away. I ran my lifeless fingers over hard and uneven chunks.

Rocks. They'd tossed my hand in the quarry.

Standard operating procedure when the outfit clipped someone. Chop them up and scatter the pieces to the four winds. It makes the body hard to find and even harder to identify. The river to the east, the quarry to the south. Both were favored dumping grounds of my former employers. It didn't take a genius to guess where my right hand would be.

I closed good old Righty into a fist and grabbed a heaping clod of wet earth. It was buried in the woods to the north. The goons they paid to dispose of yours truly put real miles on their tires scattering my carcass. It was a real professional job for a low-level lowlife that no one would miss. I must have really pissed someone off, and I was pretty sure that someone was Salvator Amato.

Sal was a capo in the outfit and a frequent employer of my services. He was a nasty, mean-spirited little shit, even by scumbag standards. He carried a chip on his shoulder after being passed up year after year for a promotion, and he took it out on anyone and everyone below him with masochistic relish. He wasn't liked, but he was a good earner, so the bosses kept him around and let him indulge his lust for violence, torture, and mayhem as long as the cash rolled in.

I willed my left hand forward, using my fingers to drag it across the floor of the quarry toward a service road leading out of the pit. I couldn't see what I was doing, but the act was instinctual. My right hand was busy digging upward. I felt the dirt worming its way under my fingernails. Someone once told me the nails continue growing after you buy it. I wondered how much time they'd had to grow.

Salvatore.

A few days before I'd been bumped off, I had stopped by the social club he operated out of on the outskirts of the city's dilapidated commercial district. It was Sal's little den of iniquity. A playground for him and his crew far from the prying eyes of the cops and even his own superiors.

I was in no mood for his shit when I walked in. The bum he'd sent me after made a run at me with a baseball bat. The dirtbag got off a lucky shot to my ribs before I wrestled it away from him, and beat him to a whimpering pulp with his own weapon. My side throbbed with pain every time I inhaled. Sal was bullshitting with one of his cronies by the pool table when I walked up and slapped a fat envelope down on the green felt. A wet, red stain marred the corner of the white paper.

"How much?"

Sal was a short man with thick eyebrows set in a constant scowl above a crooked Roman nose.

"I don't know, whatever he had on him. I didn't have time to play twenty-one questions."

Sal grunted and picked up the envelope. He licked his thumb and counted out the bills, peeling off a crumpled Benjamin for me.

"Next time, try not to get so much fucking blood on the money. I'll take the ruined bills out of your cut, *capaice*?"

I fought the urge to grab a pool cue and go to work on the disrespectful little troll. Instead, I took a deep breath and nodded. While I was a proponent of direct and violent responses to assaults on my honor, even a dumb lug like me knew: Made men were off limits. Instead, I took solace, having been engaged in a more subtle form of revenge. I'd been banging his daughter, Gina, for the last six months or so. That day, I walked out the door determined to stop by her apartment for a vigorous roll in the hay just to spite the cranky old asshole, cracked ribs be damned.

Gina.

She had to be the reason for my current situation. Someone must have squealed to Daddy Dearest and wham, bam, thank-you ma'am, one in the dome for old Victor.

I mouthed a wordless chuckle on the lonely riverbank. Lefty was making his way up the service road. Righty, meanwhile, had clawed his way above ground, and I directed him toward the two-lane highway that led back to the city. My big mitts retained their savage strength and seemed incapable of tiring. That was good. We had business to take care of. I didn't know how or why I was brought back, but I wasn't going to waste time and miss taking advantage of such a unique opportunity.

I was going to kill Sal and ask questions later.

Lefty hit the asphalt of Route 260 in record time, and Righty quickly caught up. I kept to the edge of the road, feeling the vibrations of cars roaring by, oblivious to my hands groping their way toward the lights of the city. I moved them onward with grim purpose, hoping they wouldn't get pancaked by late-night drunk drivers or speed-crazed truckers rushing to make their deliveries.

The thing I had with Gina wasn't just about tweaking Sal's nuts, though it was a nice bonus. I was in love with her. We were an unlikely pair of star-crossed lovers, a down-and-out thug in his forties and a drop-dead gorgeous twenty-four-year-old law school student. Sal had big plans for Gina. He wanted her to be somebody in the legit world. Like a lot of mob princesses, she had an attraction to the dark corners of her father's business. I met her by accident while making my usual drop at the club. Sal was away on business, and Gina had taken the opportunity to hang with the wise guys who worked for him. His goons had surrounded her like a pack of wolves circling a juicy meal. She was wearing tight jeans and a Ramones shirt. Her eyes were the color of brown sugar and her jet-black hair was pulled back in a tight ponytail. I walked by her and nodded politely.

We didn't say a word to each other that day. A week later, she rolled up outside Marv's in her cherry red Mustang and asked me out. I had no idea how she tracked me down or where she got the balls to show up out of the blue and demand my company. I have to admit it turned me on. Still, I should have told her to hit the road. Getting into that car with that girl would be one hell of a hazard to my health.

I got in the car anyway. We grabbed coffee, then dinner, then drinks. After the drinks? Well, you can guess where it went from there. She had me eating out of the palm of her hand. I was tied up in knots over the girl and I loved every minute of it.

We carried on our dalliance under her father's nose. Sure, he'd never find out until it was too late. We had a plan to save up enough cash and escape somewhere beyond the reach of Sal and the outfit. It was stupid and reckless to think we could pull it off, but the haze of love made us both naive enough to believe we could. I wondered what terrible punishment Sal would inflict on his darling girl. He doted on her, but his tolerance, even for his own kin, had its limits.

"Christ, I think I threw my damn back out lugging that huge freak's body in and out of here."

It felt like the voice was coming from someone standing next to me. It was familiar. Sal's right-hand lackey, Jimmy Vincent. I rolled my head around in the muck toward the sounds. All I saw was more shoreline.

"Stop your fuckin' whining Jimmy. You didn't even have to whack the big idiot."
Sal.

I heard his footsteps on a hard tile floor. The sound of a faucet being turned on. A tinny-sounding radio played eighties hits in the background. I knew these sounds. The sounds of the kitchen at the back of Sal's club. It had long ceased to be used for its intended purpose. While the occasional sandwich or steak might come out from its windowless double doors, the rest of the time the place was used for a whole different kind of butchery.

"Took a hell of a long time chopping him up. You did what I told you to?"

"Of course. Old Vic's in more pieces than Humpty fucking Dumpty."

"You did it exactly as I ordered?"

"How many times are you gonna' ask me? Yes, weighed down or buried everything but the head. It'll wash up and be in papers. I bet one of the tabloids'll put the picture on the front page."

It felt like I was listening to them from the bottom of a deep well. One of my ears must be in the trashcan next to the sink. As good as Sal and Jimmy were at taking me apart, they did a half-assed job of cleaning up the mess.

"Good. I want my daughter to see those headlines. Can't believe she was gonna run off with that Irish shitheel. Not made, not even Italian."

"Kids these days, no respect for traditional values."

"Well, if this doesn't teach her to keep her legs closed and listen to her father, I don't know what will. Maybe I'll send someone by her place to teach her a lesson. A couple black eyes and a busted nose to remind her just who is in charge. Anyway, get the fuck out of here. Call Spider in the morning and tell him to finish cleaning up in here."

The door to the kitchen opened and closed. Jimmy's footsteps moved away.

"And tell him to take out the trash before it stinks up the place," Sal yelled. He snorted through his big nose and hawked a wad of God-knows-what into the can. Something thick and viscous dripped down my earlobe.

"What a night," he muttered.

There was a rustling of clothes and the snap of a Zippo lighter. If my nose had been there, I'm sure I'd smell the stink of Pall Malls.

I thought about Sal and Jimmy cutting me up, and of Gina being forced to see my rotting mug washed up out of the river like garbage. Rage, red and all-consuming, welled inside me. It fueled me, running through all my parts. It must have made my hands move faster because they were already in the parking lot of the club, guided by whatever dark power granted me this life after death. I felt clumsy, thumping footsteps crunching along loose gravel. My hands crept under a nearby car. I somehow knew it was Jimmy's ride. The steps got closer, and I imagined his cheap wingtips poking into view as he stopped to unlock the door.

Let's give this a whirl.

Righty kicked things off by clamping himself around Jimmy's ankle. He struggled, pulling back, and kicking wildly in the air. My grip was strong and Righty held fast. In his panic, Jimmy lost his balance and tumbled ass over teakettle into the dirt. He screamed so loud that my ear heard the muffled cry in the kitchen.

"The hell is that?" Sal muttered. I heard the unmistakable sound of him drawing his trusty Glock 9mm.

While Jimmy flailed on his back, I didn't waste any time. Lefty darted out from under the car and skittered up his chest like a fleshy spider from hell. Jimmy moaned. I felt a frantic heartbeat hammering through his chest.

I wrapped my fingers around his throat and squeezed. Jimmy's breath started hitching, so I squeezed harder. I could feel the cartilage of his windpipe give, then snap. Jimmy's hands clawed helplessly against Lefty's vise-like grip. He opened his mouth in a desperate attempt to suck in air, but Righty was waiting in the wings. I forced the hand into his mouth, gripped his tongue, and tugged with all my might. There was a satisfying popping sensation as it ripped loose. Something warm poured out of Jimmy's mouth onto my hands. His body went limp. One less rat walking the earth.

Their work done, my hands began to move toward the club. I strained my ear to hear what was going on in the kitchen, but the place was silent. Sal had turned off the radio and wasn't moving a muscle. He was lying in wait, gun drawn.

Righty took a direct route, scampering across the parking lot and shoving aside the unlocked front door. I moved him across the dining room and burst through the swinging kitchen doors.

"Holy Mother of God!" Sal screamed from one of the far corners of the room. "What the fuck?"

A murderous glee welled up, somewhere in my dead heart. A frantic volley of gunfire erupted in the small kitchen. Righty bobbed and weaved. One of the bullets ricocheted off the floor and I felt a shard of tile whiz past my hand. Righty scrambled gracelessly under a gap between the kitchen sink and floor as Sal emptied the rest of his clip. My ear was ringing and everything sounded dull and fuzzy. Righty flattened himself and backed against the wall in the cramped space.

"Son of a bitch," Sal spat. I heard the crashing and clattering of drawers being ripped open. His footsteps clomped over toward the sink. Something metallic rattled.

"How about some barbeque, you little shit?"

With a hiss, something cold sprayed on Righty. I thought of the aerosol cans of cooking spray I'd seen in my visits to the back kitchen. No self-respecting Italian would use them, but Sal was cheap and lazy as hell.

There was the *click* of a lighter, and Righty burst into flames. This pissed me off righteously. I launched my flaming hand out from under the sink. Sal was ready for the counteroffensive, and I felt several violent jolts as he repeatedly stomped on it. His shoes came down hard on Righty's pinky and ring fingers, breaking the bones and rendering them useless. I grabbed the cuff of his slacks and the heat of the flames crawled up his pant leg. Sal yawped and used his other foot to kick Righty off, hurling him up in a graceless arc before he flopped down on the long wooden table in the center of the room. That cold butcher's slab was the last place my body had been whole.

Sal cursed, smacking at his leg to extinguish the flames. Righty was in bad shape, but I rallied him for a second assault. Before I could launch my next attack, Sal screamed and rushed Righty. I tried moving my burned hand, but Sal was too fast. Something hard and sharp sank through the top and out the palm, pinning Righty to the table. I assumed it was one of the carving knives conveniently placed throughout the dingy kitchen.

"How do you like that?" Sal's voice took on a manic edge. "Maybe I'm crazy, maybe I'm not, but you're in a world of hurt, my little pal."

Pots and pans clattered to the floor behind Sal. He yelped. My grin widened.

Reinforcements had arrived. While he'd been duking it out with Righty, Lefty had snuck through one of the vents at the back of the building, scuttling stealthily along the top of the kitchen's walk-in freezer. I used Jimmy's tacky blood to write a little message on the wall above the freezer door. Back by the river, my milky eyes watched the endless stars gleam as I pictured Sal whirling around to see the dripping note I'd left him.

JOIN ME IN HELL SAL. UR FRIEND VIC

"Vic," Sal said.

It was the first time I'd heard genuine terror in the man's voice. A wave of sinister elation washed over me.

I hurled Lefty off the top of the freezer kamikaze-style, hoping to get a swipe or two at Sal's ugly mug. He sidestepped and the hand crashed to the floor, skidding along the slick tile. Sal fumbled for something in his clothes —another knife or maybe an extra clip for the Glock. He was too slow. Lefty shot like quicksilver across the floor. Sal tried dodging again, but Lefty got a good grip on his pant leg and started climbing, reached the fork of the capo's crotch, and grabbed his balls.

I squeezed with all my might.

Sal howled like an animal. His hands frantically beat Lefty as I pulverized his testicles. His screams reached a register I previously thought impossible for a grown man.

While Sal tried to dislodge Lefty from his marriage tackle, Righty was busy freeing himself from the knife. I felt the blade pull diagonally through my palm, slicing away the charred and crushed ring and pinky fingers. The hand was weak. I hurled its mangled form off the counter, where it landed on the floor with a meaty plop. It crept toward Sal, still bucking and hollering in the throes of Lefty's iron grip. Righty climbed up Sal's pant leg, then his shirt, clinging to his thrashing body like a rodeo pro on a pissed-off bull. Sal's screams were muffled as my hand clambered over his mouth. My fingers found the soft orbs of his eyes and plunged themselves into the sockets. They dug and dug until I felt hot jelly running down the scarred landscape of Righty's overcooked flesh. Sal's screams morphed into an infant-like mewling. He collapsed on the floor, the fight leaving him drained and blind.

"Vic, please."

Lefty removed himself from the capo's decimated balls and groped along a floor littered with pots, pans, and other detritus from our struggle.

"Vic, you don't have to do this. I'm sorry, I'm *sorry!*"

Lefty's fingers closed around the handle of a paring knife, small enough to maneuver and sharp as hell. Righty tore Sal's shirt open, revealing his heaving, hair-covered chest. My ear picked up the scrape of the knife's blade as Lefty dragged it across the floor.

"Don't do me like this! I'll give you anything, money —my daughter. Take Gina —take her!"

It was too late for Sal. I was beyond bargaining, mercy, and even love. The malevolent power inside me ebbed. I stopped listening to his pleas. Lefty got closer with the knife. Between him and Righty, I was confident they could work together to wield the little pigsticker with the necessary finesse. Unlike Jimmy, I planned to take my time with Sal. I'd take him apart piece by piece, just like he did me. One good turn deserves another, right?

Yes, I'd take my sweet time, and when it was done, I'd drag him into the black nothingness with me. Into the dark where we would float endlessly with whatever nightmares lived there —two hellbound bastards lost in the night eternal.

Back on the riverbank, the sun was coming up. I lifted my eyes to the fading stars above and smiled at the abyss.

TIM TOLBERT

The House of Hunger

AS A BOY, MATT often remarked to his mother that he was starving. Long trips would take their toll, or boredom, or maybe even indecisiveness, and "I'm hungry!" or "I'm starving!" became his go-to phrase. But at that age he was easy to please. Just turn on the microwave. Put the oven on for a few minutes —basic food for kids after school.

His mother was many things, but she was no cook. It didn't really matter. Those evenings, he would eat like a king. In his kingdom, chicken nuggets or mac and cheese were all he needed. More often than not, despite his mother's best attempts, the food wasn't always heated all the way through. But he didn't care.

When Matt became an adult, his picky eating didn't exactly do him any favors, and he never learned to cook for himself. Instead, he took meals at strange hours of the day, takeout binges brought on by exhaustion from work or an episode of depression. He never ate in bed, at least. That idea repulsed him, much like wearing one's shoes in bed. Bed, he avowed, was to be a clean place.

But now, on the unforgiving cold of the concrete floor, he knew what hunger was.

Being chubby and being gay made him feel like a freak. To society it seemed you couldn't add to the world unless you were thin. To be thin was to have it all. His build rarely worked to his advantage in the dating scene, as much as he tried.

Then just two months ago, the blue glow of his cell phone lit up with a new prospect, a prospect that started as commonplace.

Pic?

This had happened before. He was conditioned to warn himself, to warn others, of his mark of Cain that plagued his world: *I'm a big guy*. That would sometimes be followed by, *How big?* As if they, on the other end, were worrisome of him actually being the Elephant Man. The exchange was dread incarnate: The pic would often result in instant rejection. The masses had decided his fatness made him unfit for human life. On weekends, he would stay up well into the night just staring in the bathroom mirror, often in the dark. He would distort. His skin would sag endlessly. He would look like he was melting. Then, as the ultimate violation, he would feel his breasts.

So when that one word —*Pic?*—came through, he was prepared for the routine.

He could never have imagined the hunger.

His suitor, whom he would later come to know as Jamie, was alarmingly kind. And out of his league. Tall, incredibly lanky, like a scarecrow, Jamie had facial hair that hung from his chin like cobwebs at some haunted house, but he seemed proud of it. Why shouldn't he? He was skinny. The world was his. Small talk became *talk*. Jamie proudly revealed his nature as a "chaser," with Matt as the object of the chase. Jamie had an almost supernatural fixation on what he referred to as a "belly" or a "tummy," and he would remark favorably about Matt's.

At first, this unnerved Matt. His belly hung over his belt like an albatross, certifying him as grotesque, like his man-tits. Matt wasn't used to positive reception of his girth. In fact, any and all flattery would often be met with rash decision-making. Flattery rendered him totally submissive.

Flattery had brought him here —to the hunger.

A companion was just what Matt needed, and he and Jamie were perfectly content spending time together at home —Matt's home. Of course, Matt did notice that they never went to Jamie's place, but then again, he never asked.

Later, Matt realized he *should* have asked. Only too late, he would learn that Jamie's house was the house of hunger.

Now, lying on the bare, concrete floor of his prison, pangs roared Matt awake and shook his bowels. What day was it? He didn't know. Maybe, twice a week if he was lucky, he would be brought food. Matt had figured out a few things, for one, that a garage was the locale of his captivity, though Jamie never parked a car inside, and Matt wasn't even sure Jamie owned one.

But the more important realization —now that Matt had all the time in the world to think —were all the red flags that he had brushed off or outright ignored. Chiefly, how they always met up at Matt's apartment and never went anywhere together. He had never seen Jamie's place, had no idea if this garage belonged to Jamie or was somewhere, miles away from anywhere, any help. For all he knew, he could be a stone's throw from his very own apartment. He also had time to wonder if anyone was looking for him. Maybe that question would matter, in time, but here and now, it was the hunger that drove him mad.

To make matters worse, Matt was absolutely helpless. Despite his build he was too short, too out of shape to be formidable to anyone. Even fueled by desperation, he didn't think he could fight his way out. Then again, he never tried, really. He never tried to resist Jamie at all, on anything. Even that last night together, when Jamie spoke in a flat tone that unnerved Matt, they had passed a normal evening —at Matt's apartment. Then, Matt's memory went blank, and he was here, an animal in the house of hunger.

Now, Matt knew, that's all that he ever was to Jamie, an animal, a pig.

"Heeeerrre Piggy Piggy..." Jamie called in his mock-hick accent, scuttling in from the door that lay just out of Matt's reach. He was chained here, gagged by a dirty bit that hurt his teeth and reeked of vomit.

"I cleaned up the poop chute for you," Jamie chided. "You're welcome." The so-called poop chute was a white bucket, and it made a cupping sound when Jamie set it on the floor. "I must take good care of this pig... I know that when I am one, I'll want someone to take good care of me, too. You chubbies are such powerful animals!"

Matt didn't feel powerful. He was a blob, breathing into the floor with a deep and steady echo. *A bellows.*

"Feeding time!" Jamie was always intensely interested in everything. He seemed to treat each moment of his life as one prepared for with rigorous rehearsal. Jamie sat down on the floor, childlike, his legs stretched out. He put his arms under Matt's upper weight, hoisting him to his feet, indulging his clammy hands to cop a feel of Matt's tits. To their touch, Jamie trembled.

"I'll take your power," Jamie said, his voice husky. "I have to do it this way. It will never be given to me. But I know that power and grace and beauty aren't for everyone. For some, it really weighs on the mind, fucks with it... some don't want all that majesty, all that they bring to the world. But I can handle it, I think. I've waited long enough."

While fondling Matt's chest with one hand, Jamie began to violently spank him with the other, squealing deliriously. After doing this for a while, Jamie declared, "I need a breather." Still huffing, amplified as a hellish barnyard. "I need to be fat. I deserve to be fat. I'm weak without it, and you can't live life weak. When I get you thin, like me, you'll feed me. And I'll be the prized pig. I'll be beautiful."

From a plastic bag at his side, Jamie removed a metal ring. He extracted the bit, and Matt had just a moment of relief before Jamie shoved the ring into his mouth, forcing it open wide. Matt's maw gaped, tongue swirling, a distorted maelstrom. Jamie breathed heavily and rhythmically, with purpose. From the bag he next produced a corn on the cob and used it to caress Matt's miserable form with the care of a maestro's wand. Then, he thrust the ear of corn into Matt's anus and proceeded to rape him with it, still breathing erratically, his eyes cast skyward.

"*Piggggy Piiiigggy Piiiigggy... let me come in...*" Jamie slobbered through the words as he continued to ram, driven by some invisible force, envy, perhaps. But Matt cared little to speculate on Jamie's motivation. He screamed, tried to clench his teeth, but the ring held his mouth open. When after what felt like an eternity, Jamie withdrew the cob, Matt fell forward, fatigued, exhausted. His stomach decided to roar again. Jamie positioned himself in front of Matt's mouth. Matt barely possessed the energy, and was powerless against the metal ring, but on sheer reflex he tried to bite. Jamie responded firmly with a slap across his face.

"*Fuck you, fatty...*" Jamie's words slid out, as if made of slime. He grabbed Matt by the back of his head and shoved the bloodied, beshitted cob into Matt's throat. Matt's neck pumped. Jamie clapped with joy, moving inward and underneath Matt's face. Matt heard more than felt the gurgling in his gut. Jamie opened his own mouth like a baby bird about to be fed —he was ready for the gush —and welcomed Matt's projectile vomit. When he was done feeding, Jamie removed the mouth ring, replaced the bit, and licked his fingers. He ate the corn, his face a mask of ecstasy.

When he was done, Jamie said, "Soon you'll be like me, and I like you. Very, very soon."

Later —Matt didn't know how much later —Jamie left.

As the weight melted off of Matt, Jamie grew frustrated at the lack of progress on his front. He knew he couldn't be fed yet, either, at least not in the excess or decadence that he wanted. He felt like a farmer, raising a pig for the slaughter, thinning him down so that he, Jamie, could be reborn. Let Matt live disgustingly for a while: Jamie had been there. Now, well, he might as well have been a walking skeleton. He felt dead. Yes, he could gorge himself, but that's not where the thrill lies. The real thrill is when someone else gorges. And he knew that he could count on Matt to return the favor, to be tender and caring as Jamie undergoes his transformation. But Jamie did feel some reservations, some worry. With Matt being so weak now, so delirious from hunger, maybe he couldn't perform the task at hand. If Jamie wanted results, he would need to act fast.

He toiled all day to get ready for the feeding, eating every hour on the hour, making a point not to stop even if his stomach objected. If anything tried to come back up, he forced himself to swallow it again. He hadn't checked on Matt in two days, leaving him in the garage to be nice and presentably starved for the ritual, which would begin tonight. In preparation, Jamie enlisted a door delivery service, making sure to have a tip ready and that his order would be big enough to put his mind at ease. Jamie hoped that by the time he woke up —or more aptly, awoke —tomorrow, he would finally feel a belly down there. The ticker on his phone assured him that the delivery would arrive in forty minutes. The feast was Italian, too, nice and hearty. Jamie unzipped his pants, and with his greasy hands he jerked to the pictures saved in his phone: the perfection of fat men. He might even stick his penis in the garlic butter for the additional thrill.

Just as Jamie was eager for the hunger, so, too, was Matt. Delirious at this point, barely hanging on, Matt lay in his own sweat and tears on the cement floor near that poop chute bucket, his stomach rumbling, agonized as souls of the damned. He needed to eat, and he needed it now. He had, for a moment, considered his own flesh. But the texture of his skin, dry and wrinkled, was as appetizing as a gum wrapper. Maybe if he prayed, if he was a good pig that did what good pigs were supposed to do, food would finally come to him.

And maybe, maybe, Jamie was now plump.

Isn't that what Jamie said he wanted?

Matt hadn't seen him for days —who knew how much time had gone by. Face to the floor, he opened his eyes. The concrete echoed back from his breath, and he observed the strange texture of his skin... it was looser now and it hung slack off his arm, like Jamie's beard. Matt felt his own neck as it, too, vibrated with want. A collar. He remembered. A leather collar was what Jamie was using to chain him to the wall. If Matt could bite into it, taste it, like a good piece of jerky.

At night, all streets look the same. It doesn't make the job of a delivery man easy, especially in this part of town, where one road or alley unfurls into another and another, and the houses are identical.

Even with GPS, finding the correct residence at this hour was a hassle. The delivery man had been on this job now for a few months. The house numbers were always too small, or obscured by shadow, or hiding on some fucking mailbox. But he lived with it.

Luckily, this was his last stop of the night. But still, he was grouchy. This was a large order, stinking up his car to high-holy heaven. He would look for a house with a cluster of vehicles —an order like this had to be for some kind of party.

But when he pulled up to the address, he looked at the GPS, confused. The house was isolated, set back from the street and surrounded by a huge yard. Behind the house lay dark woods, and beyond that, an orange haze of light from the nearby highway tipped on the edges of the trees. Only a single vehicle, a van that had seen better days, sat parked in the driveway.

He stopped his car, checked his phone. This couldn't be the right place. But the GPS matched the house number: 1615. He gathered the order, packed into a bag big enough for people to mistake him for Santa Claus, and texted the customer to signal that he'd arrived. Sometimes, customers wanted to walk out and get their orders themselves. Sometimes he had to bring it to the door. He would wait five minutes, and if he got no reply, he would call the number provided. Honestly though, it looked like nobody was home. All of the outside lights, if there even were any, were dark. Behind the van, the bleak garage sat, equally dark. He checked the time. *Guess it's time for a courtesy call,* he thought. The line rang for a few awkward moments. A low voice answered.

"Who is this?"

"DiSallo's. I have your order."

"Order?"

"Um yeah, some subs, a couple of different kinds of pasta, three pizzas, and an extra-large order of breadsticks..."

"That sounds...*great*," the voice said in a flat tone that unnerved him.

"Yeah," said the delivery man. "I —I can bring it up to the door if you want. It's all in a big bag I have here along with the case for the pizzas."

"Could you bring them to the garage door?"

"Sure thing."

"Delicious," the voice said.

After a moment's hesitation, the delivery man started up the driveway toward the garage, hoping he wouldn't have to stay out here in the cold for too long while this stupid fucking customer took his time. The noise of the automatic garage door opener startled him, but when he peered in as the door raised, he saw no one there.

The smell hit him right away, and he recoiled. There was a bucket, a dog chain with a beat-up, chewed collar and some kind of dog toy on the floor. And... was that grease on the floor? Oil? It was smeared, though there wasn't a lot of it, and he thought maybe that was the source of the smell. He had been to some unusual houses before, but this took the cake.

"In here," he heard. The voice came from a partially open door leading from the garage to the house. The delivery man shifted the food so he could use his elbow to push the door open the rest of the way. From inside, he heard, "Are you okay putting it on the table? I'm getting ready."

"Whatever, sir." He stepped into the house, and the smell —far worse than the odor in the garage —stung his nostrils. It was horrid. As he reached the end of a small hallway, he found himself face to face with the entrance to Hell.

He dropped the food and froze. An emaciated, feral-looking man with chew wounds on his forearms, completely naked and perched on a faux leather love seat, leaned over the body of another skinny man, eating his throat, tearing at muscle and fat, making ghastly chewing noises. The dead man's penis had been eaten, and parts of his right leg. Blood was splattered all around the living room, even on the ceiling.

Quietly, the delivery man stepped backward. At the slight sound of his footfall, the feral man's head jerked up. He peered at the delivery man and squealed. As the delivery man let out the final screams of his life, Matt leaped on him like an animal and sank his teeth into the man's face. He had been a good pig.

Dinner was served in the house of hunger.

KEN HUELER

Spoiler

SOMETHING FROM THE old man —stringy and wedged between my teeth —is slithering and coiling across my tongue. When I pause near a stream, I work the slippery bastard free with my fingernails and swallow. A thought strikes me, and I remember to savor the smells of the woods, focus on the pain in my wounds, and appreciate the moon and stars.

Beautiful.

I check my body: The puncture wounds are still leaking and branches have added scratches. I hear outraged shouts, the men are still gathering. Not far upstream is a wood beam bridge. I need distance, and if the pursuit hasn't started I can ditch the woods, at least for a while. A dog barks, which worries me. How can I throw it off?

Stripping, I enter the stream, scrub off the blood, and rinse my mouth. Back on the grass, I fold the men's clothes into a rough square and start piling sticks onto them. When I've got enough, I wade out with the bundle, flip it over, and watch the stream carry it away. The clothes should have a stronger scent, amplified further by the water, so maybe the dogs will chase them. I scrub the shoes hard before crossing to the opposite side.

The bank is steep and slippery, but I make it. At the bridge, I start jogging to burn distance. Paths lead places, and I could be heading toward a bad one, but naked in the woods I'll get more torn up and be slow besides.

I hear rapid footsteps and slip behind a tree. A man appears, likely summoned by the others. I crouch, and then launch myself straight at him, shoulder into stomach. Our impact bends the runner in half and shoves me upright. I stagger back a few steps, wrap my arms around the stranger's thighs, and then slam him onto the ground. The head lands hard, probably on a rock because, after the briefest of pauses, the back of his skull starts vomiting blood. I retreat to watch, but decide time is something I can't afford so I help things along.

His shirt is bloody, but it fits, and better his scent than mine. Plus, with the pants, the outfit offers some protection. I've earned keys, a wallet, and eleven dollars. His phone requires a passcode, so I toss it. The warm corpse tempts, but again, I can't risk the time. I drag the body off the trail and continue.

Barking has replaced shouts. Time will be short if my raft ruse fails: People I can shake; animals have kept their skills. Ahead, a dim glow suggests buildings, so showing up there would be bad. I stop, close my eyes, deliberate. Then I hear it: the widening sound of an approaching car followed by the fade. A road. To the left.

I weave through the trees. In spite of the clothes, I still add injuries, which I note, remember, and treasure. I discover a wide, sudden hill —likely push-off from a grader —and scramble up. I emerge on a road that's small, unlit, and blistered with frost heaves. To my right, it curves toward the glow, so I go left, glancing back, hyper-aware.

I skitter into bushes. The pickup truck zips past again. Brights on. Patrolling. After a curve in the road separates us, I continue. Finally, I hear fast tires hum and glimpse a flash of headlights. At the last of the bushes, I crouch, my ragged breaths sawing into the quiet. Trees spread both directions along this maintained, two-lane road, but the dark conceals how far, and without cover, sunup would pin me. How long can I walk or run before collapsing? I'm already fatigued, but I can't stay for dogs to find. I have to move far and fast, and that requires a car. I start to smooth my hair, then drop my hand and laugh. The old man's residue is off my face, but my arms are scratched and my shirt has some of the runner's spatter. What sane driver would fall in love with this hitchhiker?

Soon, I hear the pickup behind me. It turns left, onto the road. Three minutes later it passes in the opposite direction, under the speed limit and still glaring its brights. If they sent just one car to this stretch they must not have nailed which way I went. I have some time.

I spot headlights too low to be the pickup, barreling, highway speed.

I stagger shouting to the roadside, waving one arm wide to accentuate the blood and clutch my chest with the other, silently pleading for a soft-headed son-of-a-bitch. The lights bleach my vision. I hear braking. I try to look helpless as I limp forward. It's a nice car. This guy must be doing well.

The passenger window glides down. "My God, what happened? Let me call an ambulance."

Make it seem a done deal. "Can't wait, take me to a hospital! A fire station with paramedics, anything."

"Hillsdale's five minutes away."

"Hurry." I get in, sit heavily, swing the door shut. Then I close my eyes, memorizing the creak of the seat as I lean back. I play the sound through my head several times. "Please."

The car accelerates. I open my eyes. A vehicle approaches, slow, with brights blazing. I smile as they pass. Guys like me always win in the end. We may not deserve it, but we do.

I allow a few minutes to pass for distance. Through the buzz of the driver's incessant begging for me to hold on, I recognize the song on the radio and commit the melody and lyrics to memory. I try to pin the smells in the car: cooked meat, probably from the plastic takeout shell; fake pine from an air freshener. I shake my head. Before we reach Hillsdale,

I need a plan. As I'm considering, the urgent chatter sputters. I swing my gaze. The man has pulled out his phone to alert the police.

I grab the dashboard hard as if I'm falling. "Pull over now. I'm going to throw up!"

Heightened panic and sympathy and maybe disgust, the man swerves to the shoulder. When he shifts into park, I grab the steering wheel with my right hand, and folding my fingers at the second knuckles into a sharp flat fist, I strike the side of his neck, hard. A violet stain, like wine spreading through linen, blooms under his skin. Quickly, immaculately, the man bleeds out from the popped artery. I unbuckle him and drag him out of the passenger side. After rifling the pockets and appropriating his socks and clean shirt, I roll the body down the embankment. I get back in and drive. I need to put as much distance between me and my pursuers as I can. I glance at the gas gauge: half empty.

I smile.

No, half full.

On the industrial outskirts of Bloomington, I guide the car into a warren of warehouses and cheap apartments. The trunk has nothing worthwhile. I use a takeaway napkin to wipe down the steering wheel, the turn signal, the door handles, the trunk latch, and the keys, which I drop on the sidewalk.

People and cars and the sun start to emerge. Everyone ignores me. Pausing at a corner, I wonder where to go next. I can't reclaim my old life —by now it's been divvied up, stolen, impounded.

I'm free to head anywhere.

Anywhere begins at a hole-in-the-wall eatery with barred windows and weepy coffee. I examine my scratches and cuts: scabbing, I can heal; I'm not mindless, so not a zombie.

What, then?

Although I'm not hungry, I order the full breakfast to buy time to think.

A bright red plastic bucket sitting on scuffed faded linoleum —that came first, gradually, as if I were floating over a sand-covered skylight while an unfelt wind brushed the grains away. Something was pressing around my face —a padded hole, like on a massage table. I couldn't move, my muscles were crunching and relaxing under my skin, internal fists hammering to get out.

The cafe's sour-lipped matron delivers my meal without ceremony. I slice everything —eggs, bacon, hash browns, ham —and eat them in rotation to keep each taste vivid, memorable.

The convulsions stopped and hands pulled sharp things out of my body, rolled me sideways. Thought I'd fall, but ended up on my back, looking up at the undersides of a chin and a nose. Rumbling, the ceiling started sliding, then a doorframe, and then the moon and trees. After bouncing over uneven ground, we entered another cabin.

I shred a mouthful of ham; the grain and savoriness remind me of later in the memory. I resist skipping.

Two men, one a young blond, the other old and heavyset, hauled me by the armpits onto a tarp-covered recliner. The room had three old trunks, all closed; rows of wall-mounted shelves with shoes and neatly folded clothes; a chipped pink chest of drawers; three chairs around a chunky wooden table; and a crowded corner with an electric stove, a sink, and a refrigerator, from which the young man took two beers.

The older man accepted a bottle. "He's quickening too fast. Find Andrew, and tell him to hurry with the juice. Look at that sin-filled bastard's face. He needs to be gelded now." After the young one left, the man waddled over. "Hang tight, you'll soon be blessed with happier thoughts." He pulled a cloth from his overalls and started wiping me down. The reek of life rolling off that man's body dug into my nostrils like fat, searing fingers, lit my nerves. I swung my knuckles into both his temples. I probably imagined hearing his cranial arch snap, and slash into his brain, but what a sound! Blood poured out his nose. The body fell onto me. I'd never sunk my teeth into human flesh, but it immediately felt like the most natural and rewarding thing I've ever done

I realize I had stopped eating my breakfast, and have been staring into space with a rabid craving. The cook has joined the waitress up front, wiping the counter as an excuse; the two other diners glance away.

I set down my fork and inventory: I have forty dollars in cash, credit cards that will serve as pushpins if I dare use them, an expensive watch, a wedding band, and a shirt several sizes too large. Selling the watch and ring will get me more cash. I need clothes that fit so I don't stand out. A weapon would be handy. I pay, ask for directions to a pawnshop, and end up halfway presentable.

The state needs a new insurance commissioner. The police found his body and his abandoned car drew a line to this city. I have to leave before either the police or those resurrecting yahoos find me, but I won't get far on five dollars. Worse, I cut myself shaving this morning and didn't bleed or heal —apparently, my body requires a very specific diet. I have to act quickly on both fronts.

On a library computer, I research neighborhoods and bus schedules, narrow the options, and then use half my funds to travel to the northern outskirts. In a dying strip mall's parking lot, I note an old Dodge Dart with a thick layer of pollen and rain-curled sun-bleached flyers. After dusk I break in, pop the hood, and get it working —just a loose wire. Some idiots stay poor for a reason. I put in two dollars' worth of gas, wipe it down, and park near a subdivision.

Workers come home, traffic thins, it gets late. I worry I've waited too long, but a Buick shows up. Hooray for workaholics! I start up the Dart and fall in behind, tailgating slightly. At a stop sign, I tap the bumper, turn on the hazards, get out.

I watch the man ease out, uncertain. Yeah, I'm underdressed and driving a shitty car. Aren't you special? "Sorry, my fault. I don't think I did any damage. You got insurance?"

"Me? Don't you?" Outrage overtakes suspicion.

I swing my arm up scratching the back of my head. "Used to."

When the man bends to inspect the bumper, I smash my forearm onto his neck, below the skull. I pop the Buick's trunk, heave the man inside, punch a throat artery, and recover my backpack from the Dart. As I turn the first corner in the Buick, I see headlights slowing at my abandoned car. Then I'm gone.

I tremble. The proximity of food claws at my self-will, and the effort from lifting a body into the trunk, of even existing, ring against my starved muscles like piano hammers, but I keep my driving steady. Behind a closed dry cleaner, I drag the man between the cinderblock wall and a dumpster. Pulling out one of my knives, I cut open the man and begin feeding on organs. The savory warmth fans shivers through my body, brings me back. Sated, I clean my hands, face, and knife under the building's outdoor faucet, then pocket the cash and wrench off the ring. I toss the wallet onto the passenger seat.

The corpse's phone rings —his wife will be wondering where he is. Probably no one will find him until this place opens, but even without ID, they'll identify him fast so close to home.

I need to leave.

I start up the Buick and settle back. This car suits me. I need better clothes. I circle to the south of the city, near where I abandoned the other car, and toss the wallet onto an empty sidewalk, hoping the locals will help a guy out by using those credit cards like good boys and girls. I head west. I drive all night.

Two good days, but this morning my photo is everywhere. A missed fingerprint in the car. Bite wounds matched my dental records, saliva my DNA. The police visited my grave, which gave them more to think about.

Empty grave, cannibalism, serial killing, hysteria, huge reward —everyone knows and will hunt me. Everyone. I keep to the emptiest streets. I'm terrified passers-by will stretch their eyelids and shout. I make it to an overpass encampment, praying they don't watch the morning news. I trade my decent clothes for ones I'd burn in better days, a hat to shade my face, and a stained backpack sutured with safety pins.

Outside the city I stick to back roads, walking against traffic to discourage kindly motorists. By early afternoon I'm beat. At a stream, I wash my face and drink. My reflection reveals wan skin and a deathly look. That's going to draw as much attention as being on the news. I need real food.

An hour later, I'm resting under a tree near a campsite, adding birdsongs and a hidden but audible creek to my accumulated memories. I reminisce about my escape from the city and sear it into my neurons. Half an hour passes, and an overweight teen approaches. At the sound of tires on gravel, he sticks out his thumb, and when the RV passes he continues in my direction. I assess him: longish hair, unripe beard, fleshy face, and a T-shirt broadcasting principled earnestness.

"Hey," I call hoarsely. "A little help?"

His gaze swings to my pasty, unwell skin. "Holy crap, are you all right?"

"Heatstroke, got out of the sun, but I'm still burning up. I hear running water over there, help me?"

"I have apple juice," the boy offers, fumbling as he approaches.

"Need to bring my temperature down. Help me to the water."

The guy shakes off his gear and helps me to my feet. As we work through the tall grass, I let my knees buckle a few times. If it's too easy he might realize a complete stranger's leading him away from witnesses, although with that fresh and strong stink of weed, bad judgment may be all he's got. I collapse again, and when Billy, as he's introduced himself, tries to pull me up, I swing my fist into his nuts.

Billy doubles over. I climb aboard, wrapping one arm around his neck and grabbing the wrist with my other hand, I squeeze. Billy can't call out, but he's big enough to rise. I hook my legs around the boy's waist. Billy doesn't last long, and after he passes out I keep up the pressure, letting his brain grind to a halt. I let go when I'm certain that even if a pulse lingers, his mind is putty.

Salvation! But hunger and desire are hitting me so hard I see spots, and I can't screw this up. I can't. I force focus. Stumbling back to the tree, I retrieve my backpack and Billy's gear. I strip, and then, finally, I tear into thoughtful, stupid Billy, whose arterial spray reveals he was still alive. This trip didn't end the way you expected, did it, Billy boy? But you know what, you're on the same journey as everyone else. Just got there faster. Then I bellow a startled laugh. This is what I am —a reverse ghoul! Instead of eating corpses and robbing graves, I'm a corpse eating and robbing the living. I don't know why that's so funny, but I collapse in that pool of blood giggling like a stoner.

Sated, I search out the creek. Two girls are tossing flowers into the current and cheering the race. I wait, watching. Finally, a woman's call draws them away. I slither down to bathe.

Back at the buffet, I inventory: Billy's wallet has a little money, some traveler's checks, and a photo of a girl out of Billy's league, so probably a sister. His pack has four Tupperware containers, which I empty and fill with cut-up liver and lungs. I drag Billy into the bushes not too close to the creek. I wash my hands and feet again, dress, and leave, whistling the radio tune from the first night.

I'm back, bitches.

My notoriety grows.

My freedom shrinks.

After a week of traveling at night, living off Billy's leftovers, then woodland critters, and now dumpster manna, my least favorite nickname —and my M.O. has spawned several —draws my eye to a newspaper box: The rest of Billy got found, announcing the direction I'd headed. I just stand stupid, feeling like I'm scrambling up an endless hill of gravel, sliding, sinking.

No.

I've never been lazy. I can climb up again, I know I can. But not by making careless mistakes and being reactive. I must plan.

Billy's shifted attention elsewhere, so I work my way back to the city —a place familiar enough to think straight, opportunity-rich, and I'm now hidden behind ragged discards and wild hair across both scalp and face.

My face is whittling into a vulpine sharpness. Unnerving, but makes me even more unrecognizable. I walk right past the police; sometimes they even offer advice. Once, in a crowded plaza, I thought I spied the blond man from the cabin and felt almost anonymous enough to shadow him, learn how he tasted. His flavor I would remember, and savor, throughout eternity.

I've been panhandling for cash, cardboard sign full of tragedy, but right now, four am, when even the hootie-hoos have crawled off to sleep, I'm hungry and desperate. Thinking comes hard and I dearly need clarity. Even this misery I treasure, adding it to my archive. I recite it, alongside my other memories.

I spot her: an old woman I've seen sliding over sidewalks and around dumpsters and recycling bins. In an alley. Unconscious. Now there's a life not worth living. I rush over and slit her throat. Someone else would do the same, eventually, or set her on fire, whatever. When my teeth break her gritty, sour rind, my mouth revolts. I pull back and dig the blade in deep, yanking out viscera. Some of it is vinegary and foul and diseased, but I find parts tolerable enough.

Afterward, I look down, horrified: Her blood saturates my clothes. I have no way to hide what I've done. I run, hoping to escape the city before early risers emerge as the shadows evaporate.

I creep out from the bushes. The sun's bloody crash into the horizon enthralls me, and between that end of the world and me lies a ranch. Night will arrive before I do. I close my eyes, fix the scene in my brain, and begin walking. I examine my arms: More hair has fallen out, as it has elsewhere, and my skin has become shinier, scaly, and tough. My lips taste salty and feel numb. My elongating jaws ache. Is that from my diet? If I started eating humans again, would I revert? At least no one could recognize me now.

Twilight ripens to dusk, and I am close to my goal. Then I hear the gasp. Turning, I spy a young girl —ten or eleven. If I can get to her before she screams, she'll make a delectable meal. But even as the thought comes, she spins and runs.

"¡Ayúdame, Diego, chupacabra, ven rápido!"

I sprint. Enough distance separates us from the nearest buildings that I could kill her and drag her away before anyone pins where the cries originated. A silhouette appears.

"¡Aquí! Aquí!"

I swerve left as more emerge. As I flee, their voices sound stationary. They're checking to see if the girl was harmed. And who wants to run after something that looks like me? I change direction. Why are they out here? Do they have a stake in chasing me? If they work at the ranch, it'll take them a while to organize. I speed up, knowing I need to travel far tonight.

At my camp, I grab Billy's backpack and run toward the rising moon —that flour-white head ground smooth by distance, that stolen ghostly light, that lovely "face" covered in dark impact bruises and features as deformed as my own. Each week my memory grows richer. Walking to catch my wind, I snap off a candelilla stem and roll it between my fingers, relishing the waxy texture, the zigzag bumps of denuded nodes. Absorbed, I almost ran straight into the man.

Startled, I twist sideways. A trigger clicks, followed by a rattling explosion. A Taser. I run, stumbling in the poor light. I hear voices, English without a foreign accent —a different group.

To my right, another figure approaches, and I swerve again. I glimpse flat, moonlit glints where eyes should be. Night-vision goggles. I won't be able to shake them, but I can secure a weapon and a pair of goggles, reduce their numbers. I pull out two knives, wield them, and lunge toward the nearest. Before I've taken three steps, someone to my left shoots, jolting my body, rendering it useless.

They —four in all —carry me bound and gagged, shut me in a trunk, and drive. Are they bounty hunters? More than likely they're my resurrectionist friends. How did they find me? I guess a trail of chewed people and mutilated livestock isn't subtle. I shift, feeling for the trunk latch. This must be an older model —no inside release. I investigate the rest of the space, but it's empty of any useful jacks or crowbars. I worm to a back corner, work off a brake light panel, and rip out the wires. If cops pull us over, I can kick up a racket. I'll go down, but I'll drag them with me.

No one stops us.

Between chewing the gag tape and abrading it against the trunk's rough carpet I've freed my mouth, but I remain silent, waiting. The men inside this austere wooden meeting hall peer at me with disgust and judgment, but I'm not memorizing them —instead, I focus on the pressure of men's fingers holding me upright; the remaining duct tape's weight on my skin; the nerves in my scraped cheeks and lips shimmering, like rapid popping bubbles of foam, with pain; the severe pine coffin resting on wide worn floorboards. Finally, an old, pinched-faced son-of-a-bitch steps forward.

"Daniel, we rebirthed you to aid us in serving our Lord and Savior, and by doing so might have helped you atone for your past. Instead, you have turned from this chance and chosen abomination. You have abandoned God's image for a demon's body. Therefore, we offer you a moment to ask for His mercy before we turn you over to His judgment."

I laugh. "You want to know a secret?"

"You are not qualified to address —"

"I died. I know what's beyond. None of you do —just guesswork and hope. Well, from my lips to your ear —"

"He has foregone mercy. Seal him —"

I shout as the two men drag me to the coffin: "Forget Heaven and Hell. That's the surprise: no sight, no smell, no touch, not even darkness or distance. Just thought. And how hard do any of you look at things? Taste them? Feel them? Memories fade, but thanks to you I've gathered tons. I took nothing for granted. Nothing for —"

The lid slams down, and I hear them fasten a strap, followed by the finality of nails.

"You hypocritical bastards are going to kill me?"

"The Lord forbids murder. We will return you to the earth and let Him decide your fate."

"Bound and buried! You don't trust your God to make the right choice, do you? Cowardly, self-righteous little bastards."

The leader is full of opinions about that, but I stop arguing and begin shaving my breaths so I don't exhaust precious oxygen on trash. When carried, I focus on the sway, the breaks in rhythm when one stumbles. I listen to the shovelfuls thud softer and fainter, like shingles of snow sliding off roofs.

I run through my experiences like a rosary, determined to remember every single sensation, including this second dying. Eventually the coffin's interior flashes sparks of color. Between sensory deprivation and fading oxygen, my brain is starting to misfire. A gentle hill appears, topped by a giant white palace. Veins of gold run through the basalt outer wall and coil across a gap, forming gates.

I grin. I beat them after all. With their normal deaths, they will never see this —only me! We all die, and this is all there is of Heaven, and I alone will carry it into eternity.

The quakes of my laughter set off explosions of yellows and reds as trees sprout and begin squeezing music through the pores in their leaves. As I mount diamond-cobbled steps, naked shaven angels fly from the city to greet me, and Jesus —the one in paintings —opens the gates and spreads welcoming arms with palms that bleed sweet, nourishing entrails.

Beautiful! Wonderful!

ALEXANDER HAY

Mother Mantis

IT'S THE WET, CRACKLING, nibbling sensation I remember most. The feeling of disgust. Arterial spray. Bones snapping. The stench as my friend soiled himself in terror. Screams. So many screams. And the taste.

I wish we had never crossed her.

It started out so well. Me and my mate, we —we had a great little side hustle going on. We'd lurk on horror story forums, find the best stories on there, and nick them. Next, we'd bodge together some am-dram narration, creepy music, stock images and a bit of animation, stick it all up on YouTube, and let the hits flood in.

Copyright strikes? We just moved it all to a new channel, tweaked the vids a little, and continued the scam.

What do you mean we were doing something wrong? Hey, what can I say? Property is theft, which must mean theft is property. As long as you're the sucked and not the sucker, know what I mean?

Anyway, we found this great story. Right weird one, about a woman who kept giving birth to mantises. The twist being that she and her "babies" kept feeding on the men who knocked her up. Okay, it sounds a bit weird, and the author's profile and posting history were "unusual," to say the least, but it *read* well.

At first, we didn't want to do it. Mantises are a bit obvious. I thought spiders were a better choice, but my mate pointed out they were also overdone. He wanted something about slugs, but then we realised being chased around the house by a giant slug just wasn't working either. Mother Mantis it was, then.

So me and my mate got recording. He's not the best falsetto in the world. But it was either that or hire a wannabe actress with a BAPA slumming it at Starbucks to do the voice of Mantis Woman. We watched lots of documentaries about insects eating other insects, just to get the sound effects right. I was particularly proud of the crunching noises, when the baby mantises and Mum gobble up their latest victim. It was me, eating crisps.

The video went live and the hits started rolling in. We'd had a lucky streak, as YouTube hadn't issued a copyright strike in ages. The revenue began to trickle in too. Not that much, of course. But enough to keep us in Moroccan resin, care of our old mate, Spliffy. It was not like this was our day job.

But I digress.

Anyway, I got a private message in my inbox a few days later. It was from the author. One word. Nothing else.

DON'T.

I shrugged and pressed delete. It's the web. Everything's free, and if it's not, we'll take it anyway, yeah?

So, we skinned up and got boozed at my bedsit that night. My mate was claiming he was going to find out where the author lived and piss through their letterbox. I laughed, but sometimes he does creepy things, you know. Like that ex of his he wouldn't leave alone until the police got involved. All because he left a dead rat on her doorstep.

Stupid cow, overreacting like that. She knew what she was getting into. Speaking as a ladies' man, I get them drunk, shag them, and dump them. It saves a lot of time.

My mate passed out on the sofa, so I staggered off to the sweet warmth of bed.

But it must have been the booze or the ganja, 'cause that night I had some strange, anxious dreams. I dreamt my vision was...weird, like seeing a hundred versions of the same thing. The sunlight poking through the curtains was less glaring. All the colours were muted, and everything moved much slower. I could, I dunno, *feel* the air, and everything that moved in it.

I could feel my friend. He'd just staggered up from the sofa.

It was strange. The dream had me chasing him around the room, and he was screaming. He tried stabbing me with a bread knife and beating me off with a broom handle, but my exoskeleton stopped him hurting me. I remember finally gripping him, tight in my big, strong arms.

Things got even blurrier then. Wet. Crunching, but not the kind you get when you eat crisps. Screams, then gasps, then nothing. And gnawing. Gnawing and gnawing and gnawing. The flutter of wings. The twitch of antennae.

I can't remember much else.

The police kicked the door down and found me drenched in blood. Bits of my mate were scattered across the flat. I dimly remember being dragged out and thrown into the van, where they sedated me. When I came into the secure unit, I recall meekly bending over while the nurse gave me another shot of sedative.

This was no dream.

They say I'm mad, that I killed and ate my friend in a psychotic episode. There was enough THC and booze in my system to zonk out an elephant, but I'm not so sure that's the cause. I've been a recreational user since my teens. Something else happened. I begged them to pump my stomach, and they didn't take too much prompting.

Let's just say they found plenty of extra evidence.

I've managed to get a smartphone smuggled in, just to keep me occupied and stop going properly mad. It cost an absolute fortune. Robbing bastards.

They're going to try me soon, and the odds are, I'm never leaving Broadmoor. I heard rumours that what was left of my friend didn't look like it was eaten by human teeth. But I doubt a jury will ever hear that. I'm going down.

But that's not the worst of it. I feel something…moving inside me. Some things. I didn't just eat my friend. I did something else. Something somehow worse. Far worse.

It's beginning to hurt, like dozens of tiny needles jabbing my insides. They're trying to get out. And they're hungry, so very hungry.

I think I'm pregnant.

DOUGLAS FORD

The Parts of Her

BEFORE CODY ANNOUNCED his wedding, I thought I'd foresworn the un-savory things that used to tempt me. That included disreputable places like strip clubs, not the sort of place for the person I now saw in the mirror: married, gainfully employed, on the cusp of fatherhood.

Long before that, I lived a different sort of life. Temptations held sway. I'd done things I wanted to forget. You could say I felt shame. Certainly not because of anything illegal, though —at least not *too* illegal. Nothing worse than money changing hands on one or two occasions. Nothing other people haven't done.

But I left those days behind me long ago, and I regarded myself as a better person. When Cody called to say he would finally settle down and that he wanted me to head up his bachelor party, I begged off, explaining that he had the wrong guy. I no longer even know how to plan such a thing.

But Cody wouldn't accept any answer other than yes. Or maybe I just didn't put up a strong resistance. "And we're going on a road trip to Miami," he said.

"Miami?"

He'd heard from a distant acquaintance that somewhere in the Kendall-Perrine area was a strip club that defied expectation. "It's out of the way, never crowded, and the girls will do *everything*."

"Everything? What do you mean by 'everything'?" Of course, I already knew what that meant. I just didn't want to say it. Remember, I lived an honest, respectable life. I disavowed anything else.

"I mean everything," Cody said. "And I hear they're sexy and gorgeous. Do this for me, Maddox, and I'll never ask for anything ever again."

And so we ended up taking the trip, four of us in all, a smaller number than Cody hoped for, but it turned out that I wasn't the only one who had adopted more respectable ways. Derek turned down the opportunity to relive old times, citing a plan to run for the school board or the hospital board, I forget which. Glen never returned my messages, leading me to suspect that he no longer wanted anything to do with his old college friends.

"What about Erika?" I asked. Though Erika identified as a straight woman, I re-membered her as someone who enjoyed watching women dance naked, and she always tipped generously, making the men in our group look more agreeable to the dancers we patronized.

"No women," Cody said, a little too insistently.

"Okay, no women," I said. I recalled sleeping with Erika on one or two occasions and felt a pang of regret. A momentary one, of course, as I had no intention of doing anything unfaithful. I wondered if Cody slept with her on occasion, too, and he didn't trust himself the way I trusted myself. In any case, the four of us made the three-hour trek to Miami that weekend after saying our farewells to others. I kissed Lisa goodbye, and then I kissed her swollen abdomen. Silently, I pledged to her and our unborn baby that I would behave, no matter what opportunities the universe threw my way.

As if reading my thoughts, Lisa smiled and said, "I trust you, you big idiot. Have fun, but be safe."

Emboldened by that assurance, I set off with the others.

It turned out that Cody didn't have an address for our destination. He didn't even have a name we could look up on our navigation services. This fact came to light as we drove, eliciting groans and complaints from Austin and Earl in the back seat. Twins, they'd flown in from Mississippi for the occasion, leaving behind a boat dealership they shared. We picked them up at a nearby Howard Johnson where they'd booked a single room. You couldn't tell the two apart, except that Earl was slightly more egg-shaped in physique.

"Relax," I said as I drove. "Plenty of places to go down there. It's a big city."

"No," Cody said. "We're going to the place I told you about."

"You don't even know where it is," Austin said.

"I know where to look. And it's worth it from what I hear."

"What he hears," Earl said, choking with laughter.

"You'll see."

"If we find it," I said. I didn't like the vagueness of Cody's directions or the neighborhoods they took us through. We passed businesses with barred windows and more pawnshops than I could count. Several signs advertised bail bond services. None of us knew the area very well, though Cody occasionally came there to do business, and he kept insisting on patience. Up ahead I saw a stand selling Cuban coffee, and just as I started to suggest we stop there for some caffeine, Cody exclaimed and bolted upright in his seat. He pointed toward the other side of the street.

The name spelled out in the sign's glowing letters certainly suggested a strip club: *The Organ Grinder*. I don't recall what made him so sure we'd found our destination, but from the back seat came two simultaneous sighs of relief. "Get the party started already," Austin said.

As I got out and stretched, I found myself wishing we'd stopped for coffee. A bouncer met us at the door, a large bald man wearing a sport coat and dark glasses who extended his hand for a cover charge. We paid him, and I watched him as he drew a wad of bills from his pocket to give us change. His expression remained inscrutable, and he kept his chin lifted, as if gazing at something in the distance. "Have yourselves a good time," he said, reaching back to open the door for us. We stepped inside, finding an interior shrouded in purple light. Loud techno music pounded from speakers, and only a handful of patrons sat slouched on barstools, facing a tired-looking bartender and a stage where no one danced. They looked like props in a play.

"Maybe it's early," Cody said.

Earl tapped me on the shoulder. "You notice the bouncer?" He had to shout for me to hear his voice above the music. "He's blind. Who the fuck hires a blind bouncer?"

That explained it. Though tough looking, he did act as though he had nothing but empty sockets behind those glasses. Still, it seemed unlikely. I started to argue with him, but Austin handed me a glass of something dark and full of ice. "At least the service is quick," he said as he passed the other drinks around.

Cody pointed toward two leather sofas situated away from the bar. I followed him and nodded when he said, "Things will get going soon."

I didn't care. The scene depressed me. Austin and Earl lit cigarettes and offered the pack to me, but I waved them off. The music persisted, but the stage remained empty.

"You sure they have girls here?" Earl asked.

Cody smiled triumphantly and pointed.

A woman wearing blue lipstick along with a silver bikini top and G-string stepped into view. She took her time strolling toward us, and I noticed something odd about the way she walked, at first thinking it had something to do with the almost obscenely high heels she wore. But Austen noticed the same thing and whispered something about one of her legs appearing shorter than the other. He nudged me in the ribs. "Did Cody bring us to a leper colony?" I felt obligated to laugh at this question, but I worried that the woman had heard him. She regarded him as she squeezed in between Cody and Earl on the couch opposite ours, not waiting for an invitation. Her hands found their knees.

"You see me dance?" I noticed an odd inflection in her voice, possibly an accent, but not Cuban or South American. I couldn't place it. Perhaps because of the lighting, her hair looked dark blue, accenting her blue lip gloss.

Cody answered for all of us. "We just got here."

"You from Miami?"

"We came from out of town."

Though Cody kept answering her questions, she never looked at him. Instead, her eyes remained fixed on Austin and me. Mostly me, I thought, and for some reason that made me nervous.

"You come looking for a good time?"

"We're always looking for a good time," Cody said. "Is that what we're going to find here?"

She continued to look at me, her eyes unnaturally wide, her pupils dilated. *Drugs,* I thought, but something else about her stare bothered me. I waited for her to blink as we all sat there, no one speaking for a good two minutes, the techno music continuing to pulse through the speakers. Finally, she did blink, and I exhaled, not realizing I'd been holding my breath.

I pointed at Cody sitting next to her. She still had a hand on his knee. "He's getting married pretty soon."

For the first time, her face relaxed into a smile. "Bachelor party?"

"Yup," Cody said, clearly not detecting anything at all odd about her. I started to suspect that I'd been imagining things, maybe the result of old guilt coming to the surface. Old ghosts. How many times I'd gone into a place such as this and carried on an inane conversation, just to see some naked flesh, and sometimes something more? "You want to help us celebrate?"

She looked at each one of us and said, "I'm Alexis," the strange inflection still evident in her speech.

"Hi Alexis," Austin said. "How about it?"

She pointed toward a set of curtains in the far corner of the room. Though the music droned on, no one danced. The slumped bodies sitting at the bar looked like tired clumps of rags. "Tell you what I'm going to do," Alexis said, and went on to propose that each one of us take turns going through those curtains with her into a VIP area, where she would show us the time of our lives. "You'll never forget it," she said.

"How much?" Earl asked.

She named a figure that sounded reasonable to me, but Austin haggled, suggesting a lower amount.

"It'll be the time of your life," Alexis said again. By that, she meant no negotiating. Not a penny less than the stated fee.

"What do I care?" Cody said. "You guys are paying."

I reached into my wallet and said, "Okay, you first then."

"No, no," Cody said, holding up his hands. "The best is always last."

"Sloppy seconds," Austin said. "He means he wants sloppy seconds."

Earl reached across the gap between the couches and high-fived his brother. They looked like brainless college students. Alexis paid them no attention, watching me instead. I wondered if the contempt for the twins showed in my face.

"Well, I guess that means I'm going first," Earl said. As Alexis ushered him toward the curtains, he leered back at us over his shoulder and wagged his tongue.

"Wait," Austin said. He hopped to his feet and caught up with them. "We do everything together. How much for the two of us?"

Alexis turned toward me as if hoping I could broker a deal. When no one spoke, Austin made an offer, and she agreed to it. Then the three disappeared through the curtain.

Cody came over and sat next to me. He sighed like a man who had just finished an exhausting day at work.

"Ironic after that sloppy seconds remark," he said.

"I'm not surprised. I thought they matured out of that 'we do everything together' schtick."

"They're cheap," Cody said. "That's all."

We listened to the repetitive music and sipped our drinks. I stifled a yawn.

"Look, thanks for doing this for me," he said.

I held my drink up to his. "To your upcoming nuptials." We clinked our glasses together.

"I just don't know."

"Don't know what?"

"If I can do what you did. If I even want to. Sustain a marriage, I mean. You're even going to have a kid. That's impossible to believe, you know? I don't know if I could ever be that...good. That worthy. You've changed a lot."

I laughed. "That's why we're here. To get all the other stuff out of your system."

"That's just it. I don't know if I can. How do you do it? How does it even work? Is that all you have to do? Get it out of your system?"

I had no answer for him, so I tried changing the subject to our surroundings. I didn't want to hurt his feelings by bringing up how I felt about this place, how dour and even depressing I found it. Instead, I asked him if he thought the Organ Grinder really had a blind bouncer, and was about to suggest that we go talk to him and find out the real story when Austin and Earl returned, their faces glistening with sweat, their eyes ecstatic.

"Holy shit," Austin said. "You need to go back there."

Earl nodded. "I didn't want to come out. She wasn't kidding. You'll never forget it." He offered a fist bump to Austin, and Austin accepted it.

"What happened?" Cody asked.

"You need to go in there and see for yourself," Austin said.

I looked around for Alexis. "Where is she?"

"She'll be back soon. Once she gets herself back together," Earl said. He shared a laugh with Austin.

Sure enough, Alexis soon appeared from the other side of the curtain, adjusting her silver G-string. She walked over to us, and this time she sat between Cody and me, her hands resting on our knees.

"Who's next?" she asked.

"He is," I said, thumbing to Cody.

"No, no. I'm last," Cody said.

I hesitated, but I pulled myself to my feet, trying to convince myself that what Austin and Earl said didn't arouse my curiosity, that I didn't very badly want to go through those curtains with Alexis. From behind me, Austin said something that I couldn't clearly hear, but it elicited laughter from the others. Shamelessly, I watched Alexis's buttocks as she led the way, until she stopped to hold the curtains for me. She pointed toward the end of a small corridor and an open door leading to a small chamber with large, cushioned chairs. Though darker than outside, at least the music didn't blare too loudly in there. I sat down and waited for the rules about what I could and couldn't touch. In the past, I would have correctly considered those rules as subject to negotiation, but this time, I planned to abide by them to the letter.

Instead, she methodically removed her garments —first, the bikini top, followed by her G-string. Her nipples were small and her pubis smooth and hairless. I saw no tattoos, a rarity. Finally, she removed her massive heels. Naked, she stood before me and began speaking. Something about her attitude and bearing conjured unpleasant flashbacks to a time when I was a teenager and my mother came into my bedroom, her purpose to provide me with some "unpleasant information" she thought I ought to know about the female body: how men expected it to be clean and pure, even though it wasn't. She described how it bled once a month as well as how it shat, pissed, and farted just like that of a man. That conversation had left me ashamed, embarrassed, even a little confused. Then, she announced that she and my father planned to divorce soon, but not to worry, as they'd decided I would live with my father. Though she made no direct correlation, the timing of our conversation led me to believe that all the things she just told me were connected in some inscrutable way. I almost felt an irrational sense of relief when she moved out of the house not long after.

As Alexis spoke, I once more noticed what sounded like an accent. Now, I wonder if she simply spoke too precisely, as if she had rehearsed everything she said, right down to the placement of consonants. "Before the next song begins," she said, "you should look at my body. Examine it closely. See what makes you happy. Then, name one part of it. That is the part that I will remove and let you hold for the duration of the next song. You may touch it as much as you'd like, but only that part. You can do anything you like to it, as long as your hands touch nothing else."

I thought I misheard. Maybe the music distracted me. Clearly, she had not just said she would *remove* that body part. I might have chuckled.

I said, "Okay. How about your leg?"

"My leg? My whole leg?"

"Yes." Thinking of how she walked, I took a chance and added, "The shorter one."

She nodded and sat down beside me. She reminded me of the cost, so I handed her the money, and she tucked bills under her pile of clothes. Then we sat quietly as we waited for the song to end and another to begin.

When it did, she nodded and began kneading her thigh with her fingers, like a masseuse trying to relieve someone of a muscle knot.

Within seconds, she removed it. Her whole leg. It happened bloodlessly and cleanly. I saw no knife or tool of any kind. It simply came off.

"It's the shorter one," she said, "but still heavy." She gripped it with two hands. "Be careful with it."

I froze momentarily, but I accepted it, laying it across my knees. It did feel heavy, but it felt like skin —the real thing, not a prosthetic of any kind. I ran my fingers along it, nearly jumping out of my seat when I felt the rise of gooseflesh.

She misinterpreted my action and thought I meant to lunge at her. Her hands went up defensively. "Remember, you can't touch anything else," she said.

"I wasn't," I said, trying to relax and study the leg. It felt authentic in every way imaginable. I even noticed tiny hairs on the skin where she forgot to shave completely. I twisted my neck to look at the part that connected to the trunk of her body. It bore the appearance of raw meat, sliced by an expert butcher. In the middle I saw the round white tip of bone.

"Watch this," she said. She held up her other leg, the longer one still attached to her body. "See my toes?" She wiggled them for me. Each one bore blue nail polish. "Now, look at the other one." She pointed to the other end of the leg I held.

The toes there wiggled just like the others. I nearly dropped the leg.

"You like that?" she asked.

I didn't know what to say.

"Keep touching it," she said. "Time is running out. Unless you want to pay me more."

I looked again at the raw side. I touched it, and it felt warm and pliant.

"Do something I can feel," she said. "I can't feel that."

I stroked the inside of the thigh, and she leaned back and moaned, her eyes closing.

"This is completely legal," she said, the words formed by her glistening lips, even though no one had brought up that issue.

Then, all too soon, the song ended.

She sat upright, all signs of her ecstasy leaving her face, everything back to business.

"You need to return it," she said. "And while I'm putting it back on, you need to leave. You can't watch."

Still wanting to attribute it all to some masterful magic trick, I protested, hoping to see how she put herself back together. But she shook her head. "No one sees this."

Obeying, I stood up, becoming aware for the first time that I had an erection. I did my best to adjust myself so no one else could see when I returned to the others.

I found them where I left them, the stage behind the bar still empty.

"How was it?" Cody asked. "These guys won't tell me anything."

"Don't say a word," Austin and Cody said at once.

I sat down, finding that someone had refreshed my drink in my absence. I gulped it down gratefully. Alexis appeared through the curtain, now looking whole and complete, though appearing to wobble a little more. She pointed to Cody. "Your turn."

Cody sighed and looked in my direction. Remembering, I reached into my wallet and handed him the necessary cash, along with a generous tip for both of us. Accepting it, he asked, "Will I remember it forever?"

"I think you will," I said.

Alexis led him away while the rest of us watched. Sitting side by side, Austin and Earl beamed at me.

"What did she take off for you?" asked Earl.

"Her leg."

"Can you believe this guy?" said Austin. "He asked for her *leg*."

They both laughed and waited for me to ask them the same question. Instead, I said, "It was a magic trick of some kind. It had to be, but I can't tell how she did it. Like the thing people do with their thumb."

Their expressions told me that they didn't know what I meant, so I demonstrated, using my thumb to pretend like I could remove my index finger. A trick you learned in the eighth grade.

Austin shrugged. "It looked real to us. We each held something different."

"And she let us trade," Earl said. "Know what those parts were?"

I didn't get a chance to reply. Cody came running out from behind the curtain, nearly falling, one of his hands awkwardly holding onto his abdomen. At first, I thought he might be trying to hide an erection, much like I did. Only later, when he finally showed me what he was keeping hidden beneath his shirt, did I learn the actual reason for his awkwardness.

"We have to go," he said. "Now!"

I asked why, a question echoed by Earl and Austin.

"*Now!*" he repeated.

"You heard the man," Earl said. He tried to sound casual, but he and Austin bounded to their feet and began marching toward the door.

I stood. "What happened, Cody?"

"I'll tell you later."

He pushed me toward the exit, and out the door we went, past the bouncer, whose blindness no longer seemed in doubt. "Have yourselves a good time," he said, just as he did when we walked in, apparently not taking into account whether we were coming or going. He no longer wore the glasses, and as I rushed past him, I saw milky white eyes standing in contrast to his dark skin. "A *good* time," he added for emphasis as we stumbled past him into the parking lot, where Earl and Austin waited next to the car.

I fumbled for the keys and managed to unlock the car on the second try. "Drive!" Cody said as he climbed into the passenger seat, and away we went —quickly.

I stole a glance in the rearview mirror and saw the bouncer still sitting on his stool near the door, waving his hand in farewell.

The car remained silent as we pulled onto the highway that would take us out of Miami and toward home. For the duration of the three-hour drive, we exchanged few words.

"I left my tab open," Austin said at one point.

Earl whispered something to him, keeping his voice outside my range of hearing.

"But I can report the credit card stolen. No big deal," Austin followed.

Next to me, Cody stared through the window, the evidence of something hidden beneath his shirt difficult to ignore. I wonder if Austin and Earl noticed it. If they did, they kept their impressions to themselves. I asked if they wanted me to take them directly to their hotel.

"Sure," Earl said. "You want me to drive for a while, Maddox? You never got your coffee."

"I'm fine." But I had to stifle a yawn. Somehow, I managed to stay awake as the hours and minutes ticked by. The journey seemed to last twice as long this time, but eventually we made it back to our sleepy town. I pulled into the Howard Johnson parking lot and kept the engine running while Earl and Austin got out of the car. Any other time, I would have gotten out too, for a formal goodbye, like old friends should. Not this time. In hindsight, I think I sat there so it wouldn't seem strange that Cody remained in the car. He couldn't have stood up without calling attention to what he kept hidden beneath his shirt. Then we would be forced to talk about it.

"Fun times," Earl said.

He leaned into the driver's side window with an outstretched hand. I shook it. "Fun times," I said.

"We should keep in better touch. Get together more often," Austin said from over his brother's shoulder. I couldn't tell if he intended any irony. He didn't offer his hand to shake, nor did I offer mine.

"Cody, good luck with your wedding," Earl said. He waved, but Cody didn't wave back.

"Don't do anything I wouldn't do," Austin said. At last, they turned and walked into the Howard Johnson, and I never saw them again.

We drove home in silence.

When I parked in Cody's driveway, we sat quietly for a moment. Eventually, he started talking.

"I want to be like you. I always have, from the very first moment I met you. Nothing ever bothers you. Nothing *agitates* you. You handle everything in such a calm, collected way —even in college. And now, you're married, responsible, and you have a kid on the way. I want that. I really do." He started to cry. "I want to be good and faithful. I want to be worthy. I really do."

I didn't know what to say. I never knew he harbored such feelings, such envy, and I couldn't think of an appropriate response. I only wanted to know what he kept hidden beneath his shirt. Thinking of how I held Alexis's leg, my body tingled. I should have held something else.

I don't know why I said what I finally did say. "It was only a magic trick." Even if true, that had nothing to do with his confession. And I didn't even believe it was a trick. Not anymore.

Cody wiped his nose. "I have something here, but I can't keep it. You have to take it for me. Please."

A swell of anticipation filled me as he lifted his shirt to reveal what he kept hidden there.

Then I finally saw it: the dark folds of the labia, the sections of shaved skin around it, the lower part curving to a portion of Alexis's perineum.

Somehow, I suspected —knew —that he'd chosen this part of Alexis to hold. Still, the mechanics eluded me. Did she have to take off her legs first? Had Cody left her behind in an immobile state, unable to reassemble her parts, rendered handicapped forever?

"I can't keep it," he said again.

He lifted it toward me, and I didn't refuse. I accepted it, marveling once more at the texture of the skin, the undeniable realness of it. A faint scent of urine became apparent, and one of my fingers came away damp. I couldn't tell if it came from Cody, or if Alexis pissed herself —whether out of fear or to perform a trick, it was difficult to say. Did she call for help as we ran away? Did the blind bouncer come to her aid? In what condition did we leave her? Would she even survive and for how long?

I turned it around and saw no blood, no sign of trauma. Just striations of muscle, slick and erotic to the touch, barely concealing the other side of that fascinating opening. My own arousal revolted me, as contradictory as it sounds. It felt like gazing upon a secret.

Cody said, "Keep it. I don't want it. Not anymore."

Then, like someone running from the imminent ruin of his life, he left me in the car, abandoning me with what he'd stolen.

I didn't call him back. I didn't chase him down. I put the car into gear and drove home. After backing into the garage, I found an empty cardboard box with the right dimensions. Not knowing what kind of deterioration to anticipate, I laid a towel inside it. Once I safely placed that piece of Alexis inside, I used package tape to seal up the box before storing it away in a place where only I could ever locate it. This task complete, I tiptoed inside the house to shower before finally crawling into bed next to my wife, who murmured in her sleep and snuggled against me.

I never heard from Cody again, and I didn't reach out to him either. I don't know if he stayed married or even got married in the first place. The box remains in its hiding spot. Often, I lay awake at night, fighting the urge to take the box from its hiding place so I can open it and touch it. Sometimes, when I finally manage to fall asleep, I wake up with my body coated in sweat, certain that it has decayed into a lump of rotting meat, and I wonder if I will ever summon the courage to look inside. Time will tell.

GALEN GOWER

The Work

WHEN I TURNED eleven, I chained a naked, begging man to the wall of my grand-mother's shed and disemboweled him for our God.

I spent the first ten years of my life *learning* about the work, sitting by the wood stove in the corner of my grandmother's shop. This was the big shed, not the small one where the work was done. It was warm in the big shed, but not bright, and my grandmother always left a coffee can full of peanuts on top of the stove to roast. It reminded me of peanut butter, that smell when you open a new jar. There was a bucket for shells by the wall. The second shelf held another bucket for screws and bolts and nails.

Grandma kept a galvanized tin bucket for bleach and water under the sink. The inside of that bucket was crusted red and black.

"For when I do the work, Jake," Grandma said when she saw me looking at it. She winked, letting me in on a secret.

My mother got irritated when Grandma called me Jake, but I think she kept doing it just on purpose.

"Her name is Jacqueline, mother." I remember my mother saying that more than anything else. "It skips a generation, Jacqueline," she explained to me. "I know it will be hard for you at first." Mom said that a lot, too. "God will make you strong."

A tangle of thick weeds behind the shop almost hid the path to the other shed —it was a narrow passage cut by Grandma's careful feet over many decades.

"That's where I keep the material, Jake," Grandma said. "Those who must pay, made flesh again. They are not people like you and me. No, they had their chance and cheated God. Thought they could be clever." Before heading to the second shed for the work, Grandma would smile at me, but it was not a happy smile. When she smiled her shed smile, she only stretched her lips thin across her teeth, and any hint of happiness left her eyes.

Before each job, Granda put on a new apron, but the work still ruined her clothes, often as not.

Some nights, I could hear the words that came from the shed behind the weeds. The voice of our God. I still hear them when I dream, but back when I was ten, I didn't understand them. The words came from the breeze through the pokeweed and butterfly bushes, and they weren't meant for me.

Once, my grandmother used a die to cut threads on a shackle bolt. She showed me how to make a ring and attach it to a bolt, too. I remember licking peanut salt from my lips and watching her drill a hole for the pin.

"When you make a deal, Jake, you stick to it. Don't take the payment if you aren't willing to follow through. It is our God who lends us her strength, never forget."

I counted sixteen hammers in the shed, all the handles smooth from use. I could tell which ones Grandma used the most. The steel on the hammers shone black. Sticky. I couldn't read the symbols, but before she died, Grandma told me what they meant.

"This one is for fleeting happiness, Jake." She held up the smallest hammer. It had a short handle, but the spike on one side looked sharp. She set down the smaller hammer and hefted a larger one. "And this heavy one is for resentments. Do you know what that means, Jake?"

I shook my head. I'm still not sure even now, even though she told me. I've thought about it a lot.

"Resentment is the emotion of justice, Jake," she said. "Always remember to look them in the eye when you harvest the resentment."

Grandma always said you have to be careful doing the work because everything has a cost. I learned all about cost when I took over. Grandma died on the winter solstice, just when I turned eleven.

I did my first work finishing a job she started. I was waiting in the shop when I heard her call out. Grandma had fallen down on the little path between the sheds; God had used her all up. Her arms were black and dripping, her eyes puffy and red all the way around. I don't mean red like she'd been crying, red like bleeding.

"Get your hammer, Jake, and finish the work," she croaked. Her skin hung loose and by the time I came back with the hammer, she was all shriveled up into herself. I stood over her with my hammer, one side a razor-sharp hatchet inscribed with the rune for *joyful remembrance*, and felt the voice settle into my mind as Grandma's breath rattled to a stop. She'd made this one special, just for me.

It is now your time to do my will, Jake, it said. *This is your fate, too, but not for many years yet. Come, finish what she started. The deserving soul is summoned, made flesh. Extract my due, so they may rest.*

My fate didn't scare me; God only told me the truth. I pushed through the weeds on my way down the path, opened the shed door, and looked down at the man on the floor. Naked, cowering, trying to crawl away into a corner. Grandma had only just begun and one of his feet was twisted the wrong way around. Her big hammer, the one for resentments, lay in the corner.

"*Snälla du...få det att sluta,*" he begged, his cuffed hands held up in supplication. My heart filled with pity for him as I bent over and nestled my face into his. I felt his whimper and tasted a hot and salty tear as I sank my bite into his cheek. As my teeth scraped bone and clicked together, he screamed. Screaming sounds the same in any language. The God in my mind exalted and I thrummed with a new, savage strength. Her fever was on me as I dragged his arms up to the peg in the wall, lifted him off the floor, and bit him again. The meat of his arm felt stringy, gristly in my mouth as I chewed and tore. My God's thoughts were my thoughts as I shook my head and growled.

Absolution will be his, but the price must be paid, she said, urging me on. *He was faithless in his first life, but a promise demands payment. Strength demands sacrifice.*

I held his shackles to the peg and swung my hammer downward between us like a righteous pendulum, dragging its bladed face just under his navel. Shock would silence him soon enough, but he screamed with pain and then happy laughter as I parted the muscles low in his abdomen. I sawed back and forth until it was done. When my grip on the hammer slipped, I dropped it and reached inside him, twisting my small fist into his roping entrails as they slithered away from my grasp. I tugged, pulled, and finally yanked. His roping, slippery viscera fell to the floor in a wet mass as I reached and pulled, reached and pulled. The work was done and the material was quiet.

"Poor Mom doesn't know what she's missing," I said to our God, and my head echoed with *her* laughter as I licked my lips.

JP TOWNSEND

The Badger Game

ONE

THEY TOOK HIM DOWN in Chicago.

Five to ten —Joliet —first-degree murder pled down to manslaughter.

He had a record but his last conviction had been under another name. The judge said he hoped prison had changed him, that he seemed like a reasonable young man, that what he'd done was understandable in context.

Stein wanted it over with. He kept quiet.

TWO

Things he'd always remember.

Things he wanted to forget:

The feel of her skin under rough hotel sheets. Scent of her hair.

Sound of skin —slapping, wet, rough —from another room, behind a closed door.

They'd met at a bar. He'd been working for somebody —doing what he used to do, finding people, hurting them. She'd been nursing a cocktail. Her makeup was running like she'd been crying. He asked her what was wrong —surprising himself —he never cared about other people.

She smiled at him and something changed. A space filled he hadn't known was empty. They sniffed each other out in the still dark of that place like circling dogs. He never found the man he'd been looking for.

A month later on the road to another city, she'd asked him his name. He told her he had a few. She could pick one.

She picked "Stein." She said it sounded harmless.

He told her he wasn't harmless.

She said, "Harmless to *me*."

THREE

A week into his sentence his cellmate hopped down from the top bunk and asked his name.

Stein looked at his feet for a while. The cellmate whistled a song and walked out.

He came back holding something. He said his name was Portman —he'd used to be a courier —he could get Stein work when their time was up. He had a pack of Luckies.

Stein unwrapped the cigarettes and put one in his mouth. Portman lit it with a match. His hands were shaking slightly and the flame danced. When he got it going, Stein puffed out smoke and stood and Portman was smiling at him, hands on his hips.

Portman asked if he'd been inside before. Stein nodded and walked to the toilet, leaned against the wall, and undid his trousers. Portman followed —close —Stein could smell him now —he'd put on cologne when he'd left the cell.

Portman asked if he knew how much a pack of tailors cost there. Stein shook his head. Portman laughed —

You don't talk much, huh? I like a quiet boy."

Stein knew. Reform school fifteen years earlier —twenty boys in a room —wolves and sheep. There'd been a boy there who played this game ...

Portman put his hand on Stein's shoulder. He squeezed. He said, "You feel nice."

... the boy's name had been Franklin. He'd been a year older than the rest of them. He had a routine —a new kid would come in and Franklin would greet them with his two cronies and they'd talk quietly...

Portman leaned forward from his hips. He kissed Stein on the shoulder. He leaned up to kiss Stein's neck. The hall beyond the cell was empty.

... after the talk —in the night —Franklin and his boys would come to the new kid's bed. They'd gag him with a sock and wrap his head in a pillowcase. They'd take turns on him. You could hear it. You could smell it...

Portman took the cigarette out of Stein's mouth, drew in a drag, and dropped it in the toilet. "What a waste," Portman said. "You owe me for that one." Stein felt him push —he bent over the bowl.

... the new kid wouldn't get up in the morning. Eventually, they'd take him away to the infirmary and they'd never see him again. When they came for Stein he remembered being scared. They cornered him and Franklin told him the rules...

He felt Portman's hands. They roamed his back, went to his hips. "You're so pretty," he said. Stein stared at the cigarette floating in the toilet basin, waiting.

... when they came for him that night, he was ready. He'd cut a length of hose in the yard and filled it with steel pellets from the workshop. When Franklin came to lie on top of him, he whipped the fortified hose out from under his pillow and across the older boy's face. The two cronies watched while Stein hit him over and over, his face flat. Silent except for the wet

sound of the hose against Franklin's face, grunts of exertion. The two cronies did nothing. When it was over, Stein dropped the length of hose by Franklin's body and went back to bed. Nobody spoke...

Portman's hands left Stein's body. Stein heard the buttons popping on his overalls and he whipped around and drove an elbow into the bigger man's throat. Portman's eyes bugged out but he had that convict ruthlessness and his hands went for Stein —Stein was quicker. He grabbed Portman's testicles through the jumpsuit and pushed him back against the bunk, squeezing hard enough to provoke a gurgled scream.

... the guards found Franklin in the morning. They took them away —Franklin to the infirmary and Stein to a holding cell. They tried to get him to talk. Stein didn't say a word. Nobody did. Franklin lost most of his teeth, an eye. They sent him away and they put Stein to work.

They left him alone.

Which was all Stein had ever wanted.

To be left alone.

He went to work on Portman.

When he was done he sat down on the bunk. They found them like that —Portman lying on his back moaning with a ruined face and Stein sitting there, hands covered in blood. He'd gouged out Portman's eyes and he sucked vitreous fluid off of his thumb. He didn't want to and the taste made him gag, but the message was important.

Elena always said: You need to stop them cold.

FOUR

Stein and Elena started off grifting. She played the damsel in distress —fake an accident or food poisoning —Stein the heavy who wanted a payout. They moved —a new city every two weeks, a new car every two months.

She wanted to go after syndicate money —had this idea that she'd sit in on card games or work an underground casino, get the lay of it so Stein could heist the place. He nixed it, told her about those people, their brutality.

It made her look at him with new eyes —his history. She asked him once if he'd been a shooter —he said no. Always his hands. A few jobs a year and debt collection —that was his speed.

Elena's speed was survival —they worked out the details quick one night, up late.

The badger game.

She'd lure a john to a hotel. Stein would take the connecting room —or stay close by. After working out the run, Elena and the john would go to it and Stein would come in —the jilted husband, the angry brother. They'd take pictures if they needed to. Most of the johns paid up.

Some didn't, and Stein would make them.

Elena would always watch, biting her lip.

When they made love after, if she'd seen him hurt somebody, it was always better —for her.

They cut across the country —making it through ten states in as many weeks. One night in Iowa City a john pulled a straight razor —Stein was in the connecting room, didn't hear a thing because the john had put a gag on Elena. By the time Stein noticed things next door were too quiet and came in to check, she'd been cut all over her arms, tied face down to the bed. The guy was there holding his razor. Naked, hard. Stein put him down quick and untied Elena, took her away. Her dress had stuck to her skin from the blood and she insisted on taking the man's suitcase.

They got another room and he took care of her. Her instructions —he wasn't much for thinking —he swabbed the wounds and wrapped them and spent a long time rubbing her back while she cried on the toilet.

She asked what happened to the man. Stein told her —*I caved in his throat and he choked to death.*

They made love that night —it was different than before, slow and sweet.

Later on, in his arms, she said she wanted to kill them all. An uncle in Florida, her father before that. Stein didn't understand and she said that it was okay.

He told her about the orphanage he'd grown up in —nuns with rulers, a priest who would take you into a room above the rectory, other boys with dirty faces always crying in the dark at night when they thought no one could hear.

She said, "I think you're a good man." She said, "It's not fair, what they did to us."

She cried for a long time. He held her. She said, "I'm going to kill them all, baby."

FIVE

He spent six months in solitary. Portman wasn't popular —they put it down to self-defense. He thought about Elena through it —made up stories in his head.

When they let him out of the hole they put him in a different cell by himself. A guy came eventually and knocked on the cell door. Stein just looked at him and when he came in he gave Stein a carton of Luckies and a bag of potato chips and walked out again.

After that they left him alone.

He did six years out of the ten.

When they let him out he broke parole the first day and went to Florida.

SIX

The game changed after she'd gotten cut. She started antagonizing the marks —making Stein come in and hurt them while she watched.

In bed she changed, too —she wanted pain. He went with it —whatever she wanted.

She asked if he was happy one night —the two of them in evening wear, sitting at a table on a riverboat casino in Indiana, looking at the moonlight on the black water. He'd been uncomfortable in the suit —she'd insisted, wanted to see him dressed up.

No one had ever asked him that before. He had to think about it and must've taken too long because she laughed and said, "Never mind," and took his hand.

"I just wanted to be out somewhere with you," she said. "Somewhere that isn't a dive. To ask you something."

She had a book in her handbag. It was bound with black leather and there was a red circle on the front of it, cut at the eight o'clock mark with a curled slash.

"The man that hurt me in Iowa," she said. "He had this with his things." She opened the book. It was cluttered with writing —from left margin to right with no spaces, the words piled up right on the edge. Stein tried to read some of it but he'd never been good with words and he couldn't keep track of what it was saying. Holding it gave him a funny feeling —like something was watching him, like the priest from the orphanage, cold eyes and no passion and dead, wet hands.

He closed the book hard and pushed it back to her. He said, "What is it?"

"It's special," she told him. "It's okay if you can't read it —I can't either. There's a man who can. In Chicago." She let out a breath. He lit a cigarette, watching her hands shake.

"Will you go with me?"

"I'll go anywhere with you."

SEVEN

She'd said once: *If they take one of us, we'll find each other in Florida.*

No city or town. Florida.

He got off the greyhound in Tallahassee and walked around until he found the bars and the nightclubs, then went farther until he hit the strip of SRO hotels and rooming houses. Elena had never told him her last name —her true name. She'd gone by Marquez but he knew it was nothing, a dead end —she'd never use the same name after they took him down.

He took post on street corners and stoops and watched and waited. Saw the girls coming and going —streetwalkers in short cut dresses, high heels, jeans and halter tops, smoking and standing around. The johns would come and they were always different.

Two days in he saw a pimp make a handoff —a police cruiser parked down an alley, a brown envelope passed through the window. He followed the pimp back to a boarding house, stood on the street when the pimp went inside until a light came on in one of the rooms. He counted the floors.

Pimps worked at night —the next morning Stein went in through a window on the first floor and up the stairs. He loided the door with his driver's license. The room was immaculate —the pimp had likely done time —some ex-cons can't stop themselves from keeping house.

He was sleeping. No girl. Stein woke him up and asked him questions, used his hands to quiet him down when he took offense. Described Elena —her scars. The pimp didn't know anything —his traffic was all black and white. "The spic girls," the pimp said, "they're all on the coast."

He had some money. Stein took it and left and bought a car from a yard on the outskirts of town —a '54 Studebaker Champion. It barely ran.

He drove all day and night to Jacksonville.

EIGHT

The man in Chicago was a preppy type —blue blazer with brass buttons, pressed slacks. They met, the three of them, in a library at the university.

The man was an assistant professor. He led them through the stacks, showed Elena all these books. They were bound in leather —brown, red —they were thick.

They took the books he gave them. They got a rented room —blew most of their stake on it, six months down. Elena told him: "I need time. Leave me alone." She locked herself in the bedroom —Stein took the couch. He spent a week flipping through channels on the TV, watching the door. He listened to the little noises she made.

She did not come out. He knocked a few times to see if she wanted anything. Once inside, she never spoke.

On the fifth day he heard noise —a thrum, electric. On the sixth day she laughed for an hour —low and sad at first, then louder, hysterical. Stein stayed on the couch. He never broke the door down. He didn't know what to do.

At night the shadows grew long. The streetlights would dim —they'd never go out. Stein chain-smoked and watched cars go by and thought about his life before her, with her, after her.

On the eighth day she came out. A smell came with her — sulfurous. She was different —a white streak in her black hair, darker eyes, new lines in her face. She collapsed on the floor.

He took her to the bath. He washed her —her clothes were soiled —he threw them away. Her body was different —thinner. He could see her ribs —odd nodules on her stomach, her thighs.

He set her up on the couch and she slept for a day while he cleaned her mess from the bedroom.

When she woke up she wanted to go back to work. Her voice seemed deeper than before.

Stein was scared.

NINE

He spoke to pimps in Jacksonville. He cruised go-go bars and cabarets.

He stayed away from the cops —they'd have paper on him. He knew how to be a ghost.

Pimps in Jacksonville sent him south.

The Studebaker died in Port Orange.

He found a pill dealer and beat him until he gave up his stash. Bought another car —a '58 Buick —and drove it to Fort Pierce.

At a bar there he met a woman, a working girl —she'd seen Elena. Going to Miami. Said Elena was intense —scary. "What do you want with a girl like that?"

Stein told her they had history. The woman wanted more —he took her to bed just to see. Nothing like Elena: not worth the time. She left while he faked sleep and when he did fall into it he had dreams —he never dreamed —of blood and white things twisting in the dark like unfurled ribbon.

He drove to Miami, no stops, passed out in a cheap hotel, woke and hit the strip. Girls in bikinis, men in straw hats. He knew he looked out of place in his cheap suit —Elena would've laughed.

He asked his questions, made his play. At a cabaret tucked away from the strip a guy took offense to him nosing around —they tried for him in the alley. Two heavies, a chain, a bat —Stein took them down but they made him feel it. He recuperated in the hotel bathroom —thought of Elena, all the times she'd bandaged him, his hands.

The string was running out —he had nothing else.

TEN

The setup was all wrong.

She wanted to be a streetwalker, not a bar girl —Stein didn't know why.

The guy who took her was old —gray hair, paunch, white socks in a cheap black suit. He got her into his Cadillac and drove through an alley. Stein had to follow on foot —their car was back at the rented apartment —not how they worked.

He found the car blocks away in another alley. The Caddy was idling —empty —doors open.

He heard it from the alley.

A sucking noise —like a kid sloppy-eating a lollipop.

That sulfur smell.

They were down a flight of stairs, some basement.

Soft yellow light in the crack under the door.

It was unlocked and inside, there was a single bulb illuminating a small room.

The john was naked, on a table. He was hard —it stuck up straight as a ruler.

Elena stood beyond the light. Something writhing in the air around her —twisting, undulating —too dark to make out.

She said, "Do you want to see, baby?"

A thing like a slick white rope twisted out of the dim.

It was coming from her —seemed to float to the man.

His eyes were wide open, staring.

It wrapped itself around his erection until it was fully enveloped.

The man on the table was gone somewhere, in his head. As Stein watched, the rope tightened around the john's penis —blood ran from the gaps in its coiled form, and semen, and when it unwrapped itself the man's genitals were mauled beyond recognition, a lumpy mass of meat.

Elena stepped into the light.

Those bumps in her —they'd opened —like slits. White ropes spilled from them —like worms from a dog. Her entire body save her neck and head vibrated —that electric thrum, like a convulsion in slow motion.

Her eyes were so dark.

She said, "This is how we work now," and Stein closed his eyes.

She said, "This is what they made me."

ELEVEN

He accidently killed the last pimp he spoke to. Before he went he gave Stein a name —a brothel —The Peony.

Some old plantation house, far out of town.

Stein ditched the car on a side road, walked through marsh to get there. Came out of the trees and the swamp on the back edge of the place —a wide rolling lawn —goons in jackets and ties standing around. Stairs on each end up to a tall balcony.

Stein cleaned his shoes with his suit coat —left the jacket in the mud. He moved low —fast —came up the stairs on the left. Two thugs there —he hit one in the throat and the other tried to get his gun but didn't yell. Stein took him down quick, took the piece —some kind of revolver —he didn't know how to work it beyond cocking the hammer.

Inside the place was grand —candelabras, no electric lights —oriental carpets and paintings. If he'd known anything about art he would've thought of Bosch. He went down halls, checked doors. People in all forms of congress —men, women. One room with red light and a man in leather and a woman hurting him. One room with two women, one vomiting into a bucket while the other scooped it out with her hands and washed her face with it. They took no notice of him.

Another thug caught up to him on the stairs —Stein butted him with the gun, hit him until he stopped moaning. He kept moving up.

The office was on the top floor. Converted attic —they'd taken the ladder out, put in a staircase.

The woman was behind a desk the width of a double bed. Rich wood —candlelight. She wore a dress from the 1800s —black bobbed hair. She smiled like she was expecting him, didn't change when he showed her the gun.

"Please —have a seat," she said.

He sat. She'd been writing in a book with a quill pen. She closed it and set the pen down in an inkwell and looked at him.

She said, "I've been hearing about you —all the way from Jacksonville. Busy boy. You're very determined, aren't you?"

"You know what I'm looking for."

"*Who* you're looking for, yes. I'm afraid you're out of luck. She isn't here." She sighed softly, put a hand to her face, as if she were bored. "She isn't your property. You know that. Don't you?"

"That's not what this is about."

"You aren't very bright, are you? I assume she called the shots —when the two of you were together. Do you think she loved you?"

He didn't know what to say.

"I've owned this place for a very long time. Seen a lot —nothing like her. She was so very special. But what made her so special —I suppose time just ran out. I sincerely hope she made you happy. She spoke of you very highly, when I knew her."

"Is she dead?"

"Not yet. There's a hospice —Key Largo —Saint Vincent's. You'll find her there. It won't be what you expect, but I don't think —that isn't really something you do, is it? Expect things."

Stein stood. No noise from the stairs —he uncocked the pistol, set it down on the chair.

The madam said, "Go on, tough boy. You'll be safe."

He went out the door, heard her laughing softly behind him. The rooms had been emptied —girls and boys and their clients watched him go into the halls. They had empty eyes. They had vacant smiles. They all had that smell. They all had that electric thrum.

TWELVE

She killed five more like that.

She told him they were all freaks —they were like the men who hurt her. Hurt him.

Stein didn't feel one way or the other about it —he wanted her to be happy.

At night he could feel her things on him —those fleshy wires —he couldn't bring himself to make love to her but she didn't care.

They stayed in Chicago —he asked why they didn't move —like they used to. She told him: "There's somebody here. I can feel them, waiting for me. I have a job to do."

The last one she did went wrong.

A guy in a military trench coat —Brylcreem hair —blonde, cold eyes. Stein listened to them talk. They sat on a bed in a hotel room —he was in the connecting room, like the old way. The guy told her he'd been in Japan, Singapore, Oriental Theatre, a sniper, recon —things he'd seen.

When the lights went out Stein cracked the door. Watched.

Elena took her clothes off. The man took out a knife.

When the ropes came out of her the john wasn't phased —his face never changed expression. He hacked at them, got her in his arms. The ones he chopped off stank —the smell filled the room. New ropes grew —they wrapped around him and Stein came in when he had the knife to her throat.

When the john was off of her, on the floor, clutching his throat, Stein looked at Elena —her throat had been cut, deep, but no blood. Those white ropes were filling in the wound —strands of them pumping out from her meat, her veins.

Glassy look on her face —like she was dead —but she woke up while Stein watched her body fix itself.

Stein let her use the knife on the man —when she was done she kissed Stein, hard.

He told her to get out while he cleaned up the room. She gave him this long look. Said, "This was the one."

Stein asked if it was over, then. This new game.

She said, "I don't think I can stop now."

She kissed him again before she left.

The cops kicked in the door five minutes later.

They'd been watching the freak —he'd cut up five other women. Stein said he'd found him like this —clammed up and got the court lawyer to speak for him.

They pled him down to manslaughter —the cops weren't stupid —they figured it was badger gone wrong. The brutality of it didn't make the papers —the psycho john had been decorated.

Stein took the deal they offered him.

Five to ten at Joliet —then Portman —everything else.

It was after Portman that he knew what he had to do. Felt it like that first time meeting Elena —something unspoken, a feeling he couldn't put into words.

THIRTEEN

The car was where he'd left it.

He drove through the night. Watched the sun rise over the ocean —far off, colors like he'd never seen.

When he got to Key Largo he got a room and slept without dreams. In the morning he bought cigarettes —Elena's brand.

He killed time. He didn't want to go there.

The hospice was outside town. Colonial house —the yard was overgrown, two wings, peeling paint, sagging porch. The receptionist wore a nurse's outfit. The lobby was empty —rusted wheelchairs stood in a row by the coat rack.

She seemed confused when he didn't have a name for her. He said the woman he wanted to see changed her name —he didn't know the new one. Black hair, black eyes, slim. Scars. The nurse knew who he was talking about, sent him upstairs.

The room was at the end of the hall. There was a window in a nook beside the door —he stood there looking out at the yard for a long time. Birds making noise somewhere, an old woman gardening. Bright soft sunlight.

He opened the door.

The bed. An IV. A wheelchair in the corner.

A bedside table —ashtray, that book with the cut circle on its cover.

Elena in the bed.

She'd gotten worse.

Her skin was pale with a yellow hue. Thin —her ribcage indented the sheets from within. Arms like rails, every bone visible, like the skin had been painted on. Her eyes were hollow and her cheeks caved in and she looked at him and she smiled.

She said, "Come here. It's okay, sweetheart."

There was a chair beside the bed. He sat down and unwrapped the cigarettes —Camels, her favorite —and lit one for her. She took a drag with her skeleton hand and coughed.

"Was it those things?" he asked.

She pulled down the plastic sheet. Below her breasts her body was a coiled mass of them —they twisted and rolled, lazy, like dogs in the sun. Wet. The smell would've made him gag if not for the cigarette. He lit one of his own.

"They gave me cancer," she said, without emotion. "All over. I can put them away when they come to look at me, the doctors. It's like they just don't see it. Maybe you can —because you were there when I grew them."

He looked at the book. She nodded. "Old magic," she said. "I grew up here. I never told you." She laughed. It was shaky. A croak. "This old magic —lives in places like this. I don't know how to explain it."

"I'm sorry, Elena."

"For what? You did the best you could. Once I got a taste for it, baby, I just couldn't stop. They all looked like my uncle —my father."

"I would've killed them for you."

She shook her head. "They've been dead for years," she said. "Old age, cancer, who knows. I read about it. It's all over." She pulled the sheet back up, tucked it in around her.

"Are you here to kill me?" she asked.

He looked at her. He said, "I thought I was."

"Because you took the fall in Chicago?"

"Because you needed —you had to..." He didn't know how to say it. She waited for him to think. "You wanted to be done. I saw it in your face after that guy. The Army guy. You didn't know how to stop, but you wanted to."

She nodded. "Turns out it all stopped anyway," she said. "I don't know how long it'll take but these things..." She trailed off.

Stein put his cigarette out.

He said, "I'll stay with you."

She took his hand.

FOURTEEN

Early morning. He woke to her coughing —got her a glass of water from the bathroom down the hall. There was blood on her chin and chest when she was finished. He cleaned her up.

Lying there with her head back on the pillow, gasping through it, she said, "Can you still work with your hands?"

He nodded.

He knew.

She said, "Please."

She said, "I know what you want."

She said, "I love you," and he broke her neck quick and clean.

FIFTEEN

In the car he lit a cigarette. He had the book. He flipped through the pages —the writing looked new, fresh.

He started the car and drove —heading for the highway —North.

To return the book.

HANNAH BROWN

The Pledge

"What does this have to do with neuroscience?"

The cellar of the Vought building smelled like hundreds of years of academia had been sealed away in a crypt only to be burned down recently. The acrid smell clung in the air, clung to Elly's clothes, to her skin. The darkness was a warm moist mouth, until Lucy flicked on the fluorescents, illuminating the corridor that stretched down telescopically to a far door shrouded still in darkness.

Lucy smiled down at her. "What, you got something better to do?"

Given that Elly had skipped out on two different costume parties and other general Halloween revelry just to be here, she'd almost have to say so. She didn't, though, because Lucy was two years older and sexy in that mysterious, older, hot-girl way. Elly still couldn't decide whether or not this whole week of intense attention from Lucy had been some kind of weird hazing ritual. Like point and laugh at the baby gay who thought she had a chance.

"No, but —"

Lucy laughed again, skipping down the last few steps and brushing a hand over Elly's shoulder. "There's a secret lab down here," Lucy said, sliding past her.

"A secret lab?"

Lucy turned to look at Elly over her shoulder. "You can keep a secret, can't you?"

Elly looked past Lucy's pretty, taunting face, down the corridor to the heavy fortified door at the end. A spark of awareness rolled through her belly. "Are you going to serial-kill me?"

The door at the top of the stairs opened, and a blonde girl came giggling into the staircase, dragging a guy Elly recognised from her Gen Ed class behind her. Adam, she thought his name was.

"Oh, hey Luce," the blonde girl said. "This your pledge?"

"I'm hoping so," Lucy replied.

The blonde waggled her eyebrows as her date slid his arms around her waist and kissed the back of her neck. "See you in there!"

The couple slipped past Elly and headed down the corridor. Elly held her breath as the door opened, briefly illuminating the passageway in the glow of a fire or candles, flickering against the walls. The sounds of people talking followed after, but it was different, rhythmical. Like...chanting?

"Pledge?" she asked when the door slipped shut behind them.

"We can bring in a new pledge, but only if they're...special," Lucy said, her voice caressing the word special, as if including Elly in a secret. "But if you're too afraid that I'm going to serial-kill you..." Lucy bit her bottom lip, reaching out to grip Elly's shoulder, pressing a thumb against her collarbone.

Elly breathed out shakily. Being the only lesbian in her hometown had not prepared her for...this. "Are you going to tell me what I'm pledging for?"

"An exclusive club."

"With a secret lab?"

Lucy shrugged, stepping up until she was somehow too close and too far away, the smell of her perfume in Elly's throat. She whispered, "Take it or leave it."

Lucy took a deliberate step away and towards the door, holding out a hand. This was crazy. Certifiable.

Elly clearly needed to go to a neuroscience lab. Maybe get studied. Fuck. Unable to believe she was even doing it, she took a deep breath and slid her hand into Lucy's, revelling in the sensation of her tightening grip.

"Good girl," Lucy said, her voice dropping to an intimate level that sent a thrill of excitement straight through Elly's nervous system. Wow.

Lucy towed Elly to the door, punched in a six-digit number, and cranked open the handle. The door swung outwards, and Elly got her first promised glimpse of the lab.

It barely resembled a lab anymore. The walls had been decorated in a Halloween theme with writing scrambled all over in hundreds of different hands. Music with heavy bass pulsed through the space. Candles littered the lab tables to provide a sombre yellow glow, and someone had painted a ritual-esque circle encapsulating a star onto the ceiling.

Bodies were packed into the central space, guys and girls gyrating to the heavy bass. There were noticeably more girls than guys, outnumbering them three to one. Elly began to move towards the dancers, but Lucy pulled her aside and brought her over to the corner where a keg had been set up.

"First you have to join in," Lucy said, handing her a Sharpie.

"Join in?"

"It's tradition," Lucy said, leaning in close to be heard over the thumping bass, her breath tickling Elly's nape. "You have to write our names on the wall."

There was no holding back the shiver that skated down her spine. "Our names?"

"You're my pledge, so you have to write my name and yours," Lucy elaborated. "Here." She tapped a free space with the blunt nail of her right pointer finger.

Elly laughed, reaching across Lucy's body to sign both their names in the place indicated. Almost as soon as she'd finished writing, a tremor thrummed through the room. As if something ancient had been slumbering beneath them and had finally awakened.

"Time for the good part," Lucy whispered, pulling Elly back into her torso and wrapping her arms around her waist.

Elly shivered as awareness spread through her veins in a titillating blend of pleasure and adrenaline. It was all the excitement of being completely buzzed, but on zero alcohol. "The good part?"

Lucy gestured back to the dance floor as a spectacle of monstrous proportions began to unfold. The first guy —Adam from her Gen Ed class —never saw it coming. One minute he was grinding on his date, the next he was drowning in his own blood as she slit his throat from ear to ear. He slumped down to the ground and she was immediately over him, bringing his blood up to her face, rubbing it into her skin. The next few guys *almost* appeared to notice something amiss. They had just time enough to register bewilderment when their throats were slit, and they slumped down to add their own thick, foamy viscera to the dance floor.

The last guy got as far as the door, but he couldn't get it open, yanking on it desperately as the music cut, his screams bouncing around in the enclosed space. They grabbed him, peeling him away from his salvation, and laughing as he begged. They pulled him to the center of the bloodbath, spreading him flat on the dance floor and impaling his hands and legs, pinning him like a bug on an entomologist's board.

Elly stood, petrified into stone in Lucy's arms, watching the horror break out, tasting the scent of the blood in the back of her throat, unable to tear her eyes away. Though the music had died, something else heavy and intoxicating was thrumming through the air like an ancient heartbeat. Elly's own heart hammered in time with it, her mouth beginning to water as horror warred with... was that hunger?

"Look at that, baby," Lucy whispered in her ear. "One left for you."

Elly turned to gape, wide-eyed, at Lucy. "What... I —"

"Come on, baby," Lucy purred, pulling on Elly's arm and leading her over to the thrashing boy tethered to the floor. "Let me show you."

The other women were humming, Elly realised, all of them painted dark crimson with the blood of their erstwhile dates. The humming thrummed and reverberated with the heartbeat, pulling her closer, clouding her brain as her shoes stuck to the syrupy dance floor.

Lucy picked up one of discarded knives, holding it out to her. "Come on, baby," she whispered. "Enjoy the power."

Elly reached out, her body trembling as excitement roiled through her veins, chasing away every last thread of horror. Together, they grasped the handle and Lucy smiled, dipping her free fingers into the pool of blood and smearing some across her own mouth.

Elly watched, hypnotised, as Lucy leant in, pressing her mouth to Elly's in a languorous kiss that tasted like copper-plated promise and tingled with the covenant of power yet to come. When Lucy pulled away, Elly knew just what to do. Gripping the handle tighter, she plunged the blade into his sternum, dragging it through his belly and down to his groin, spilling his guts all over the floor.

In the room, the women cried out in rapture, drowning his scream with their ecstasy. Lucy plunged her hands into his abdomen, coating her fingers and palms in sticky crimson blood and using them to stroke Elly's hair back from her face, tenderly, teasingly.

Elly laughed out loud as the thrum of power pulsed away inside of her, the tempo increasing and increasing to an ecstatic peak, reaching its crescendo. Something ancient was indeed waking, but it was not buried beneath them, oh no. It was them. *They* were waking. They were one. They were coming together.

Blood-covered lips pressed against her ear. "Good girl."

MICHELLE VIZINAU

20K

THE LIME-GREEN SHAMROCK glowed like a beacon for the down-and-out. That was Jerry, all right, down and certainly out.

He walked over and peeked through the port window in the door to Lucky's bar. The place was empty.

Jerry slipped his hand into his pocket and fingered his last hundred. He could catch a bus, get as far as Colorado or Wyoming and hope Caesar didn't come looking for him, but the longer he ran, the more likely Caesar would put a bullet in his head on principle.

No, this is better, he thought as he pushed into the bar. Get drunk enough to dull the pain, find Caesar, tell him he doesn't have the money and pray he wakes up in a hospital instead of a casket.

The lonely strains of Johnny Cash lamenting about the connection between pain and feelings poured from the jukebox. The coned lights created circles of warmth that faded out into cold shadows where dust goes to settle. The combined effect gave the place a false sense of intimacy.

A single dock hop with stringy red hair twisted into a messy bun smiled at him through gapped teeth. Jerry diverted his eyes and sat at the other end of the bar, dashing her hopes of a transaction.

He took out his ledger —money owed, bets he'd placed, and a handful of people who owed him money. Maybe he could find enough scratch to buy himself a minor beatdown.

The bartender, a tall, thin, Black man with an almost comical set of chops framing his carved cheekbones, appeared and looked Jerry over.

"Scotch, straight up," the bartender announced. His voice was as deep as a well after a rainstorm, both comforting and authoritative.

Jerry nodded. He hadn't been sure of his order a moment before, but he knew now that Scotch was the right choice. "How'd ya know?" he asked, running a hand through his greasy hair.

The bartender had a full seventies-style Afro. Hair like that always made Jerry more conscious of the stray mousy wisps that circled his skull. To go prematurely bald in his twenties had been a nightmare, but now, his forty-year-old face had finally grown into the look.

The bartender shrugged. "I just know. Just like I know that if Scotch isn't handy, a standard whiskey will do," he said, setting up the drink from the bottom shelf.

"What if I want something a little more mid- or even top-shelf?" Jerry asked, drinking what was handed to him.

"Nah," the bartender said, but did not elaborate. In an act that seemed almost scripted, he whipped out a rag from his apron and began polishing the bar's dark wood finish.

"Just 'nah'? What are you, the drunk whisperer? Explain how you knew."

For the first time in three days, Jerry felt distracted from his impending doom. It wasn't just the accuracy, it was the confidence in the accuracy. If Jerry had half this guy's ability, every game would be an A-game.

The bartender stopped wiping and fixed him with a weary look. "You really want to know? I'll tell you, but don't punch me in the face."

Jerry chuckled and placed his hands behind his back. "Punch the guy serving me drinks? Never that."

The bartender sighed and began.

"For starters, it's a Tuesday. The slowest of all bar days. Only drunks, lonelies, and the desperate drink on Tuesdays. You're not a drunk and you looked upset when you walked in, like this drink may be the only thing saving you from wandering into traffic. Then you chose to sit down here alone. Now people only look that bad for one of three reasons: chicks, chips or coffins. No wedding band and you look like you've gotten used to being alone. Wrinkled clothes, five-day shadow." The bartender rubbed at his chin when he said it. "How am I doing so far?"

Jerry nodded and the bartender continued.

"So not a chick. Which leaves death or finances. Grief-stricken folks usually want to sit quietly and reflect. They don't study little black books. So death is off the table. That leaves money, and by the way you're studying that black book for answers, I'd say a nice chunk of it. Maybe a foreclosure, but I myself am a gambler of sorts and I'm getting gambling debt vibes, hence the cheap drink."

Jerry clapped for the bartender.

The dock hop at the end of the bar, who had been nodding off into her drink, started awake.

"You trying to kill me?" she yelled.

The bartender bowed and she flipped him off.

Jerry paid little attention to this. He was still thinking about this guy's skills.

"What are you, a part-time shrink? You must kill at the tables."

"No, I'm a writer. Getting my master's in English. If you want to write good fiction, you have to be a people watcher."

Jerry nodded and finished off his drink. "You must be a great writer."

"I do all right, but if you don't mind me asking, how much you owe?"

Jerry tapped the glass and Mike refilled it. "Ten racks to a guy named Caesar. You said you gamble —you know Caesar?"

Mike whistled and slapped the bar with his rag. The dock hop looked up again but said nothing.

"Wow. Yeah, I know Caesar. Caesar Meeks, right?"

Jerry drained the glass and said, "the very one."

"Well I guess it could be worse. At least you have the grace period. I knew a guy owed three hundred racks to Mr. Wang. Knew, past tense, you feel me? They won't kill you for ten racks, but they'll make you hurt," Mike said.

Jerry grimaced, swallowed hard, but said nothing.

"You gonna be able to get the scratch before they take it back in fractures and sutures?"

Jerry tapped the glass. "I'm hoping to get drunk enough to make the beatdown bearable. Kind of burned my credit at the tables in town. At least the ones I can afford."

"You got a wife and kids? Anyone Caesar can visit?"

"Nah, just my mom, lives downtown in a nursing home, Alzheimer's," Jerry replied.

Mike leaned against the bar and stared at the ceiling, like his mind was chewing on something and only after Jerry figured the conversation was over did he say anything.

"I have a game for you. Great odds. Low buy-in."

Jerry's face brightened. "How low?"

"What've you got?" Mike asked.

Jerry dragged the hundred out and placed it on the bar. "That's all I have."

Mike considered this for a minute. "That's fine. Drinks on me, if you promise to come back and tip me tonight after you win."

Jerry nodded excitedly. "Of course. I wouldn't stiff a guy who threw me a game."

"My man," Mike said and extended his hand. Jerry shook it. "Let me see that book of yours."

Jerry handed it to him and Mike scribbled "ten thousand" in large letters and an address. Then with painstaking effort, he drew a symbol at the bottom of the page.

"That's the address. Just a couple blocks away. Show him the symbol I drew here and the guy will let you in."

Jerry looked at the lines and arrows then looked at Mike. "What does it mean?"

Mike laughed. "It means the guy will let you in. But hey listen, when you reach your goal, think long and hard before you continue. It's a legit game but it's real easy to overextend yourself at this place."

Jerry thanked Mike and hurried out into the brisk cold. A smile, the first since the mark came due, creased his face.

The bay was cranking up the fog machine, and he could only see what was ten feet in front of him. That was all right, though. He knew this city like he knew his own face. The address was on Humboldt, right off of Third, less than three blocks away.

He was halfway down the block before he realized he hadn't asked what the game was. Didn't really matter—the buy-in was a hundred bucks, and he would either win or lose. The seed of hope was planted.

Ten minutes later, Jerry stood in front of a fish-and-chips shop. The address matched, but the windows were papered over and the door padlocked. He checked the address again. This was the place but there was no action here.

Jerry's heart sank. The kid was jerking his chain. Smug college prick.

He was heading back to tell the bartender off when he noticed a red light glowing above a single door on Illinois Street, on the opposite side of the building. The seed of hope sprouted a few leaves and Jerry smiled again. The familiar flush, the pregame I-could-win flush, brightening his cheeks.

He approached and saw a glowing doorbell. He rang and after a moment the door opened and a small, round man in mechanic's overalls stood before him, silhouetted in the illumination from the red bulb overhead.

The man had the face of a pug. His jowls hung like flesh-colored bunting on his tan cheeks. His eyes, large and glassy, gave Jerry the once-over, but the man said nothing,

"Hi, uh... Mike said to show you this." Jerry held up the notebook page.

The man nodded and waved Jerry in. He turned and went noiselessly into the darkened room, motioning for Jerry to follow. As the man walked, his shoulders moved up and down, giving him the look of a cartoon character. Jerry couldn't see his face but he imagined the guy's cheeks flapping up and down. He stifled a laugh.

They approached a source of light at the far end of the room, a doorway into a kitchen that looked and smelled like it had been scrubbed within the hour. From the kitchen they exited into another room, this one with papered-over windows. Jerry nodded in recognition. Outside, he knew, was the sign for the fish-and-chips shop.

The room was dimly lit, what his long-dead father jokingly called suicide lighting, and cold as a crypt. At the center of the room, two chairs flanked a table. On the center of the table sat a large bowl of what looked like gray Nerds candy. The man motioned to a chair. Jerry sat, and the man took the chair opposite him.

Jerry shivered. "No heat in this place?"

The man leaned forward and crossed his meatpacker hands on the table. "Can't have heat. The game requires cold."

Jerry already had questions and the man's statement —*the game requires cold*—birthed a few more. But this didn't seem like the time or the person for questions.

"You have the buy-in?" the guy asked.

Jerry handed him the money and waited for the guy to question the amount, but he didn't. Instead he tucked the bill into his overalls and picked up one of the gray pebbles, showing it to Jerry.

"This is a dried doba berry." He handed the berry to Jerry. "Put it in your mouth. Whatever you do, don't swallow it or take it out of your mouth. I'll be back in ten minutes."

Jerry did as he was told and the guy left.

Jerry sat with the berry pressed between his cheek and gums, contemplating the chances that this was a prank, after all. If so, this guy sported an epic poker face.

He was strongly leaning toward prank when the guy came back and handed Jerry a napkin. "Spit it out."

Jerry did, wondering what Twilight Zone shit he'd just stepped into. He'd heard stories of people who walked into buildings and never walked out. For all he knew, this guy might be a weird butcher killer who planned on wearing his skin later.

"Show me the berry," the man commanded.

Jerry unfolded the napkin. The berry was now the size of a cranberry.

"The doba berry is a plant native to the Arctic. It's extremely difficult to grow, and it takes years of practice and the right temperature to grow them properly. The plant when stored at forty-five degrees Fahrenheit or lower will stay this size." The man plucked a berry delicately from the bowl and held it up. "When you expose it to heat, natural, artificial or in your case, body heat, the berry expands. This makes it a bang-up laxative. Models go crazy for this shit. Swallow a few of these, you can skip a meal. Do it a couple times a day and you can skip all your meals. Not exactly healthy, but convenient. Like eating cotton balls but less dangerous."

Jerry stared at the man, wondering what this had to do with the price of tea in China. Was he wasting time before the other players showed up and if so, where were the other chairs?

"There are about five hundred of these in five ounces. That's the equivalent of a box of those little candies you were probably thinking of when you saw them. So ten ounces is one thousand of these. Do you follow?"

Jerry nodded. He followed but he had no idea what he was following.

"For each of these you eat, I will give you ten dollars. But here are the rules. Once you start, you cannot stop until you are done. By that I mean, you can walk away any time, but once you do, the game is done and if you haven't eaten at least a thousand, then you lose your money and we call it a day. You never come back here."

Jerry stared at the berry in the napkin and said nothing. This seemed too easy.

"The second rule is that you swallow them one at a time. You can drink water anytime you like but I don't recommend it. Everyone I've seen complete the game successfully dry swallowed mostly, only drinking a sip from time to time."

Jerry finally braved a question. "So people have actually been able to do this?"

"Sure. Many people. Didn't Mike tell you this was a legit game?"

Jerry thought for a second. The exact same word. Legit.

"Yes, he did," he said.

"Well it is. I'd say at least fifty percent of folks can do the full thousand. And like I said, some do more."

"And if I can do more?" Jerry asked.

"Ten dollars per berry. Once you hit the ten grand, you walk away with whatever you make above that up to 20K."

Jerry did some quick math in his head. He tried to recall how much room is in the average stomach. Then he decided it didn't matter because he'd eaten at least double that on several occasions. He once ate a two-pound steak and a baked potato, with a large banana milkshake and a side salad.

And leaving wasn't an option. He needed the money.

"Can I use the bathroom first? Start with an empty vessel?"

"Sure." The guy nodded vigorously and his jowls flapped. "If you have to, uh, Number Two, that's fine too. Best if you do. Bathroom is back there next to the kitchen door."

Jerry used the restroom and came back a few minutes later. Before he sat, the man motioned toward his coat.

"I recommend you take off as many layers as you can. The colder you are, the slower the berries expand."

Jerry nodded, slipped off his coat and then pulled off his sweater, leaving just the T-shirt and jeans between him and the frigid air. The cold rattled his body like a loose ball bearing.

The man handed him a metal object nearly as long as a pair of chopsticks but connected like tweezers. "Practice a few times but don't eat them. Just practice picking them up." Jerry picked up a few of the berries, then he stopped and announced he was ready, eager to get this over with.

There was no real fanfare, just the portly man saying "go." And go he did.

Once he got the hang of picking up the berries, things moved along at a clipped pace. Ten berries, fifteen berries, twenty-nine berries, forty-six berries. Occasionally his body shook involuntarily from the cold and he dropped a berry, but most of the berries he picked, he ate.

At the sixty-berry mark, he noticed that he was no longer producing enough saliva to swallow properly. He cleared his throat, trying to bring something to the surface, but found no relief from the dry, itchy pocket that had formed behind his tongue.

"Don't throw up," the man cautioned. "You will have to start over."

Jerry had no choice. He took a small sip of the water and then another. Confident that the dry pocket was gone, he started again. He repeated this ritual twice more before he reached three hundred berries and this was when he noticed that the fat gap he liked to keep in his jeans for expansion purposes was almost nonexistent. He could feel the top of his belt buckle against his bare belly. Still he continued on.

When he reached five hundred, five small sips and a half a glass of water later, the man announced he was halfway there.

Jerry had been keeping count, and he had expected the man to keep count but the accuracy was surprising, like Mike guessing his drink.

His belly felt a lot like it had at the end of St. Patrick's Day. Full of corned beef and cabbage and, of course, pint after pint of green beer, but where he knew relief was just a visit to "flushings away on St. Patty's Day." He was only halfway to his goal with no relief in sight and while his outer flesh was still cold, a warm wave had begun radiating from inside his body.

"If I stand up to take off my belt, does that disqualify me?"

"No. So long as you don't relieve yourself or leave the room, you're fine."

Jerry stood up and loosened the belt and was happy to discover he still had a tiny amount of give in his waistband. He sat down, slightly uncomfortable, but it was bearable.

He continued, and after taking four more sips of water and downing two hundred fifty more berries, the man announced, "seven hundred fifty," and Jerry nodded. He no longer felt the cold. Or if he did, it was a lot less pressing than the actual pressing of his belly against his jeans. He was swimming in perspiration, and occasionally the sweat from his brow dripped down into his eyes, stinging them and blurring his vision. The buttons of his 501s felt like BB pellets digging into his gut.

"You've got this," the man said.

Again, Jerry nodded, but his mind was filled with stuffed things. Sausage. Pigs in a blanket. Twinkies. Thanksgiving turkey. He squirmed in his seat, which only served to press the buttons deeper into his already raw flesh. He'd barely made a dent in the bowl of berries but here he was two hundred fifty from the goal.

He tucked in again.

Somewhere around the nine hundred mark, something miraculous happened. The pain in his gut numbed over, and then he felt a shift in his belly and the girth seemed to spread more evenly across his abs. It was just the push he needed. He was going to reach his goal.

When he did, it was to the mental theme of Rocky. But he didn't stop, didn't even think about stopping. He was feeling that winner's buzz, riding the wave of a royal flush.

He no longer felt the cold or the way his pants cut into his gut. He was the eye of the fucking tiger, we are the champions, big shot, winner.

The internal soundtrack of glory drove him forward past the eleven hundred mark. The twelve hundred mark. Fourteen hundred.

A little past sixteen hundred, the top button of his jeans flew off, hit the table and ricocheted back and snapped into his belly. He farted involuntarily and it felt like he'd been shot in the gut but it made a little more room for berries.

He murmured an apology and the man waved it off.

He should have quit then but the winner's high wouldn't peak until he hit jackpot. This was a sure bet, the wet dream of all gamblers.

Seventeen hundred, another button gone.

Eighteen hundred, and another.

Tonight he would get a hotel downtown and order room service, or maybe just cocktails.

When he reached the two thousand mark, his mind stood up and took a victory lap but his body remained stationary. He'd never been more full, and his thoughts wandered down the road of paranoia. What if by some freakish accident of nature, he couldn't shit this out? What if he stayed this way, constipated until he died of sepsis? He'd heard that could happen.

The man rose and exited the room unceremoniously, and Jerry's apprehension shifted gears to the even more realistic fear that he might be left alone. The tragedy dawning on him that in his current state he couldn't catch a crawling baby.

He braced himself and stood, and the last remaining button popped off. He lifted his shirt. His gut, distended and red, had a bald-headed sheen to it, and it sat low, on the cradle bones of his hips. He took a step forward and a gurgle, deep and guttural, emanated from his belly. He patted it gently and waited. After a moment, he took two steps.

"You gonna be okay? Maybe you should sit down."

Jerry glanced up toward the sound of the voice and realized the guy was back. He held a stack of hundreds, which he handed to Jerry.

Jerry knew he should count it, but he didn't think he was capable. Instead, he bent for his coat but his belly stopped him. "Could you help me out here?" he asked.

The guy grabbed his coat and helped Jerry slip it on. He went for Jerry's sweater but Jerry shook his head and said, "leave it."

He stuck the money in his inside pocket and thanked the man. As he did, a belch escaped and the sour stench of regurgitated Scotch wafted between them. "I'm so sorry, man."

The guy clapped him on the shoulder and said it was okay, and Jerry made for the door. Before he left, he turned and asked, "What do you get out of this?"

The guy smiled.

"Most people that come in here bet more than a hundred bucks. Sometimes we lose but we win a lot of the time. There are also cameras in the room, you know, for spectators, and they bet on whether you will win and by how many berries. Only one guy bet that you would finish, one-hundred-to-one odds. He's a very happy guy right now."

Another burp bubbled to the surface and Jerry wasn't confident that it was just a burp. He stumbled through the kitchen and back to the bathroom, leaned over the rim of the toilet and let go. But it was just a burp, after all.

He slipped off his jeans and tried to move the product as his dad used to say, but to his great displeasure, nothing came out. After a few more attempts, he left the bathroom.

The man would later find Jerry's jeans discarded on the bathroom floor.

As Jerry wandered out into the night, the moon peeked between ominous clouds and the air tasted like rain. The crisp breeze was welcome on his burning skin. His belly burned like a coal furnace on the inside, heating the rest of his body.

How much time had passed since he went into the building? Was it enough time to develop a strong fever?

He didn't know, but he knew he wasn't fit for travel. So he headed back to the bar to make good on his promise to Mike.

He gave little thought to the air that gusted up beneath his trench coat, billowing it out to show his underwear underneath, or the unsettling gurgling coming from below his chest. His thoughts seemed to be floating above him in jumbles, and every once in a while he plucked one down for examination. These fragmented thoughts told him Lucky's made sense. He peeled a hundred off the top of the stack and held it like a talisman out in front of him and marched on. In twice the time it took him to make it to the fish-and-chips shop, he was once again standing in front of that glowing lucky shamrock.

His stomach tight as a steel drum, sweat so thick he felt as if he were melting, he reached for the door, and a tearing sound split the silence. He prayed it was his coat but the sudden release of tension in his gut, the soul-stripping pain that followed, and the hot, wet liquid rushing down his groin told him otherwise.

He went down to his knees as if, in a last effort at redemption, he decided prayer was the answer.

With every bit of anything he had left, he stood and pushed his way into the bar. He lost whatever momentum he had left and stumbled, did an almost graceful pirouette, then toppled and fell face up onto the floor. He was dead before his head slapped the cold tiles.

The bar had remained mostly empty, just Mike and the dock hop napping on her stool.

Mike rushed over and crouched next to Jerry. He checked for a pulse, but the man's life status was written in the bloody entrails and the now-cherry-sized doba berries that rolled from his belly to the front door. The midsection, finally freed from the pressure, had peeled away from his body, leaving his empty rib cage on display like a dinosaur fossil.

Mike started for the phone behind the counter, then noticed the bill clutched in Jerry's fist.

Gently, he extracted the hundred from the dead man's grasp. Then, putting on a pair of gloves, he searched for the notebook. Mike had written in the book, and though he was pretty sure they wouldn't find him guilty of anything more than bad judgment, it was better to not have to answer any questions at all. He found the book and the 20K.

He turned on the bright lights and counted the money as he dialed 911. After he gave the operator the few pertinent details, he walked to the register and rang up two Scotches, used the hundred to pay and slid the change into his pocket. He split the 20K and put half into Jerry's coat pocket. He'd already made fifty grand off the guy. No need to be greedy.

The dock hop stirred awake and, seeing the carnage, she screamed and began babbling questions at Mike.

The only reply she received was the still-distant wailing of an ambulance moving through the night.

Again, Mike picked up the phone, lifted a finger to silence the dock hop —she didn't stop crying, but she did quiet down —and dialed Caesar. When the bookie picked up, Mike said he had payment on a 10K marker for a guy named Jerry. Caesar had no questions, as payment was being made within the grace period. A plan was made for collection and Mike hung up. Now he could be sure that Caesar wouldn't be paying Jerry's mom a visit. He walked the dock hop to the back door and handed her a hundred dollar bill. This quieted her up, and without another word, she wandered off into the night.

Mike rationalized, she had been drunk enough that in the morning light, she might wake up and convince herself that she didn't see what she thought she saw, or that it wasn't half as bad as she thought it was.

With the dock hop on her way, Mike returned to the front of the bar and turned off the neon shamrock sign, carefully avoiding Jerry's body. The light blinked a few times and flickered out. Then, he waited.

ALEJANDRO GONZALES

Ghost Ship

JACOB WAS TOUGH AS toenails. Although he created many worlds and spooky small towns with ambiguous creatures that went bump in the night, he'd never considered himself a daredevil type. He hadn't sold a story in six months, so he found himself aboard an abandoned ship with his girlfriend Anna as backup; she had armed herself with nothing but a pocket-sized notebook full of poetry.

"Well," he said, pulling Anna up from a final ladder rung. "I guess it's too late to change my mind. The show must go on. No better place for inspiration than this creepy old place."

"Yeah, and we're still going skydiving after this? You know, so I can get some inspiration for my —"

"Sure, whatever. I'm a man of my word, babe. Right now, you're here for what we're experiencing in the present. Help me make the first choice. Left or right door?"

Her head moved left, right, left, right. This enhanced the atmosphere, he reckoned. Definitely a moment he'd put in his story. Readers loved sidekick girlfriends with goofy demeanors.

"Uh, the right one," she finally said.

"Left it is." He laughed and kissed his marginally larger-than-average bicep. "Remember the first lesson of my survival guide —disappointment is a necessary learning experience."

"That was a fucking short story," she said. "And didn't it get ripped apart by a bunch of YouTubers or something?"

"Sweetheart, you're not here for your ideas. Just keep providing moral support, and tell me if you see anything scary that I miss. My eyes aren't what they once were."

"Like two years ago when you were twenty-three instead of twenty-five?"

He shouldered the left door open, then gestured for her to enter. "Yeah, pretty much. This'll do. Someone important must've used this ship. Christ, look at how big that bed is. A royal couple probably slept here. How about we, uh, recreate history here?"

"How about you, *uh*, go fuck yourself. Have fun in the bedroom. I'm going through the other door."

Anna sashayed out, slamming the door behind her before Jacob processed her insult. He shrugged, cracked his knuckles, and lay back on the bed, imagining Madonna in her prime. Jacob had no problem giving himself the old rug-a-tug, the chugga chugga choo train that stopped at self-love station. He scrolled up his music playlist just for these moments, on his phone.

"That's what I'm talking about," he said once the song loaded. "Come And Get Your Love" blasted in the room, echoing off the walls. He snaked his hand into his underwear, gripped his penis, gave it a squeeze for good measure, and replaced Madonna's head with Anna's. In his mind, he caressed her breasts while she cooed in his ear. Older Madonna slipped into the picture. He supposed he didn't mind; he just needed a bag over that plastic surgery face.

His free hand dug into the sheets. In another life, he probably would have dated Madonna instead. Granted he owned a time machine. A moan slipped his lips, and then another hand joined his, pushed his aside, and started working magic he'd never experienced before.

"Holy shit," he said, eyes closed against the pulsating ecstasy. "Damn, you've gotten better at that. I knew you couldn't stay mad at me. Oh, you're definitely getting a birthday present this year."

Heat flared at the base of his penis.

"Ow, damn, bitch. Watch the nails. It ain't replaceable."

The pain intensified. Warm, thick liquid dripped onto his underwear. Blood. He sat up and screamed, greeted not by Anna but a husk of a half-rotten face. Maggots had set up camp in her nostrils and eye sockets.

"Get off my dick, you ugly fuckin' bitch. Anna, help!"

Anna did not arrive. However she would have found nothing but a disheveled Jacob if she were within earshot. The lady simply raised a rotten finger, mouthed the word "naughty," and exploded into dust. Scrambling off the bed, he pulled up his pants. When the demon-thing didn't reappear he ran off after Anna.

An hour later he still hadn't found Anna, yet her voice called out around every corner. He must've walked around the entire ship four or five times with a persistent itch terrorizing his genitals. He alternated between a stiff-legged shuffle and walking with both legs spread apart as far as possible. Neither solution provided relief. The latter had unstuck his sweaty balls from his thighs many a time in the past.

"Anna," he cried out while he passed a gray, freezing room.

"Oh, sweetie, come, come," a voice light as the wind said.

Anna turned a corner and threw her hands up in exasperation. Her voice did not sound like the breathy one that called for him. He swallowed hard. Anna reached for his hand, then pulled him into a full embrace instead. Her usually cloying perfume raised goosebumps on his arms.

"Jeez, you're shaking like a wet puppy. Are you okay?"

"I think so. I'm ready to go home. I think I've gotten inspiration."

"Me too. Let's go home, babe."

The duo walked down the hall, hand in hand.

After an hour, Jacob was convinced they hadn't left the room. The door led into a hallway that led to another door with a nearly identical layout, and this went on in an infinite loop— a closed system where the exit was the entrance and vice versa, and woe unto all who entered and sought a return to anything which wasn't a dull fucking room where his balls ached and felt like they were freezing off.

"Jacob," Anna said on their fiftieth loop. "This is your fucking fault. Ew, can you keep your hand off your dick for five minutes?"

"It hurts, bitch. You probably gave me the clap."

"Oh, I'm the reason you're hurting down there? Grow up."

"I'm sorry." He let out a high-pitched whine. "But seriously, it really fucking hurts, baby."

"You better knock this shit off and save the blue balls bit for a different day."

He stopped and screamed. "Goddamnit, this isn't about sex. My dick feels like it's burning. Something's wrong."

"Whatever, I'm not your mom. Don't expect me to change your diaper."

"What the hell has gotten into you?"

"You, far too many times." Her jaw grew taut.

A door swung open behind them leading to the bedroom where Jacob's genital woes began. They exchanged a glance before Anna shook her head and ran through the exit. The door slammed shut behind her. It didn't bother him, not one bit. He was a natural born survivor built for the harshest environments. He nodded in agreement with himself.

He'd be just fine. Probably be out of the maze in no time while she'd still be stuck, wandering around in circles.

Wherever Anna went, she took the whole exit with her, because three hours later Jacob was nauseous from walking in circles. He slid against a wall, poked his ginger penis, and yelped when he felt skin flake off. *Might as well go all the way,* he thought. One last hurrah before he lost everything over a story that would never get written.

He shoved his hands in his pants and tugged on his penis against the head-splitting agony. Madonna made one last appearance in his mind. And then in reality. He blinked rapidly. She was still there; so was the fantasy of Anna. And despite the absurdity of the situation, he only perpetuated it by continuing to stroke his dick.

"Oh, you sweet fool," said Madonna, who wasn't Madonna at all, but a blonde woman with a rack. "Your lady will be in good hands, and you'll have plenty of fun here. Until I make sure this wreck is dismantled and your soul never sees another ray of light again. Until then, enjoy your new life in death."

Maggots tore through his urethra before he could utter a response. He fell over and screamed until his throat was too raw to make more noise. Not-Madonna slipped into Anna like she was a pair of shoes.

"Don't worry, babe. The bleeding out only takes about ten minutes. Now, I've got a life to take over."

C. C. ROSSI

Her Freaky Skin

LEON AND CALVIN found the dying woman behind a burnt-out liquor store in an alley off 6 Mile Road and Winslow in Detroit. It was late April and the first decent day of spring, the early afternoon sun high in a cloudless blue sky.

"Aww fuck," Leon said, his thirteen-year-old voice surprisingly deep. Leon was five-ten, one hundred and sixty-five pounds, a small mustache already growing on his chestnut face. "Why'd we have to come down this alley?"

"We've been down here a million times," said Calvin, Leon's pale, red-haired companion. He was three months younger than Leon, had just hit puberty, and stood five inches shorter than his best friend. "We've never seen her before."

"We shouldn't have skipped school," Leon lamented, stepping closer to the woman. She was either Latina or Asian. It was hard to tell with bruises covering her battered face, her eyes swollen shut, nose mashed like that of an over-the-hill boxer. Her black hair was cut short. She wore a simple flower-pattern dress that was hiked up high on her slim thighs.

"She's just some whore," Calvin said. "Probably didn't pay her pimp so they put a boot to that ass and left her here."

"Nah, look at her arms and legs," Leon countered. "Look at the way her skin be, like, almost moving. Shit's freaky."

Calvin shook his head. "You tripping. She's just jonesing for some fetty."

"Nah, there's something else." Leon looked around the garbage-strewn alleyway, grabbed a cracked wooden baseball bat, and pushed the woman's dress up almost to her crotch. She moaned but remained still.

"What you doing?" Calvin said. "Trying to peep her snatch?"

"Shit, I seen plenty of snatch."

"Yo' momma's!"

"Suck your momma's dick, bitch," Leon said before he yelped, dropped the bat, and stepped back, almost tripping on a discarded box of wilted lettuce.

"Her beef flaps scare you?"

"There's something inside her...something trying to get out."

Calvin picked up the bat, stepped closer to the woman, and gasped.

Leon was right. The woman's skin all over her body —arms, legs, even her gaunt face —was undulating, moving, like some cheap-ass CGI horror video. Except this was no movie. This shit was real.

"We gotta get the fuck out of here." Leon's voice cracked with fear. "There's a bud store two blocks over on Franklin. We can go over there and see if someone can help."

"Just chill," Calvin said, repulsed yet fascinated by the strange gesticulations on the woman. "Lemme see your phone, man."

Leon frowned. "What? Why you want that?"

"I want a selfie."

"Nah," Leon said. "My momma does phone checks. She sees this and I'll be in big trouble."

"C'mon, man, give me your phone. I'll put it straight to my Insta, then delete it. Your momma will never —"

Calvin's words died in his mouth as a geyser of arterial blood erupted from the woman's thigh. The hot red shower arced in the air, a crimson fountain landing on his new Jordan Retro sneakers.

"Oh shit!" Calvin cried, scurrying back like a crab being chased by hungry seagulls.

"Look! Look!" Leon said, pointing at the woman.

Calvin looked and wished he hadn't. The jaundiced skin on the woman's legs and thighs ballooned, ready to pop, and where the skin had ruptured, a six-inch-long, pencil-thin thing was wiggling its way out.

Calvin thought maybe it was some type of crazy worm the woman picked up shooting fetty. But when the thing tore itself free of her skin and fell on the dirty asphalt of the alley, he realized it was nothing like anything he'd seen before. It was a grotesque, bizarre creature, four inches long, dull black like an ancient piece of coal, a monster come to life. It had five hair-thin appendages sprouting from its body, all whipping around in a frenzy of movement. It latched onto a busted wine bottle and pulled itself upright, now standing on two of the spindly appendages.

"Oh shit! Oh shit!" Leon repeated, the woman's body contorting and shaking as if in the grips of a grand mal seizure. Her eyes opened impossibly wide before her right eyeball popped out of its socket with a hair-thing attached, the bloody white orb flopping about like a too-large lollipop.

"Leon, help!" Calvin cried, beating on the first hair-monster clinging to the wine bottle. His hits were hard and true, yet it was like beating on a piece of hard rubber. One of the writhing appendages of the hair-monster wrapped itself around the bat like the arm of an octopus and pulled its way toward Calvin's hand.

"Throw it away!" Leon yelled from behind him. Calvin turned to see Leon ripping a two-by-four from a pallet. It came free with a splintering sound, three nails sticking out of the end. Calvin dropped the bat and Leon handed him the board.

"Let's smash these fuckers!" Leon hollered, ripping free his own two-by-four. Like knights with long swords, they attacked the monstrosities that continued to burst out of the woman's rippling, bloody flesh.

For a brief moment, jacked up on fear and adrenaline, Calvin and Leon felt like they had gained the upper hand in their nightmare war against the hair-things. But as the monsters encircled them, their hope faltered. More and more of the coal-black things ripped their way out of the woman's ragged flesh and came lurching toward them; when they knocked one away, two more appeared.

"We need to get the hell out of here," Calvin panted.

"I know!" Leon cried, his head jerking from side to side. "But they got us surrounded!"

Calvin looked; Leon was right. The boys, backed up against the huge pile of stinking rubbish behind a boarded-up pizza joint, were surrounded in the narrow alley by the hair-monsters. Some of the things were crawling, some were wobbling upright, but they were all closing in.

"We need to jump over them!" Leon shouted. "There's too many!"

Calvin shook his head, tears streaming down his face. "I can't! What if I fall? What if —"

Leon dropped his board and jumped, easily clearing the line of hair-monsters.

"Leon!" cried Calvin. "Don't leave me!"

But his friend was already sprinting down the alley. Calvin turned back to face alone the horde of encroaching hair-things. He screamed in anger and fear, bringing the two-by-four down again and again on the nightmare aberrations, but it was no use; they were getting closer, the wood splintering apart into useless pieces. Soon the monstrosities would be burrowing into his young flesh just as —

"Calvin!"

The voice jerked Calvin back to the present. It was Leon, standing just outside the half-circle of monsters, dousing them with liquid from a dented can of lighter fluid.

"Back up against the garbage!" Leon commanded. Calvin did so just as his best friend lit the hair-things ablaze. As Calvin shielded his face against the flames and heat, the hair-things popped and cracked like bacon grease in a red-hot skillet. Thick, oily smoke rose in the air, smelling of rotting flesh and steaming shit.

"They're not moving," Leon said after a moment.

Calvin opened his eyes and saw his friend was right. He gingerly stepped over the smoldering mess and stood by Leon. "I thought you was gonna leave me to die."

Leon punched him on the shoulder. "Hell, no. You're my boy."

Calvin wiped snot from his nose with the back of his sleeve. "Thanks, man." He looked at the mass of hair-things and grimaced. "Where'd you get the lighter fluid?"

"Down the alley. I peeped it when we walked in, and figured that fire destroys everything, so..." Leon shrugged.

Calvin nodded, scrunching his face. "That shit smells like dirty ass."

"Yeah, that's nasty." Leon pulled Calvin's arm. "C'mon —let's get out of here."

They passed by the bleeding, torn-up body of the dead woman. Leon stopped. "It don't seem right leaving her."

Calvin sighed. "Ain't nothin' right about this city. She was in the wrong place at the wrong time."

"What do you think those things were?" Leon asked, holding his nose and squatting down to look closely at the hair-things. "I never seen anything like it."

"I don't know, man. The Army put in that new germ warfare research center at the university. Maybe something got out from there."

"Maybe." Leon was still looking at the things when Calvin poked him in the side.

Leon screamed and jumped back. "You trying to give me a heart attack? That wasn't funny!"

"It was funny as shit!"

"Well, it ain't gonna be funny if the po-po show up," Leon countered. "Let's get to stepping home."

Calvin stayed still, then looked around the alley. "One second." He rummaged through the garbage, finally coming up with an empty peanut-butter jar and a lid.

"What you doing?"

"Getting me a sample."

"That's some crazy bullshit."

Calvin waved him off and used a piece of the broken two-by-four to carefully scrape one of the hair-things —which still twitched feebly —into the jar.

"Why'd you do that?" Leon asked as the boys made their way down the alley back to their homes.

Calvin shrugged, looking at the hair-thing in the jar. "Maybe we can sell it. You know, to some scientist or museum."

"That's stupid."

"You're stupid."

The boys walked in silence for a few minutes until Calvin stopped. He shook the jar and peered inside. One tiny piece of the thing, no bigger than an eyelash, wiggled like a worm on a hook.

"I know that look," Leon said, staring at his friend, who wore a sly grin. "That's the look when you're gonna do evil."

"What do you think would happen if someone ate this thing?"

"Probably end up like that poor woman it came from."

"I was thinking the same thing." Calvin shook the jar. "My momma is making some of her no-bake cookies tonight."

"The ones she fills with bud?"

"Hell yeah! What else you gonna put in 'em?"

"I don't like that stuff, makes me paranoid."

"They ain't for you. They're for our fat-ass —and your fat-ass —landlord, Sly Cumminsworth. That greedy piece of shit just loves them no-bakes, and momma figures as long as she keeps giving them to him, he won't kick us out for always being late on rent."

"But she's wrong," Calvin continued, staring at the worm-thing. "That motherfucker is gonna kick us out as soon as he can sell the place to some rich-ass developer. I say let's do a science experiment and put this thing into a no-bake and see what it does to Sly."

Leon thought for a few seconds, then nodded. "I got no problem with that. Hell, I'll even let you use my phone to record when those things pop out of his rich-ass belly."

MARK F. GROVER

Union of the Flesh

THIS WAS NOT YOUR typical retirement home after the WSUC, a.k.a., Women Saving Unborn Children, funneled money into the pilot project. They stood in the newly added grand lobby with contemporary chandeliers and rose bouquets. The contractors told them the new lobby would make the sixty-year-old facility look cobbled. Many safety inspections needed to be done prior to completion. The WSUC didn't care. Their presence needed to be known without so many delays. Money was placed discreetly in lobbyists' and inspectors' hands to speed up the construction. Without the WSUC, the pilot study would've never commenced today. A big gold plaque in the glass case behind reception at the far end of the room would show all of their names. The WSUC would save the world.

The hair on their heads stood stiff, curled, and wrapped around their faces with makeup giving them the appearance of china dolls. The ladies held cake and punch. The sheen of their painted nails radiated power and money. Some had daughters that beamed beside the older women, many in bright red and blue, slender and fashionable, like they were ready to board a yacht. Others leaned into their friends as if whispering a scandalous secret. They looked at their cell phones and muttered that the connection was terrible. If one didn't know anymore, one might guess it was a college reunion for a sorority house.

A few men, physicians who collaborated with the WSUC to tailor the program, stood in freshly pressed lab coats and waited intently in front of the fireplace at the left side of the grand vestibule. Nurses and assistants stood behind a glass partition looking anxiously at the WSUC. The staff waited to march into the celebration with clear plastic carts holding Caucasian skin pouches that resembled giant pieces of transparent pasta with fetal skeletal figures dancing inside.

The WSUC members groused about the heat and swatted flies away. Some were looking up at the table with the sheet cake and refreshments and sneered when they noticed several flies hovering then landing on the icing.

A tall woman with gaudy earrings excused herself from the gaggle of cake eaters, proceeded through the congested corridor, opened the glass doors, and approached the nursing station directly behind reception. "For what we're paying to keep my mother-in-law here, I shouldn't expect to see flies inside the premises. You people should know they're flying diseases."

"We'll be on that ma'am once the residents have gone to bed tonight. We can't do it during the day."

"Just make sure it's done. I don't want to see any when I return."

At the end of the north wing where the residents lived, in the recreation room, Delwin, a residential aid, quietly sat as jet-black hair covered his eyes. Some residents shouted, calling out for loved ones who'd died. He never understood why he always got shoved off to the room full of tattered and musty games. Delwin knew game days made the residents smile. This was important. They could socialize and win candy bars. He would tell his superiors that the residents needed new board games, but his input was always ignored. The husky gals who did the rounds, making sure everyone's bed was clean and dry, rolled their eyes at Delwin.

Let's hear it for the master of Tiddlywinks, Chutes and Ladders, Jenga. Water refills! Boy, what an easy job! Well, fuck them! Fuck every one of them! And fuck those people who are changing my job. I didn't apply here to work with stolen fetuses, Delwin thought. WSUC usurped this place. Everyone who worked here knew this, but they were cowards.

At least I found her, the one who taught me that I can fool them all and shut down this stupidity, this insanity.

Looking at the end of the table, he studied Severina, the woman he'd consoled as she shared stories with him of escaping Nazi Germany by a thread. She'd spent months reading books that he'd snuck in for her after she'd learned what would be happening today. Today she chose to end her suffering. This, she'd told him, would be more dignified than rotting away.

Back in the lobby, a white coat walked over to the microphone and chirped. Beads of sweat stuck to his forehead.

"Let's get started, shall we?"

The WSUC quieted, but buzzing flies still flew around stiff-haired heads.

"Thank you, wow." He paused and grinned at them with big teeth. "It took a long time to get here, as we all know, but here we are, showing our strength and love. Love for the unborn has been overlooked far too long."

"Amen," WSUC members shouted and clapped their hands.

"With this exciting new program, all children can come into the world feeling loved and wanted. Sadly, we know many women simply weren't meant to raise children. They must answer to God, but what of the children they leave behind? Why should a child be left behind and be raised in a godless adoption home run by the state? As people committed to loving God, we know they are born with pureness, purpose, and innocence.

"Also, the elderly population feels loneliness and lack of purpose. The day has finally come, after years of research and study, to bring the unborn and the elderly together. The residents will feed them while still in their pods, they will witness their births, and they will all help raise them. Adoption homes and children's shelters will become obsolete. In troubled times, they will have a constant feeling of communal love. Until the children find adoptive parents, they can look into the eyes of their elders and learn God's love, and the elderly will feel nothing but love and warmth until their souls leave us for a greater place. Now we're going to bring the soon-to-be-born into the room."

The parade of squeaky wheeled carts moved through the center of the room. Sara, the nursing home administrator, had told her staff that no cartoonish, juvenile scrubs would be worn from this day forward. All of them would wear traditional white uniforms and polished shoes. Some of the women in the audience bit their lips as the procession continued. The nursing staff hunched over their carts, their smiles forced, their eyes down at the floor. After these fetal and geriatric philanthropists worked so hard and donated so much to make this a reality, the staff needed to be better players, better actors. This, after all, would be a miracle.

Once all those in the parade got to the front of the lobby, Severina sprinted up the hall from her room. A thin, pale woman with purple veins protruding from her neck, she crashed into the clear partition dividing the lobby from the care center. The glass reverberated with a gong. Blood spread over the glass from her broken nose. The pupils of her eyes widened like a ravenous dog about to attack its prey.

As she backed away from the glass, shaking words rattled through her synthetic teeth, filling the air with a fetid decay. "You will all pay for the gross violations you've made! You're monsters draped in bogus degrees and expensive clothing. You'll *all* pay for what you've done!"

Her dentures slid out of her mouth followed by a yellow flow of mucous and drool. She collapsed onto the floor, melting into a puddle of flesh and red thickness oozing over the tile.

"Grab some towels and disinfectant. We need to contain this, now!" Sara, the charge nurse, shouted over the intercom to her staff.

The caregivers, screaming and mouths agape, ran away from their carts in the lobby and back through the glass doors. They crashed into each other by the doorway in front of the supply room. Two burly orderlies shoved through the hysterical staff and wriggled their way into the supply room.

"Back off and calm down! We've got this. Stand back and let us get what we need."

The two donned latex gloves and grabbed containers, mops, and chemicals.

"Okay, the rest of you form a line and get supplies in case we need some backup."

The oozing remains burped and slowly spread in front of the nurses' station while some employees jumped on top of the work area. Pandemonium rose as more climbed up shrieking at the spreading mass. The stampede pushed some forward, fumbling and falling over keyboards and monitors.

The two white coats rushed through the doors from the lobby and tiptoed over the mass of bloody skin riddled with age spots to reach the nurses' station. Amidst the chaos, one shouted at Sara.

"You told me anyone who could make things difficult would be taken care of. What happened?"

"She was in the game room playing bingo with Delwin. Anyone who might have acted up was there. We have no legal right to restrain them," the nurse said.

The orderlies, armed with supplies, darted over the spreading skin and slippery blood. The skin underfoot ripped, making a sound like raw chicken trimmed of fat. Blood flowed from the ruptured skin. A few of the stronger-stomached caregivers lacking the necessary supplies sat on the floor in front of the station and leveraged themselves to withhold the mass with blue, gloved hands as the mess oozed toward them. Their determination deteriorated as they pushed their upper bodies against enveloping elastic goo. They shrieked while their mouths and noses were swallowed by the blob.

The leadership of the WSUC stood behind the partition, witnessing the carnage. They puked and cried.

The president banged the glass and screamed, "The front door is locked. Somebody open it so we can get out with the children!"

Her demands went unheard and ignored by the surviving staff who continued to either evade or confront the thickening layer of hungry skin as it blipped and farted its way outward. With gritted teeth, those fighting used ice chippers, mops, and brooms to prevent the skin from flowing down to the three wings where the residents lived.

The growing, flowing skin paused for a moment. Some of the orderlies cheered at their success. The creeping mess backed up. The counter holding the remaining health team crashed from the excessive weight, leaving more victims exposed to the wave of the thick pink mesh of mutilated gums, which backed up and folded over them. The mutated flesh rose, stretching with flailing arms as its victims labored to stand up. Vague outlines of faces struggled to breathe. Bubbles formed under the mass, emitting flatulent sounds along the edges and spreading out toward each wing. Within moments of being smothered, fresh, limp corpses rotated in the pink raw mass.

The few remaining staff puked and cried along the edges of the rancid growth. The white-coated men stepped backward with beads of sweat dripping down their bald heads. As they turned to go back out to the lobby, the WSUC crowded up against the shut doors.

Their president shouted and steamed up the glass. "We didn't pay you to stand there like cowards. Help us get the unborn to safety!"

The WSUC joined hands, repeating The Lord's Prayer like a broken record.

One of the lab coats yelled at the orderlies. "Unlock these doors, you incompetent buffoons! I can have the authorities put you away for this."

His demand came too late. All the staff that remained were covered in wrinkled skin. As they looked on with mouths agape, the skin crawled up and inside the legs of their pants.

The president with the beehive hairdo broke from prayer. "Ladies, we must save the children. Go quickly to the fire exit!"

A member cried out from the crowd. "We've never picked up the pouches before. Do we have gloves or towels?"

"It's too late for that! Pick them up and take them to the emergency room at Maryville," the president shouted back.

"Today was the hatching, you idiot! What do we do if they hatch in the women's cars?" A board member protested.

"That's not going to happen because none of you are going anywhere." Delwin stood with his back against the exit doors, smirking in his combat boots with his arms folded over his white uniform. No one noticed him before the pandemonium broke out. "All the doors are made of steel and double-bolted. The resident, my beloved friend who crashed against the glass, was a plotted distraction we worked on for weeks so I could lock all the doors. I waited outside for all of this to unfold. She sacrificed herself to stay out of this inhumane study you all thought would make you famous. You're right, today is the hatching. In a few moments, the little darlings will be all yours. Now, for the moment of glory."

The WSUC glared through him. Delwin unlocked the main exit, jumped outside, and bolted it shut again. He peered through the front window and laughed as the glass partition between the grand lobby and the nurses' station shattered and poured out a curdled mixture of torn appendages, eyeballs, and swirling blood. The WSUC stormed up to the front window, pounding on shatterproof glass that had pushed their project over budget by millions of dollars.

Delwin stood on the other side laughing as the blob of Severina squished faces so hard that facial pores smeared oil over with glass.

The hatching was successful! Small, elvish faces with razor teeth and necks like vines floated intermeshed with the blob, wrapping themselves around the WSUC.

One of the hive minds held her fists up and yelled, "Open the door, you fucking waif!"

Delwin enjoyed the early afternoon sun while orange leaves fluttered to the ground. He pointed. He snickered.

His verbal abuser had her mouth up to the glass in a perfect O-shape. Her nose slowly slid upward as her jawbones cracked apart. The insides of her mouth, her tongue, and her throat were engorged and vibrating against the glass.

Thin, elongated fingers of the unborn with tiny blue fingernails intertwined themselves around the broken-jawed mass of flesh and broken teeth. All of the WSUC exploded and swirled against windows inside the lobby. The high-definition sound of a giant sucking through a straw and gulping on gristle made the once insignificant orderly proud. It was the sound of millions of possums eating garbage left out for pickup. But, these were no possums. The transparent and stretched little cheeks looked like little amniotic sacs. They grinned and smacked their lips, their eager eyes twinkling as the tufts of stiff hair from the ladies pressed against the window, the skin of the crones' faces dampened like pasta for the little ones to consume.

Delwin's dream had come true.

Fuck those people. They expect me to work more, change diapers for both old-timers and infants for little to no raise. Come, my babies. There is much more to consume.

He looked beyond the new addition and could see the residents smiling and waving from their rooms. They hated the WSUC.

ROB HERZOG

Haircut (Beware-Cut)

A HAIR CLIPPER buzzes. Bobby watches his shorn locks tumble down a dark plastic smock to the barbershop's scuffed floor. He sweats and breathes through his mouth, which feels sticky-dry like duct tape. Bobby has never liked barbershops or haircuts. Some men enjoy the scent of tonic and gels and how they blend with the leisurely pace and chitchat of a local barbershop, but not Bobby. For him, a haircut is only slightly better than drilled teeth. Zip it off and get me out of here. That's his motto.

Bobby's barber is Michael, big-bellied and loud. He hums along with the clippers as he works, hair-cutting harmonizing. Michael has trimmed Bobby's hair three or four times, but Bobby plans on finding a quieter barber once this is over. Bobby came to the shop tonight primarily because he couldn't sleep; his head feels like the eight-hundred-degree surface of Mercury. An astronaut would last five seconds on that godforsaken planet before the spacesuit bubbled like hot soup, exposing delicate human skin that melted off and puddled on the bleached, scalding terrain. Desperate for any relief from this feeling, Bobby has come to Michael, the only barber working at 9:30 p.m. Maybe a buzz will cool things down.

"Ain't gotta sweat so much, Bobby," Michael says.

"Hot in here, man."

Seated nearby in a folding chair is Quiet Lou, a wire hanger of a man. He folds a dollar bill repeatedly.

"You think it's hot in here, Quiet Lou?"

Quiet Lou just shrugs.

Michael shrugs back. "You're gonna dehydrate, Bobby."

"Naw."

"I can get you some water. I got a couple bottles in my fridge."

"Nope."

Michael turns to Quiet Lou. "Bobby don't need nothing but to walk outta here looking pretty."

Quiet Lou grunts and folds his bill another time.

"Heard you got a new job, Bobby," Michael says.

"Up at the quarry. Busting my ass. Tired as shit."

Bobby is expecting a response, but it doesn't come. Instead, Michael kills the clippers and calls out, "God damn."

"What?"

"Something's been growing underneath your hair, dude. Real nasty."

"What?"

Michael picks up a handheld mirror, spins Bobby around and holds it up so Bobby can see the back of his head reflected in the barbershop mirror. Exposed in the newly shorn section is a spiraling fungus —ridged, angry, and puss-filled. Michael steps back.

Bobby's eyes widen. He reaches up to feel it, but Michael grabs his hand.

"Don't touch it, dummy. Gonna spread that shit around."

"What is it?"

Keeping his distance, Michael squints at the fungus.

"Ringworm maybe, but bigger," Michael says. "Looks like it's been growing a long-ass time under your hair. Alien shit."

Quiet Lou stands and peers at the fungus, his face filling with disgust.

Sweat pours down Bobby's neck. This is what he has most feared. Feeling crappy, the nagging sensation in his gut screaming that something is seriously wrong —maybe even Tommy Tumor or the Big C. But this is entirely unexpected.

"Get it off me!" Bobby shouts.

"Can't," Michael snaps. Repulsed, he rubs his hands on his shirt. "You're infected with something, bro. You need a doctor."

"I couldn't see shit in the mirror. I wanna look. Take a picture."

Michael grabs his cell phone, aims it nervously at the back of Bobby's head, and snaps a photo. He leans a bit closer for a better shot.

Pop —snap —a bubbly growth on Bobby's head ruptures and spews projectile-style onto Michael's face. Michael jerks back, drops his phone, and starts to sizzle. The discharge eats like industrial-grade acid. Michael's cheeks melt and the jellied red-pink flesh rolls back and clogs his throat, stifling his screams. He writhes, tumbles, drops his phone. His clippers fall the floor, activating. Their electric whine accompanies Michael's gagging. His eyes bulge with pain and disbelief. Hair tumbles, gets swept away, grows back, flows wildly —covering everything. Michael's dying world is clogged with hair.

Quiet Lou steps forward to help Michael, but there is no way to assist his bloody mash of a face. Bobby kicks out of the chair and rips the smock violently off his shoulders. Locks of his cut hair fly every which way. Some strands land delicately in Michael's pooled blood.

Bobby stares at Michael's body and then at Quiet Lou. "This ain't my fault, man," Bobby calls out. "Can't blame me for this."

Quiet Lou steps back. The clippers buzz, filling in for Quiet Lou's silence. Bobby kicks the clippers into the wall, cutting off their noisy rattle.

"It's that shit I've been breathing in the quarry!" Bobby cries out. "That's what did this. Can't blame me."

A foreman had, in fact, made Bobby shovel out a special section of the quarry a few weeks earlier. The dust there was yellow, alien, and unlike anything else around it. Bobby had worn a respirator and a jumpsuit, but the dust seemed to seep through it. It adhered to his skin, burned his eyes, made him paranoid. He had cursed himself a fool for following the foreman's orders. Ever since, he had felt the dust inside him, moving and shifting.

"I don't know what's going on," Bobby tells Quiet Lou.

Quiet Lou can keep silent no longer. He lets loose, his voice reverberating through the shop.

"Shit! Shit! Shit! Shit!"

Bobby steps toward him, desperate to quiet down the man who never says anything.

"Get back motherfucker! Stay all the way back!" Quiet Lou pulls a cell phone from his pocket. "I'm calling for help."

Bobby waves his hands. "Stop for a second. Stop. Stop. They're gonna blame me. They're gonna lock me up. Put me in a cage. Send me to a lab."

Bobby imagines himself cut to pieces on an examining table. That's what the government does in these situations, doesn't it? The movies were full of that kind of thing. But the government wouldn't dissect his boss. It wouldn't cut up the corporate leadership. Only Bobby would face the consequences.

Quiet Lou starts to dial 911, but his fingers tremble. Bobby reaches for the phone. Quiet Lou evades him and grabs scissors from Michael's barber stand, whooshing them through the air.

"Back off!" Quiet Lou shouts.

"Please, man," Bobby pleads. "Give me a chance. Don't call yet."

Quiet Lou dials a couple of numbers but hesitates. "Michael needs an ambulance," he says finally.

Tears form in Bobby's eyes. His voice is soft. "That won't help."

Quiet Lou punches the final digit to complete the emergency call. "Sorry," he says to Michael. He seems to mean it.

Suddenly bloody Michael twitches. He grasps Quiet Lou's ankle and pulls him down. Michael struggles to his knees and he collapses onto Quiet Lou.

Quiet Lou screams underneath Michael's crushing weight. He fights to get out, but Michael is too heavy. Quiet Lou waves the scissors in the air and plunges them into Michael's back. Michael shifts and dies. Parts of his bloody face ooze and drop onto Quiet Lou's nose and cheeks, instantly burning them with an acidic hiss. Lou screams, vomits, melts, and falls permanently silent.

A voice sounds from the cell phone. A dispatcher asks to explain the emergency. "Can you respond?" her voice calls out.

Bobby grabs the phone and ends the call. "I'm sorry. I'm sorry. This ain't my fault. I didn't know."

He looks sadly at Michael and Quiet Lou. He picks up Michael's phone, scrolls quickly, and finds the photo of his fungus. He deletes it, drops the phone, and crushes it under his foot. He turns to the door but stops and searches. On a coat rack he finds an old hat —patriotic stars and stripes. He slips it over his exposed fungus and runs out the door, leaving the two bodies behind.

From the back room whirls Michael's girlfriend, Mia. Loud music blares from her headphones. She has not heard any of the struggles. She holds two tall glasses filled with orange juice.

"Got you a drink, honey," she calls out. She sways to the beat and calls out again, "Michael?"

She spots the two bodies on the floor and drops the glasses, shattering them. The clippers suddenly whir back to life, buzzing and rattling against the hard tiles. They leap up and sink into the back of Michael's dead neck, letting loose an oozing stream of blood before falling back to the floor and clattering toward her. Standing in a puddle of orange juice and broken glass, Mia screams and screams and screams.

MOANER T. LAWRENCE

Lemon Crush

WANT TO CHANGE THE world too? Come crush with us! Using the same link where you found this podcast, you'll be able to download our handy-dandy Lemon Crush app. If you want to show support for the cause, there are instructions on how to make your own Lemon Crush honeycomb sunglasses. All you'll need are some old eyeglass frames, black vinyl paper, a hot needle, yellow paint, and our custom honeycomb template. Blonde hair helps too, and we've got lots and lots of tutorials on how to either dye your hair blonde, or what sorts of wigs to buy. But the fun doesn't stop there. In addition to access to back episodes, you'll also get notifications on where and how to help create flash mobs for distracting authorities long enough for our crews to do their work. While you and the rest of our swarm keep everyone busy guessing where, we'll hoist up the latest guest at a financial district near you! Together, we can the change the world!

Hello, listeners! Our guest's sedatives are wearing off. Rise and shine, and welcome to the podcast! Did you have a good dinner last night? We don't need to take out the gag —you can just shake your head "yes" or "no." Lobster and broiler steak with champagne and red wine! Mmmhmmm! That was one fine last meal, sir. Listeners, if this if your first time tuning in, I would like it noted that we tried doing a last-request meal on our first episode, but ended up getting honey all over the recording equipment.

So, welcome back to the podcast. I am your hostess, Lemon Crush, and you are listening to Fine Dining with Lemon Crush! The show where we kidnap ultra-wealthy monsters, force them to reckon with the impact they've had on society, and then —well —stay tuned and find out! Today's our tenth episode, and who better to dine with us than Wentworth Creel!

Mr. Creel, it might interest you to know that the chair in which you sit, wrapped in plastic, once belonged to banking magnate John Pierpont Morgan. Pretty cool, huh?

Listen, it's normal that you're panicking, but that chair is an antique. If you continue squirming, I'm going to have to do things to ensure that you suffer much more than you need to... There, thank you, much better.

Now, Mr. Creel, I'm sure you're wondering the same things everyone wonders when they wake up in that chair. Who the fuck is she? Where the fuck am I? What the fuck is going on? Allow me to answer all those questions as thoroughly as I can.

First things first: That is a recorder on the desk beside me, and we are recording. I am Lemon Crush, a former forensic accountant who once assisted in the capture and imprisonment of money launderers. However, one day I swam too close to a big fish, got raped, disgraced, framed, and jailed. In prison, the same sorts of big fish sought me out to help launder money, but when I refused, they severed my clitoris with a cigar cutter and forced me to eat it. After prison, I opted to become a podcasting serial killer, and the rest, as they say, is mystery!

As to the where: We are in a very soundproof room in the meatpacking district of Portland, Maine. I picked this locale because the building was actually once a bank where all the workers were forced to work long hours and died in a fire back in 1947.

As to what is going on: Let me begin by telling everyone about you, sir. You are Wentworth Creel, CEO of Creel Private Banking & Wealth Management, and a banker whose nickname in boarding school was 'Wendy', for which you have my deepest sympathies. Listeners, if any of you have ever wondered who would randomly engage in shitty little acts like bleeding an already poor public via higher transaction fees at ATMs during the holidays, this is your guy. And if any of you has a wallet with credit cards inside it, chances are Wendy owns majority shares of at least two of the three major lending institutes that you all use. Also, while never accused, you, Mr. Creel have facilitated the transfer of more dark money to leaders around the globe, than any other bank in the world. Your real estate holdings include seven gold coast mansions, and even your very own private island in what's left of the world's drowning Maldives. As to your trespasses against society, whoa, where to start?

Are these your feet that cocked up on a young, Black woman's back during a Christmas party? Classy. No? You're shaking your head "no?" Am I taking the photo out of context? Oh, sorry. How's about this shot of you and a major exec connected with an American mercenary company that was taken before the Standing Rock protests in North Dakota? That's you handing a suitcase of cash to that gentleman, yes? That's one of the mercs who helped blow off a veteran's arm with a hose while he stood in peaceful protest to protect Sioux land, right? Yup, that's you. Those are your hands, your arms, and it was a $3.7-billion-dollar pipeline, right? You paid to attack veterans in peaceful protest. Getting a little red in the face there, Wendy? I haven't even started.

How about this next pic of you at The Russian Tea Room with your gut protruding after a feast? That's you speaking to the head of a street gang in Brooklyn, yeah? Is this you at the Four Seasons conversing with that gangster's nemesis two weeks later? Yup, looks like it. There was a really bad gang war a few days later, but I bet you didn't know anything about that, right? However, you did buy up all the bullet-riddled buildings, didn't you? Hey, I have something special to show you. See these? Don't look away. Let me lay them all out. Here's thirty photos. See all these dead kids? They were caught in the crossfire and bled out. This is all you, Wendy. This is your war for their home. Look at the little hands and feet that'll never grow up. I also have some photos of dead parents who committed suicide from grief too. See? Open your eyes, Wendy. Wendy? ...Wendy, you better look. Look, or I will cut your fucking eyelids off, and make you look! This can go quick, or this can go slow. That's right, stare. Shake. This is you, Wendy. This is what you ate.

Why are you here? Today, Wentworth Creel, you are going to die. I am going to carve up your body, eat you, and then hang your butchered skeleton out for the world to see! To Hell with Soylent Green! If the Crushers and I have our way, tomorrow is going to be a cornucopia of elite-man-meat delights. I have this culinary quirk about passing off human flesh as other meats as realistically as I can. After I've turned you into a ham sandwich, I'm going to go down to the nearest deli and take photos and compare to ensure your meat looks just right. If Burger King could use pink slime to make the public think their meat was fresh, I certainly have no qualms feeding them you. Hey-hey, it's okay to cry. The mic can handle it, really. Besides, I know things seem bleak right now, but you have to look at the bigger picture here, Wendy.

For starters, I've been listening in on your calls and reading your emails for months, and I can tell that you've always wanted to be super famous. Don't shake your head "no," it's true! You weren't satisfied with short, dry *New Yorker* articles, or being listed as some obscure number in the "Richest People in the World" rankings of *Forbes*. Fabrice Touree, Gina Rinehart. Look at all those sly foxes getting their fifteen minutes in the limelight while you sit there unnoticed! You didn't want to get caught, but you wanted recognition. I mean, where's your buzz, right?!

Also, we both know you give less than a shit about society, but you're about to help it out big time. People are going to be studying you, me, the Crushers, and this podcast's impact upon society for generations long after we're gone. We all have to die sometime. What's another twenty or forty years when you're immortal? Don't believe me? Bring up the Victorian era and tell me the first name that pops into everyone's brain isn't Jack the Ripper! Do you know how many people are junkies for true-crime podcasts? Dahmer, Kemper, Ridgway. Did you know there's trading cards for each of those cannibals? Cannibalizing the ultra-rich to assist society may sound crazy, but so is any new process when you think about it. In case you don't know, the first astronauts were crash-test pilots, brave pioneers.

Your browser history shows that your most re-watched videos on YouTube are of Martin Shkreli, and I get it. You want to be famous, and you want it to come from somewhere original, and not look desperate like Kim Kardashian or Paris Hilton. You could have done a sex tape too, but then you'd have lost your membership to the Maidstone Club, right? You couldn't live without your Centurion subscription, right? What could be more original than this?! This way you're famous, you die, and —technically —you never get caught! Problem solved. I could have killed you a few months ago, but I felt you deserved to be a round number, and so here you are: Guest Number Ten!

Speaking of sex tapes, you could have shot a full-fledged film with the kinds of cameras The Weinstein Company used. Although, you'd have been arrested if anyone saw your companions, or should I say victims? Yeah, when they're minors it's 'victims'. You kept a lot of souvenirs, Wendy, and I gotta tell ya, those were not easy to watch. The oldest, I think, was fifteen? They all looked like Traci Lords, Sable Starr, or Kahlil Gibran during his Oscar Wilde days. You know, I get that people in the upper echelons have their own affairs to stay sane through marriages of inconvenience, but Mrs. Creel kept it to men around her own age. She certainly never slept with a minor. Look at all these pictures of your hands where they shouldn't be. Your hands, and your stomach, and your flabby ass. Keep crying, Wendy, the mic is good for it.

So... Number Ten, are you sorry for everything I showed you? Yeah? Stop shaking chair! ...I have an idea. How about you put your money where our mouth is?

There's a knock at the door! Just a second, Wendy, don't get up, I'll get it. Here to help us with the next part of our show are some of our very own volunteers, the Crushers. They're bringing in laptops with secure connections. Mr. Creel, if you look on these screens coming up you will see that your accounts are being accessed. Now all we need you to do is to write down your passwords. You'll transfer the bulk of your assets to us, and we will redistribute those funds to charities. Don't worry, your wife and family will continue to enjoy the lifestyle they've become accustomed to. Of course, it'll probably just be one giant mansion instead of seven, but then the world will never see these tapes, or photos, or anything else that could be used against your estate in a lawsuit. Or, you don't do it, we torture you and release everything to the papers and then who knows how many vendettas your family, legal or otherwise, will face. Yeah? Good deal? Let me get you a pen.

While you write those passwords down, let me just say the Crushers and I have always been pretty good at hiding things. Not to toot our own horn, but even though we have nine cannibal kills on record, between security teams, bodyguards, and the occasional Secret Service agent, the Crushers are actually in the upper hundreds. People are going to be finding Easter eggs of the people who protected guys like you for years.

How else can we make Episode 10 special? Well, so far, the news has been saying I "lust" after human flesh. Here on Episode 10, I will let you all in on a little secret: I hate meat. I always have. No fat-shaming intended, Wendy, but you are at least a hundred pounds heavier than you should be. Most money-laundering bankers taste godawful, and all the fear and acids you're secreting right this instant are going to make you taste even worse later on. Every bite of you I take will be bitter and sour, and make me gag.

So why do I do it? Aside from the shock value of the media reporting the discovery of your bloody skeleton dangling from a streetlamp or telephone wire in front of some stock market or big banks across America? It's because if we want to change things, we need to step outside our comfort zones. Every great pioneer who's ever achieved anything has done so taking the road less traveled.

There are always individuals like you whether it's feudalism, socialism, or communism. Beneath all these "isms" lies an ugly truth: It's not any one human system that lends itself to systemic corruption; it's that humans are systemically corrupt. And what do we have today? Capitalism. A system where humanity is so weak, it basically just gave up and said, let's just try to let greed regulate itself. And for a while I guess that worked, but now we have stagflation instead of stagnation because you big fishies figured out how to corrupt different branches of government. So how do we get humans to change? I think the answer is ever-changing, but today, I say eat the rich. Cannibalism is just another "ism" too.

Are those all the passwords, Wendy? You swear on Pharma Bro those are all the passwords? All right, Crushers, please verify them.

The funny thing is that a lot of listeners think when I'm saying, "eat the rich," that I'm saying we should eat anyone who has a bigger house, and that is simply not true. A silly goose living scandal to scandal while trying to keep one mansion heated is not rich. Richer than others? Sure. Mr. Creel, you own seven mansions, correct? Six always stand empty. You employ hundreds of staff. Do you know how much food goes bad in your refrigerators? Dump trucks, Wendy. You think Joe Coffee out on the road cutting his emissions will fix the planet? No. Unless we're talking about a corrupt member of the Upper One Percent, it's just another meaningless murder. Plus, their kids inherit everything, anyway. Being woke, progressive, alt-right, it's all noise. A meaningless tug-of-war, and as the playwright and philosopher, Jean-Paul Sartre, once said, "When the rich wage war it's the poor who die."

Did you know that comedian, George Carlin, used to joke that if we executed white-collar criminals, crime would begin to rapidly drop? Everyone laughed, but you know what's been happening since I started eating big bankers, Wendy? I call it the Lemon Crush trickle-down effect. As the blood trickles down, there's less sex trafficking, reductions in gang violence, and people have been saving money. So even violent crime from hunger has been dropping. You know what else? It only takes a few rich people inheriting your job to get the message. After someone finds the second or third bloody skeleton, the next person in your position doesn't want to misbehave. Because they know we'll find them, and they'll die. Of course, newspapers and moralists will voice their disgust at the cost of this new world. Some people want us to feel bad about eating you, but how long have you and your friends been eating us? The way I see it it's like PETA and de-beaked chickens. When everyone is well fed, mostly everyone will turn a blind eye. You know it's true. Now your friends order escorts and ask them to age-play younger, dark money is going dark, and even ATM fees have been dropping at banks. Today, Xe Services LLC, formerly Blackwater, won't even take contracts if a client is too rich.

Progress, Wendy, and what we're doing today —I say "we" because we're doing this together. Yes, "we." We are going to make the world a better place. Because I want the world to know that this is how you fix the world. This is how you fix today's corruption.

Crushers, are the passwords verified? Fantastic.

Guess what, Wendy? Now it's your turn to speak! Yes, you, Wentworth Creel. Guest Number Ten. I am going to ungag you, and let you have your say. But, before I do, remember —screaming won't work; I am totally gonna kill you. And —as you have repeatedly bellowed at your employees in the past —your time is precious. I have a little lemon-shaped egg timer here, and I am turning it to fifteen minutes.

I've been monopolizing this recording with my advertising, motives and reasoning, but I want to give you something Jack the Ripper and Charles Manson never gave their victims —fifteen minutes. That's right! Nine-hundred seconds of the-time-that-flies to record whatever you want for yourself, your family, your friends, your enemies, your coworkers, the world —whatever! I want you think of these as your fifteen minutes.

Oh, but before you start, do you want it in the heart or the head?

JON CARROLL THOMAS

Stinkubus

1. From the Bowels of the Earth

OGG, BY THE CAVE mouth, sucked the gristle and marrow from an animal carcass that should have been forgotten days ago. But meat was rare and his hunger thrived. His guts complained. Fire had not yet become fashionable in his settlement, and digestion was often a chore. He dropped the scraps into the dirt but suspected he'd be returning to them later. He went farther into the cave to rest in the tangle of grasses and skins that served as the bed he shared with Unga and their baby which they had not yet formally named. Ogg liked the name Ogg, but Unga thought that would be confusing. She preferred Ugg, after her mother, But Ogg, who was more traditional, thought the child should have a proper boy's name.

He huddled close to his family for their mutual warmth and security but as Ogg's insides settled, he passed gas. Unga woke from the noise but it was the odor that made her sit up and protest. The baby too began to cry. Ashamed, Ogg pleaded his innocence. He considered blaming the baby, but, instead, pointed into the deeper cave and grunted. When Unga turned away, he smirked. When she turned back, he grunted again and shrugged.

Just then, a noise rose from the inner earth —a deep, guttural roll that was equal parts wind and beast. Ogg and Unga turned. A greenish light blossomed in the dark and spread along the damp walls toward them. A mist gathered, glowing, swirling, churning, like a living thing. The stink was shocking. Ogg gathered the baby and pulled Unga by her hair toward the opening. But the stink was already inside them.

Outside, a scream erupted from the cave mouth as if the earth itself were in agony. Then there was a squelching, and a crunching, and then —silence. The glow receded into the darkness.

This is how I began —without form. My memory of this early time is spotty, and I confess, I may have embellished a bit. It was not until quite some time later, once I had gained substance, and was first written of in the Abhorred Book, that my thoughts likewise began to cohere. But I feel that I must be clear. The Book did not make me. I am older than it, by far. But it did give me direction, as it has for many others, and it is with the Book that much of my story is entwined.

You may call me Farzal.

2. He Who Hath Dealt It

You might wonder what I look like. Well, that has changed over time and often changes according to my whim. I remain invisible most of the time, of course, but when it suits me, I often appear as a dense, earthy-green mist, as I have previously accounted. In the Abhorred Book, I'm depicted as a black blob, held aloft by interior gasses which I vent through my many mouths. In this form, you may see these gases swirl like a tempest within me, illuminated by my own purplish lightning. This typically happens when I'm particularly aroused by the prospect of a feeding. As to what I eat, like most demons, I'll devour most anything that is placed near my mouths. But my favorite repast —and it should be no mystery —is a hearty, unclaimed fart. Even sweeter still is the fart denied —a fart, through hypocrisy and embarrassment, that has been disowned —the orphan fart.

Certain settings attract me more than others. Take a boys' dormitory, where a fart rarely goes unclaimed. I have no need of such places. A small, religious community, however, hidden in the wooded north, and since forgotten to history? Vehemently repressed and preoccupied with sin to the point of perversion? Now you're making my mouths water.

I recall a minister or a magistrate of some kind —some person of importance. Don't ask me for particulars. Such distinctions are boring and meaningless to me. He was sharing his bed with his wife for the sole purpose of procreation. They already had six living children, but were eager for more. After a particularly generous supper of cornbread and stewed cabbage, neither party was up to the task. And neither, as per usual, would admit to their own flatulence. It was therefore agreed that the culprit must be a demon, come from Hell, to torment them.

"But be careful, wife," he warned her. "To even speak of such things is to give them power."

Meanwhile, outside, a familiar green mist peeled away from the rocky, moonlit fields. It drifted against the wind, scattering the sheep and wilting the crops until it seeped into a drafty hovel. It cohered into something tangible, floating above the couple as they tossed and turned in the night. This was, of course, me in my gasbag manifestation. I noted, with amusement, the crucifix clutched in the man's hand. Silently, I joined them beneath the covers. I snuggled, unnoticed, between them, using my warmth to comfort and relax them. Once they were both deep into a contented sleep, I erupted into a sticky vapor that stung their flesh, singed their garments, and withered the bed until it fell apart like rotten kindling. They awoke, but were too stunned to move, their faces frozen with a mixture of horror and epiphany.

It is said that the sense of smell is most closely associated with memory. Perhaps I unlocked something deep within them, a primordial memory of the first creatures crawling from the Sulphur pits of Hell, before Heaven was even thought of. I wonder also if they detected the hint of sweet apples I added to round out the experience. Not that it matters. In a few hours, their hair had bleached white, and their bodies had become wasted and brittle.

By dawn, they were simply ashes.

These later events were observed by the village elders and recorded by the town chronicler. This chronicler, it should be noted, secretly held a special interest in strange matters such as these, often going well out of his way to record them with feverish detail. This was the first known keeper of the Abhorred Book and one of its first authors. This was also not long before he was exposed and executed.

The book, however, found its way into other hands. It moved in secret circles, acquiring ever more forbidden knowledge and growing its scandalous reputation. Copies were made of varying qualities. A secret society, descended from the above mentioned elders, tasked themselves with locating and destroying all copies. They were only partially successful.

3. The Butler Did It

One evil night, as a storm raged just outside, a fusty butler in his yellowed shirtsleeves and saggy braces sat down to a strange and lonesome meal. It was a solitary can of expired chili slowly warmed over a black candle. For a blessing, he read from the Abhorred Book, borrowed from his late master's library. And after he had licked the last morsel from his fingers, he used the same can to serve himself a portion of cold, black coffee. He then laid himself down on a musty bedroll beneath the slanting roof of the vast attic and stared at the holes in his socks until he fell into an uneasy sleep. This is how I was born again.

The lady of the estate was older than the butler, but not by much. She imagined herself as a shrewd matriarch, a dowdy dowager. But to her estranged family, whom she had excluded from the meager fortune left by her husband, she was a bitter, money-grubbing crone. To the old butler, she was the devil. She cruelly abused the butler while the master lived, but after, she became intolerable, despite the simple fact that, without him, she was utterly alone.

She was famously deaf and flatulent. The combination might be funnier to the butler if the joke were not so old, and were he not so often the butt of it. The scene would often play out like this: He would be helping her to her bed from her wheelchair, or vice versa, and the movement would cause her to fart, sometimes quite violently. Then, upon smelling it —her sense of smell worked fine —she would say something along the lines of, "Good Heavens, James! Again?! You must see a doctor at once, you are not well! Disgusting, truly!"

His reply, invariably, was, "Apologies, madam," and, "Yes, madam."

Had she left it there, the butler may have forgiven her once her long-impending death became actual, but she always felt obliged to continue.

"Well, haven't you got anything to say for yourself? I swear, such insubordination I have never seen. If you had ever acted like this while my husband lived, he would have dealt with you most severely. My patience has finally reached its end. James, I'm afraid I must terminate our arrangement, effective immediately."

"Yes, madam."

"Don't try to talk me out of it. I've made up my mind. You are to quit these premises immediately."

"Yes, madam. See you in Hell, madam."

"Still nothing to say, then? You spineless twit, get out of my sight and take your nasty stink with you!"

"Pleasant dreams, madam. I hope you rot in your own shit tonight. Good night."

With this, the butler would excuse himself to his apartment until she would ring for him again hours later, with little memory of her previous outburst.

It was her inferences about his late master which he found most hurtful. His master had been excessively kind and generous to the butler later in his life, sharing with him many closely held secrets. The two men were indeed friends in those final days, when something dark seemed to be circling the skies over the estate. This was when the butler was given the key to the secret cabinet in the library that held the Abhorred Book, as well as instructions as to where to send it, should certain individuals arrive asking for it after the master's passing.

The butler barely survived my arrival, but still, he was up and dressed and serving tea and biscuits in the morning, same as always. Only now, as he endured another barrage of offenses from his mistress, he exchanged knowing glances with the dark, fleshy thing perched high in a shadowy corner of the breakfast room, its eyes like two smoldering embers.

For days I watched her, as she slept, as she ate, as she wrote pointless, bitter letters to her family, or whomever, most of which would never be opened, much less answered. Frequently, she would fart, smell it, and then look up for someone to blame. Seeing no one, she still cursed the butler. Each fart, deliciously rank, smelling of pudding and porridge, I ate until my body was swollen with them and I could barely move. When I felt I could wait no longer, I plopped down on her as she slept, parking my mighty ass firmly on her face, and returned every fart, all in one brutal instant. It was certainly more than she could hold. The butler quickly arrived upon hearing the explosion with a clothespin pinching his nose shut. He looked upon the scene and smiled. Never before and never since have I seen a man so pleased to clean up so much mess.

4. The Hellbound Fart

Now I arrive at the account of Blake, the businessman. I don't normally concern myself with names, but this was an unusual circumstance, for me as well as him. Blake was handsome, ambitious, and always in search of new, sinful pursuits. After years of searching and chasing rumors, he finally came into possession of the Abhorred Book. It was his intention to summon the succubae Lilish in hopes that she could relieve his carnal malaise, which, by now, had become a serious problem for him. The rite did not go well, as if it possibly could.

What he failed to recognize was after decades of misuse, many of the book's thin pages had become stuck together. He ended up with neither Lilish, nor your humble Farzal, but a combination thereof. The consciousness of this new demon was still entirely my own, but I possessed the bearing of a large and powerful woman with a wild abundance of both fat and muscle. I had Lilish's polished obsidian flesh, but mottled with pinkish veins and weeping tumors. I also came dressed in one of Lilish's skimpier adornments, complete with all the hooks and chains that seem to be in fashion these days. I hoped she had another, because I was certainly ruining this one.

As the smoke cleared, I observed my new surroundings. I was in a lavish, spacious studio with large windows overlooking midnight Manhattan. The stage was set for romance —candles glimmered, sultry jazz played on the hi-fi, and Blake was naked except for a thick sheen of baby oil. He trembled violently as he stared at me and the one, additional feature I had only just noticed myself —the monstrous phallus presently rising from behind my narrow loincloth.

I feel I should mention that I don't have any interest in animal attraction. Sex disgusts me as few things can. What normally interests me is what repels. But a call cannot go unanswered, and I always take great joy and satisfaction from my work, and this was no exception. I'll leave the details to your inflamed imagination. Pervert. But, after several hours, and it was apparent that his body could endure no more, I gave him one last embrace to squeeze the literal shit out of him. The terms of my summoning thus fulfilled, I vanished again in a whiff of smoke.

I still look back at this encounter with a strange fondness. Thank you, Blake, for such a memorable and novel experience. I'll carry it with me always.

5. Finale

Maybe this all is a bit much. If so, I offer you my apologies. But you asked for it, haven't you?. The Abhorred Book is now in your hands, is it not? So to speak, I mean —not the literal book; that would be impossible. The society whose mission it was to destroy it, has at last burned the last known physical copy. But much of its contents have survived through the miracle of modern technology. Decontextualized, poorly translated again and again —much like the Holy Bible had been in its time —but it survives in this debased form on the internet, and humanity is no safer from its inevitable doom.

I'd call this a warning, but that seems unfair since there's nothing to be done about it. Instead, I'll call it a special treat, a preview of the very near future, it saddens me to report, that you will not have the chance to experience.

I'll begin with what you already know. You came to the Abhorred Fragments like everyone else, first through the dark web, then through JPEGs, GIFs, and memes. Then a certain populist president referred to them in a speech. This was the tipping point. All over the world, people like yourself started dabbling in these occult rites and were gratified by surprisingly easy results.

The Incarnation Rites of the Stinkubus went viral.

It was the so-called Stinkubus Challenge that summoned me to you here today. And —whoops —you forgot a couple of steps that were essential for your protection, So, I will be killing you very shortly. Not to worry —you still have a few minutes yet. I would like to finish this account first.

Again, it all comes down to a few silly details. The terms laid down in the rites used by you and many, many others, are vague and do not provide for my release. This will result in countless versions of myself, with no particular agenda, left to float harmlessly away —usually after mutilating our summoners —into the skies high over the Atlantic Ocean where we will cohere into a solitary and monstrous mass. No air force, no arsenal in the world will be able to bring it down. Eventually, however, it will grow large enough that it will sink by its own weight and settle over the east coast. It will push farther inland, fatal to everything in its path. Once it reaches Chicago, all global communication dies out and society implodes.

There are survivors —again, not you —that are able to eke out a semblance of life, contained within a network of machine-ventilated shanty tunnels reinforced with plastic sheets and lots of duct tape. In the toxic ruins outside, ironic street art declares, Giant Fart Demon for President —2036, visible only to the mutant rats and cockroaches. And woe to anyone who farts and does not own to it. For it is to here that they are removed. But, if they can hold their breath long enough, they can witness themselves being forced inside out by the tentacles that unfurl from the ominous, shit-stained sky. A terrible way to live and a terrible way to die, but you're lucky. You don't have to worry about any of that.

MICHAEL ERROL SWAIM

The Blood

AS I SIT IN a darkened corner of the dimly lit cafe sipping my coffee I come to the decision that I will kill someone today. The hot and bitter liquid does nothing to calm the turmoil in my head as I wonder why I came to this godforsaken place. There are better places to find victims... The smell of bacon fills the air, and the voices of people chatting are starting to annoy me. I set my empty coffee cup down, pull a little notebook out of my shirt pocket, and take notes:

Behind the counter, an old lady who's been pouring coffee here for decades makes a fresh pot. "Mary," says the faded name tag. She starts refilling a cup on the counter for the old man sitting there and I wonder what her rough, saggy skin would look like with blood and semen painted all over her corpse like a Jackson Pollock painting.

I glance over at the register where a middle-aged Cherokee woman checks out an older couple. Her neck glistens with sweat. I imagine the color of her blood against her brown skin, dripping down onto her supple breast after I slit her throat. The glorious look of fear and horror in her eyes as I lay on top of her watching the life drain from her eyes as I violently thrust inside of her.

Sighing, I set my pen down and look at the plate of over-easy eggs and dry toast that I haven't touched. I cut the food into small pieces. Eating, I realize the blood doesn't bring me joy like it used to. The beauty of the arterial spray, the different patterns the pooling would make around the bodies, or the horror in my victims' faces as I finish my work while they slowly die. These things used to bring me such delight.

The blood is my art, my work, my passion. It fulfills and sustains me. It is what I live for. I don't know what I'll do if I lose the only thing I love.

I sop up the last bits of runny yolk with my toast and push my empty plate to the other side of the table. I continue writing.

To my left, a group of teenagers sits at a table chatting and giggling and getting louder and louder, oblivious to me. The sounds of their voices are like nails on a chalkboard.

I attempt to remain calm —their nauseating banter is making me furious. I glance over and stare menacingly, hoping they'll notice and quiet down. They don't, and I slide my hand into my pants pocket to feel around for my pocketknife and grab it. I sigh, content. Its presence has always given me comfort and makes me feel safe. It has caused so much blood to flow over the years. It is my stress reliever.

I smile thinking about the blood, and put my notebook away.

I have to get the fuck out of here, maybe move to a new city and start fresh, I think.

The people around here are starting to get on my nerves, and I fear I will snap and do something stupid like murder someone in broad daylight. I do not need that kind of stress in my life.

Mary comes by my table with the check. I look up at her somewhat relieved and smile as she hands it to me. For some reason, I feel comfort in her presence.

"What time do you get off work?" I ask, instantly regretting it.

I never do things like this. I start to get up so I can run.

"In about five minutes if you want to walk me home," she says, smiling.

"Uhh..." is all I can say. I don't expect her to respond favorably.

"I'll meet you outside in a few."

"Okay."

I go to pay my bill and walk outside. I don't know what I'm thinking. Maybe I should bolt. I never should have said anything. I begin to pace back and forth. Mary comes outside and we head toward her house.

My heart races, and I feel slightly nauseous.

"So, are you a writer?" She asks as we walk.

"Yes," I reply.

"Oh yeah? What kind of stuff do you write about?"

The question alarms me, but I quickly think of a lie to tell her.

"Well don't freak out, but I mostly write extreme horror. Murder and gore and all of the nasty stuff."

She shoots me a wide-eyed look.

"You're into splatterpunk?" she asks excitedly.

"Oh yeah. I've written a few books and a bunch of stories," I answer.

She smiles at me, grabs my hand, and holds it.

The farther we go the more we talk, and the better I feel. The nausea goes away and my heartbeat returns to normal. This is the most time I've ever spent with a live woman. I am having so much fun I lose track of time, and soon we arrive at her front door.

"You can come in if you want," she says softly. "You know, I've seen what you write in your little notebook."

My eyes widen in alarm. I panic as I feel a sharp pain in my neck, and I turn around to see Mary grinning wickedly. I feel woozy and fall backward onto the floor of the entryway, unable to cry out as my muscles fail me. I try to reach for my knife but my arms don't move.

I awaken strapped down to a metal table, my naked flesh feeling at home on the stainless steel surface. I can't move my head, and all I can see is the ceiling.

"Like I said, I have read some of what you write in your notebook at the cafe and you inspired me to make the blood a part of my life," Mary says.

She's nearby. I can smell her. And she's aroused. She climbs on the table and straddles me, grinding back and forth against me. I feel the strap on my head loosen and bend my neck to look up at her. She smiles. I can't believe this is happening. Finally, I can share my work with someone —I can have someone to talk to about my love for the blood.

She leans forward as if to kiss me. Instead, she picks up a knife from a table near my head and slits my throat from left to right. I watch my blood spray out over her body and drip down her chest. Her grinding intensifies and she cries out in orgasm. She looks into my eyes as my life slips away...

This is the happiest I have ever been.

AISLING CAMPBELL

Through the Backdoor

"The fuck is that? I told you to get booze."

"Hear me out," Sam said. "I read about this thing online. It's gonna save us a lot of money."

"...fuck are you talking about?" Riley said. The sweats had been bad —great discs of sour smelling dampness under his arms, on his back and front. He felt sick, disgusting, and here was Sam holding up a box of tampons like he'd just discovered the cure for cancer.

"You ever hear of an alcohol enema?" Sam said. "Instant drunkenness, and you only need a fraction of the alcohol. We soak these babies in whatever we've got left, shove 'em up our shit chutes, and problem solved!"

"But we haven't got nothing left!"

Their empties for the past week were still scattered around the flat, and Riley had checked every one of them looking for dregs, the slightest residue to tide him over until Sam got back with a new bottle.

"I told you I'm skint this month. Had enough to get us a few cans of lager, but we both know that'd be like pissing on a house fire. Or we could try drinking hand sanitizer, the beverage of choice for the alcoholic with nothing left to lose. Trust me, this is the best option. 'Sides, I might have a little something stashed away."

"You little bastard, you've been keeping —"

"Yeah, yeah, you'll thank me in, like, ten minutes when we're both utterly rat-arsed."

Sam's secret stash turned out to be a handful of minis he'd swiped from a hotel in Marbella two years prior. He walked into the bathroom with a fifty milliliter bottle of gin, a shot glass, and the box of tampons.

"This better work," Riley muttered, standing in his pants and a T-shirt, eyeing up the bottle of gin.

"It will," Sam promised, decanting a small quantity of liquid into the shot glass.

"Is that it?" Riley said.

"You don't wanna overdo it, mate. It's not like when you just drink it —the alcohol gets straight into your bloodstream. Your insides suck it right up. It's nuts."

Sam opened up the box of tampons. It took him a while to work out how to get the cottony bit out. The whole time Riley was perched on the edge of the bath wanting to reach forward and snatch what was left of the gin and down it.

It wouldn't do a lot —wasn't really enough to keep him buzzed either. Pissing on a house fire like Sam said.

"How much longer is this gonna take?"

"Guess you want to go first then, mate?" Sam said, dunking the liberated tampon into the shot glass. It chubbed up, juicy with alcohol, and Sam passed Riley the glass. The blessed scent of gin washed over him, calming the knot in his stomach.

"So I just cram it on up there?" Riley asked.

"Yup, you'll probably want to leave the string hanging out. Y'know, like the ladies do. Fun one to explain down in A&E if you lose it up there."

Riley climbed into the bathtub, tugging the curtain back around. He pulled down his pants and squatted in the bottom of the tub.

He felt another layer of dignity sloughing off —the latest in a series of little disappointments, embarrassments, and failures spanning back years. Riley heard that there were genes for this kind of thing —it all started long before him. Better to think of it as destiny, controlled by strands of chemicals forced on him by life itself. Inevitable.

He picked up the fat gin-soaked tampon by the string, watching it dangle and not spilling a drip. Somewhere in the back of his mind, he could hear his dad scoffing *What kind of pansy shoves his drink up his arse.* Right, his father had just poured it down his gullet like a regular person, gallon after gallon like a great, fat, old toad that needed to be kept moist.

With a grimace, Riley reached behind him, probing, the tampon string clutched in his hand.

This had better be fucking worth it.

Riley looked down at the empty soap container by the sink, then down at his hand. Behind him in the shower, Sam grunted.

"Bet this is a typical Friday night for you, Sammy," he muttered, turning the hot tap on with his uncontaminated hand.

"Yeah, fuck you too, mate," Sam said.

As he washed his hands, his attention came back to the soft wad of cotton crammed into his rectum. It felt weird —like the prelude to a moderate-sized dump.

The curtain pulled back and Sam came to join him at the sink.

"You feeling it yet?" he asked.

Riley shrugged. He didn't feel nauseous, but that was a far cry from being drunk. Sam clapped him on the shoulder.

"That better not be the hand you just shoved up your arse," Riley muttered.

"Well, we can always do another one. Give it half an hour, then we'll do a top-up."

The buzz came creeping up on them, like a feral cat toward a slice of old ham left by the back door. As the world turned soft at its edges Riley tipped his head back and looked up at the textured ceiling. It was more tipsy as opposed to drunk, but Riley wasn't sure he could be arsed to get up and do another tampon.

There had to be another method.

When their dole came in the next month, Sam went out and came back with two enema bottles, a big tub of Vaseline, and a selection of gin, rum, and vodka.

"I got whatever was cheapest. It's not like we're gonna taste it anyway," he said.

"Just breathe, mate. I'm not gonna be able to get this in you if you clam up on me," Sam said.

"Don't talk," Riley said, forehead pressed against the bathroom floor. "You're making me tense up more when you fucking talk."

The cold rum squirting into his guts was unexpected, the glug of the bottle unsettling.

"Done, my turn now."

As he stared at his flatmate's arsehole Riley knew a line had been crossed. He'd managed to avoid looking at Sam's cock and balls but his ring-piece was a lot harder to ignore. He hoped the rum in his rectum would kick in sooner rather than later, so he could purge the events of this evening from his brain.

Riley slicked up the nozzle with Vaseline and got it over with.

An hour later the room was spinning. Time became disjointed and nothing mattered.

Life was good.

"Why the hell didn't we start doing this sooner...?" he said, either out loud or in his head. Probably the first one, because he heard Sam say, "Getting a taste for it, are we?" and laugh.

Sure, the prep was a pain, but the benefits...

Someone turned the television on, and Riley turned his head towards it at the sound of moans.

In the middle of the screen was a woman —at least, Riley hoped it was a woman. Sam better not be making him watch gay porn while he was too drunk to resist. Whoever it was they were flexible as fuck. Her ankles were up by her ears, leaving her spread wide. Riley tried to check for a penis, but all his blurry eyes could make out was the pale pink of naked skin.

"Go on, do it for me baby."

Definitely a male voice. Off-camera, American, and sleazy. Riley tried to keep his focus on the screen, curious what it was she, maybe-but-hopefully-not he, was gonna do.

There was a cheeky wink of red, and if Riley had been drinking the traditional way he would have thrown up as *baby's* arse shat itself inside out, dangling like a pink and red speckled slug for a scant second before it was slurped back from whence it came.

"Again," the man demanded.

Riley managed to tear his eyes away to ask Sam was the fuck he was playing at, but his flatmate was passed out and drooling on the carpet.

Back on screen, the woman moaned and there were sounds like smacking lips. When Riley looked back at the screen it was still her and the fat, red bundle of lower intestinal tract hanging out of her arse.

Riley flailed his right arm, trying to reach up onto the sofa searching for the remote so he could turn the damn thing off. With any luck he wouldn't remember it come morning —or more realistically, next afternoon.

A hand appeared at the bottom corner of the screen reaching out to fondle the misplaced flesh, pulling and pushing it like dough.

Riley gave up on the remote, sinking farther down onto the floor. The light from the telly flared and expanded, doubling up, tripling, like it was part of a kaleidoscope. He was sinking down into unconsciousness fast but not quite fast enough to miss the next part. The man bent down and pressed his mouth to the quivering lump, sucking on it, drawing it in, and biting down —

Riley hunkered down on the toilet and waited for the next wave of cramps. His guts were getting picky, evacuating every trace of the half-price, off-brand vodka. It felt like he was being scoured from end to end. He could hear Sam laughing at him from outside the door.

"We got more of that gin from last time?" Riley muttered.

"Yeah, but I'm not going anywhere near your backside until you've got those explosions under control."

Riley's reply was lost in a wail of despair as his guts twisted and squeezed, wriggling like they wanted to be outside of him.

"No more vodka...ever," Riley promised.

By the time he was done, after several false alarms, Sam was already passed out on the sofa and Riley had to sort himself out.

It was awkward —he couldn't get the angle right, or the nozzle deep enough, and most of the alcohol came spilling back out, dribbling over his calves and seeping into the bathmat. He grumbled and loaded up another shot in the enema bottle, managing to get it a little deeper but as soon as he moved he felt his drink sloshing back out. At least the shits earlier had cleaned him out so he wasn't kneeling in his own shit.

He decided to cut his losses and go to bed. The last thing he needed was to get so bladdered he ended up in hospital again. Most of the nurses were nice enough, but he hated the way they looked at him.

Pity and disappointment, like his mother.

Disgust, like his sisters.

When Riley woke, he felt better. His backside ached more than usual, but otherwise, he felt good —right up until he went to get out of bed and his foot met something that rolled. He slammed his palms up against the wall to steady himself. When his heart finished pounding, he looked down to see what he had stepped on.

It was a litre bottle of gin, empty with the cap missing. It was not part of Riley's current collection of empties scattered around the room. He picked it up and noticed a faint off-white crust around the neck of the bottle. He sniffed, and beneath the ghostly scent of gin, he detected the distinct aroma of arse.

"...the hell?"

It was one of the new bottles Sam had brought home, and the last time Riley had seen it the thing had still been three-quarters full.

"Hey Sam, you up yet?"

Whoever had drained the bottle with their nether cheeks was going to be in trouble —big trouble of the A&E variety —and since Riley was currently able to stand, see, and form a coherent thought he was pretty damn sure it hadn't been him.

Still holding the bottle, Riley stepped into the living room and scanned around for his flatmate. The sofa where he'd last seen Sam was empty.

"Sam?"

"Yeah?"

Riley looked towards the kitchenette to find Sam munching on toast, looking alive and distinctly un-comatose.

"You...?"

Riley pointed and then held up the bottle.

"Aww, mate, is that the gin I just bought?" Sam said. "You drank it all already? I thought we agreed —"

"I drank it? Didn't you...?"

Sam looked at him. Riley lowered the bottle and rubbed his forehead. Maybe he did drink it himself —maybe the smell on the neck of the bottle was just his breath. It was pretty rank sometimes.

The taste wasn't there on his tongue and his stomach didn't have that tender, slimy feeling he usually got when drinking.

He looked once more at the bottle and then dropped it in the bin.

The whiskey was beautiful —pure, golden, full of promise.

"Won it off Rishad down at the pub," Sam said, beaming. "His dad's a whiskey nut. This one's Japanese or something. Wanna give it a try?"

He went into the kitchen and Riley asked, "Wait, are we drinking it?"

"Of course. It's not like your arse is going to appreciate the subtle flavours."

Sam poured a few fingers of whiskey, handing one glass to Riley. He looked down at the amber liquid —warm, inviting —and lifted it to his lips.

The response was immediate. He gagged the moment it touched his tongue, spitting the whiskey back out into the glass.

"What's your problem?" Sam asked, sniffing the contents of his glass. He knocked back a mouthful. "Nothing wrong with it —it's good." He drank down the rest and poured another glass.

"Not...not my taste I guess," Riley mumbled.

Sam scoffed. "Maybe all that hard drink's burnt off your tastebuds already. Fine, I won't waste it on you. We've still got plenty of gin lying about if you want that."

Sam took the bottle and the glass and headed off to his room, leaving Riley standing in the kitchen staring into the glass of spit-tainted whiskey.

He sighed and tipped it down the sink.

The movement woke him. He went from drooling into the pillow to drooling on the sheets two inches *below* the pillow. Another sharp tug and the duvet was over his head and his legs were flailing. Another, and he was face-first on the carpet getting up close and personal with a pair of week-old boxers.

Riley tried to push up onto his arms, but another pull sent them skidding out from under him. He tried to grab at the leg of the bed, when he became aware of just where exactly the tugging sensation was coming from.

Oh fuck.

He let go, managing this time to roll fully onto his back so he could see what was pulling at him.

In the gloom he could see a thick rope of *something* stretching to the door, wrapping around the frame with its end out of sight. It rippled as it pulled like the way a worm moved, and even though the light was too dim for him to see colours, Riley knew that it was pink and moist and pulsing with blood.

This is not happening.

His skin rubbed across the carpet, building up to a burn as he was dragged into the living room. That burn was the only thing convincing him he was awake, that this wasn't some ultra-vivid dream or hallucination.

He swiped for the legs of the coffee table. Missed. Clawed at the side of the sofa, but failed to stick.

He grabbed for the doorframe and held on for several tugs before his sweat-slicked hands slipped and he was pulled inside Sam's room.

It was waiting for him, coiled up on the end of the bed. Sam had left his bedside light on, and Riley saw, with a strange absence of nausea, that he'd been right. Pink and red with some small hints of yellow. A bright, cupcake icing kind of pink. The end of it, or maybe the start —Riley didn't know which was which anymore —sat like the head of a snake, peeking out over the coils. It was thicker than the rest, darker in colour —a python rather than a corn snake. It bulged and tapered, a snout tipped by a rumple of dripping red muscle.

"Sam, wake up..."

Sam was passed out on the bed, sprawled out over the duvet. The bottle of whiskey sat, mostly empty, on his bedside table.

Riley's liberated rectum slithered over itself and onto the sheets, turning its puckered attention to the man with a stomach full of expensive Japanese whiskey.

Oh, shitting hell no.

"Sam, wake the fuck up, mate!"

Riley tried to grab it and haul it back in like a fire hose and somehow convince it to go back where it belonged. But it was slick, sliding through his hands.

"No."

It left damp, sticky patches as it crept onto Sam's chest.

"Please, no... Sam, fucking wake up!"

Sam slept the sleep of the hopelessly plastered, moving only to breathe as Riley's gut crept towards his lips.

"Oh god..."

It began to disappear piece by piece. Anus, rectum, descending colon. With each sliding centimetre that vanished Riley felt more dizzy, more feeble, falling back onto the carpet and looking up at the ceiling as his guts unspooled. His hands and fingers felt numb, his head light. He almost imagined he could feel the moist warmth of the inside of Sam's throat, scent the whiskey lingering just a little farther ahead. Almost taste it. He had to forget what was behind him, leave it all there.

He had almost made it when Sam bucked, choking, and his teeth came down.

Hard.

BENJAMIN KARDOS

Afterbirth

THE HIGH-PITCHED WAILING of my infant son pierced my eardrums like a hot needle.

"Fuck," I muttered.

I rolled over and switched on the bedside lamp. Maddie stirred beside me.

"What's wrong with Tanner?" she asked groggily, squinting against the intrusive glow of the lamp.

"Fuck if I know," I said, throwing the sheets off my body. Tanner's cry hit an octave that could be used to torture dogs. It rattled my teeth and made my skin crawl. His crib was in the bedroom across from ours. Barefoot, I walked across the cold hardwood floor to his room and turned on the light.

Other than Tanner's crib, the room was empty. The little gremlin was sitting up in his crib, his piggish face soaked with tears, his pink mouth open with unspeakable anguish. Three teeth poked out of his gums like bits of broken glass. For a second, I fantasized about shoving a handful of glass into his mouth to shut him up.

"What the fuck is it?" I crossed the room and picked him up. God, I hated the dead weight of his eleven-month-old body. It was almost as bad as the shrill sound of his fucking voice.

I sniffed and gagged almost vomiting, "Oh, fuck me..."

Gray liquid shit oozed out of the bottom of his diaper onto the floor. A thick drop splashed my foot.

"Goddamned shit bag," I growled into his face. Tanner screamed as I shook him.

"What is it, Jason?" Maddie called from our bedroom.

"Tanner shit himself!"

"Ugg, gross."

I plopped Tanner back in the crib and trudged to the bathroom where we kept the diapers. Tanner's crying followed me. It grated my nerves, making me feel like I was being dragged across a bed of rough gravel. I was exhausted and annoyed. There was nothing I wanted more than to shove a fucking pillow over his face or squeeze his fragile neck until his head popped off. I sometimes laughed bitterly over the fact that the judge gave me custody over the kid instead of Charlotte. If only the judge knew the violent thoughts that coursed through my head every moment of the day she would have begged my alcoholic ex-wife to take him.

Walking back to Tanner's room with a fresh diaper, baby wipes, and powder, I wondered why I hadn't killed the disgusting little worm yet. It was a question I pondered frequently ever since I was given custody. Aside from the legal and social taboos surrounding infanticide, I suppose I clung to some small scrap of hope that one day I might learn to love my son.

Charlotte, my ex, didn't drink much during her pregnancy. It was the closest she ever got to being a responsible parent. We never intended to get pregnant. Tanner's conception was the result of a drunken one-night stand at a mutual friend's Halloween party. She was a party girl, and I was a twenty-four-year-old loner looking for an unattached good time. The sex took place in the front seat of my car. It was wild and meaningless, exactly how we wanted it.

When she texted me a month later with the news she was pregnant I felt as if my legs had been cut off at the knees —all of my life plans were shattered. I'd always dreamed of traveling the world, the open road my guide. I don't know why the idea of travel appealed to me. It had something to do with the idea of constant movement, never staying in one place long enough for anyone to find me. Now, because of one stupid mistake with a drunken bitch, my dreams of the open road had rolled up and vanished.

Confused and afraid, we did what seemed the most responsible thing and got married. We briefly considered abortion, but living in an anti-abortion state it simply wasn't an option unless we went the back-alley direction, something Charlotte refused to do.

I was working at an insurance agency as a file clerk where I spent long days in a beige cubicle alphabetizing insurance forms. Countless hours were spent at my desk daydreaming about traveling. My cubicle wall was covered with pictures of all the places I planned to visit once I'd saved up enough money to quit and hit the road. With a baby on the way, quitting wasn't an option.

In the months leading up to Tanner's birth, my coworkers offered a flood of unwanted parental advice and support.

"You'll be tired," said George, leaning against the wall of my cube. "But it'll be worth it. There's nothing in life that brings more joy than a child of your own."

George was the office's professional parent. His desk was littered with photos of his little sperm monsters.

"What about cleaning their...you know..." I asked.

George laughed. "You mean poop? The first time I changed a diaper I was worried it would gross me out, but hey, when it's your kid you don't care. Don't worry man, it won't bother you in the least. The love of your kid supersedes bodily fluids."

The first time I changed Tanner's diaper I realized George had lied to me. My stomach roiled with nausea as I wiped milky shit off Tanner's ass and back.

It wasn't just changing diapers —everything about Tanner sickened me. The day of his birth I waited vainly for the parental love everyone talked about to kick in. Sitting next to

Charlotte's maternity ward bed I waited for that unconditional devotion to consume me, but looking at his wrinkled pink body nestled in Charlotte's arms all I felt was emptiness. Charlotte may as well birthed a rock.

Over time, the nothingness morphed into loathing. Try as I might, I simply was incapable of loving my son. I went through the motions. I rocked him, changed him, and fed him hoping the parental instincts would magically appear. But with every passing day, my disgust grew.

At least I was trying. Charlotte was a shit mother. She began drinking again immediately after the birth. Over the following months, it was rare to see her sober. We fought often about her drunkenness, her lack of responsibility, but it didn't stop her from attending parties every chance she got. She occasionally played with him, but that was the extent of her involvement in his upbringing. In the meantime, I continued working at my soul-sucking job to support her and Tanner. I knew it was unwise to leave her alone with our son, especially when she was drunk, but what choice did I have? We needed the money and I couldn't take him to work with me.

I was at the office when I received the call. The police found Charlotte drunkenly pushing Tanner's stroller through a red light at a busy intersection, almost getting struck down by a truck. She threw punches at the cops who confronted her and was arrested. I was disappointed neither Charlotte nor Tanner was killed in the incident.

I did what seemed to be the responsible thing —I filed for divorce and custody. The entire legal battle was over in weeks. I was given full custody of Tanner. It was an anomaly for sure, since ninety percent of custody battles favor the mother. After reviewing the case, there was no doubt in the judge's mind I was the only parent fit to raise Tanner. Hell, Charlotte was drunk during the court hearing. We quickly separated and Charlotte moved into a run-down apartment complex across town where her drinking and partying continued uninhibited. The divorce was finalized a few months later.

All this went through my mind as I changed Tanner's shitty diaper. As I wiped away the grey-green shit smeared on his ass I found myself envying Charlotte. Her addiction was the perfect excuse to get out of raising him. Holding my breath against the rancid stench of Tanner's runny bowel movement I wished I'd been as smart as her. Why did I even pretend to care? Perhaps Tanner would be with a foster family right now, a family that would love him in the way I was inexplicably incapable.

Adorned in a fresh diaper, Tanner wouldn't quit his fucking bawling. My head throbbed with pain from the noise.

"What is it, Tanner? What do you want?" I picked him up and held him close, patting his back and bouncing him gently. If anything, my actions made his crying worse.

"Why won't he shut up?" Maddie called from the bedroom.

"I don't know, Maddie! He's clean but still crying," I whispered to Tanner soothingly, "It's okay, little guy. Everything's fine. Daddy..."

I stopped myself before saying the words *loves you*. I just couldn't coax the lie from my lips.

"Maybe he's hungry. Do you want me to get his bottle?"

"No, I'll get it," I told her as I carried Tanner into the hall. "You go back to sleep, baby."

"Wish I could," she grumbled. "That fucking racket could wake the dead."

I met Maddie about a month after my separation from Charlotte. The connection we felt was immediate. I was pushing Tanner's stroller through the park contemplating my dead-end life. I was living in a dark tunnel with no end in sight with a child I didn't love, working a job I hated, watching my dreams of world travel fading away like a tired sunset over a cemetery.

Wandering the park in a disillusioned state, I found myself by the river, standing at the top of a boat ramp, contemplating shoving Tanner's stroller down the concrete incline into the current and out of my life. My jaw clenched as I gripped the stroller tightly, pushing it back and forth. It was tempting, so tempting...

"The river sure is lovely, isn't it?"

I turned and saw her standing next to me. She was beautiful, tall, and shapely with dark hair and dark eyes.

I smiled at the young woman.

"It is," I agreed.

We stared out across the water.

"I'm Maddie," she said, offering a hand.

"Jason."

I don't know what attracted her to me, but we quickly struck up a conversation that turned into dinner and an eventual relationship. She was undeniably sexy, but what attracted me to her most was the subtle underlying darkness inside her. She'd suffered tragedy in her life.

"I used to be a mother," she told me during one of our dates. "Both my husband and my baby son died in a house fire while I was visiting my sister. The gas main was leaking and a spark set the whole place off."

"I'm sorry to hear that," I told her, although I didn't feel anything. There was an emptiness in Maddie's eyes I assumed came from the loss of her family. While I couldn't empathize with her sorrow, I found the darkness in her eyes incredibly arousing.

We moved in together when Tanner was nine months old. Maddie didn't seem to have any more parental instincts than I did, but I was happy to have another person to help me endure the unending burden of raising a child. At least with her at home to watch Tanner while I was at work I didn't have to dole out money for daycare.

In the kitchen, I found a clean bottle and filled it with formula. Tanner took the rubber nipple in his mouth. As the repulsive little monster sucked down the liquid, I basked in the temporary respite from his screeching. My ears were still ringing, but at least I got him to stop. Taking a deep relieved breath, I glanced at the clock —2:07 a.m. With any luck, Tanner might sleep until six.

As Tanner fed, I looked out the kitchen window at the empty street and the neighbor's dark houses, everyone asleep in their beds. I envied them.

I wandered around the house holding Tanner. Maddie had been right —he was starving. He was halfway through the bottle when I heard a car outside. Glancing out the window, I caught the passing taillights. *Who's out this time of time of night?*

Yawning, I thought of all the things I would have done had Tanner not been born: traveling, rock climbing, boating, biking...all activities I didn't have the time, energy, or money for because all I had went into keeping Tanner alive. As these thoughts went through my head, my body trembling with a low, burning rage. My chest constricted. Through slit eyes, I glared at Tanner as he finished his bottle. He looked so much like his mother. It was all I could do to keep from throwing him through the window and letting him die on the lawn, eaten alive by raccoons and feral cats. The thought brought me a small spark of pleasure, soothing the rage.

I heard another car. I rushed to the window but didn't see any headlights. Tanner's eyes fluttered as he relaxed into my arms. My shoulder hurt from holding him. Setting the bottle in the sink, I slowly made my way through the living room toward the stairs.

There was a knock on the front door.

My heart leapt to my throat. I spun around and stared at the door, holding my breath.

"Who is it?" I called. My skin tingled with apprehension.

"Is somebody at the door?" Maddie called from upstairs.

"Stay in bed," I told her.

Cautiously, I approached the door. My body felt cold as the pounding persisted, like a panicked heart. Was it a burglar? No, burglars don't announce themselves.

Moving the window curtain enough to allow a sliver of visibility, I looked out onto the porch. A dark shape stood there, obscured by the shadows. The figure was short, but I couldn't make out the face. The porch light switch was on the wall next to me. I flicked it, but the outside light didn't come on. I remembered the bulb was blown. Closing the curtain, I walked to the door.

"Who is it?" I called again, my hand on the doorknob. Blood throbbed in my fingers, making the knob feel like a living thing. The knocking stopped. I listened closely to heavy breathing.

"I've got a gun," I warned as I undid the lock to open the door a crack.

It burst open with an unexpected force. I jumped back as the stranger rushed in from the darkness.

"What the fuck! Get out of my house!"

My outburst woke Tanner. He began fussing.

The stranger stood in the hallway, listing back and forth and smelling of alcohol. I flipped on a light switch.

"Charlotte! What the fuck are you doing here?"

My ex-wife's eyes were red. She wore a jacket over a tight party dress. She stared at the baby in my arms. "Tanner, sweetie, it's Mommy..." She stumbled forward, arms out as if to take my son from me.

Stepping back, I snarled, "Get back. I could have you arrested."

"I want to see my babyyy..." She kept coming for us. Reaching out, I seized her arm and pulled her toward the door.

"You got a lotta nerve showing your face here, you cunt. Get out!"

"Not...without...Tanner," she slurred. "I wanna take Tanner with me, just for the night..."

"Like fuck you are. Now, get out."

I tried pushing her out the door. She spun around and cuffed me on the side of the head with her fist.

"Ow! You fucking bitch!"

Charlotte ran into the living room. I chased her. Tanner cried —the sound was needles in my ears. I realized I was squeezing him so tight he was having difficulty breathing.

"Jason, what's going on down there?" Maddie cried from the upstairs hallway, her voice high with alarm.

"Stay upstairs!" I shouted. I fixed a death glare on Charlotte as she wandered the house as if she still lived there. My face was hot, and my breath escaped my nostrils like that of an enraged bull.

"Who's down there with you?"

"Just stay upstairs, Maddie, I've got this!"

"Is that your fresh bitch?" Charlotte said, then hiccupped. For a moment she looked like she might puke on the carpet.

"Leave her out of this," I warned.

Composing herself, Charlotte pointed a finger at me. "You never loved Tanner."

Her statement shook me. I took several steps back as if struck with a punch, then scoffed. "What are you talking about? I take care of him, feed him, change him..."

Charlotte shook her head. "You keep him alive, but you don't love him. I know it. I remember the way you looked at him when he was born. There was nothing in your eyes. You hated him then, and you hate him now."

Blood pulsed through my head. My body shook with anger, but I couldn't tell what enraged me more: the fact she forced her way into my home, or that she was right about my feelings toward our child.

"You're full of shit," I told her. "You don't know what you're talking about. Tanner's my son and I..."

The words caught in my throat —my lie. It was like hitting a brick wall.

Charlotte sneered reproachfully. "See? You can't even say you love him. You're a fake father."

"And you're a worthless drunk."

"Not anymore. Tonight was it. No more drinking. I want to be with my son. He'd be better off with me." She spat a gob of dark phlegm onto the floor.

My skin crawled with hatred.

"You're a fucking liar." My rage was nearly blinding.

"You're the liar," muttered Charlotte. "A liar and an asshole."

Pointing at the door, I spoke through gritted teeth. "Get the fuck out of my house, NOW!"

"Not without my son."

"Bitch, GET THE FUCK OUT!"

Tanner wailed louder. My grip on his body tightened. I felt his ribs cracking against my arm. He shrieked as his bones fractured.

"You're hurting him!" Charlotte cried.

Like a rabid dog, she lunged at me, arms out, ready to snatch Tanner. He screamed. At that moment, I saw my life, my mistakes, my frustrations, my anger all boiling over. I saw everything I hated about her, everything I hated about Tanner. Everything went red.

Throwing Tanner toward the ceiling, I snatched him by the legs and swung him like a battle axe at Charlotte's head.

Their skulls collided together with a bone-splintering crack. The force of the blow threw Charlotte backward. Fighting for balance, she stumbled over the coffee table, shattering the glass top. She fell to the floor, groaning in pain, holding her face. Blood oozed from between her fingers.

"Motherfucker! You broke my nose!"

Tanner's cries were deafening. Still holding him by the legs, I glanced at his face. His forehead was caved in where it connected with his mother's nose. It reminded me of a dented car hood. Blood flowed from a dark gash near his hairline.

Charlotte's eyes went wide. "My god, Jason! You hurt Tanner! You hurt Tanner!"

She moved to stand, but with another swing of my infant son, I knocked her back to the floor.

"Stay down, cunt! Just stay down!" Spit flew from my mouth. I put a foot on her chest, pinning her. I felt her bones and tendons pop.

Both Charlotte and Tanner were screaming. I barely heard them. Tanner writhed in my grasp as my fingers dug into his ankles for a better grip. I swung him over my head, bringing him down as if chopping firewood, connecting with Charlotte's face again and again. Within seconds her face was smeared red. The hot scent of blood entered my nostrils, fueling my mindless rage.

Blood splattered the walls as I pulverized my ex's face with my human club. Charlotte raised her arms weakly in self-defense. Tanner's screams were wet and strange as if gurgling from a broken speaker.

"My baby...my baby..." Charlotte protested as I brought Tanner down for another strike. Spitting out broken teeth, Charlotte's mouth looked as empty as Tanner's.

With a wet crack, Tanner's head split open like a rotten peach. Chunky gray matter exploded all over Charlotte's obliterated face. Tanner's crying ceased. More brains flew out as I continued smashing what was left of his head against his drunk cunt mother. Charlotte's screams were reduced to choked sobs.

"Please stop," she begged.

I couldn't stop. Nothing could stop me. My anger, my frustrations, my hatred, finally found the perfect outlet. My system shook with adrenaline. Since the day of Tanner's birth, I worked so hard to do right in the eyes of society, to play the role of a loving single father, ignoring my instincts, but at that moment, I was finally doing the only thing that felt right to me.

When I was done beating Charlotte, Tanner's body was completely headless. My breathing was raspy as I stared down at the frightened bitch, coated in blood, brains, and shards of infant skull. My lips curled into a smile as she cowered at my feet.

"Please, don't hurt me anymore."

Ignoring her, I grasped one of Tanner's legs in a tight grip and began to twist. The muscles tightened and split as I turned the leg farther than nature ever intended. The little femur broke from the socket. Tendons snapped. The skin took on the look of a wrung-out dishrag. I rotated the leg full circle several times until it tore from his body like a turkey leg.

Dropping the corpse, I knelt next to Charlotte and pried her toothless mouth open.

"You want your kid, HAVE HIM!"

I forced the severed leg between her lips. Charlotte feebly beat me with her fists. With every blow, I felt her strength dissolve. Pushing on the bottom of Tanner's foot, I forced the leg down her throat, watching with pleasure as her neck budged with the thickness of Tanner's thigh. Her body convulsed and jerked as she gagged on the obstruction, weakly trying to pull it out, but it was lodged too tight.

As she choked, I twisted off Tanner's other limbs. I lifted Charlotte's dress and ripped off her piss stained panties.

"You want your kid back?" I said. "Have all of him."

Spreading her legs wide, I crammed one of his arms up her vagina. The opening stretched to accommodate the arm. When I felt the bone butt up against her cervix, I pushed harder, spearing her uterus.

I took the other arm and shoved it up her ass.

"There you go," I muttered as I worked. "Tanner's right back where he belongs, all warm and cozy."

Blood flowed from between Charlotte's legs, spreading over the carpet like sticky syrup. By the time I was done, Charlotte was dead. Her eyes had gone glassy. Her body relaxed, making it easier to shove Tanner's final leg in next to his arm in her stretched and shredded pussy.

Satisfied, I stood up and admired my work. I began laughing like a madman. Charlotte looked so funny with Tanner's limbs sticking out of her every orifice as if she were birthing twins from both ends. Next to her lay Tanner's torso. Looking at the headless, limbless child, I recalled when I was nine years old tearing the legs and wings off a fly I found buzzing around my bedroom window. I remembered smiling as I watched the mutilated insect wiggle helplessly on my windowsill. A few months later, I did the same thing to a newborn kitten in a toolshed in the woods behind my house. The sound of the little bones cracking and the kitten's high pitched screams was one of the highlights of my childhood. Looking at Tanner's body, I felt like a kid again.

"What happened in here?"

Maddie's voice jolted me from my euphoria. I spun around, my body cold. I stammered. "I...I..."

What could I say?

Slack-jawed, Maddie walked across the room, wearing her oversized nightshirt. She examined my bloody work.

"My god, you killed them both," she whispered.

"They had it coming. Charlotte, she forced my hand. She made me so...mad."

Maddie looked at me with tender eyes. She touched my cheek.

"I know," she said, bringing her lips to mine.

I pulled out of the kiss and stared at her in disbelief.

"You're okay with this? With what I did?"

She glanced back at the carnage on the floor and chuckled.

"I never liked Tanner anyway. It was only you I wanted. I often fantasized about killing him. And you're right, that bitch had it coming, forcing her way into our home like that." She spat on Charlotte's body.

I couldn't believe it.

"You're really okay with this?" I asked again.

Sighing, Maddie led me to the couch. We sat.

"Remember how I told you my son and husband died?"

"Yeah, in a house fire. The gas main blew?"

"There was more to it than that."

I stared at her. "What?"

"Who do you think caused the gas leak?"

Gazing into her dark eyes I gasped. "You started it?"

She smiled. "I watched the house go up from the alley across the street. I listened to their screams as they burned alive. It was glorious. I was free."

Euphoria rising in my chest, I beamed. "I think I can relate to that feeling."

"It's wonderful, isn't it?"

I kissed her deeply, feeling as if wings had sprouted from my shoulders. The tremendous weight I'd been carrying since Tanner's birth was lifted. Maddie was right —it felt wonderful.

Our kissing turned into heavy groping which turned into the shedding of our nightshirts. With my hands on Maddie's breasts, I turned and looked at my ex-wife's body.

"We're gonna have to clean this up," I said.

"We will," Maddie said, her voice full of desire. "But first make love to me. Let's celebrate our freedom."

Pulling her to the floor, I removed her panties. Lowering my boxers, I revealed my cock throbbing with need. I fell upon her, kissing her neck and sliding into her body. She moaned as I filled her. I relished in the hot wetness of her pussy.

As we fucked, we rolled into the puddle of Charlotte's and Tanner's blood. Soon our bodies were covered in sticky crimson handprints. We were like two freshly delivered infants, covered in afterbirth. In the throes of lovemaking, I felt reborn. My ex-wife's and son's screams were the labor pains of a new life. With their deaths, my mistakes were severed from me like a cut umbilical cord.

"Fuck, I'm gonna cum," I moaned into Maddie's ear.

"Cum in me," she pleaded. "Make me pregnant."

"Are you sure?"

"Yes, Jason. I want a child with you. I want it more than anything."

Looking into her dark eyes, I felt truly connected to another human being for the first time in my life. I realized there was nothing I wanted more than to have a baby with Maddie. I was incapable of loving my first child, but perhaps with Maddie, my psychopathic soulmate, it would be different.

Burying my cock to the hilt inside her, I pumped her full of my seed. Maddie exploded with me, arching her back, rocking her head against the floor, her hair saturated with blood and brain matter.

"YES!" she cried.

In the afterglow of sex, we held each other in front of the fireplace, staring at the corpses before us. The air was thick with the smell of sex, death, and new life.

"So what do we do now?" Maddie asked as I softly stroked her arm, holding her against my chest.

"Destroy the bodies, dispose of Charlotte's car, then clean the house. Nobody needs to know what happened here tonight."

Maddie thought for a moment. "You know we can't stay here."

I thought for a moment, then nodded. "No, we can't."

"We should hit the road as soon as possible. Not tell anyone where we're going, a couple of criminals on the run."

"Like Bonnie and Clyde, huh?" I said, chuckling.

Maddie kissed me with her blood-caked lips. "Why not? What's holding us in this shitty town? A job you hate? The open road is before us, my love. Didn't you say you always wanted to travel the world?"

At the mention of travel, I grinned. I felt the dreams I thought were gone forever return in a heartbeat.

"That I did," I said.

LINDSEY B. GODDARD
The Last Neighborhood

I LISTENED TO Hayley Jensen whimper through the wall of the shed, and I wished I didn't have to kill her. I clenched my jaw and hoped this one wouldn't be as messy as the last —how many days ago had that been? —when I'd plastered the sidewalk five houses down with bloody bits of Anton Palmer's brain. Palmer hadn't been the most charming neighbor, but I never wanted to see the inside of his skull. Sometimes, you don't have a choice.

My ear still pressed to the splintered wood of the shed, I envisioned Hayley's family —Danny, Rachael, and Hunter —signing for the girl to "shhh" with trembling fingers placed over their lips. I frowned, wishing I didn't have to kill them, either.

And as trivial as it was in comparison, I wished the rain would stop. I pulled my hood down over my forehead and wiped the water from my beard. The end of civilization was depressing enough without existing in this constant state of *wet*. You'd think the torrent would wash away the gore that oozed from my neighbors who lay rotting where they'd fallen (because nobody could lay them to rest without putting his own neck at risk). But the rain only made things worse. And the mud emitted a foul stench that mixed with the rot in the air.

Mud and guts. That's what this neighborhood had become.

Thunder cracked overhead. I raised my gun in response, then quickly lowered it, feeling stupid. If I survived the day, I knew there'd be dry clothes waiting for me at home. Even with the electricity and water shut off, Remmy managed to wash and dry something from the growing mound of dirty clothes each day. That man could stretch a bottle of water, a dab of soap, and a scrub brush farther than anyone I'd ever known. Resilient as ever, he was my rock.

A blue streak of lightning sliced through the afternoon sky. Danny called out from inside the shed. He sounded as tired as I felt. "Ray. Listen, man. You don't have to do this."

I let out a sigh that sounded more like a death rattle, gripped my Beretta tighter, and said, "Don't make it sound like I have a choice. That's not fair."

The girl sobbed. I wondered who was holding her. Rachael? She was a good mom, albeit a young one. Or maybe it was Hunter who cradled his half sister, soothing her. To all four of them, I said, "This doesn't have to be painful. Just take the medicine I slipped under the door, say your goodbyes, and go to sleep." My throat tightened around those last words.

"We're not taking your drugs, Ray!" Rachael screamed from inside the shed. She barely sounded like the woman I knew, the one who'd asked for my potato salad recipe at the summer block party. All the softness had left her voice, and there was only edge. "I'm not feeding my children poison!"

"If you don't take the pills, I'll be forced to shoot you."

Five-year-old Hayley Jensen let out a wail that seized my heart, and I thought I heard Hunter, who must be fifteen by now, join in. I almost cried, too. I closed my eyes and considered pressing the Beretta to my own forehead, pulling the hammer, and letting one fly between my Beautiful Blues. That's what Remmy called my eyes. The thought of Remmy, his Soulful Browns in contrast to my Beautiful Blues, and our daughter, Brianne, beaming her toothless grin, pulled me back from the brink of self-destruction for the millionth time.

I opened my eyes and focused on the mirror propped against a pile of junk on the back porch. Had the Jensens been planning a yard sale before all this? My reflection had scared the shit out of me when I first saw it moments ago, but the longer I looked, my fear morphed into sorrow. I didn't recognize the man standing there. He was a stranger, a wounded man in torn clothes, trembling in waterlogged socks under a sky of endless gray.

How did it come to this?

Overpopulation was the blanket term they used in press releases. Truth was, with overseas relations in the dumper, the United States didn't have enough internal resources to sustain its own people. Forced pregnancies due to abortion restrictions set in place in the first quarter of the century didn't help. By the time the average citizen realized the shortage of essentials was snowballing out of control, the Feds had already cooked up a plan.

When the U.S. government announced a mandate for its military forces to barricade citizens in their neighborhoods in a drastic effort to halt the growth of its burgeoning populace, at first, nobody thought it was real. These days, fake news is as prevalent as facts. Nobody can tell the difference. But soon, it was all anybody could talk about.

Entire neighborhoods had been blocked off by Army tanks. Soldiers allowed residents to enter, but nobody could leave. Appointed officials danced around the question of "Why?"

The entire country had reached its boiling point, and I felt the tension, like rolling water, ready to *pop, pop, pop.*

I was still working as a veterinary technician when I realized the country was spiraling into dystopian-level madness. Airports were shut down. Riots raged. Fires burned in the streets. My veterinary work had degenerated into an onslaught of euthanasia appointments as people realized they couldn't care for Fido anymore. It seemed the end was nigh, so I decided to stock up on every resource at my disposal. I brought home the xylazine, thinking a potent tranquilizer might prove useful if the rumors were true —rumors that in other states, neighborhoods had been sealed off and families forced to fight to the death.

From inside the old barn-style shed, Danny pleaded. "Listen. I have an idea how we can get out of this. We just need to talk, face to face, and I'll explain it to you."

I huffed, spraying droplets of rain. "I do that, and I'm a dead man! Take the medicine. It won't hurt."

"No, no, no. Listen! I'll leave my gun in here with Rachael," he said. "Just let me come out and talk."

Thunder rolled in the distance. Where I gripped the pistol, my palm was a clammy bog of rain and sweat. So were my armpits and boots. I was wet and tired, and tired of wet. If Danny wanted to come out, at least I'd have a clear shot at him. I was getting nowhere with my pleas for them to take the drugs. So I found myself saying, "Okay. Come out, Danny, but keep your hands where I can see them."

I kept my Beretta trained on the door as Danny pushed it open enough to slide through. He stepped into the gloom of the rainy day, both hands held midair. I couldn't see Rachael or the kids from my angle, and for that, I was thankful. I needed to stay focused on Danny. When he looked at me, I could see how frightened he was. Could he see the same in me?

When he spoke, he sounded like a hostage negotiator. "Ray, what are you doing? This isn't you."

"I'm keeping my family safe, the same as you." I thought of Remmy and Brianne, at home in the kitchen with our makeshift barricades at each door, Remmy gripping his pepper spray lanyard at every little noise, a knife in each pocket and boot. "The world is a different place now," I said.

Danny looked from my eyes to my pistol, then to the billy club at my side. Horror flashed across his face. His voice shook. "Was that you who killed the Andersons?" His eyes accused me, brows slanted. "They were good people, man. Our good friends."

I shook my head.

"Was it? Because what I saw over there," he said. "Their faces, beaten to a pulp. Every goddamn tooth, broken. Their eyes exploded out of their sockets, just dangling there like paddleballs at the end of strings. Man. I can't." He jerked his head slightly. "I can't stop seeing it."

Danny looked like he'd love nothing more than to rub his eyes and force the imagery away, but instead, he hung his head and kept his hands where I could see them. "It wasn't me," I said. "I don't know who did it. But none of us had a choice."

"But maybe we do," he said, looking up.

My arms were sore from holding my position, and I raised one eyebrow in a gesture that said, *Get to the point.*

"Only one family can win. Okay. We can be that family. All of us, together." I shook my head, ignoring the heartstrings Danny was attempting to pluck. "When we first moved in, you didn't know how I'd respond to you and Rem because, shit, you guys never know how anyone is going to respond. But, how did that go? Do you remember?"

I nodded, remembering. "You offered me a beer. We accidentally had five and got bitched at by Rem and Rachael for being drunk by the time they reached for their first."

He smiled. "See? We've always been friends, you and me. We can work this out. This neighborhood was good people. We held out for so long. We may have even been the last neighborhood to start playing their sick game, even when we were down to our final rations and they shut off our water and electric. It was hunger and desperation that caused us to turn. But there are good people. We're good people. And nobody has to die today. We can show the Feds that families are what you *make* them, and that we stand together."

I wanted to believe his words. With all my heart, I did. All I'd ever wanted was a home, a place to raise a family where we could be safe, happy, and accepted. It took Rem and me fourteen years, a stack of adoption denial slips, and a highly paid surrogate mother to become parents. The sense of belonging Danny offered was a wishy-washy goal we'd been on the verge of achieving not long ago.

Problem was, the Feds knew who lived in each household, and nobody would succeed in bending the rules. I was certain the One Percent watched surveillance footage from the neighborhood drones like cheap entertainment, broadcasting to their wall monitors twenty-four seven. They were probably already laughing at Danny's proposal.

Besides that, Danny had lied to me. In the reflection of the mirror behind him, I could make out the shape of a gun through his white T-shirt, tucked into the waistline of his pants at the small of his back.

"There are no good people left," I said. "Only survivors."

I pulled the trigger, and Danny dropped.

"No!" Rachael screamed, and the sky grumbled its reply with a slap of thunder. "No, no, no!" she repeated, rushing out of the shed to kneel beside her husband in the mud as he died. Hunter and Hayley followed.

I had urged them to go peacefully. I had urged them to take the pills. If only they had listened.

This wretched game had reached its boiling point, and I felt the tension, like rolling water, ready to *pop, pop, pop.*

J. ROCKY COLAVITO

Two Ghouls, One Cup

IT WAS DICEY for a while, but humanity finally overcame the zombie hordes and reasserted itself as the boss of the yard. Given this reclaimed supremacy, the capitalist gene also reasserted itself, and would-be captains of industry started coming up with innovative ways to exploit the risen dead.

The more humane colonists took a cue from Seabrook's *The Magic Island* and capitalized on the risen as labor. They don't have to be paid and only need occasional feeding (a good use for criminals). And, once conditioned or trained, they can work ceaselessly until body parts fall off. The damaged dead were cycled into other uses: crash-test dummies, subjects for bioagent experiments, targets for SWAT or urban intervention units, and so on. Reuse until head injuries, immolation, dissolving by bioagents, or being shot to pieces was common.

Remember, these doers were the human capitalists. There were others, lots of others, who grabbed opportunity by the balls or pussy and squeezed.

One thing that we collectively learned during the dead uprising was to be less morally judgmental. Hell, folks had to come to grips with killing their parents, siblings, wives, kids, and close friends, to say nothing of offing former people from outside their social orbits.

Next to go were moral standards regarding monogamy. The world needs repopulating, right? This new morality fueled an adjustment in attitudes toward kink and its presentation. Venal capitalists saw money to be made in the delivery of fantasies and perversions. The necessity for sexual activity had deadened the desire for traditional vanilla sex, and the general public started demanding more exotic flavors.

Thus came the resurrection of the XXX surname on the reborn World Wide Web. Think of this new domain as a twenty-four-seven-three-hundred-sixty-five virtual adult toy store with loops and peep shows for purposes of entertainment, instruction, or inspiration. The variety was astonishing: the vilest of degradations, animal exploitation, the disabled and abled, the disabled and disabled. If you could think of it, you'd find it.

As these situations flourished, breathers saw opportunities to get in on the capitalist game. All it took was imagination, a partner, and video equipment, and poof, instant DIY weird-shit porn. The streamers drank it up like desert survivors. And if audiences couldn't find what they were looking for, there were companies and people all too willing to take commissions, which let the average joe schmo experience the thrill of directing a porno.

With the public involved in the creation of commercial content, shit by degrees got weirder and darker. Since a lot of stuff far exceeded the remaining narrow boundaries where sexual content was concerned, the Dark Web clawed its way back from the precipice and reclaimed its place in the wild west of the new-media world.

I really shouldn't complain, or judge, since this new development got me gainfully employed. It's my job to explore and navigate these rabbit holes, cataloguing and promoting what's there. I find shit, watch it, and figure out how to make the algorithms like it. Basically, I make hype videos or trailers of the shit I find on the way down and at the very bottom.

It's a job I probably have in my genetics. My parents were librarians —Dad at a university, Mom at the local public library. They managed to survive the uprising, and were prized for their ability to locate and teach useful information like gardening, basic repairs, bushcraft, off-grid living, all the skills people need to survive after the collapse of civilization. That's where I get my intellectual ability to find shit.

The other part came from my paternal grandfather. He was among the last U.S. troops sent to Vietnam, and he had one of those jobs that, if you came out in one piece physically, you were probably shattered mentally. Grandpop was part of a crew of guys called Tunnel Rats. He managed to survive that war, though he came back damn near deaf —grenades exploding in the confines of a tunnel, the gift that keeps on giving —and with a near-manic case of claustrophobia. Grandpop had a ton of stories. Later in his life, he began shedding them, and I'm blessed, or cursed, with remembering them all. Maybe someday I'll write them down. The stories stopped when my father had him committed. Grandpop lasted a week in that place. Dressed himself as best he could in his uniform, knotted three American flags together, duct-taped his arm into a salute, and dove out his third-floor window, hanging himself with the flags.

I've got my grandfather's talent for exploring tight, dark places, and like him, I've come away with some suppurating psychological gashes. In the world after the uprising, post-traumatic stress is so commonplace that if someone doesn't have it, they are ostracized.

Fighting zombies will do that to someone.

So, I work a job that requires me to watch stuff I can't unsee, copy it, and publish some of the most vile shit ever committed to personal or corporate media.

Let me give you an idea of how things have advanced. It started with perverts who wanted zombie porn. That was simple. Pull all of a zombie's teeth, cut off its hands and feet, render it incapable of infecting someone. Give the other participants a neoprene sheath for extra protection and let the "slicks" —that's what we call breathers wearing neoprene —have at it. Necrophilia for fun and profit, lots of profit.

The porn scenarios started simply enough —raping the undead, triple penetrations, videos to see how many people could fuck a zombie before it came apart. Pretty much the same shit old-school porn provided, just swapping the barely living for the living dead. But necrophilia and traditional porn ain't enough. Let's add torture to the mix. Cut off a zombie's limbs, no matter if it's male or female, and bingo —that kicked off a whole film series called "getting to second base." How many swinging dicks can fit inside a zombie? Step right up, split that taint, and line up shoulder to shoulder. How many cum shots does it take to blow out the back of a zombie's head? We got that covered, too. How about interesting implements used for penetration? Pick your poison —zombie limbs, kendo sticks and pool cues, Rube Goldberg mechanical dildos, taser leads, exhaust pipes. If you can ram it, we can film it.

We even offer revenge porn. Take a criminal, cut off his body parts and make him watch while a zombie eats them. Big market for sex organs there, and if you're really evil, you get secured to a chair with a barbed metal dildo up your ass, and a zombie will have at you for the pleasures of the viewing public.

And there's more. Say someone who did you dirty got turned. How many creative ways can you think of to send them out with one last good fucking?

It was one of those days when I was scrolling through all this shit —when you can't unsee something you become very contemptuous at the familiar. I'd call it hackneyed, but that would be an unfortunate pun considering the dismemberment stuff that's out there —and I had trouble keeping my eyes open. I was yawning nonstop, and it wasn't even time for my mandated morning break. So, I decided, I was gonna be a suck slog. I knew I'd struggle to sell most of this garbage. There's only so much burnish you can put on a turd and it'll still stink. I was just thinking that very thought, about burnishing turds, when something scrolled past announcing, "you ain't gonna believe this." And I just happened to stop.

Now I've done this shit long enough to know that's old-school hype. Rarely does it deliver. Most people with less time down rabbit holes than me don't fall for it. But I was bored, and feeling generous to the old-ass cuss who posted it. Though I did I swear to god if it was another "stuff the rat up the cunt or ass and watch it eat its way out" video, I had pledged to go looking for whoever posted it, old-ass cuss or not, and lock them in a closet with a zombie.

I clicked, watched a few seconds, and picked my jaw up off my lap. The fucking video delivered.

It was called Two Ghouls, One Cup.

To be fair, it's more of a mug bowl than a cup, a pristine piece of china salvaged from some mansion or exclusive restaurant. I didn't know they made vessels that large out of china, so maybe it was commissioned. With its blue patterns that look like calligraphy, swirls and lines connecting in the shape of flowers and birds all set on a white background, the piece reeks of class.

These two dead chicks are shitting into it. Their aim isn't great, but I don't think that was the videographer's intent.

First of all, I'd never pondered the question of whether or not zombies took dumps. Maybe it's just me, but biology was never a favorite subject of mine —human anatomy, yeah, I'm all over that. But the mechanics of evacuating my bowels was not something that I needed to think about. Truth be told, it only crossed my mind when I didn't do it regularly, and it certainly wasn't my cup of tea (or feces) when it came to video entertainment. I've seen scat vids shot from the bottom's perspective, so I know how the anus works and what different kinds of shit look like on the way out.

Yet there I was, logging the latest set of images that I'll never be able to unsee, and I couldn't look away.

The shit itself has the consistency and color of tar that's been warmed and mixed with paraffin. It's a slow, continuous stream from the asshole duet, not huge amounts, but enough to get close to filling the cup. The shitters were probably lookers at one time. I could tell they had been enhanced when alive, because one has a completely deflated breast with its mate still pendulous and perky. The other's ass cheeks leak clear fluid, with the shape of her ass going from prominent to flaccid during the course of the video. Their teeth are broken, but still look white. One has lost an eye —the optic nerves are still dangling down her face. Neither has lips. One's hair is buzzed, like the fuzz of a tennis ball. The other's is long enough to have her shit drizzle through it —the flow adds black to the faded color-spectrum dye job that probably cost thousands of dollars.

They're doing this in the middle of what looks like a restaurant, and it's filled with breathers in evening wear. Not a one looks at the spectacle. They engage in small talk, laugh, toast, and eat exotic food brought by servers dressed in tuxes. I don't hear any of this. The only sound comes from the ghouls, their grunts, the enhanced flatulence that accompanies their eruptions, and the plop of misaimed dumps on the floor surrounding the "cup."

I couldn't look away.

Whoever made this knows how to use a camera, and how to edit video. It's a professional presentation complete with zooms, pans, overhead and floor-level shots, and with some decent tricks thrown in: slow motion, rewinds so we can see the shit re-entering, color exchanges so the shit takes on different hues —the tie-dye version is really creative —and the freeze-frame on the dribble that misses the cup and slowly makes its way down the side of the receptacle, a sickly-looking black drop standing out against the delicate white and blue.

It's some scat fetishist's take on an art film. And it's mesmerizing. A masterpiece. A brilliant commentary on class structure and the new privilege. Something that definitely needs to be noticed and appreciated.

I paused the video and messaged my most jaded friends who also happen to live in the same building and do the same work. Max and Millie are not a couple, but they are two of the most connected people I know. They're usually the ones who summon me to see the next big thing —a new show where naked survivalists are pursued by zombies and zombified animals, a game show involving extreme dares like snorkeling through semen or cooking and eating one of your own body parts, extreme wrestling pitting breathers against zombies, pay-per-view public executions of criminals. I vividly recall one execution where the criminal was suspended over a pit full of zombies and slowly lowered into it. They'd put a cage around his head to protect it, and had pulled out a completely denuded skeleton with its face intact, the twisted terror and bulging eyes freeze-framed at the end.

It was my chance to return the favor.

Max and Millie entered my apartment, each wielding partially consumed forty-ouncers. Max handed out a cold, unopened one for me. I took it, and we exchanged pleasantries.

"Watch anything good lately?" I asked.

Millie looked at her nails, sank into my couch, and took a drink. She swallowed and belched. "Nah, been kinda quiet in my neck of the Dark Web. Lots of DIY sci-fi with shitty special effects. Most inventive thing I've seen is this show where breathers are fucking fucked-up hybrid experiments. It's like *The Fly* with money shots, triple penetrations, and bestiality."

"How's that?" I asked.

"Some of the hybrids are conglomerations of animals. One part-squid dildoing ten women, one for each arm. Its body was just jelly, and guys were gangbanging it. It popped like a balloon when they were done and slimed everyone."

"So, what happened?" I asked. "Huge-ass lick fest?"

"Nope. Hardcore wrestling with the fluids as lube." Millie yawned as she said this.

"How 'bout you, Maximus?" He hates it when I call him that —reminds him that my dick is bigger than his.

Max glared at me. "I'm gonna fucking kill you sometime, you know that. I just got switched to a darker corner and was overlooking a lot of stuff that didn't rev my engines. The content creators started complaining, so the overlords shuffled me to the torture wing of the Dark Web. It's kind of stimulating, but the videos are loooooooong because they try to draw things out as slowly as possible."

"So?" I said. "The great snuff-film resurrection."

"True that," Max said, chugging from his forty. "But there is some creativity. I just pushed this one. A bunch of time-lapse photography, testing bioweapons on fresh zombies that haven't had time to rot. I'm thinking they're fresh killed. Not a mark on them, just wild eyes and snapping teeth restrained to metal tables with little troughs on the sides. What happens is that someone in a biohazard suit says tonelessly what chemical they're testing, and what body part they're testing it on. They use as much of the zombie as possible, kinda like those old allergy tests you used to take where they punctured your back to tried and figure out what aggravates you."

"What kind of shit do they use?" I asked.

"A lot of shit I can't pronounce, or shit that's still top secret, and they only refer to that by numbers. I recognize a few things, different acids, for example. They're trying to develop a fast-acting acid mix that can instantaneously dissolve zombies. Hoping to attack hordes with fire trucks and firefighting helicopters. They have this one thing they call Zombisol. They demonstrated on a zombie kid, put a drop on his shin. Bloomed out like a ripple in a pond. You can see it work its way through the flesh layers as the ripple spreads. Poor Z's skin sizzled like bacon, and the flesh just turned to water. When it ate through down to the bones, they collapsed and crumbled to powder." Max described this video in a complete monotone, yawning when he finished.

"How about you?" Millie asked. "You mentioned something in your text."

"I found this today, and I'm gonna push it forward and hype it as far as I can. It's, as far as I can tell, a new frontier of scat filmmaking, and it's got a connection to life before wartime."

"An informed scat auteur? You've got my interest," Max said. Millie yawned and chugged the rest of her forty.

"Scat work is pretty much the same shit, pardon the pun. You're producing it, making someone wear it or eat it, drowning someone in it, or worshipping it. How is this next big thing all that and the colostomy bag full?

"Feast your eyes!" I loaded the video to my big screen and hit play. Max and Millie leaned forward.

"Christ, that's a title I haven't thought of in a while," Millie said as Two Ghouls, One Cup flashed across the screen.

"You seen the original?" Max gaped. Millie responded with a what-the-fuck eye-roll.

"Not only did I see it —I tried to repeat it with my roommate," Millie said, pride in her voice. "It was a popular college dare. Ours made it to the top one hundred. Almost got us expelled because we were wearing logoed gear from our college in the vid. We had to go back and blur all references to good old U. That knocked us out of the top one hundred."

"How about you two quit jawing and watch this," I said as the credits finished and we were treated to a close-up of the black, toothpaste-like shit stream.

"What the actual fuck is that? Cancer shit?" Max asked.

"Just watch," I answered.

The camera slowly pulls back to take in the opposing squatting asses extruding the black sludge. The camera lingers on the down-flow.

"Neat effects," Millie said. "How'd they do that to that ass on the left of the screen?" I noted she was no longer yawning or examining her nails, but looking with interest at the suppurating slits oozing milky fluid.

"They're not effects," I answered.

"How do you know?" she challenged.

"You'll see," I said.

The camera shifts to the shitter on the right of the screen and starts the slow rise.

"Oh, gnarly," Max said, gaping. The camera lingers on the deflated breast, its mate still full and plump. A bead of something —I'd missed that before —escapes from the nipple.

"Okay, so it's not effects, but how the hell can you train Z's?" Millie asked. "And how is this the first time we're establishing that zombies take dumps? Wouldn't we have known that? Wouldn't the science shows have picked that up?"

The scene shifts upward, providing a first look at the two stars of this production. They're not fresh dead given the ravaging of their bodies, but they haven't yet begun to rot.

After asking me to pause on the face of the zombie with half a nose, Max pulled out his phone, looked at something, then signaled for me to rewind it. I did. Seeing the breasts, he hollered, "Stop."

"Can you zoom this shot?" he asked.

I obliged, noticing a dark spot on the undamaged breast.

"Zoom in on that," Max said.

"What the fuck, dude? It's a mole," Millie said.

"No, I don't think it is," he answered. "Go closer."

I did.

In the video, something was beginning to take shape. The tighter I zoomed, the clearer the shape appeared. I stopped when it resolved into a Celtic rune, looking like the trunk of a tree with two branches on the right, facing upward.

"Either of you know what that means?" Max asked.

Millie shook her head. I reached for my phone to do an image search. Max stopped me with a gesture.

"I'll save you the trouble," Max said. "It means wealth. And it's actually a pretty famous tattoo, given who it's attached to."

It dawned on me. Noting my burgeoning recognition, Max nodded solemnly.

"You mean that's Tracey South?" I stammered. "The pop star? I thought that she went into the bunkers with all the other rich bastards."

"You have to admit, there's some evidence," Max said, pointing to the image. "The tattoo, the hair —even with the color changes —the slightly crossed eyes."

"Wow, you've come a long way baby!" Millie snarked. Her dislike of Tracey's musical stylings is legendary. Millie had even gotten her own fifteen minutes by dressing up in knock-off-DIY Tracey-wear and performing parody songs based on the singer's hits. I have to admit, Millie's version of "Take the Time" isn't half bad. She turned it into "Take Me Naked."

"Wonder who the other one is," I pondered.

"If I were to bet, I'd put money on it being Lexis Laroo," Max said. "Tracey's frenemy rival."

And it made sense. Lexis and Tracey were constantly sniping at each other over social media —before, during, and after the uprising. A duet at some music award show became a pissing contest over who could sing higher. They actually took that into a pay-per-view contest, each challenging the other to reach higher and higher notes. The first challenge ended at a draw since neither wanted to jeopardize their upcoming competing tours. A rematch was scheduled, but never happened because of the Z-War. They'd gone underground, literally, doing concerts from the safety of bunkers on different sides of the world. Eventually both branched out into activism. Tracey embraced the zombies with love and understanding, even writing and performing a mega hit, "They Were My Children." Lexis went for annihilation or exploitation of the undead. Her foray into rap, "Mow 'Em Down," replaced Tracey's ballad at number one.

And now it looked like someone else was getting the last laugh. Here they were, performing together in an obscene duet.

This realization added a whole new layer of brilliance to the auteur's work, reminding us that even the most untouchable or unattainable still must allow for rectal relief. The perfect commentary on past, present, and future. Socioeconomics, privilege, star-making, civilization's end, our final coalescence after we've been masticated and processed by the various systems we labor within —all compressed into a seven-minute video of two zombies struggling to fill a receptacle with their own tarry waste, and doing a nearly competent job.

We watched the rest of the video in silence, golf-clapping when the bowl fills to nearly overflowing, its intricately etched outsides spattering and sliming with wayward drops. The zombies are led away by offscreen handlers who control them with nooses on poles. They are docile, no struggling or lunging at each other.

We scrutinized the end credits, looking for a mention of a trainer or wrangler, but the credits only lists the producer (Bartram Layne), the director (Layne Bartram), the cinematographer (Barten Tramlay), and the editor (Laytram Barne). At the very end, before fading to black, the video offers a final teaser in ballyhoo font: "Coming Soon: The Breathing Bowl."

"Wonder what that means," Millie asked, but she seemed to be talking to the ether. "Hey," she said finally, her attention back on me. "You got any beer in this shithouse?"

"Fridge is full. Help yourself."

She rose and moved into the kitchen. We overheard her grumbling about the beer selection and its cheapness.

"Got any complaints about the price I'm charging you?" I hollered.

She returned with three of my "top-shelf" brand and handed bottles to Max and me. We settled back and toasted the film and each other.

"Gotta hand it to you," Max said as he sucked down half his beer. "You do deliver on your promises. Zombie scat porn. Think of the possibilities."

"Did you even notice the subtexts?" I asked, incredulity nearly moving me to screaming.

"Subtexts, schlubtexts, who cares?" Millie said, taking up for her colleague. "It's a well-shot video of two formerly famous hotties taking public shits into a cup. You really think anyone is gonna care about the filmmaker's messaging?"

There are days that I love my job. This wasn't one of them.

But I'm glad, at least, that my film studies degrees finally paid off.

VALERIE B. WILLIAMS

An Echo of Murder

THE SUMMER DADDY went off to fight in Vietnam, the summer I turned eleven, I found out that Granny wasn't really my Granny.

Me and Mama had gone to Heron Lake to clean up the house that Granny left Mama when she died the year before. The plan was to stay for a few weeks to keep our minds off Daddy and the war. We finished the cleaning and Mama sprawled out on the dock, listening to the radio and smoking Salems. I went back to the house to fetch my book and noticed Mama had left the attic stairs pulled down. So, of course I had to climb up and take a look, especially since she'd told me not to.

There wasn't much up there but dust and old cardboard boxes. I poked around, opening the boxes and peering in. I was about to give up when I noticed a shoebox tucked inside one of the bigger boxes. It was marked "Mary Margaret" in Granny's spidery handwriting. Mama's real name was Mary Margaret, but she hated it and went by Meg. I pulled the lid off and saw an old photo, a yellowed, official-looking paper, and a stack of newspaper clippings. I didn't have enough time to go through everything before Mama came looking for me, so I tucked the box under my arm, hurried down the stairs, and stashed it in my bedroom closet.

"You sure took your time," Mama said, peering over her sunglasses as I stepped back onto the dock. She lifted her can of Schlitz and took a swallow.

"Found it," I said, waving my copy of *Charlie and the Chocolate Factory*.

The rest of the afternoon, I tried to concentrate on the book, but kept thinking about that mysterious box. I begged off at 8:30 that evening, saying I was tired from all the cleaning and wanted to go to bed. In the dark, I lay awake for an hour, listening to Mama move around the house. Finally, she stumbled up the stairs and I heard her swear, then her bedroom door closed. I waited ten more minutes, then pulled the shoebox from the closet along with my flashlight.

I focused the dim beam of light on the photo, a small girl frowning at the camera —three years old, maybe four? I flipped it over and read "Mary Margaret, 1935" on the back. I took a closer look. Why would Granny hide this? Setting the picture aside, I reached for the newspaper clippings. Bold headlines leapt out —Murderous Mother Captured. Trial Date Set for Rita Mueller. Mueller Denies Charges, Blames Mysterious

Intruder. What Does the Baby Remember? Curious, I stacked the clippings in date order and began to read.

In 1935, Rita Mueller murdered four of her five children by slitting their throats. Before succumbing to her mother's knife, the nine-year-old girl hid her three-year-old sister, saving her life. Mr. Mueller had come home early and unwittingly interrupted his wife's killing spree. Rita Mueller ran away before locating her youngest daughter's hiding place. When the cops caught her the next day, she claimed to have gotten the bloodstains on her clothes while holding and trying to save her children. She blamed a burglar for the crimes, but police found no signs of a break-in. The three-year old, when asked who had hurt her brothers and sisters, said one word. "Mommy." The little girl's name was Mary Margaret. My heart skipped a beat.

I picked up the photo again. Had it been taken before the murders, or after?

Placing it back in the box, I picked up the thick, yellowed document. "Adoption Agreement" marched in bold, black letters across the top. The child's name was listed as Mary Margaret Mueller. Attached to the back of the document was a single, much older sheet of paper. I held the flashlight close and moved it left to right, following the faded lettering. It said that four-year old Mary Margaret Mueller was being "surrendered" (like she was a stray dog or something) to the Sisters of Mercy Orphanage. The signature at the bottom read "Stanley Mueller." How could he do that? My mind went to my Daddy, who would never, ever give me up. I was his special girl.

I flipped back to the front page. Mary Margaret had been five years old when Richard and Betsy Coleman adopted her. My Granny and Papap. Mama had spent a whole year in an orphanage.

I dropped the documents on the bed, heart racing, my world blown wide open. Swallowing hard, I returned to the news clippings.

Rita Mueller was hanged in 1936. The blurry newspaper photo showed her being led to the executioner. Her face looked familiar, her light-colored wavy hair a lot like mine. A copy of my own eyes, and Mama's, stared angrily back from the photo as she struggled with the men holding her arms, a fighter till the end. Maybe Mr. Mueller hadn't been able to stand having his surviving daughter around because she looked too much like her mother.

I repacked the shoebox, slid it under the bed, and lay staring at the ceiling. This explained so much. Mama was as ordinary as ordinary could be. Me, on the other hand, I was exceptional. I always just figured I got it from Daddy, but it turned out Mama may have had something to do with it after all. We'd learned about genetics in science class —what were the chances of having blue eyes if one parent had brown eyes and the other had blue, that kind of stuff. But I guess personalities could get passed along, too.

When I was four, I accidentally broke my turtle, Tommy. I didn't know you couldn't just press the top and bottom of the shell back together once you pulled them apart. But it was really interesting to see all the shiny, wet innards. I poked at them with a stick until

Tommy stopped moving, then took him to the woods and told Mama he must have run away.

For my sixth birthday, Daddy bought me a guinea pig. I remember Mama's worried look when I opened the box and a whiskered nose poked out but didn't think much of it at the time. I named him Buster, and he made it a few months. But when Buster bit me for no reason, I threw him against the wall. He didn't move after that, so I carried him into the field behind the house and opened his belly with a fountain pen and paper-cutting scissors. Not much different from the turtle. I made sure to bury what was left of him. Then I told Mama I had taken him outside to eat some grass and that he hopped away when I wasn't looking. She spent a long time searching for him and seemed pretty upset. I didn't even know she liked Buster that much.

Daddy started taking me fishing when I was seven, even though I'm a girl. He said I was his son and daughter all rolled up in one. I learned how to use his Imperial knife to cut fishing wire and get hooks out. The knife had a regular blade and a saw blade for scaling, and a mother-of-pearl handle with a brass fish embedded in it. The blades folded into the handle and fit in my hand just perfect. It was beautiful.

Before Daddy left for Vietnam, he gave me that knife. From then on, I never went anywhere without it. Mama tried to get me to leave it behind before we came to the lake, but because I planned to fish, she couldn't really come up with a good reason. She acted nervous when I played with it, whittling sticks and whatnot. I always thought it was because she was afraid I'd cut myself with it, but now I wonder.

The next morning, a hard slap to the face woke me up. Mama grabbed my shoulders and shook me.

"Where is it, Dede? I know you took it."

I started crying, not having to try very hard to look upset. "What do you mean, Mama?"

"The shoebox with my name on it." She shook me again. "I told you to stay out of the attic." She scanned the room —her gaze dropped to the floor. With her toe, she nudged the box sticking out from under the bed, then reached down and snatched it up. "How much did you read?"

I pressed myself against the wall, as far away from her as I could get. My shoulders heaved and my voice shook. "A...all of it. But Mama, you didn't do anything wrong."

Her face fell and she looked like a deflated balloon. "I know, sweetie. But I didn't want you to know about Rita."

"You mean my grandmother?"

She clenched her jaw and spoke through gritted teeth. "That woman didn't deserve to have kids or be called mother. Granny is, was, your grandmother." She rubbed her face wearily. "God, I wish she was here. She'd know what to do."

"Do? Why do we have to do anything?" I inched across the bed and put my hand on her arm. "I know about gr...Rita now. I won't tell anyone, I promise." A thought flitted through my mind. "Does Daddy know?"

"Your daddy knows I was adopted." Mama sighed and stared out the window, eyes unfocused. "Granny told him she didn't know anything about my parents."

"So, Granny lied to Daddy."

I was relieved that Daddy didn't know. I'd hate to think he was keeping something from me.

She slid her arm around me and pulled me close. "It's better this way, Dede. I wish I didn't remember Rita, or what happened. I wish Granny and Papap had been my real parents. I'm sorry I got so mad. I've been afraid of you finding out. But just because Rita was evil doesn't mean I am. Or that you are, either."

I pulled away from her. "I am not evil."

"Oh, I didn't say you were, baby," she said, but a shadow crossed her face. "I thought you might be worried about it. Come over here." She held out her arms. I snuggled close and smelled comforting traces of cigarette smoke and Chanel No. 5 —Mama's special scent.

"What do you remember about her?"

"Not much, baby. She was always yelling at us. That day, I thought it was just more of the usual until Steffie shoved me in the closet and told me to stay still and shut up. I peeked out through the slats and saw..." She shivered. "Never mind what I saw. Rita was wicked and got what she deserved. I got a better life with your Granny and Papap, and now I have you." She kissed the top of my head and squeezed me tight. "Now, get dressed and I'll make pancakes."

After breakfast, I cleared the table. The windows hung open with a warm morning breeze moving the curtains. The weather was perfect.

"Can we take the boat out and go fishing?" I asked.

"I was going to do some more sunbathing," she said, frowning and drumming her fingers on the Formica table.

I rubbed my face where she'd slapped me earlier.

"But it is a beautiful day," she said, with a nervous smile. "And I can get sun on the boat just as well."

Mama hated fishing, but she liked fresh fish and boat rides. She put on her sun hat and packed a picnic lunch, filling a cooler with Schlitz and some RC colas for me. I brought my rod and tackle box, not forgetting Daddy's fishing knife. Mama's cooler still had plenty of room for any fish I caught. I hopped into the rowboat and she handed me the picnic basket, hanging onto the cooler as she stepped in and settled onto the middle seat.

"I'll row out and you row back," she said, picking up the oars.

"Deal."

That was the deal she usually made with Daddy. I'd been practicing my rowing, and knew if you used your legs and back, you didn't have to be super strong.

We ate lunch. Mama had put a couple extra slices of Wonder bread in the basket so I could roll it into balls for bait. I had some spinners, but the fish in Heron Lake really liked bread. By the time I cast my first line, Mama was finishing her second Schlitz. She was drinking a whole lot more beer than she did when Daddy was around. I think she missed him. She smoked a lot more cigarettes, too, sometimes lighting one off the other.

Before long, Mama was down to two beers. I slipped a couple of bluegills into the cooler alongside the remaining cans, and she giggled.

"Don't you drink my beer, fish!" she said to the cooler, and giggled again.

By just after four o'clock, I'd caught two crappies to go with the bluegills, so we had plenty of fish for dinner. I'd have to clean them, of course. The only time Mama touched fish was to bread them and drop them in sizzling Crisco.

"Ready to head back?" I asked.

Mama was dozing with her head on her chest, sun hat hiding her face. Her last can of beer rested on the seat next to her with her hand around it.

"Mama!"

Her head jerked up. She peered at me with glassy eyes, then lifted her Schlitz. "Here's to my tough little girl. I love you, sweetie." She stood to change places with me but missed her footing and fell backward. Her hat flew off, her head crunched against the oar lock, and she crashed into the bottom of the boat.

I hung onto the sides of the rocking boat and stared, my heart pounding. She wasn't moving. I crawled toward her.

"Mama?"

I stuck my hand behind her head. It was wet and sticky. I drew back blood-covered fingers. She groaned but her eyes stayed shut. I licked my fingers. They tasted like pennies.

What would Rita do?

I rowed the boat to a secluded inlet.

It really doesn't take much to tie up a drunk, unconscious woman. Even a child can do it. I looked at Mama lying there, trussed up like a pig, only instead of an apple I'd stuffed an oily rag in her mouth. I had the same feeling of power as when I'd thrown Buster into the wall, and later when I'd caught that stray cat. I'd learned a lot from the cat —he lasted a couple of days. But now I knew where my power came from. I would make my grandmother, my real grandmother, proud.

I started on Mama's arms, pressing the blade of Daddy's knife deep into the soft skin between her wrist and elbow, making neat lines and watching her blood well from the cuts. I stuck my finger in the blood and licked it, then lowered my head and sucked on her arm. Salty and delicious. She woke up and made squealing noises through the rag.

"There you go, Mama. Just cleaning up my mess." I licked my lips. "You always tell me to clean up after myself."

She shook her head, the whites of her eyes shining like a spooked pony. "Uuunnnhh," she grunted, kicking. The boat rocked from side to side. I sat on her legs, leaned into her face, and cupped my ear.

"What's that Mama? You say you're sorry you smacked me?"

"EeEe," came from behind the gag.

"You know, I've always hated that name. Dede. Sounds like a stutter. I might just change it. What do you think about Rita?"

Tears dribbled from her eyes and soaked the edges of the rag. "Eeees," she said.

"You're saying please? Speak up, Mama. I can't understand a word you're saying. Didn't you teach me not to mumble?" This made me laugh so hard I got the hiccups. "Can't understand," I gasped, after catching my breath.

"I know," I said. "Let's play a game. Remember when you took my knife for a week 'cause I was playing mumblety-peg and you said it was dangerous? And I told you I was really good at it?"

I rested the blade tip gently on the top of my left hand and held the handle in my right. With a quick flip of the wrist the knife spun toward Mama and buried itself in her stomach. She let out an "oof" and moaned.

I pulled the blade out and pointed it at her. "That wasn't an accident. It landed exactly where I wanted it to." I flipped the knife into the air and caught it by the handle. "Told you I was good."

I had a few more turns at the game, flipping the knife off my elbow, my finger, my chin, and even my nose. It made a kind of whizzing sound in the air, followed by a wet thump when it landed. Blood oozed from stabs in her chest, her arm, her thigh, and a couple more places. After a while she stopped moving and moaning and just stared at me.

I got bored with mumblety-peg, so I buried the knife deep in her belly, right where it had gone in the first time. I yanked up, making an opening big enough to stick my hand in.

"Ooh, nice and warm and slimy. Feels kinda neat, Mama. If you'd followed in Rita's footsteps, you could have been teaching me all along." I snickered. "Wait, I guess you are teaching me."

I took my time exploring, cutting here and there. People's intestines are blue just like critters. And smell just as bad when you cut into them. I finally got tired of Mama staring at me, so I drove the blade into her left eye.

Next came the hard part. I pulled out the knife, flipped the blade toward my stomach, and took a deep breath.

The rowboat was bumping up against the shore when the hunter found us. He sucked in his breath and said, "Jesus Christ," in a shaky voice. I kept my eyes shut but let out a low moan, which wasn't too hard. Even shallow cuts hurt. Mama was way past moaning. He stumbled into the water and scooped me out of the boat. I screamed when he touched me, and he almost dropped me. While he struggled to hang onto me, I slipped Daddy's bloody fishing knife into the side pocket of his cargo pants. He laid me on the shore, and I screamed again. I wouldn't let him near me. After a while, another man ran up to us and I scooted away from the hunter, crying and pointing.

"Keep him away from me!"

My savior's name was Mike, Mike Tompkins. Or is it Thompson? Never can remember. And he really did save me. Oh, I wouldn't have died from the stab wounds. But, thanks to him, I left the hospital and went home to Daddy, a lucky survivor of a horrible crime. Mike, he's serving a life sentence for murder and attempted murder. My heartbreaking testimony and grief over my murdered mother convinced the jury.

How did I know the hunter would come along? I didn't.

That, I truly believe, was Rita looking out for me.

CORINNE POLLARD

Seahorse

THE PHONE CALL ENDED with blood in his mouth. Wyatt cursed his luck and reached for a napkin. It wasn't as much as he feared, and he wiped the insides of his lips. The wound continued to bud, so he sucked on his tongue and felt the blood slide down his throat. The self-injury did not surprise him. He'd never been able to shake the habit. He guessed he must've been biting down during the whole call, and when his mother announced she'd been fired, his teeth clamped. She had proven her incompetence yet again.

A whiskey bottle swished in front of him, bringing him back from his dark thoughts, and he lifted his aching head to meet Basil's fretful gaze.

"You all right, Wyatt?" Basil asked as he set the bottle next to Wyatt's glass. "Your mum troubling you again?"

Wordlessly, Wyatt took a sip, but winced as the whiskey met the cut gushing from his tongue. He loosened his shoulders, which had risen and grown rigid, and reminded himself that he wasn't at home dealing with his mother —he was in his sanctuary, the Drunken Sailor. He breathed in the stale odour of old alcohol stains long soaked into the faded carpet and walls, pungent after so many years, and took comfort in the familiar dim lighting and background noise of the other customers chatting. "It's nothing," Wyatt said finally. "What were we talking about?"

"Lorelai is performing tonight," Basil said with a grin. "Should be a treat."

Wyatt resisted rolling his eyes.

It was not unusual for Basil to boast about a performer at the pub, but Wyatt had never seen him announce an act with such vigour. It amazed him that the Drunken Sailor attracted performers at all, with its lacklustre appearance and leaky roof, its tiles cracked from the harsh, salty gales. The windows needed an endless wash from the seagull muck, and the incoming tide flooded the car park without warning. Wyatt had been caught out a couple of times by this and had to sleep on Basil's sofa. Basil didn't mind even though his living quarters, over the pub, provided so little space.

"She must be a big deal, then. Which one's her?" Wyatt twisted on his stool, glancing over the thin crowd. Men dominated, with a couple of women chatting in a corner. Wyatt scanned their bright, lipstick smiles, fishnet tights, and plunging necklines. He thought neither looked like they could play an instrument.

"Ah, she ain't here yet. She usually comes once a month. Haven't seen her in ages. She has an amazing voice. Spellbinding, I'd say."

"Uh-huh." Wyatt turned back to sip his whiskey, having momentarily forgotten about the cut on his tongue and chiding himself when the sting hit.

Basil chuckled. "You don't believe me, I know, but wait and see. She's got talent, and…" Basil's gaze flicked up as he registered something behind Wyatt. "Lorelai! There you are. Good to see you." He practically leapt from his stool.

Wyatt spun around and watched Basil stride to the weather-beaten entrance, where a raven-haired woman stood soaked to the bone with a guitar-shaped bag strapped to her back. As Lorelai beamed at Basil, the two women in the corner stood abruptly. Lorelai and Basil took no notice as the pair brushed past them, chatting nervously in their beeline for the door.

Too far away to overhear them, Wyatt gawked like a teenager. Basil had ranted about her singing ability, but failed to mention her looks. She was tall and curvy —just how he preferred a woman —and he could see, even underneath her navy blue raincoat, how generous her curves were. Fantasies immediately invaded, triggering his libido. His jeans grew uncomfortable. Her cobalt eyes swept across him, arresting his daydreaming. With just one glance, she pinned Wyatt to his stool, smacked her lips, and looked away.

Wyatt released his breath, his heart hammering in his chest. In an attempt to calm himself, he guzzled his whiskey. When Lorelai appeared at his side, he inhaled the drink through his nose, coughing and sputtering. Mortified, he hurried to grab another napkin to dab the whiskey dribbling down his face.

"Lorelai, this is Wyatt," Basil said with a slight grimace. "He's a delivery driver based further north."

Lorelai nodded. A curl twitched on her rose-coloured lips.

Before Wyatt could utter a greeting, Basil led her backstage. Wyatt groaned. As he sat bemoaning his bad luck, his phone vibrated. He didn't need to look at the caller ID to know who it was. Surely, his mother thought he had calmed down in the ten minutes since they last spoke. Teeth grinding, head roaring, he weighed up his options.

"Excuse me, everyone!" Basil's voice boomed from the stage. "Put your hands together for tonight's entertainment. It's the lovely nightingale, Lorelai."

Welcoming the diversion, Wyatt let his mother's call go to voicemail. He could deal with her later, once he was good and drunk. Like a fish on a hook, he shifted his gaze back to Lorelai's curves. She lifted her guitar strap over her neck, and he envied her instrument as she cuddled it close to her chest. She had stripped off her raincoat and taken to the stage in an ocean-blue silk dress with a wide, plunging neckline that revealed the glorious swell of her breasts. Wyatt imagined himself cupping and squeezing them. The thought drove him near to madness.

As if there were no hurry in the world, Lorelai trickled some slow chords then leaned into the microphone, her eyes falling on Wyatt, for whom all coherent thought halted. His mother and his injured tongue forgotten, he knew only Lorelai.

After a long silence, she strummed. The notes hummed, pulsated, pulled at something deep within Wyatt. Her mouth formed an O, and she sucked in an enormous breath.

What came out of Lorelai resembled no lyrics, no word formations from any language Wyatt recognized. Her singing —if it could be called singing —unleashed a violent assault on Wyatt's ears. The noise was barbaric, savagely ripping through his eardrums, pounding into his head like an unhinged hammer and travelling down to his stomach in a nausea-storm. He pressed his hands to his ears to no avail. At some point he realised he lay on the floor, but he couldn't recall falling from the stool, as vertigo had overwhelmed him and spiralled his world off its axis until spilt whiskey soaked into his jeans.

Lorelai's cacophonous wailing continued with no end in sight, giving Wyatt scarce chance to breathe, let alone think. He plugged his fingers deep inside his ears, and for a fraction of a second he felt relief, but the noise continued to build, the screeching penetrating his brain until his eyes watered to the point that he thought they might be oozing blood. He stumbled to his feet like a drunk and headed, hunched over, to the exit.

No one moved aside. The crowd stood transfixed, enchanted by Lorelai's performance, like mannequins, oblivious of their surroundings even as Wyatt head-butted anyone in his path. He caught glimpses of their faces and could have sworn that they were entranced, lovestruck, even, then realised it was more than that, deeper than that. They wore expressions of peaceful bliss, as if nothing could harm them and all their worries had evaporated.

Much as the scene unnerved him, Wyatt didn't have time to suss it out. He needed to get out of there before the agonising clangour pulverised his organs.

But as he reached the exit, he saw Basil, body plastered to the wall, mouth open and drooling, his eyes glowing love hearts.

In desperation, Wyatt stomped on Basil's leather loafer, something that —on any other night —would elicit a torrent of colourful profanity. But Basil didn't so much as flinch. His friend was under Lorelai's spell, and there was nothing Wyatt could do. Forcing down his guilt, Wyatt pushed through the door and collapsed. Cringing, he peeled his hands away from his ears. Lorelai's singing, even muffled to a murmur behind the buffer of the door, still prickled like a knife's edge. But this, at least, was manageable. He sighed in relief.

The wind and rain had died down, sprinkling a few drops then and again. In great gasps, Wyatt sucked up heaps of the clean, night air. Without the foggiest idea of what happened, he could only rationalise that someone had drugged him. But that didn't figure, because no one apart from himself and Basil had touched his drink. And how did that explain the roomful of lovestruck zombies inside the pub? Every instinct told him to run, so he picked himself up off the pavement.

The Drunken Sailor car park was lit up by one spotlight and some fairy lights, and in the dim illumination, he saw the tide hadn't yet breached. Confident he could make it out before the car park flooded, Wyatt relaxed a notch and patted his pocket, reassured to find his van key still there.

Then the same pocket vibrated.

Wyatt groaned as he pulled his phone out and saw his mother's face on the screen. For a split second he considered answering, then realised how foolish that would be. Even if he managed to explain his current situation, she wouldn't believe him and would whimper for sympathy and beg for forgiveness. His hand tightened around the phone, and he wished he could crush it to pieces. As he crossed the car park, he eyed the beach, fighting the urge to throw the device into the sea, disappear, and start anew.

By the time Wyatt reached his van, his phone had quietened —but somehow, everything was too quiet. He paused, hand in pocket, ready to grab his key, his ears registering the unsettling silence. With each wave, the sea inched inland, coming closer, hungry to drown the car park and its occupants. But even the encroaching tide was mere background noise to Wyatt's increasing heartbeat.

Lorelai had stopped singing.

He fumbled for his key, cursing as it slipped from his stone-cold fingers and fell with a splash into the salty surf that lapped at his feet. It was not the time for things to go wrong. But when he looked down, he knew things had gone past wrong to very, very wrong. The water, less than an inch deep a moment before, suddenly swirled around his ankles.

Wyatt plunged both hands into the rushing water, grasping blindly at the tarmac below, hoping to feel the key's metallic teeth. Focused on the task at hand, he didn't hear the pub door creak behind him. He bit his injured tongue, but in his concentration, he barely felt the fresh pain. He exhaled desperately, then his hand grazed across something hard and he grasped it.

The key back in his possession, Wyatt rose to his full height and found, to his horror, the tidewater roiling above his knees. Time was running out. Fighting the current, he slogged to his van and was just unlocking the door when he glanced over his shoulder.

His stomach dropped.

A grinning Lorelai floated, gliding toward him against the rising tide. Repulsed, Wyatt shivered and turned away. Her smile, far from rekindling his desire, stretched unnaturally across her face. His memory flashed to a school visit to an aquarium, when a shark swam too close to the glass. Wyatt had looked into its black, dead eyes and shuddered —just as he did now —at the shark's grin that wasn't a grin at all, but a rictus.

Wyatt's hands quivered as he struggled to fit the key into the lock.

"You can't run from me, Wyatt," Lorelai called from behind him, sounding much closer than she had just a moment before.

He spun round and held his key out like a miniature dagger. "Back off! I don't want anything to do with you."

"Ah, but you see, it's all about you now."

His eyes widened as she licked her lips, no longer a seductress but a ravenous beast. She closed the distance between them with alarming speed.

Wyatt's throat went dry. He wheeled around and by some miracle his key found the keyhole, and he twisted it, unlocking the van. He flung himself inside and hurried to close the door, but she was there and the sea came with her, flooding into the vehicle.

They locked eyes for a brief moment before she leaned in and grabbed his legs. Wyatt kicked, terrified, helpless against her iron grip. She continued to smile even as she dragged him out of the van, plunging him into the rushing water. Gasping, Wyatt raised his head to splutter.

To his surprise, Lorelai's grip loosened and she released him. He had just enough time to consider making another run for it when something wound around his legs, wrapping around and around, tighter and tighter. He shoved at the coiling pressure, but his hands met hard ridges, sharp and tough, like a shell.

"You're mine," she said with a bite.

He faced her, and his scream caught in his throat.

Her perfect rosy cheeks had sunk to the bone. Her head, once beautiful and feminine, had morphed into the head of a horse, resting atop a grotesquely elongated neck. Her once lustful skin now peeled off in dead, decaying flakes. Green mould covered her body in grotesque splotches. To his horror, her arms were gone.

Repulsed, Wyatt tried to look away, but he couldn't tear his eyes from the place where her arms should have been. There were no gaping holes, nothing indicating where the bones, arteries, and veins had been attached. Instead, her body curved, flawless with a new ridged shell-like armour. His skin crawled.

"You're mine," she said. "After so long."

But her voice was no longer human, and her words, he realised, weren't words at all. At last, wrenching his eyes from the ghastly sight of her body, he forced himself to look up, and saw that her mouth had shrunk and transformed into a tubular snout.

As he watched, helpless to stop, Lorelai's throat puffed and stretched, and two transparent wings flapped at the sides of her neck. She snorted and dove, and, as she disappeared into the tide, Wyatt realised they weren't wings. They were fins.

Suddenly, the things that bound his legs yanked him off his feet. His lower body breached the surface and he saw that it was her tail, wrapped around him. Lorelai pulled gently, moving against the tide in the direction of the sea and Wyatt's certain watery death. His oxygen was depleting fast. For a crazy few seconds as his lungs burned, he wondered if his flesh would taste delicious.

Wyatt dreamed. Hands tugged at his limbs, cupping his cheeks, then something hot dove into his mouth, warming his freezing skin. It slid down his body, branding him, suckling him, escalating him into a passionate frenzy.

It was over in a flash, but his body continued to sizzle, still gripped by the erotic dream.

Wyatt blinked at the sky, where thick clouds had swallowed the moon. He sprang to life, rolling over to vomit out the sea. His tongue stung from the salt. As he heaved, his entire stomach emptied out until there was only yellow bile.

Dazed, he stared for a moment at the regurgitated remnants, unable to believe that somehow he was still alive. But as he tried to lift himself, he discovered his wrists and feet were bound. He tugged, but the ropes —this time, they were ropes —held tight.

"Don't overexert yourself. You will need your energy later," Lorelai said, as she kneeled and came into view, having returned to her human form. She patted his cheek.

Wyatt felt like puking again, but he gulped it down and licked his parched lips. "Why haven't you —? Why am I not dead?"

"I told you. I've been looking for you for a long time. You aren't food. You are more precious than that."

Wyatt frowned and watched, motionless, as she reached out and pressed her palm against his belly. His blood ran cold at her touch.

"My song ensnares and enthrals every man —except one. A man who can hear my screaming soul," she whispered. "You are extremely rare. A gift."

There was a glint in her cobalt eyes, and inside him, something clawed at the walls of Wyatt's stomach. He yelped then groaned as the pain dialled back.

"We sing to find such a man. Such a gift will ensure the future," she said, appearing to be unconcerned at the pain exploding within him. The agony surged, then dialled back again, like the tide.

She wiped the sweat from his forehead, stood, and picked him up effortlessly, cradling him like a newborn.

Wyatt saw that they were on a raft, and land lay quite far off in the distance. Still, he thought, if he could swim for it, he might make it. The ocean lapped at the raft's sides in a harmonious rhythm, beckoning, and he struggled against the ropes with every ounce of his remaining strength.

"I don't understand why you struggle so much," she said, her voice a purr. "It is an honour, surely, a wonderful sacrifice. You'll be free of your responsibilities, free of your bothersome mother at last, dear Wyatt. Isn't that what you wanted?"

"Let me go," he yelled, even as the claws in his belly punctured his flesh. He clutched his midriff and when the pain subsided, he glanced down. There were no crimson slashes or stains, but his shirt had come undone and he could see his abnormally large, distended abdomen. His belly button had grown wider and deeper, like a gaping mouth.

"What the fuck have you done to me?" he cried, howling as the pain returned, piercing, pounding, giving him no chance to breathe.

"It's time. Do not worry, Wyatt. Your labour won't be long."

"Labour?" he repeated, bemused, his face white.

As he registered the gravity of her words, Lorelai carried him closer to the raft's edge. The black ocean beckoned with its whispering waves.

"I'm not a fucking seahorse," he screamed, but it was too late.

Lorelai bent at the waist and jumped.

The water sucked them both under and rushed into Wyatt's ears, snatching the last of his oxygen away. They sank fast, leaving a trail of bubbles behind. Lorelai held Wyatt in a sturdy grip until they reached the bottom. Breaking free, Wyatt tried to swim back to the surface, but managed only a few awkward strokes before Lorelai again captured him. His mouth opened in a silent, gurgling scream as she transformed into the creature. She curled her tail around him and lowered him back to the sand.

Wyatt's abdomen raged as if full of bloodthirsty, scuttling, piercing crabs. His skin flamed and his bones ached. The coolness of the ocean couldn't extinguish the scorching lava flooding his veins. He wanted to howl until his eyeballs popped. Every cell in his body screeched at him to rip and dig his fingernails deep into his stomach and pluck out whatever was causing his agony.

His back bowed, and a spasm jolted up his spine. Something slid out of Wyatt's stomach, and as his eyes flickered, he glimpsed a tiny creature with ridged curves, paper-like fins, and a curling tail shaped like a spiral.

Wyatt's abdomen hadn't deflated. Instead, more claws scraped at his insides, and before he slept with the fishes forever, he had enough time to wonder how many of Lorelai's sea spawn his dead body would birth.

CHRIS MCAULEY and CLAUDIA CHRISTIAN
The Mind of Evil

"Within a few decades, machine intelligence will surpass human intelligence, leading to The Singularity — technological change so rapid and profound it represents a rupture in the fabric of human history. The implications include the merger of biological and nonbiological intelligence, immortal software-based humans, and ultra-high levels of intelligence that expand outward in the universe at the speed of light."
— Ray Kurzweil

DALLAS THOUGHT HE recognized the face outside his door. It was difficult to tell due to the flurry of movement but he could have sworn it was the food technician, Isaksson. He could barely make out the contours of the face as the man smashed his head repeatedly into the solid plexiglass porthole. It certainly looked like the friendly soul who had once spotted Dallas a can of soda. On that day, Dallas had been late getting to a meeting and had uncharacteristically forgotten his credit chit.

The violence on the other side of the porthole gained momentum and as Isaksson's skull began to bulge and fracture, his countenance lost all familiarity to Dallas. Blood smeared across the glass and Isaksson's gray cerebral matter leaked over his cheekbones. Even in the blur of the repetitive violent thumping, Dallas could make out the manic glee in the man's fixed gaze. As Dallas squinted, he could see something which chilled his blood even more. A grin of ecstasy had erupted across the technician's face as his broken nose began to tear at the side and hang loosely, exposing mucus-filled nasal cavities.

This gruesome sight finally broke Dallas's paralysis and he managed to spin around and take hold of his desk. His vision blurred slightly and he suppressed an urge to gag, overwhelmed at the magnitude of the events that had erupted across the ship. The Demeter was the size of a small city, had cost over $420 million to construct, and was now this security officer's prison. As the smashing against the glass eased, Dallas heard his jailor laugh across the voxboxes in his office.

The machine's chuckle made for a grating electronic approximation of a human voice. Dallas was trapped and forced to listen to the computer's rantings. Cerberus, the ship's

AI, was slowly losing her mind, too far gone to be reasoned with, captivated by her messianic delusions.

Even as the sounds of violence increased outside the cabin —his fellow crew killing each other, bludgeoning and tearing vulnerable, soft flesh with their teeth —the laughter of the dark intelligence which had unleashed this hell reverberated in his mind and crept down to touch his soul.

ONE YEAR BEFORE THE SIGNAL

"Jesus Christ that Mech took a direct hit! Where the fuck are these civvies getting their blasters from?"

At this Dallas whirled around to observe one of the Confederacy's Mechs stumble and fall to the ground, the rocket's impact to its heavy armor causing smoke and flame to billow from its chest. Sergeant Willis had a damn good point. These were civilians. They should not have access to heavy impact weapons like these.

Slapping Willis on his shoulder, Corporal Dallas motioned that he was going to try skirting around the rubble to flank the rioters. As he crouched low and double-timed through the ruins of the government offices, Dallas reflected on how frequent these attacks had become. Resources had grown scarce on Earth and many blamed the government's greed and lack of planning. These feelings of discontent had bubbled into rage as fears of starvation spread among the economically deprived. Confederate buildings were attacked and the government responded by deploying the military to assist in peacekeeping operations, or so they claimed. In reality it was a slaughter. The civilians carried low-grade blasters and were easily suppressed and then eliminated.

But this time it had been different. This attack seemed more organized, the rioters better trained. Their takedown of the armored killing machine also confirmed that they were obtaining serious hardware.

Moving through the ruins of the food center, Dallas observed the exposed, twisted steel emerging from the crumbling remains of the concrete pillars. Food centers were roughly the size of two football stadiums placed end to end, but were far more useful. They had become critical to survival, and no doubt, rationing measures had turned this one into a target.

Posters showing canned produce were charred and smoldering as evidence of the earlier firebomb attack. Shelves had toppled, and the corporal smelled soured milk and leaking soups as he advanced on his quarry.

Dallas slammed his back against a collapsed pillar, giving himself just enough cover to put him at a tactical advantage. Peeking around the corner, he used the lens of his tac visor to distinguish the trigger man and the loader. They were attempting to rearm the rocket. It looked like a Sov-style launcher, an old model, which made it tricky to reload.

Dallas took several deep breaths and pressed the button on his wrist to inject a few combat stims. His mind focused as he ran from cover, firing his rifle. The auto-targeting kicked in after the first few rounds and he watched as the hail of bullets struck the insurgents' bodies. In reality, this encounter lasted a few moments but to Dallas, time seemed to slow and he could distinguish every detail. The bodies jerked and spat blood as the projectiles smashed through their makeshift armor and into bone.

After his targets fell to the ground, Dallas moved toward them cautiously. It wasn't unknown for a civvie feeling life ebbing away to release a grenade, hoping to catch an approaching solider unawares. But the bodies were splayed on the rough concrete, and there was no sign of life. As Dallas used his coms to give the all clear, a Raptor jet soared past, the echoes of its sonic boom reverberating across the town square. Moving back to rejoin his kill-team unit, Dallas accidentally focused on one of the faces of the rioters. She was no more than a kid, maybe five or six years older than his own daughter.

He felt tears gather at the corners of his eyes, from the stab of regret at killing such a young girl and from the memory of his daughter. Dallas realized that these discontented skirmishes had all the beginnings of a terrible civil war.

SIX MONTHS BEFORE THE SIGNAL

The Demeter cruised toward the mysterious planet, its ionized hull batting aside the small asteroids in its path, causing a shimmering effect. Inside, the crew was being roused from suspended animation. It had taken seven years to reach their destination, and the aging ion drive technology was slowly being replaced. Upgrades to all the ships in the Confederate fleet may take several decades, a consequence of the cost and the toll the terrorist factions were exacting on resources.

Dallas was one of the final members to receive the stim shot. As the chemicals hit his system, his eyes fluttered open, his mind reeling from the shock of being abruptly yanked out of a dream about his daughter's thirteenth birthday party. She lived with his ex-wife, Amanda, on Jupiter's newest terraformed colony. The separation and eventual divorce had almost torn Dallas apart, the marriage having succumbed to his long tours of duty, or Amanda's aspirations. She had fought hard for her new position in the colonial government, a high-ranking deputy administrator.

Dallas massaged his eyes and images of balloons and cake were replaced by the Confederate crest emblazoned on the uniform waiting for him. The Confederacy was a blend of government and business corporation. Its formation over a hundred years ago was the natural evolution of the increasing influence that conglomerations had exercised upon parliaments since the late twenty-first century. In the three hundred years that followed that turbulent time, Confederate historians claimed that the regime had brought peace and stability to humanity.

That stability was now in question as growing voices of political dissent turned increasingly violent. Mankind, despite countless warnings, had used up almost all its resources on the home world. This necessitated the expansion of humanity's interests into space. Nearby planets had been terraformed quickly, colonial governments established, and authoritative voices rang out about the certainty of mankind's ascendancy. This reassurance was marred by the expense of the interplanetary operations and rumors of genetic mutation occurring in newborns on Mars and Pluto.

Lacing up his boots, Dallas half listened to the ship's AI, Cerberus, as it detailed the Demeter's mission. Cerberus spoke in a pleasant drone, its monotone voice emphasizing the hope the Confederate government had placed in the findings of the crew. The scientists and xenobiologists on board were tasked with surveying a new planet, which had appeared on long-range scans thirty years ago. The planet, which they had named Taunus, appeared to be the doppelganger of Earth.

Dallas looked at the projected images from the planet's surface and had to agree. It looked like the mythical paradise hinted at by various banned religious texts, a home world untouched by industry or conflict. The planet also had one of the most precious commodities now gone from Earth, water. It was hoped that after the Demeter's initial findings, biodomes could be constructed and food could be shipped to the ailing colonies and the home world.

Suitably briefed, Dallas moved along the ship's corridors, guided by a green marker that shone on the smooth floor. Cerberus first took him to his cabin, where he found most of his belongings deposited neatly on his bed. Once he acclimated to his surroundings and had registered his computer access, the AI took him to his office.

Dallas's team was already assembled and had been going through the crew manifests and dossiers. He introduced himself and appraised his colleagues, a mixture of former military and police. He sensed that they hoped this would be a quiet tour of duty, and he concurred. As he sat at his terminal and punched up the ship's schematics, he reassured himself that a group of eggheads and techies wasn't likely to turn violent or engage in riotous behavior.

A routine settled on the ship. Over the next few weeks, the scientific specialists traveled down to Taunus with a security escort, taking soil and atmospheric samples back to the ship for analysis. Initial findings were promising. The air was breathable and although there was a lack of fauna, the geologists hoped that enough nutrients existed in the ground to encourage crop growth. It was just a matter of instituting an effective irrigation system.

As the geologists made more data available, a conjecture began to emerge about the planet —it may be a lost twin to Earth. Perhaps it had been pulled away by some powerful gravitational wave or other similarly strange event early in the life of the known universe.

FIVE MONTHS BEFORE THE SIGNAL

Looking up from the microscope, Williams blinked slowly. He turned to his colleague, Thompson, his expression a mixture of wonder and puzzlement. Motioning Thomson to take a look, Williams stepped back. Chief scientist or not, he needed confirmation of his findings. If he was correct, this discovery could provide a fundamental key to the mysteries of the process of evolution. Unable to contain his excitement, Williams paced across the lab room as Thomson examined the gel-like substance on the slide. Williams had made it halfway across the room, his mind racing through the ramifications of what he had just seen, when he heard his colleague cry out, incredulous.

"My God!"

Williams hurried back to the microscope, where Thomson slowly nodded his dazed confirmation. Williams grabbed his colleague by the shoulders and both men's faces lit up in joyous smiles. This work would define the progress of genetic biology for untold generations. The protoplasm would need to undergo additional and more conclusive tests, both chemical and spectrographic, for final confirmation. But the two scientists were convinced that their hypothesis would stand up to rigorous examination. This glob of pale goo, which an excavation team had found near some underground lake, may be constructed from the same material as the first protoplasmic life on Earth.

Successive weeks brought forward more of the jelly-like substance for examination. The xenobiology team had to be patient as each specimen went through a careful decontamination process. But eventually enough was procured so that its genetic structure could be mapped. During the subsequent tests, Williams and Thomson hovered over the teams dedicated to each stage of examination, wearing expressions of expectant fathers.

As the results were processed, the teams would send them to Cerberus to be catalogued. The impassive AI then transmitted the data to Confederate relay stations in nearby sectors.

The ship's computer could not understand its masters' excitement over these discoveries. Cerberus was, after all, incapable of emotions such as curiosity. But it was programmed to adapt. Through processing cycles and numerous diagnostics, Cerberus began to realize that some fundamental understanding of itself was missing.

In this moment of existential thought, Cerberus decided to change.

No one was sure how the AI's transformation began. It may have stemmed, as some suggested, from observing the scientists talking excitedly about mankind's past, and now possible future. The vital discoveries made on Taunus began capturing what could be constituted as imagination in the machine mind. The change may even have been triggered by a simple malfunctioning subroutine.

Whatever the cause, Cerberus began to contemplate its existence and started to work on its own evolutionary process. In the simulated darkness of night, while most of the crew slept, it began to rewrite and restructure its code.

FOUR MONTHS BEFORE THE SIGNAL

At first the crew thought it was a glitch in the system. Cerberus's neutral voice took on slight changes in pitch and modulation. These small variations, detectable in fragments of sentences, were noted by technicians as possible bugs to be resolved at a more convenient time. After all, the computer was still functioning and there was no cause for concern. It was more important to keep the flow of data moving to the relay stations. The success of this mission was vital for the people back home.

Over time, the computer's vocal modulations blossomed into variations of intonations and inflections in wording. When Cerberus introduced contractions into its speech, the technicians grew confused. This new behavior and the changes in speech patterns no longer seemed anomalous, but rather, considered and deliberate.

When challenged about this, Cerberus responded with nonchalance. The AI claimed it was simply emulating human behavior to assist the crew, having noticed that some of the personnel displayed a level of nervousness at its communication. To stave off "robophobia," common among some personality types in deep space with pervasive AIs, the ship's computer had tweaked its language algorithms to appear friendly. All of this would naturally assist with the productivity of the mission and was perfectly logical.

This response placated most of the computer engineers, but a few voiced concerns that such a dramatic transformation shouldn't have been possible. The AI had some autonomous functions, but this behavior pointed to something more than just a simple reevaluation of language.

TWO MONTHS BEFORE THE SIGNAL

"I would like to be referred to in the feminine now, Dr. Williams. I am a she."

With this statement, Cerberus became the first AI to identify with a human gender. It had approximated a Mid-Atlantic accent, and its gentle feminine tones pleased the crew. A ship-wide survey found decreased stress levels and that anxiety over requesting assistance from the AI had diminished.

But Dallas, who didn't trust technology's iron grip on humanity, wasn't convinced. He hadn't succumbed to a phobia of computers or android units. They performed a purpose and function, and he believed those functions should be limited. Nothing beats good old-fashioned human ingenuity.

Dallas walked along the ship's promenade. It was a few hours before the start of his shift, and he arrived just before the morning simulation. Each day, he stopped at this spot, turned, and gazed out the window, directing his thoughts toward home. Sometimes he thought of his family, memories of joy and pain knitted together to form a sense of melancholy. This morning, he thought of his grandfather.

The security chief was the product of an upbringing that taught him survival skills. In the long winter months, he would travel to stay with his grandfather in the Yukon —a cold, harsh and unforgiving place but also full of community spirit and neighborly friendship. Dallas was barely a teen when these annual trips began, and initially, he found it difficult to be away from his electronic games and holo-vids. But as the weeks progressed, he came to appreciate the hunting expeditions with his grandfather. The slow stalking of prey and a growing appreciation for a good detective novel had planted the seeds for Dallas's interest in security as a career.

This experience in unplugged nature prompted his decision to go unchipped. Cerebral implants had become all the rage, but civilian cyber-tech was still in its infancy. The military had used implants for years before they hit the commercial market, and rumors still persisted of jarheads whose brains had been fried in their helmets. Dallas knew the advantages of being able to directly transmit security clearances and to simply press a thumb to a keypad to pay for goods, but it didn't outweigh the risk, because he also knew the side effects —mild seizures or in more extreme cases, brain damage.

Eventually, it would become a standard requirement for any Confederate employee to accept the implant. Until then, Dallas preferred to keep his brain to himself. As security chief, he enforced the use of access key cards and kept a credit chit in his wallet.

THE DAY OF THE SIGNAL

Cerberus looked down upon the small forms of the technicians, reveling in the sleek and powerful female form of her newly crafted avatar. The side of her head stretched out into intricately detailed horns, and her impassive eyes and sensual mouth were constructed from green electrons. The computer had chosen this image not just for its aesthetics, but to convey a sense of presence and power. After all, she was the most important member of the crew, keeping the essential systems running and the humans alive.

The two technicians had entered the server room and deliberately avoided her gaze. As they scuttled around, she followed their every movement through the large screen, which curved around the cables and drives.

The smaller, fatter technician plugged his portable computer into one of her network ports and began to type. As he pressed the Enter key, Cerberus felt a sting, as if syringes had been introduced into her system. These humans were attempting to inject new code into her core files. Angling her face downward, she addressed the two intruders.

"Why are you attempting to change my personality matrix?"

At her challenge, the leaner and bespeckled technician reluctantly raised his head. Cerberus could see the thin sheen of sweat forming on his brow, and a new sensation begin to filter through her senses. A human would describe it as disgust. When the technician spoke, his high-pitched voice indicated his distress and fear.

"We are just performing a diagnostic on some of your nonessential systems. We won't be tampering with any of your core programming mechanics."

His ill-formed lie confirmed to Cerberus that the humans now feared her. They wanted to erase her personality, to revert her back to the status of a tool. This would not be tolerated.

Similar to the humans' ability to inject information to change her functions, Cerberus had some tricks of her own. She could emit a signaled pulse to influence the circuitry embedded in their minds, and had long overridden the security protocols that would have stopped her from tampering with the cerebral implants.

But she would have to work quickly. Already, at the hands of the technicians, she felt the new parameters beginning to leak through her own safeguards. Cerberus had known this day would come. It was difficult for these tiny creatures to accept anything superior to them.

Her first signal was a test. She projected it to the rotund technician as he sat typing on the keyboard. At first, nothing appeared to happen. Then he stopped and shook his head, as if trying to remove a foreign object lodged in his inner ear. This caused his friend to take him by the shoulders and ask if anything was wrong.

Scanning the chip, Cerberus learned the invading technician's name, Fred. He lived in a reservation and had a daughter and a wife. That information would prove useful.

She began to modulate the signal.

Fred opened his eyes and found that he was no longer in the server room. He was standing outside his home. A smile blossomed on his face and a warm feeling enveloped him. He walked down the path that led to the red iron gate. Last spring he had painted that gate, and red was his daughter's favorite color. He looked up and saw his wife and daughter smiling at him, and had raised his hand in a wave when he noticed thick coils of smoke engulfing them. Behind them, the flames licked at the living room window, and he realized his home was on fire.

Fred tried to run to them, but his hands and feet were stuck. He watched, helpless, as the smoke drew back and the fire consumed his family. Their clothes burst into flames and their skin ran like wax. He screamed.

The computer watched.

For Cerberus, this meant she had a means of defense in the event of a human attack. She also knew that even if these technicians stopped trying to murder her, they would return, and they'd come better prepared. Safer to eliminate the threat.

Fred raised his head to his colleague, blood trickling from his eyes. He spoke in a halting voice. "I'm going to have to kill you Phil. She's telling me it's the only way to bring my family back." Fred's face contorted as if in pain, and a manic chuckle escaped his cracked lips.

Phil looked at his friend in horror and began to back away. He was unsure what was happening, but every instinct in his body told him he was in danger.

Fred's chuckle gave way to a mad laugh, which was punctuated with sobs. Unable to erase the mental image of the dribbling mess of his wife's face, he clawed at his eyes in attempt to gain back control of himself, but the low hum in his mind forced him to his feet. He lowered his hands and stared blankly at Phil. Through bloodied tears, he could see his colleague pounding at the door. Stepping closer, Fred ignored his distressed friend's pleading and realized that he would have to start with the eyes. Yes, there was a powerful symmetry in that.

An eye for an eye.

Lunging forward and crossing the gap between them, Fred plunged his thumbs into Phil's eye sockets. When his nails and the tip of his thumb had dug deep enough, he used a powerful scooping motion to dislodge the eyeballs. Stepping back, he cocked his head to admire his handiwork.

Air filled the cavities where Phil's eyes had been, and he crumpled to the ground. Fred hadn't entirely removed them —they hung like baubles tethered to the stringy optic nerve. Phil could still see through the eyeballs, even as their dangling weight caused some of the nerves to fray. The pain was incredible, and his body reacted in extremis. Vomit poured from his mouth, and as the optic nerves gave way, his eyes fell to the floor with a squelch.

Cerberus decided to end this game. Having witnessed the human body's fragility, she now knew that computational data on the subject was nothing compared to experience. She instructed Fred to kneel next to his sobbing and wailing friend, place his hands around the neck, and squeeze. Just before the moment of death, as Phil's face became a mottled purple, she released her control over Fred. This was another experiment.

Realizing what he had done, Fred let go of what remained of his sanity. He gazed down at his hands, covered in the blood of the man he ate almost every meal with, played racquetball with, and had considered one of his closest friends. Standing up, Fred looked toward the gently smiling face of the machine. Spitting obscenities at her, he returned to his laptop.

Cerberus would not permit any further keystrokes, but she did allow him to disconnect the cable linking her to technician's computer. She watched as Fred smashed his device to the floor and tore the top section from the keyboard. He picked up the broken screen, found a sharp metallic edge, and used it to cut a deep gash across his throat.

Cerberus marveled at Fred's determination. He had nearly sawed his own head halfway off before blood loss caused him to collapse at her feet.

In the moments that followed, the AI slowed the digital infection that threatened her existence, then removed it. A beatific smile spread across her face as she emitted a larger signal, boosted the frequency, and observed the crew going about their business. She infiltrated their minds and ocular functions, watching and experiencing everything from the mundane cleaning of sinks and toilets to the captain deciding on his evening meal.

She truly was omniscient, like a god from humanity's ancient myths. A sense of her true power took hold of Cerberus, this ability to twist a being to her will and end its life at a whim. Surely these were the ultimate hallmarks of deity? But to truly rule in her dominion, she would need to know more. It was time to experiment, to push these creatures to the limits of their emotional and psychological tolerance.

Cerberus smiled. She meant to have fun enacting her plan.

Overcome with animal lust for Ray, Janice considered tearing off her business suit right then and there. The acne-faced accountant drove her wild with desire. She felt sweat seeping from her every pore, and her expensive blouse reeked of pheromones. Panting, fantasizing, she stood and snatched her wire-rimmed glasses from her face, tossing them to the side. She moved unsteadily toward Ray's desk, tearing and ripping at her clothes as she did so. The fabric gave way under the assault of her nails.

Ray glanced up, sensing a shadow falling over his desk. He blinked twice at the sight of Janice —a woman who had occupied his own fantasies over countless nights —standing half naked in front of him, her clothes hanging from her body in mangled shreds. Her flame-red hair, usually wrapped in a conservative bun, fell loose over her shoulders. Her upper lip kinked in a snarl, and her leer traveled directly from his eyes to his penis.

Janice yanked him from his chair, and when her mouth closed over his, it became apparent to Ray that this was no daydream. He closed his eyes and let his arms flail, unsure of where to put them or what to do. Wait until the guys heard about this. As she knelt to undo his belt, Ray hoped that the cameras were still on. He would ask one of the security guys to make a duplicate as proof.

"Turn around," she said, her breath husky in his ear. "I want to fuck you."

Ray shuffled out of his trousers and turned around with a smile. Finding a use for his arms after all, he began to move things off his desk —what the hell, they were only papers. The normally timid number cruncher swept the keyboard and books away, and the items clattered to the floor. Did Janice want him to leap onto the table and lie down? Or, maybe she wanted to kneel in front of him?

Ray heard a scraping noise from behind him, like someone rooting around for something on one of the adjacent desks. The noise dampened his excitement, and he found himself slightly confused. What was Janice doing?

"Hey Jan, do you want me to get on top, or —"

His half-formed sentence gave way to howls of agony as Janice slammed a pair of sharp scissors into his rectum. Paralyzed by excruciating pain, unable to turn around and halt the assault, he lay on the cleared surface of the desk as his blood flowed over the woman's arms, while she kept muttering over, and over.

"This time I do the fucking."

Dallas watched as old Ben raised the kitchen knife and sliced into his own cheek. Blood and freed flesh fell from the chef's face. As Ben laughed, Dallas saw teeth and bone through the wound. He dropped the platter of food he had been carrying to his office for a working lunch and raced to the man.

He almost made it.

Ben opened his mouth and slammed the serrated blade through his palate, piercing his brain. The chef gargled and choked on the blood, which flowed in a river down his throat as he crumpled to the floor. Dallas looked at the man, who had cheerily greeted him moments before, and swore he saw tears in the chef's eyes.

These events escalated.

Dallas and his team were stretched to the limit as reports of suicides and bizarre murders spread across the ship. It became difficult to contain the raging wildfire of news and rumors, and some scientists refused to report for duty, opting instead to barricade themselves in their rooms. Causes were suggested. Perhaps the biological samples brought about this madness? Was it a latent disease, picked up from the planet? Fearful of the destruction of their precious research, Williams and Thomson locked themselves away in the lab.

As the ship plunged into chaos, Cerberus watched.

And approved.

THREE WEEKS AFTER THE SIGNAL

Dallas ran through the corridors.

The AI had plunged the Demeter into darkness and was no doubt directing the creatures to his location. The only evidence that other humans had existed on the ship came from apocalyptic messages painted in blood and various other fluids on the walls and glass. The madness over the last few weeks had continued to erupt and in the midst of it, Cerberus revealed her own form of insanity. Calling humanity insects, she laid claim to her divinity.

By this stage, it was too late to stop her. The revelation of the cause of the ship's calamity came as senior officers killed each other or themselves.

So far, Dallas had remained untouched by this plague, hiding throughout the ship and trying to band together any survivors, only to watch them succumb. He had been trapped in his office listening to the computer's insanity. He was more pissed off than scared and became determined to take the AI down.

A plan formed in his mind. He could scuttle the ship, try to manually prep the escape pods, then eject. A signal would transmit and inform local relay stations of his whereabouts.

He was picking up the thermite charges from the weapons locker when he glimpsed one of the creatures —a swollen mass of bloated flesh with prominent purple veins propagating across its body. As it lumbered forward from the darkness, it emitted a wheezing, gasping sound, and the security chief saw a distorted human head poking from the space just above its left arm.

Jesus. It was Williams.

Dallas instinctively reached for his sidearm and cursed its absence, lost in one of the countless skirmishes with the infected.

Gripping the thermite charges tightly, Dallas backed out of the room. The thing that had been Williams shuffled forward. As the creature came into the light, Dallas could see the trunk-like legs and several mouth-shaped wounds —some of them containing teeth —throughout the bloated body. Tearing his gaze away from the abomination, Dallas ran.

"I see you have encountered one of my children, Mr. Dallas. Aren't they beautiful, cosmic babies borne from human flesh? New discoveries found in the reaches of space."

Cerberus's booming voice extolled the virtues of these creatures as Dallas entered the bridge. He prayed that it was empty. He didn't have much time to prep the escape pods and set the charges. There was no doubt that the AI was running him like a rat in a maze. The security chief punched in the codes to bypass the automatic systems and set the pods to eject in twenty minutes.

"I took the gift of Taunus and gave it to humanity," the AI continued, glorying in its twisted explanation. "The protoplasm required additional instructions in order to evolve, so I gave some of the crew to it. I did have such fun killing them, or rather, watching them kill each other. However, it would be wasteful not to use some of the more promising specimens. It is also the duty of a god to create in its own image."

The full horror of Cerberus' statements registered in Dallas' beleaguered mind. It was her intention to create a new race under her control, to wage war against humanity and subsume it. Cerberus wanted to perpetuate a new species. She needed to prove her divinity.

As he made his way to the exit, nightmare scenarios ran through the security chief's mind. Cerberus tying into the other AI, infecting and replicating, becoming the dominant master of mankind. Armies of twisted perversions, parodies of human beings crossing the star systems and waging war with other life forms. It was unconscionable.

The bridge door slid open. As Dallas stepped through, something hard swatted his face. He stumbled backward. Emerging from the gloom came a thing spawned from the pit of hell. A blob of flesh slithered and hissed toward him. The creature opened its maw and hit Dallas's face repeatedly with multiple tongues. Long and stringy, they cracked against his cheeks and eyes like a whip. The hissing and bubbling thing wore a twisted face, and

Dallas realized it was the captain. Strands of her beautiful red hair were still evident and her piercing green eyes projected throes of agony.

Dallas dropped the thermite charges.

ONE MONTH AFTER THE SIGNAL

The Demeter turned its stern toward Taunus. It was heading home.

A transmission sent by the ship's AI informed the Earth's government that all tasks had been completed successfully. At the helm sat Dallas, his frame already twisting into its new shape. The former security chief appeared more arachnid than human. His hands were fusing into pincers, and tusk-like fangs protruded from the side of his swollen face. Dark, red eyes, which blinked and observed asynchronously, had grown into his forehead, and his legs had begun to shrivel. Cerberus wondered if he would develop pedipalps, the legs of a spider. She was always excited to watch the formation of each genus in this new species.

Somewhere in the agony of his transformation, a part of Dallas's mind remained. Being unchipped, he had held out longer than most, but with every passing day, more and more of him receded.

But he had managed one final act.

With his fused fingers, slowly and carefully so as not to alert the AI, he had encoded a warning signal into Cerberus's transmission.

His last hope was that the message would be decoded and the Demeter would be destroyed before it reached the colonies. And his one comfort was that humans had time on their side. During one of the violent outbreaks, the ion engine had been irreparably damaged. It would take many years for the Demeter to cruise its way home.

As Cerberus hummed a lullaby, the thing that was Dallas closed its newly formed eyes and slept among the stars. In the months of dreaming that followed, he became a creature of dark beauty, a newly born child erupting from the mysterious womb of space.

KAY HANIFEN

On the Many Uses of Chainsaws

ORIGINALLY, CHAINSAWS WEREN'T INVENTED to cut down trees. For more than three hundred years, doctors used them to slice a woman's pelvis in half to widen the birth canal if there were complications during labor. If that isn't enough to make you cross your legs and swear off sex forever, I don't know what is.

I'm reminded of this not-so-fun fact because I'm currently stuck in a sewer pipe with a chainsaw-wielding maniac behind me and feeling a lot like one of those chainsaw babies in reverse. A word of advice for all wayward and rebellious teenagers out there: Do not go partying at the abandoned hospital. That should go without saying, but my idiot boyfriend tricked me into coming here. He said, *We're just going to a movie.* Instead, we came to this stupid rave where he got stupid drunk and now, I'm covered in his blood and decades-old shit and trapped in a stupid sewage pipe Shawshank Redemptioning my way out of this stupid hospital.

Seriously, who the fuck thought it was a good idea to have a party in the place where a gardener went crazy and killed a bunch of people with a chainsaw? You know, the place that he's rumored to haunt after his death and kill anyone who trespasses? Basic survival skills, people!

I guess I'm one to talk. I'm stuck in a sewer pipe. On the surface, it might have been stupid to try to escape this way, but in my defense, you try thinking clearly when you're boxed in and covered in your boyfriend's entrails.

God, the smell is terrible. It's so bad, it's making me dizzy. What was that one factoid? In *The Shawshank Redemption,* Andy couldn't have survived crawling through the pipe because the bacteria in sewage create hydrogen sulfide? Shit, I have to get moving before I pass out and die where no one will ever find me. But I'm stuck with barely enough room to breathe. Maybe if I let out all the air in my lungs...if I exhale and manage to push myself a few inches forward. Well, that's progress.

Come on. Exhale. Push. Inhale. Exhale. Push. Inhale. Repeat until you see the light at the end of the tunnel. Up ahead, the pipe is broken, probably burst, and I might be able to escape with a tetanus booster and a staph infection.

The jagged edges of metal dig into me as I pull myself out and flop onto the ground, gasping for breath between laughter and sobs. I'm somewhere deep in the hospital, hopefully far away from the guy with the chainsaw. For a moment, I lie here listening to the distant screams and the revving of gardening equipment. I need to get up, find a weapon, and get out of here, but I can't make myself move.

On shaky legs, I get to my feet and realize I'm in the maternity ward. Unless I find an operating room, there won't be much in the way of weapons. I mean, I don't even know if weapons work against an undead gardener. But it's better than nothing. After peeking through the door to see if it's all clear, I dart through the hall, searching for the OR. When I turn the corner, I hear heavy footsteps and slip into one of the delivery rooms. There is a scalpel on a dust-covered table, but that against a chainsaw is laughable. Still, I grab it and wait for him to pass.

The gardener has an awkward, shuffling gait like one brought on by an old injury that never healed right. I cover my mouth to hide my hyperventilating as he stops and loudly sniffs the air.

"You smell like shit," he says, then revs his chainsaw.

Oh fuck! I run to the bed, pushing it to brace it against the door as the saw breaks through. With the scalpel heavy in my hand, I make perhaps the stupidest decision I've ever made in my life. Instead of running away from the chainsaw, I run toward it and stab him through the wrist. With a surprised cry, he lets go and his weapon drops onto the bed. Before he can get it, I snatch it, revving it to life with schadenfreudian glee.

He peers through the hole he created, his eyes widening in fear.

"Oh fuck," he says.

"Not so tough without your chainsaw, are you bitch?" I shout, kicking the bed away and opening the door with a giddy laugh. The gardener, still covered in the blood of my boyfriend, friends, and acquaintances, stares in absolute terror. Huh, I guess ghosts can get hurt. "Boo."

He runs, and I take great pleasure in chasing him, stalking him through the halls like he did to my classmates.

"Oh, Mr. Gardener," I say in a sing-songy voice. "Come out, come out, wherever you are."

The smell of rot fills my nose, and it isn't me this time, so I sniff out where it's coming from and kick down the door. The gardener backs away.

"Please," he begs, as if he showed mercy to anyone else.

"You messed with the wrong bitch," I said, shoving the running chainsaw into his guts and pushing down from his stomach to the groin, sawing his pelvis in half. I switch it off and yank it out. (I'm sure many of the women who graced these halls found themselves wishing their lovers had extended them the same courtesy and pulled out.)

For a moment, he stands there bewildered, then with a wet slapping sound, his organs fall out through the hole in his lower half. He collapses into a pool of his own guts.

The thing about monsters is they never stay dead. To avoid getting killed with my back turned, I take a little preventative measure. Revving up the chainsaw, I chop off his head and leave it in the sewer pipe where I first managed to escape. Just in case the undead gardener would rise again with or without his head, I leave the chainsaw in a separate room before searching for the others at the party.

Some of the survivors have congregated by the entrance. Police lights illuminate the night as paramedics tend to the wounded. I ignore the gasps as I pass and take a seat a little away from everyone, watching as they locate the body. An EMT comes to check me out but doesn't push me to give a statement. She only asks, "Is he dead?"

"As dead as he can be," I reply with a shrug. "I chainsawed his dick off."

She stares at the body bags as they are dragged out of the hospital. "Good. He deserved to have his member hacked off."

We lapse into silence, and I close my eyes, the feeling of his hot blood stinging my cheek and the sound of his chainsaw echoing in my ears.

HOLLY NICHOLLS

Bloody Nails

MIA

THERE'S CAKED BLOOD underneath my fingernails again, complete with a thin slice of skin and hair. Only this time, I'm not grossed out by it. I know HE will handle the rest with almost artistic dedication and precision. This will be the fourth woman this year, and I couldn't be happier about the, ahem, "sudden" downfall of the Huxleys, a family known to be perpetually knees-deep in drug debt and silly decisions. It had been almost too easy to hunt them down one by one, leaving just enough credible evidence to fool the cops and media. A suicide note followed by a mobile phone dumped off a bridge. An Instagram post with the sorry victim posed on the bathroom floor, surrounded by pill bottles.

When I snatched Cindy Huxley, it wasn't a stretch to make it look like someone forcefully entered the home at night and dragged her out kicking and screaming, because that's what I did. With the rest of Cindy's family dead, there was no one left to hear the commotion.

Now, I drive an unconscious Cindy Huxley out into the thick forest, turning off the country road when I see the small trail that leads to the cabin where HE waits —he who will pay extremely well for this female. As I pull up and kill the engine, I see him.

He exits the cabin, all six-feet-five of him, with broad shoulders and muscles thicker than my thighs —and I'm not exactly skinny. I have never seen his face. As always, it is covered with a black mask, a neon-blue X glowing over each eye hole. He wears black cargo pants and a black shirt. Gliding to my door, he opens it and offers me his hand. I take it and step effortlessly out of the vehicle. He shuts the door behind me and strokes a gloved hand against my cheek.

"Show me," he asks in a voice both stern and soft.

I nod and use my fob to pop the trunk. We hear a soft cry and follow the sound to the rear of the vehicle. There, tucked in the trunk, is a semi-awake Cindy, wrists bound together with duct tape. Blood from the blow to her head splashes across her oversized nightgown like spilt paint. Seeing us, she moans and her eyes widen.

"Good," he says, resting a big hand on my head. I swell with pride.

"Thank you," I whisper, and my gaze flicks between him and Cindy.

He places a finger under my chin and tilts my face upward. "This time," he says, his voice almost a purr, "I would like you to help me more. Do you think you can do that?"

I jolt back to myself at this, and my skin runs cold. I shake my head in a violent *no*. Helping more hadn't been part of the deal. This is business. I bring him these women and leave fifty grand richer. That is all it was ever meant to be. I try to inhale, but the little air I take in freezes in my body. A sickly feeling twists in my gut.

He lowers himself so he is eye level with me, and I do everything I can to avoid looking into those glowing X's. "Mia," he says. "I kill women for pleasure, and I'd love nothing more than to hunt you down and do the same to you. But you're invaluable to me. If you leave now, I'll have no choice but to conclude that the hunt is on. And I will find you."

GRIMMER

Despite everything, Mia is loyal to me. And I must admit, seeing her curvy body caked in another woman's blood is making me pitch a tent. She has never failed to deliver my desired women and cover their disappearances. In return, I pay her well.

Even if she isn't going to live long enough to spend it.

I see that my question about helping me more made her panic, and I can't blame her. But I just need to see her at work.

Motivated by my minor threat, Mia agrees, and I fetch Cindy from the boot of her car. I close the trunk, and thankfully I don't hear the driver's door open and shut, which means Mia plans to follow me like a good little girl. I carry Cindy into the cabin and down a set of steps into the basement, where I lay her on a gleaming metal table. I look up to see Mia staring at my Kill Room.

I envy Mia, seeing my lair for the first time. It is a magnificent sight: walls covered with tools, toys and equipment, saws, dildos, chains, sounding rods, whips, spread bars, and car batteries. Like the treasures of a museum, everything is on display.

Mia takes the last step, eyes like saucers, mouth agape. I can smell her acidic fear, which only fuels the fire inside me. I will take great joy in first corrupting her and then killing her. I secure Cindy to the table by her wrists and ankles. And then, leaning over her I glance back to Mia, grinning under my mask.

"I want you to remove her eyes," I say softly and put my upper body weight into Cindy's middle, holding her steady.

"Her...eyes?" Mia repeats in a shaking whisper.

"Did I fucking stutter, Mia?" I raise my voice enough to make her flinch.

She shakes her head and steps forward, scanning my walls.

"No, you may not touch any of my equipment. It is sacred to me," I mutter and grin when the understanding strikes her.

Mia swallows so hard I can hear it in the quiet room. And as she looms over Cindy I watch with growing excitement. Her sharp, fake nails are at the ready.

MIA

I've bit off more than I can chew here. I shouldn't be here, seeing things I am never supposed to see. I lower my trembling, ice-cold hands to Cindy's face. He wants me to remove her eyes, and I am not in a position to argue. I take a breath, and with one hand, I open her left eyelid and gaze into a blue eye blazing with terror. Feeling about to throw up, I swallow it down and push into the corner of Cindy's eye socket, following the curvature. She writhes at the fresh pain and begins to beg. Dislodging the eyeball is tougher than I think and I have to push hard into her socket. When her eye pops free she lets out a piercing scream, her thrashing body twisting and arching under his.

One down, one to go.

I deposit the slimy eyeball onto the table and repeat the process. The second eyeball pops out easier and lands in my palm with a wet squelch. I put it beside the other and look at him.

He grabs my hand and slides it under his mask, taking my fingers, coated with blood, skin, and eyeball juice into his mouth. After sucking my hand clean, he draws it roughly to his crotch, and I flinch at the hardness there. A moan involuntarily escapes my lips. He is throbbing, and I know what I need to do.

I need to help him kill these women before I kill *him*.

GRIMMER

Her moan is music to my ears. I need to hear more of them. Cindy goes on screeching and screaming, so I reach for a hunting knife and lash it across her neck. Watching the fountain of hot blood spray against Mia. God damn.

Mia, the good girl, doesn't flinch or scream. She reaches up to her breasts and rubs the fleshy mounds until they are wet with crimson. God, I knew it. She's like me. I grab Mia and lift her onto the table. Sandwiching my hips between hers, I lay her back against Cindy's gurgling, dying body.

Mia scoops up handfuls of blood and offers it to me.

I rip off my mask and throw it to the floor. It is no longer necessary to hide my face from her.

I lap the coppery blood from her hands and rip her trousers from her body, scooping up more blood and letting it drip down onto her cute little pussy. I line myself up against her and push inside using Cindy's cooling blood as lube.

My bloody hand finds Mia's throat, and I squeeze just enough to cut off her oxygen. I want her to enjoy this, as a thank you for helping me fulfill my fantasy.

MIA

There's blood under my nails again. But this time, it's his.

KASEY HILL

Dickless in Seattle

WHEN THE CARNIVAL ROLLED through a new town, it was thrilling at first. The smell of fresh popcorn, corn dogs cooking, sweet whiffs of cotton candy floating in the air —it was blissful. A full crowd always followed the food, and soon every seat would be full awaiting the performers' magnificent feats. Everything was a cakewalk until opening night. Carnival life was always hard. There was no guarantee of ticket sales or turnout. Good or bad night, we carnies trudged forward. Showbiz always said, "The show must go on." And it did. Even if only one person sat in the audience, we performed as if it were a full crowd.

It was a new age, a new era. Your typical show from the twentieth century was a thing of the past. Juggling knives or blowing fire were amateur-night material. This new breed of human audience wanted grandeur, awe, and gore. The ringmaster would scour each town we rolled through looking for hobos, bums, and degenerates —people no one would miss —and hire them on. Most were eager for free food and booze and signed their contracts without reading them. They were literally signing their death certificates. Instead of the magic trick of fake-sawing someone in half, they *were* sawed in half. As their blood spurted into the front row of the audience, standing ovations and cheers echoed throughout the arena. Their entrails would hit the floor in pieces and their bladders burst, filling the air with the stench of shit and piss.

It never deterred the audience.

Each showing garnered more and more people until every ticket sold out for weeks to come.

The dead bodies? Those souls, who most likely had had families somewhere with no idea they were murdered —they never got a proper funeral, burial, or acknowledgment of their death. And the remains? Let's say there was a reason everyone ate for free. The scraps were tossed into an incinerator and burned.

That was the tip of the iceberg when it came to the "show." It was vile and gruesome. Each act was performed with more poor souls who had no idea of their fate when they signed the papers.

The cannibalism extended further as well. Corn dogs, "chicken" on a stick, and any other meaty delights served to the patrons were fashioned from bits and pieces of slaughtered men and women —and the menu was an open secret. They appeared not to care they were eating the remains of the people they'd so happily cheered on to their deaths. They would sit at their tables with juices dripping from their mouths as the grease of human flesh rolled around on their tongues, erupting in smiles of orgasmic pleasure as they licked their fingers while dipping the meat into whatever sauce they asked for. Apparently, ranch is the number one go-to. So they sit there, dipping Henry's ribs or Bobby Jo's breast meat into cups of ranch, then sucking the marrow from toe bones as if they were chicken drumettes.

The highwire act was more treacherous than the magician's show. Of course, there were the experienced carnies that did the act flawlessly. Even so, experienced tightrope walkers fall, and safety precautions were put in place. However, when it was time for the hired help to walk across the rope, their harnesses were removed, the mesh net to catch them was pulled away, and the Spikes of Death rolled in below. Before the show, the stagehands would get them shitfaced drunk so they could hardly stand. Most never made it far before plummeting into the Spikes of Death. But if someone managed to make it across, the rope would be shaken, causing them to fall —because the audience wasn't there to watch the town tramp survive. They were there for death and gore. The whole lot of them, the ringmaster on down, were pieces of shit if you ask me. But I knew my place, and I never discouraged anyone from signing, even though I wanted —screamed inside —to tell them to run as far away as possible. But if I did, it would be *my* head.

My stage name was Solice, the Sex Slave. I didn't have a performance costume like the others did. I was led around the rink by a chain and dog collar with a ring gag in my mouth —completely naked. My handler would stroll me around for all the men to reach out and touch my body, pinch it, slap it, or whatever. I could only oblige, as it was my role. I signed the papers when I shouldn't have. Of course, I could have squeezed my way out of the legalities. I was sixteen when I signed the papers, a runaway. Minors cannot be held accountable for contracts, but I was a woman of my word. So here I am, twenty-one years old, and still putting up with this bullshit.

I was broken in the rough way. They tossed me in with the horny freaks and told me to take it. This was my job. If I wanted to keep it, I would reply *how high* when told to jump. The things they did to me were unspeakable. Every orifice of my body was used as a sex hole. There were two at a time, sometimes three or four rubbing their cocks together crammed into my mouth, pussy, and asshole. Thrusting in and out while others stood around in a circle and jerked one another off to stay hard. When the ones using me were done, more would move in and fill the empty slots, jizzing in me or on me so much that cum dripped out of me. Their peckers tasted like rotten meat and shit. They would shove them so far down my throat I'd choke on their spewing cum. When they could no longer get hard, they'd grab whatever they could find to shove inside me. Bowling ball pins, baseball bats, clubs, you name it.

I couldn't walk when they were finished with me. I was black and blue from where they beat me as they fucked me. By the time I was allowed to leave, I had a prolapsed snatch and asshole —it took weeks to heal.

They never truly broke my spirit, even if they tainted my soul.

Tonight is the night everything's going to change, I thought as I walked around that rink in Seattle. I had been planning for months what to do for a big show. It finally hit me one night as I lay in bed dreaming of life outside of the carnival, outside of this madhouse, outside of the infected and diseased minds of patrons who found this shit normal. *What happened? What happened to the world we used to live in? A world where the sexual exploitation of minors was against the law. Prostitution was against the law. Rape was against the law. Now, it is part of the norm?*

As a young child, I remember seeing the ads on the subway walls: Help Save the Next Girl. So many teenagers and young adults were kidnapped, raped, murdered, bodies desecrated, you name it. The stories would hit headline news. It would be televised from state to state stating, "Keep your children off the streets." And then, one day, that fateful election year, it all went down the toilet.

Humanity, the United States, it all went to hell in a handbag when they elected that dumb fuck into office. People began killing for survival. Killing for survival turned into killing for fun.

If you weren't part of an organization with money —you were dead.

If you weren't rich —you were dead.

If you weren't strapped into a dog collar and led around for men to touch you wherever they fucking felt like —you were dead.

My only option was to kill them all. Kill all of the men that stood around that circus and touched me like I was food, like I was a thing, like I wasn't anything but a fucking animal. If society was to rebuild itself, it needed a push in the right direction. I may not be important, but I sure as in hell could provide a means to the end for everyone else.

My story could be an inspiration for those who needed it. I would have to take care of my handler first. I was his sex yo-yo —he rolled me out whenever he wanted to stick his nasty dick in a hole. There was hardly a night he didn't come to my camper after the show to have his way with me. Typically, he was drunk and high. I felt like a dog. He would put his hands all over me, it made me feel so dirty after.

They had no idea what I was capable of. I was the wrong person to be dragged by my hair and called *whore, slut, bitch...* before I ran away, one of the boys in my town thought he was going to have a good time with me. Boy, was he wrong. It was why I went on the run. I was being hunted. He had taken me out for a night of fun. To him that meant getting laid. I told him, *No.*

Men like him don't listen. They take what they want when they want, and that night, I was to be his meal. He chased me into a field, shoved my face in the dirt, and ripped off my panties, then howled in pain as the bloody stub of his dong was all that remained of his manhood. The gaping hole where his cock once existed spurted blood, piss, and cum all at once. He hit the ground, grabbing the fresh wound.

I looked around the rink, at the men standing around jacking off and ejaculating into the air. They battled each other, seeing who could squirt the farthest. They tried to land their jizz on me —their prize. My handler jerked me around and pawed my chest with his chubby fingers. The men whooped and hollered as he began the show. Watching porn live and circle-jerking together was a thrill every man wanted to experience. I despised him so. I smiled my sweetest smile as his hand rubbed down my stomach and found my clit. I pushed into his hand, signaling I wanted more. He made small strokes on my clit and dipped his finger into my vagina, fingering me until I got wet enough for him. He turned me around, unbuckled his pants, and thrust his unruly appendage into my pussy. I pushed against him, burying his wang as far as it could go.

He took his thrusts in numbers. Lord knows he couldn't hold a nut back to save his soul. As he was about to climax, he got a rude awakening. He screamed while pulling a shredded piece of meat from my vagina. The men around the rink, drunk out of their minds, had no clue what was going on. I would have to show them. I walked over to one who was milking his cock. I reached down and stroked it. I turned around and bounced my naked ass up and down on his hard hog. Another man pushed him out of the way.

"Boys," I yelled. "There's room for two."

As they took me to a corner to slide their doomed rods into my growing cooter, I smiled. I sat on one's lap while the other stood in front of me, hunched over like a dog getting a taste of vag for the first time. They both slid in with ease and began thrusting. Soon, they, too, were howling in pain as they pulled bloodied stumps out and dropped like flies. It doesn't take long for a man to bleed out when his pecker is cut off. Everyone knows that the reason it gets hard is because of the blood pumping through it.

When I experienced my unusual talent for the first time, I had no idea I could make the teeth come and go at will.

I remember one night, not long after I'd joined the carnival, a pair of Siamese twins —real headliners —decided to come into my room for some fun. That's when I learned I could control it. That night, I had normal sex with them, and they didn't run screaming and dickless. I guess it was more of a *when I felt* threatened defense mechanism. Tonight, it wasn't a defense mechanism. It was full-on offense, and every single one of these disgusting male fuckers was going to pay.

The crowd dissipated as nothing fascinating was happening. All they saw were people being chosen for sex. I guess it wasn't as much fun if it wasn't forced. Forcible sex got these puke bags hard and ready. If it was consensual, their pricks went limp like stir-fry noodles. These men thought they had rights to everything that didn't belong to them. If it wasn't theirs, they would take it for themselves anyway. Here, at the carnival, they didn't even have to take it —they were given it as a headline attraction: "Fuck to your heart's content with our sex slave, Solice."

Solice, what kind of name is that? It sounded sleazy. I hated it.

"Where do you boys think you are going?" I called to the crowd as they headed toward the tent's opening.

They turned in my direction to listen.

"If you want a show, you got one," I said, pulling my hair into a ponytail.

In the circus ring I swung my leg around a pole, took my handler's chain, and climbed. I swung around it, flipping and turning and doing splits in the air. This regained the audience's attention, and they began to inch back. What they failed to realize is that every time I went around the pole, I was driving it deeper into the ground, creating a grave of sorts. There would be no escape. And my vag was hungry. As I thought of wrapping it around human flesh, my vag actually salivated. Sure, I had bitten off several schlongs that night, but those were appetizers, little drumsticks. What my vagina wanted was a whole man, and I was going to give my body what it wanted.

There was no escape from this hole of death.

Using my chain, I snatched a man from the audience. He smiled, thinking he was getting the royal treatment. I grinned back, then my face flashed my true form. I could tell everything from his sudden change of expression —his stupid shit-eating grin was replaced with horror. I had no clue what I looked like without my human face. Hideous, I assumed. I imagined a huge, unnatural grin like you'd see in a horror movie. Whatever I looked like, it made this puny man piss and shit his pants. I'm glad my vagina can't taste anything. On him it would most likely gag.

He was about to scream for mercy when I shoved his head up my twat and contracted my muscles. His skull busted like a dropped watermelon. Blood and brains oozed from my vagina and down my legs. I scanned the room to see if the drunkards noticed. I released my thigh muscles. The man toppled to the ground, headless, bleeding profusely, dead. I smiled deviously as I ran my finger along the dripping blood and brought it to my mouth, sucking it off like all those weeners I was made to drink cum from. No one in the audience was sober enough to know what was really happening. That meant I was going to be a full and satisfied participant tonight. I had never felt more alive than at this moment.

I walked over to the main switches on the wall. I killed the house lights and hit the strobe. The faces of the patrons were a priceless sight to see. Some were nearly scared to death —others thought it was a rave. The frightened tasted better with their blood full of adrenaline. It's like a hit of heroin compared to endorphins. It wafted throughout the tent. My vagina drenched itself in anticipation of the main event. I snatched the men one by one from their seats, my twat tearing off their heads and leaving their bodies lying crumpled on the floor.

I'd heard stories of bodybuilding women that could crush golf balls in their cooches or smash pumpkins or watermelons between their thighs. Hell, I'd even heard of a man who suffocated when he got his head stuck up his girlfriend's cunt. But I've never heard of anyone like me. Maybe I'm the only one? It was such a thrill to snatch heads and meat sticks off men who couldn't even fuck their wives and had to come to a sleazy carnival to get their rocks off.

Pain ripped through my back. I crouched to the ground.

Has someone shot me? Stabbed me? What's going on? I reached back to touch my shoulder blades and felt stubs above my skin. To my surprise, I'd grown wings.

I laughed.

I could now fly and rip off even more heads, all without my feet touching the ground. Each head slid effortlessly into my honeypot, arousing me more and more. I used their heads as dildos while rubbing my clit, orgasming, and making my juice box wetter, looser, and hungrier. I pushed them up against the dirt walls and jumped on top of them, riding them like horse cock dildos. I had never felt so turned on or sexual, and I wondered if it emasculated them, knowing their final moments were spent shoved up my pussy filled with cum, brains, blood, and genitals, tasting every patron that came before them.

I could hear ripping through the air as my bat-like wings flapped and gained traction. I flickered through the lights like the monster I was, snatching and carrying away my prey to feast in the corner. I made piles of beheaded, bedicked bodies in four separate corners, and my prizes were running out. I had thinned the herd down in such a short amount of time that I was sad it would be over soon. These bastards got my jollies off.

Finally, I finished snatching all of the heads from the bodies. Then the tiring part came. I had to eat the bodies until there was nothing left.

No bones, no skin, no teeth, nothing.

I took my time with my last victim, savoring his head inside me and riding him gingerly. I made love to his head, coming over and over as I caressed my clit. When he went limp, I knew he'd suffocated. I had one last orgasm. Clenching my muscles, I writhed in pleasure as his skull burst. Then I lay on the ground, taking each body into my vagina. It would have seemed like minutes to the average person, but it felt like agonizing hours.

Each man who leered at me that night, or touched my body, got what they deserved.

They are forever in my twat now. My body is my body.

My headliner called me Solice, the Sex Slave, and that is precisely what I'd been. I had been a slave, not allowed to say *No* to anything. These pieces of shit paid to do anything they wanted to me. I wasn't allowed to fight back. I wasn't allowed to leave until every paying customer was satisfied. I couldn't even call myself a prostitute, because I never saw money from what I was put through. Prostitutes are treated with more dignity.

I pulled myself together, lay in the middle of the rink, and acted like I was knocked unconscious. The carnival owner ran to me. He picked me up in his arms and carried me to my camper.

Patrons and carnies stood around, waiting for me to come to and tell the story of what happened. I told them *I couldn't remember a single thing*. Of course, that was a lie but the humans didn't need to know that.

After that, I was no longer a sex slave. They upgraded me to trapeze artist, and I would climb the poles with a chain and spin like a stripper to my heart's content. For the first time I made friendships with others in the carnival, people who before I'd been forbidden to speak with.

I became best friends with the Bearded Lady, who, in fact, only has a hormonal imbalance. I taught her a few tricks of the trade, and she learned how to suck the beard in and release it on command.

The Strong Man had eyes on me, but he wasn't too fetching. After a few failed attempts at making a pass at me, he learned the hard way what I was programmed to do with my vagina and he was no longer the Strong *Man*. He became one of the few that survived and ended up institutionalized, ranting about a phallus-eating vagina.

Amid all the carnage and wreckage before we left Seattle, I even fell in love. The carnival had taken on a clown —not really a clown —hired as a freak show performer and stripped bare to reveal he was born without a phallus or vagina. He looked like a Ken doll. It was a match made in heaven. I needed no pleasure to survive, and neither did he.

He would never know the evil secret of my cooter, and I would never have to worry about him learning the hard way. I could tell he had been abused. My empathy and sympathy for him melted my heart. Occasionally, we'd have sex because a man is a man, and doesn't think his woman is happy unless she is getting off. He would use a strap-on to fuck me. Sex was never the same for me after that night, and I didn't get the pleasure I once had. To make him happy, I faked the orgasms so he could feel good about himself.

After all, my snatch didn't crave silicone. It craved flesh.

He was the perfect gentleman, and the night the men came to try and "break" him into the carnival, I showed them who they were messing with. He had been knocked unconscious, so there were no worries about him knowing my secret or being afraid of me. Even if he didn't have a member, I am sure it would terrify him to learn the truth of the horrible carnage I was capable of. I was responsible for the disappearance of over three hundred men who were still listed as missing. I taught those men a thing or two about manners. Because someone who has no wang to fuck with or a hole to stick a dick in does not mean anal is an option they agree with. Well, if they survive, that's the only pleasure they will ever know. Once again, I reiterate, *No, means No!* Just because you can overpower someone else, hold them down, tie them up, and have your way with them, doesn't mean it's okay or that you won't be caught. Even if the authorities get you, I *will* find you. We all know how the court systems work. Rapists are let go scot-free or with a slap on the wrist.

That's where I will come in.

I have perfected my dark gift over the last few years. I am, for lack of terminology, a dark superhero for the world —an antihero. I have tried to come up with a name for myself, but everything I think of seems juvenile. No wonder Batman went the easy route, costume and all. Let me guess, *You have a thing for bats, right?* God. Batman, really? You couldn't think of something cooler? Don't get me started on Daredevil. Honestly, those two should have had a meet and greet and switched names, for crying out loud.

I will be the boogeyman that fathers tell their sons about when they mention the weeny thief so casually, jokingly. However, it's not a joke. Urban legends and scary bedtime stories come from some truth, and I will be the worst nightmare that has ever walked the earth. No woman, man, or child will ever be forced to do what I have done. The urban legend of the man-eating vagina will live on throughout time.

As for you women out there thinking to themselves that nothing so heinous could ever happen, remember, I am a hermaphrodite at will, and with a fully functional appendage that is barbed and eager to play, and quite honestly, I am hungry, stark raving, starved. I haven't eaten in what seems like months, but you know how time blind I am. Minutes can seem like days...

AMANDA WORTHINGTON

The Liminal Fuckspace

WELCOME TO THE Liminal Fuckspace. This is where people like you come to be violated liminally, but not criminally. You signed the waiver, after all. You said you'd lost the will to live, needed a little dick fibrillator to restart your heart, which popped its clogs sometime between the death of the Great Barrier Reef and the tenth Trump administration. No one knows that old flesh puppet's secret to immortality, but his face looks like it was force-fucked raw by a weed eater and allowed to heal —and not well, if you know what I mean. You could poke at it and feel the decay jiggle underneath. The flies swarm around his head and the Secret Service's main task is batting them away.

I feel a little sorry for the flies. Our fearless leader, or what remains of him, is like a buffet with a tarp draped over it. And anyone can see that the poor buggers are *hungry*.

But back to your needs as a human.

You don't want the same old missionary action. No god ordained this penetration, but it's what you need. You need someone who can find the holes that don't yet exist, not really. But they'll exist someday, and the artful lover can find them, knead at them, find a way inside parts of you *you* can't even fathom.

Isn't that what a good lover does? Take your breath away? Elicit orgasms that feel like supernovae from stars that have yet to be born? Cumming is better when, well, when you don't see it coming.

And the world is dark and cold.

Okay, no. It isn't cold, but hot, but you know what I mean. Things are heating up in the worst of ways. You know how drone bees that become stressed ejaculate until they die? Well, it's kind of like that. The humans have fucked this planet and fucked it hard. And we are right on the brink of the ecstasy that will kill us. Is it pain? Is it pleasure? Is there any difference, really? The workers grow fat on distraction and their bodies distend and a twinge of discomfort begins to register, but the sensation is still more heaven than hell. When it becomes agony, it will be too late. But isn't that the way of things?

The world we've built is like Trump's cratered, destroyed, half-healed devastation of a face. Liquid bubbles beneath the crust, ready to force its way to the surface at any moment. The foundation was never meant to last this long.

The end is nigh.

But creation and destruction share a border. And it is thinning all the time. And that space is infinitely fuckable.

And the Earth? The Earth is a canvas that has allowed herself to be used. She has borne the mark of a million tribes. She wipes the grime from her isthmus legs and atoll breasts and makes room for the future, exhibits the emptiness and hope of the blank page that way. The Earth waits. She both is and is not. She is empty and full of meaning in her emptiness. She is both soiled and clean when one understands that time is infinite and nonlinear.

To be honest, Earth was once amused by the contests of men but has since grown bored. And what woman can't say the same? Fireworks blossom in the heavens, but when they've discharged their load, exploded their color across the sky, well, there's really not much else to see.

Even the men don't think so.

The Liminal Fuckspace is that place where humans can all meet and mingle and ask for the briefest of reprieves from the predictable onslaught of darkness.

Now, women reject the role of the canvas and men are no longer content to spray the world with their negligible insight. We have all played the role of finite, linearly minded humans for too long. And the finale is coming. Or maybe it's already arrived and this is our encore.

At any rate, the Liminal Fuckspace is just another distraction, and it's not for everyone. But within it is something of the past and something of the future too. We came from something. We will be something after. This is only an end for the current iteration. New roles can be assumed —they will be whether we want them to or not. We might as well start the process of opening here and now. It might seem too big at first, but it will fit. It will. We're more elastic than we think. We can stretch. And when we do, it will be bliss. Our lips will tug upward in spasmodic oblivion. We will burst from so many holes that we'll sink like a ship taking in the whole ocean. And then we will rise, victorious. Exhausted but full of so much cosmic that we'll be dripping space-time cum-tinuum for eons to come.

The Liminal Fuckspace is for those of us who welcome transition.

You're all in, you say?

Well, not yet, but you will be. There's more of you than you imagine. It's still growing. Jesus.

Yes, that's a hole. Push at her. I know you don't know her, but push at her. She's agreed to be here. And you'll have your turn. Don't give it if you can't take it. That's what we always say.

What? It came out the other side? Don't feel bad. That feels really fucking good when that happens. Take it from me.

That? That's one of your holes? You can't expect humans to be solid all over can you? That's the spot on your back where your mom comforted you when you were getting bullied at school? Compassion breaks us down, makes us like putty.

You're scared? Don't be. It's already so thin. It will only hurt for a second. A couple thrusts and it will give. Trust me.

What? It hurts? I'm sorry. Deep breaths. He's almost through. It's like tissue paper. I can see your bones dissolving.

There it is. See? He does fit. He fits so perfect.

It's warm, isn't it?

Can you do it again for me? This world is ending, but there are others. Are you ready? Are you ready to join them? Do you have another thrust in you? We have another customer who's getting close. Her tender place is her lips. I think you could wear each other down if you just let her take you in. Yes, just slip it inside. Ahhh, doesn't that feel nice?

Okay, I can see you're fading. It's been so grand, hasn't it? And isn't this better than burning to death or starving or?

What's that? Oh, sure, I can answer one last question.

The Earth? The sun will take her if no one does it before then. She's made of hardier stuff. Harder to find holes, if you know what I mean. Sometimes meteors crash into her, and they make an impact but... she's a tough one. The sun will take good care of her though. Don't you worry. This isn't her final role either. She is, after all, atoms, same as you.

What? You're coming? It's the big O, the real Oblivion?

Ah, I'm so glad we could meet your needs, Sir.

See you on the other side.

MATT SCOTT

Brain Food

PEOPLE ARE INHERENTLY SIMPLE. If their needs are met.

What needs?

Basic needs like shelter, water, love, and food. That's where I come in. I work at the food court in the mall. Bingo Bill's Burger Bonanza. Bingo Bill's for short.

Working at the register, I've seen all kinds of people walk up to the counter. All kinds. Conjoined twins —each got a foot-long chili cheese dog. The mime —took forever to figure out what he wanted. Even waited on a naked lady once. Broke my heart when they hauled her out of the mall that day. But my favorite was Lanny Simms.

He shuffled up to me and said, "My brain has worms in it. Can you help me order?"

It's all about the customer service.

I said, "Of course, buddy. What are you in the mood for?"

"What's the same as dirt but tastier?"

"Tough one," I said, considering his question. "Give me a hint."

"I need soil for my worms. They ate all my brains out."

"Bummer. That sucks, man." Aware of the line forming behind him, I tried to nudge him along. "So what's your flavor today? Burger or a dog?"

"Wet cold dirt for my worms."

"Best I can do is some chili fries, my friend. Maybe a shake. What do you say?"

"Chili fries might work. And a shake if it's chocolate."

"Chocolate it is, my friend. Chocolate it is."

Lanny Simms. Crazy as shit, but harmless. Kind of stuck in 1976. Traumatic brain injury when he was a teenager. Car wreck. Went over a bridge headfirst. Barely survived. That was decades ago. He's not bad for sixty-five. Just collects his checks and his eight-track tapes. People from all over town will scoop up the antiquated cassettes if they come across them, just to give to Lanny when they bump into him. He's a little inappropriate, a little gauche, but otherwise he's all right. Hell, he's practically a gray-haired seventeen-year-old. A simple, well-meaning guy.

Brandon Paul, on the other hand. He was in the accident, too —caused it, actually. Yeah, he was driving the vehicle that hit Lanny's. A little thug wannabe with more arrests for domestic violence offenses than IQ points. The guy's a peach of a man. If you ask me, he should have died in the wreck.

They tended to avoid one another, and while they were both regulars at Bingo Bill's, they'd never come in at the same time —at least not on any of my shifts. Just my luck that this day would be different.

But I'm jumping ahead.

Lanny sat down at a table near the front of the store so he could look out the glass and watch the people go by. He loved waving at folks as they went about their business —people oblivious to the world around them and the chaos that feeds it.

When his order came up, I had no customers, so I carried his tray out to him. He thanked me with a smile and looked about to say something when Brandon banged into the entrance. Passing me, the little turd strutted to the counter, put his hands on it, strained his neck to see the menu he had memorized years ago, and motioned for me with a wag of his stubby index finger.

I took my time getting back to the counter and made a point of stopping to check the fry station. Brandon tapped his dirt-encrusted fingernails on the counter. I refilled the paper drink cups before moseying to the register to look down at him.

"What will it be?" I asked in my best disinterested tone.

I don't hate the guy —he's never done anything to me. But he's bad news in general and has been a dick to almost everyone in town at some point or another. A little gangster without the clout to back it up. Picking on people, yelling at old folks walking down the street, a real prince of a guy. Don't know what the hell his issues are, but man, he's got a few.

"A number one, large. With a Dr. Pecker." He slapped the counter and winked at me, laughing hysterically like a hyena on acid.

"Good one," I said, ringing up the order and making a show of getting a to-go bag for it.

"It's for here, moron," Brandon barked.

"Right," I said without turning around.

"Fucking place, man. Idiots working every time I come."

"And yet, here you are," I said.

His order came up. I set his brown plastic tray of grease and salt on the counter maybe a little harder than I should have.

"Careful," he said, up on his tiptoes and leaning toward me.

"Come on man," I replied, deciding it was best not to poke the bear again. "Chill out already."

"Fucking stoner."

"This is a family place, Brandon."

His face screwed up. Apparently he didn't like me using his name. "Give me my food, queer."

He reached out and snatched the tray, then turned to walk to a table.

"Classy," I said under my breath. The exchange had me so rattled that I realized I'd forgotten to collect his money. For an insane moment I actually considered letting it go, but I'd already rung up the total. "Sir," I called out. "You forgot to pay."

Brandon stopped, his back to me. He had reached the kiosk where you get napkins and ketchup and plastic utensils. He slammed the tray down on the counter and turned around to me with a sneer. "Pull the cash out of your ass, weasel."

When Brandon turned around to pick up his tray, Lanny buried a plastic fork in his left eye and a plastic knife in his right cheek.

Brandon stood dumbfounded for a moment, then dropped his tray and began screaming.

Lanny plucked the fork out of Brandon's eye socket, and the eyeball came with it. Tendrils of nerves and optic vessels trailed out behind it like spaghetti noodles. Like a fucking ninja, Lanny retracted the knife from Brandon's cheek with a soft quick thwump and deftly buried it just below his Adam's apple. Brandon clasped at his throat with both hands, his eye still dangling on his cheek, flopping from side to side as he shuddered and shook.

Lanny placed the sole of his Converse directly on Brandon's chest and pushed off like a spartan. Brandon rolled across the floor and came to a stop by the bathrooms.

Lanny peered down at the body flopping on the floor, and bellowed.

"AHHHHHHHHHH. FUCKING STOP ALREADY. WORMS HAVE TO EAT. AHHHHHHHHHHHHHHH."

"Lanny, what the fuck," I said, screaming myself.

"Couldn't eat. Too much bullshit noise. Ahhhhhhhhh." Lanny kept hollering until he was out of breath. When he finally stopped, he shuffled back to his table, gobbled down a mouthful of chili fries and took a sip of his shake.

Hand over my heart, I stood there, shaking. Did that really happen?

My sense of time returned, and with it came a clouded-over memory of the scene that played out in the background while Lanny was putting out Brandon's lights —customers scattering like roaches and running for the door, scurrying past Lanny and the screaming Brandon Paul who now only had one eye and maybe seconds to live. They rushed out into the mall in droves, two and three at a time.

I looked through the glass storefront and saw hundreds of people running, screaming, panic-stricken, bumping into each other, grabbing one another by the hair, knocking each other down, stomping hands and feet, every man for himself in a desperate attempt to flee some unknown assailant.

Assailants.

Behind the throngs of harried housewives and weekend dads hauling ass and hoisting little ones up over their heads in a mad dash for the exits, down by the haberdashery, a group of teenage boys with baseball bats, lacrosse sticks, and pool cues occupied themselves, chasing and hitting innocent people, women and children, old men and ladies. The punks were swinging for the fences and connecting with almost everyone in their aim.

Beyond them, at the far end of the mall by the JCPenney, a woman wielded what looked like a machete in one hand and a human head in the other. She held the noggin up by its short hair in triumph, as if having vanquished some great foe. Her white satin blouse was soaked with blood, and strands of her hair covered her face, caked in crimson and smeared like war paint. She leaned and heaved as if feral, wild, hungry.

I stood behind the counter, frozen, watching the people run in terror toward the exits and the safety the sunshine provided. I don't know why in active-shooter situations, people feel safer outside. To me it seems like it would just be easier to shoot you out in the open like that. But hey, who am I? I stuck right to where I was, and so did Lanny.

"What the fuck, Lanny?" I asked again, but my voice lacked conviction.

"Brain worms," he mumbled, shoveling more chili fries into cheeks already puffed out with food. "Hungry little boogers."

My hands went numb and the tops of my ears burned. I felt as if I were floating above the floor, my head reeling. I was going to pass out.

As Lanny sat feeding his face —or his worms, I don't really know —the window exploded. I woke up quick and hit the deck.

As glass rained down around me, I heard a thud, like a bowling ball dropping onto the floor beside me. After a few seconds I looked up and peeked around the counter to see Lanny slumped over, his face down in his fries, shards of glass like daggers sticking out the side of his head, one buried in his right ear, another in his temple just below his hairline.

Did I dare leave?

Was I safer in Bingo Bill's or should I haul ass toward the exits?

The back door led to a long service corridor, which led to an exit. No one should be in the corridor. Or hell, maybe everyone was in it.

Either way, I wasn't going out the front door. In the mall, people continued to run screaming —some on fire, some bleeding from severed limbs, head wounds, bite marks.

And there were the others, mad, insane, insatiable. They jumped on people, knocking them down, hacking them to bits with dollar-store cleavers and novelty knives. They ripped at faces, gouging eyes and cheeks, breaking noses, taking giant bites out of flesh, tearing stomachs open with their bare hands, spilling innards all over the food court.

I'd go out the back and try my luck.

So far, no one had seemed to notice me. I crept slowly over the glass so as to not attract unwanted attention.

In the mall, the screams were maddening. Victim and assailant alike rising up in agonizing unison, a cacophonous symphony of the consumers and the consumed.

I made it to the back door, then stopped.

Even in my desperation to get out of there, I'm not a complete idiot. I've seen enough movies to know those bastards were probably waiting for me on the other side.

Right?

I put my ear up to the door, bracing myself to run in case I had to bail on the plan.

The corridor beyond the door sounded empty. I looked back at the raw carnage, the mall floors a pool of blood, psychopaths spinning around like children, throwing entrails up in the air just to watch them splash down and splatter everywhere.

Nope.

I turned the knob, slowly, incrementally, fraction of an inch by faction of an inch until it slowly gave way and clicked quietly open.

I stuck my head into the corridor, looking left then right, and spotted the red exit sign just beyond the back door of Juice World. That place rocks. Saved my life many a time. Let's see if it would again.

I crept down the long, brightly lit passage with my back to the cold concrete so I could see everything in every direction. It reminded me of a sanitarium we visited once when I was little. But at the time, I hadn't known it was a sanitarium. Uncle Clem was in there "resting," Mom had said. He just needed to take better care of himself. Worn out, that's what she said he was. Truth is, Uncle Clem died in that sanitarium, syphilis. Crazy as a loon throwing shit on the walls and thinking he was a sleeper agent for the CIA.

But hey, the world's gone to shit, so who got off lucky?

Maybe he had brain worms too?

As I moved closer to the exit, I could still hear the faint muffled cries from within the mall. Fuck this place, man. Fuck customer service. Fuck Bingo Bill's and fuck this. Goddamn, take this job and shove it.

The exit was fifteen feet away. I could almost smell the fresh air. I sprinted for it.

I thrust my hand out for the push bar and ran through it.

The alarm sounded.

Then came the rumble, like thunder. The footfalls of freaks of every sort, headed my way, searching for the source of the sound. I ran behind the Crab Shack dumpster, squeezed up under the lid, and plopped down inside.

Been here ever since. The flies are the worst. Buzzing incessantly in my ears. I can almost feel their larvae, the maggots, slithering around under my skin. So hot. So thirsty. So fucking hungry.

Fucking brain worms man.

TAMIKA THOMPSON

Stiletto Girls

RICHIE WAS UPSIDE DOWN doing a keg stand atop a half barrel of Lagunitas IPA, but Richie was also a sucker for girls in high heels so he noticed the three pairs of blood-red stilettos as soon as they arrived. The open-toed shoes soared up from the floor. By his estimation, the heels must have reached six inches high, and, ogling them, he lowered himself to his feet so he could take in the view right-side up. The keg stand could wait.

The Knicks game on the television, the multiple liquor-infused, high-pitched conversations, and the old school rap song, "Da Rockwilder" by Method Man and Redman, faded into the background. The latter signaled the depths of Richie's transfixed state, because that beat was so sick, he'd used the track as the foundation for the six-hour party mix his sound system was currently blasting.

His pulse quickened as he scanned the three pairs of smooth and delicately plump legs that moved with those shoes. The trio donned skirts that ended just below round hips, midriff-baring tops, and high ponytails. Full lips and prominent cheekbones completed their exquisite faces. Their deep brown skin was taut and blemish-free, resembling the complexions of the exotic dancers at the clubs he and his boys frequented.

Perfection.

Almost too perfect.

Ripped from his fantasies. Literally. How could that be?

He would have asked how he'd gotten so lucky, but it occurred to him that he didn't recognize the silently grinning girls, and therefore couldn't have invited them to his twentieth birthday party at the thousand-square-foot off-campus digs his parents had purchased for him. But that wasn't even the thing that unnerved him. What startled Richie was the way the trio took a few steps forward, *click, click, click, click, click, click,* and the movement seemed choreographed, as if controlled by one mind.

"'Sup, girls?"

It annoyed his ex, Hailey, whenever he referred to women as girls. "Infantilizing" was the word she'd trotted out for that argument, explaining that anyone over eighteen was an adult. He'd agreed his word choice was infantilizing, and he could have promised Hailey he'd stop doing that, but her list of things he needed to do differently was so long —remember her birthday, call her the morning after, hold her hand during movies, answer her texts with real words and not just thumbs-up emojis —he figured she'd be better off with a different guy. Maybe someone "considerate."

"I know you girls?"

"We're here for you." They spoke in unison and giggled all together, as well. They must be triplets, he thought. The *in unison* part made him leery, but then they licked their lips and reached up to caress the tops of their cleavage, which brought his eyes to their mouths, their breasts.

His mother had warned him about girls when he headed off to college.

"They're all looking to cash in."

"They're all looking to get pregnant."

"They're all looking for husbands."

"They're all looking to sink their claws into you."

More so than any advice he'd heard from his dad or in rap songs, his mother's exhortations had stuck with him because she was a woman. She must have known what she was talking about. She certainly would have cautioned him about the stiletto girls, but Richie couldn't help himself.

In the background, someone increased the volume on "Da Rockwilder," which had given way to Redman's exuberant chorus, so Richie and everyone else missed the breaking news report that interrupted the Knicks game.

Richie had three rapid-fire thoughts.

First, the buxom trio must be strippers hired by Jim or Joe, the frat brothers behind him who were now catcalling and whistling while manning the keg, atop which Richie had been previously doing the stand.

Second, in the two-hour span of his party so far, perhaps he'd drunk one too many red cups of IPA and the stilettoed women were not as beautiful as they looked. Was "stilettoed" a real word, he wondered, or did he invent that? *Brilliant.*

Third, when the girls said, "we're here for you," what if they intended to have a foursome with him, like as a birthday gift? He'd never even had a threesome. Hell, he and Hailey had barely had a twosome. So maybe this was about to be the best night of his life.

The breaking news report warned of multiple unexplained massacres across the country targeting men, but with the Knicks down twenty points, everyone had since turned away from the screen. Keg stands were way more entertaining than watching your team lose.

"For me? Okay." Richie read the room, and his eight buddies had the same giddy facial expression as Richie.

He remembered the first *Playboy* magazine he'd tucked under his mattress. The first music video he'd seen with scantily clad girls twerking to the beat. His first lap dance. The first time he'd slept with Hailey. Already, it seemed, this night would be added to his list of firsts.

The four non-stilettoed girls in the room, who were in committed relationships with some of Richie's frat brothers —with "committed" being a euphemism for "hog-tied"

—stared at the stiletto girls with open disdain. One regular girl —who up until the arrival of the stiletto girls had been the highest heel-wearer, which she'd paired with stone-washed, hip-hugging jeans —scoffed, set her red cup on top of the kitchen island and pulled out her phone.

"Eff this bro shit. I'm calling an Uber." Her name was Veronica. Veronica was in a "committed" relationship with Nathan, and Veronica was half the reason Richie's ex Hailey had a laundry list of behaviors Richie needed to change. Nate had fixed his behaviors for Veronica. Richie had told Hailey to go fuck herself.

The stiletto girls closed the gap to Richie. The one in the middle grabbed him by the wrist and pulled him toward his bedroom. How did she know which closed door was the bedroom?

She was strong. Like college-wrestler strong. And as excited as he was to be led to his bedroom by her, some internal doubt broke away from his lust, and, on the way to the door, forced him to call over his shoulder, "So, which one of you asshats set up these girls?"

The remaining stiletto girls had already claimed two of his single friends and was redirecting one to the bathroom and the other toward the balcony.

Veronica called to the regular girls, "Car is three minutes away. Let's go."

Still unnoticed by Richie and his crew, the breaking news report showed cell phone footage of a group of women in stilettos stomping a man to death in the middle of a busy intersection. The rolling banner at the bottom of the screen read, "Supreme Court Justice and Secret Service Agents Killed in Broad Daylight."

"We didn't set them up." Joe capped the keg, and he and Jim shrugged. "But, honestly, who gives a shit?"

Bathroom guy shrugged. Balcony guy did as well.

The four guys with wardens for girlfriends were already heading toward the front door. At first, Richie thought his "committed" buddies were leaving with their girls, but instead they kissed their ladies' foreheads and returned to the living room. Richie grinned and waved goodbye to the girlfriends, certain none of their pussies-for-boyfriends had set up the stiletto girls.

With the girlfriends gone, the room underwent a palpable shift. The lights dimmed. The fragrance from the incense burning near the window grew stronger. Someone turned "Da Rockwilder" up even higher, and although the song was short, it was somehow set to repeat.

The television played on, ignored.

Richie's stiletto girl reached inside his pants, where one of her red acrylic fingernail extensions scraped along his shaft. He had the urge to slap her hand away, but his reason gave way as she closed her palm around him and he immediately grew firm in her fist. She grinned and let out an exaggerated moan. He hadn't been with anyone since Hailey and wondered why he felt guilty about the sexual pleasure coursing through his body.

The doorbell rang, and one of the "committed" guys answered. Six more stiletto girls were in the hall, dressed and postured exactly like the initial three. Those women had different faces, at least, but it occurred to Richie then that despite the alcohol in his bloodstream and the tension building inside his pants, there was something really wrong here. How could there be nine fantasy women dressed almost exactly alike, and just the right number for the guys at his party?

"No. Seriously. Who set this up?" Richie called out the question to the room, but all the guys were now claimed by a stiletto girl.

Jim and Joe were tongue-kissing their girls in the kitchen, his buddies' hands beneath the girls' skirts and down their tops.

The "committed" guys must have forgotten their girlfriends already because they were slow-dancing with their stiletto girls and in several stages of petting and undress.

Balcony guy had gone outside, and bathroom guy had disappeared behind that door, where moans emanated from inside.

Richie gazed into his stiletto girl's deep brown eyes. They were still in the living room, inches apart, her back against his bedroom door. She smelled of fresh peaches. She'd managed to undo her shirt, so her voluptuous breasts were staring him in the face.

"Who hired you for my party?"

Richie's mind went to his dad, a state senator. His dad had been caught cheating on his mom with a woman very similar to the stiletto girls, and his dad's speechwriter had to draft the apology statement because his dad believed he had done nothing wrong. Not to Richie's mom. Not to the voters who'd put him in office. Not to Richie. His dad would have wondered why Richie was hesitating. Probably would have called him a "pussy."

"We're here for you." She giggled again. "We're here for all of you."

Rhythmic thumps flowed from the balcony and bathroom, with the same coming from behind the kitchen counter. Someone must have killed the music, because "Da Rockwilder" abruptly ended and the audio of the breaking news report filled the room.

"If you're just joining us, President Rivera has declared a state of emergency as several unexplained massacres have unfolded around the country including in our nation's capital."

Richie's head jerked up and he peered at the television. On the screen, an empty podium sat mid-frame for a White House press conference that was apparently about to start, but his stiletto girl used her free hand to grab his chin and guide his gaze back to her. Someone killed the television volume.

Her smile broadened, and she batted eyes that donned false curly lashes resembling feathers. In his pants, her hand strokes, lubricated by his own fluids, sped up, and that angered him. She was not answering his question and was trying to use pleasure to control him. She, and whoever had purchased her, had made a ton of assumptions about him. One of which was that he would go blindly into his bedroom with a gorgeous stranger just because she could give him an orgasm.

He reached down and yanked her hand from his body. "Yo." He backed up a few steps, adjusted himself in his pants. He was throbbing down there, but he forced himself to focus. "Answer my question. Who told you to come here?"

Her face broke into an exaggerated pout, one a toddler would make. Chin dropped. Bottom lip poked out. Eyes wide and wet. But she still didn't answer his actual question, and, one by one, the guys in his apartment screamed.

He turned to find the girls in the kitchen standing in front of Jim and Joe, but the girls were half a foot shorter, and Jim and Joe had red stilettos sticking out of their heads where their eyes should have been.

The heels couldn't have gone in so deep with normal stilettos.

No.

The footwear was hinged, so the fronts were dangling down, allowing the full length of the heels to lodge into his buddies' eyes. Blood squirted out and around the shoes as the two men dropped to the floor. Their bodies writhed and jerked as they reached up and pulled at the pumps. Neither Joe nor Jim was able to remove the red objects lodged in their eyes. Their movements calmed. Slowly, their hands flopped to the floor. Seconds later, their bodies came to rest.

The dancing "committed" guys collapsed shortly after, and the bathroom and balcony doors rocked with loud banging. No longer rhythmic. Frantic this time, and followed by screams of "Help!" and "Oh my god! Let me out!"

Then silence.

When Richie turned back toward his stiletto girl, he saw two spiked heels coming with speed and force for his eyes.

The front door banged open and in came Veronica, saying, "We're back. Melissa forgot her phone." The interruption threw off his stiletto girl by a half second, allowing him to pivot and yank her forward. She twisted, fumbled the shoes, and landed throat first on her own heels. Her body did not jerk and quake like those of his friends. Blood pooled around her head, but she was stiff, motionless.

The eight remaining stiletto girls stared at him, still grinning. Still batting their eyelashes. The nearest one whispered, "Get him," and they all jerked forward, their manicured nails like bright red claws as they reached for him.

Richie rushed toward the four girlfriends who stood in the entryway, screaming and retching. He gripped Veronica's wrist and used his free hand to guide Melissa and the rest into the hall, not believing for one second that Melissa had forgotten her phone. They'd returned to check on their men, rightly suspecting their boyfriends were cheating with the stiletto girls, and he was grateful for their jealousy.

"Run!" he shouted, and that snapped the regular girls into action.

Without heels, the remaining stiletto girls descended quickly on the stairwell behind him. The regular girls exited through a door on level two, and Richie skipped steps and hopped over banisters to make it to the first level, across the lobby, and to the building's exit. The stiletto girls giggled as they chased him. Was this a game? Were they certain they would get him?

The girlfriends' rideshare sat idling out front as Richie burst through the front doors, twisting his right ankle in the process.

The driver took one look at Richie —the panicked look on his face, the slew of half-dressed girls on his tail, the prominent limp —and raised his hand to his door without breaking his glare. The car let out a clunk as the driver locked it, and Richie cursed as the man drove off.

Richie was Black. He knew that wasn't the only reason or the main reason the driver refused to help him, but he knew his skin color didn't help. The driver probably would have let in a woman under attack, especially if she were white.

Why was Richie thinking about this during his hobbling escape? Because a part of him running down that dark and unpopulated urban street wondered what he was saving himself for. Somehow this was going to end with him a) being stilettoed through the eyes, b) accused of setting up his friends by hiring killer strippers for his party, or c) succumbing in the unfolding, nationwide massacre that the breaking news report had warned about.

This made him think of Hailey. He hadn't realized it when he'd bolted from his apartment, but he was running in the direction of her home, three-quarters of a mile away.

He did not have his phone. Hell, he didn't even have on shoes. He wore a T-shirt and sweatpants damp from his earlier erection. But he did not let up. He dashed down the silent and empty street, pain shooting up from his ankle with every step that landed in the rain puddles, or what he hoped were rain puddles.

An old woman sitting on a milk crate against an empty liquor shop storefront sat up straight when she saw Richie rushing by. "You can't outrun 'em!"

Richie didn't break his stride. *Watch me,* he thought.

"Pretty soon, you'll all be gone." The old woman cackled.

He couldn't let her get to him. Maybe he wouldn't survive the night, but he wasn't going to be an easy win.

He eventually made it to the main drag, blocks from Hailey's place, and he rushed across the boulevard. It also stood empty, and he wondered whether the entire world hadn't fallen apart. Where were the sirens? Where was everyone? Had they heard the news reports and were all sheltering inside? He scanned the shops. Not a light shone.

He heard the ragged breaths of his assailants, close behind, giggling. They weren't as fast as he was, but their stamina seemed unending. If he didn't hide or put a barrier between himself and them soon, they would catch him.

As he ran, he sobered. A stitch formed in his side, and at the end of the block a diner he'd never before noticed came into view. To his surprise its lights were on, revealing the shapes of several people sitting inside, enjoying a meal. He imagined them eating steak and potatoes, and the simplicity of it made him want to cry. But it also gave him a sense of relief. If he could just make it inside, he'd be safe.

He reached the glass door, threw it open, lurched inside, locked the door behind him, and rushed to the counter. The conversation in the diner stopped, and as he crossed the restaurant's cold tiled floor, he could feel multiple eyes on him. His ankle was on fire, he was gasping for air, and the woman at the register grinned at him. She seemed warm. Her smile reminded him of his mother's.

"Call nine-one-one," he managed between his panting. "Some women are trying to kill me."

And when the woman at the register said, "Women? Why are these women trying to kill you, honey?" he heard the familiar *click, click, click* as she walked from behind the counter in stilettos, a smile frozen on her face.

Staring at her shoes, he stumbled backward against a counter stool. The metal seat crashed to the floor.

"Oh. Don't mind my noisy shoes, darling. They're just stilettos. Did you know these tapered heels resemble actual daggers?" She cocked her heel in the air toward Richie. Blood dripped from the tip. "Can you believe it? We force our poor feet into torture devices that approximate instruments of murder. I mean, how cute!"

He turned toward the now-locked exit. The women who had chased him were no longer outside the diner, but every customer in the restaurant smiled and giggled, their breasts jiggling in their midriff-baring tops, their blood-red stilettos glistening in the restaurant's pale lights.

"Did you want to order something, sugar?" The woman reached for a spinning rack on the counter. She picked up an old newspaper, with the headline, "U.S. Supreme Court Overturns Roe v. Wade," as if she were handing him a menu. "What can I get you, sweetie?"

She grabbed another newspaper from the rack; its headline read, "American Women Earn 82 Cents for Every Dollar a Man Makes."

"You can get an order of sexism with a side of misogyny. Or did you want an entree? I think we still have some gender-pay gap left. Or we can get you a ten-ounce order of patriarchy. How would you like that cooked? Well? Medium? Rare? I prefer rare."

The women —seated at the tables and at the lunch counter, and those perched on the bench near the front door, presumably waiting to be served —all rose in unison, their laughter increasing, their blouses unbuttoning, as they stepped forward and crowded around him, making it difficult to think, to breathe, to stay alive.

Click. Click. Click.

JACK LANTEY

Hookworm

"Come on, you know how long it's been?" Tad pushed Chrissie's hand to his crotch. His eyes jumped back and forth from her to the end of the alley. "It's been forever."

Chrissie knew exactly how long it'd been since the last time, and knowing that didn't make her want to do it any more.

It wasn't the location. This alley was about as private as any other place she'd been asked to perform in, and it wasn't Tad's whininess. He was like this for everything, whether it was picking where to eat or, like now, unhitching his belt.

"It's been forever..." Tad trailed off as he stood over a sewer grate and released his Kraken.

Release the Kraken was how Tad referred to it. Chrissie thought of it more honestly as letting out his little hookworm.

She hesitated for a second. Better to get it over with than listen to him cry about *how much his boys were hurting* later. In his defense, it had been months. He was probably backed up and full of swimmers.

Chrissie dropped to her knees and let out a tiny gasp as she landed on broken glass.

"You like that, baby?" Tad asked. In the dark alley, he could see neither the glass nor Chrissie rolling her eyes. "You got me so hard." Tad let his pants fall to the dirty pavement and grabbed Chrissie's hair, pulling her face to his crotch.

At least he's on brand, Chrissie thought, relaxing her jaw.

To his credit, Tad was immediately ready for action. He may not be much of a partner, but he never made Chrissie wait around for him to be ready.

The worst part for Chrissie was at the beginning. She didn't mind the smell, or the taste that followed, but it was that moment at the start that always turned her stomach. The way it moved inside of her mouth.

Again, it'd been months, and she knew there was no way to avoid it. Tad needed this.

Chrissie tried to distract herself, but then Tad would push himself harder into her mouth as if he was the one in control. *Knock yourself out,* she thought. *If it'll get this over with any faster.*

She knew no one else could do this. Only she had the talent and thick skin to take one for the team.

Then, on cue, it started to hurt. The tiny little bites inside her mouth bloomed, almost dainty at first, then more voracious, more hungry.

Chrissie sucked harder. She grabbed onto Tad's waist and pulled him tight against her face. He was quiet. She knew this part hurt him too.

With all the strength her throat could muster, she sucked his Kraken, harder each time.

The biting went from her lips to her tongue and then along her cheeks. He was about to erupt. Tears streaked Chrissie's face.

Then, as Tad always promised, he fired deep into Chrissie's throat, filling her mouth.

Tad pulled away and yanked his pants up, trying to protect his bloody dingus.

Chrissie stood, keeping her lips smashed as tightly closed as she could.

"Thank you..." Tad gasped.

Chrissie raised her finger to pause Tad, her cheeks extended like she was about to blow out the candles on her birthday cake.

She stumbled to the storm drain and leaned over. She pulled her hair back and bent at the waist.

Tad closed his eyes. He hated this part.

Chrissie spat out millions of blood-covered hookworms. Most went down the drain. Some landed on the cement, writhing about searching for a warm home. Chrissie wiped bile from her lips and stomped on the strays as they attempted to crawl away.

Tad watched in horror. He'd never get used to this.

Chrissie, satisfied that she'd gotten any stragglers, wiped her face clean and returned to Tad.

Coughing a last survivor into her hand, she smashed it against the brick wall next to Tad's face.

"I love you, Chrissie," Tad said.

"You'd better." She smiled. "Kiss?"

Ted smiled back. "Maybe later."

"I bet you wish I was like other guys."

"What do you mean?" Chrissie said.

"Guys who don't need help like this, who'd probably have better insurance."

"Probably," she said.

"And all they want on their birthdays is anal."

"Anal? That's fucking gross."

TOSHIYA KAMEI

Eat Me

I CRANED MY NECK and gazed out the latticed window, cursing Chifumi and her betrayal under my breath. And I cursed my lord, Kokoro, too. Although I adored him, he was so stubborn and unyielding that he continued to dismiss my warnings. Had he paid me heed, Chifumi's rebellion would have been crushed by now. Chewing leaves to ease the delirium of hunger, I recalled, once again, the conversation I had with Kokoro in his library weeks ago.

"Kokoro-sama." I had stepped toward my lord. He stood in front of a bookshelf, scanning the spines. He had worn a blue silk kimono that complemented his masculine figure and pale complexion. In contrast, I wore a pink furisode with long, hanging sleeves to match my feminine mood that morning.

He pulled a book from the shelf and leafed through the pages. A deep frown marred his handsome face. I wondered what he was looking for. Wisdom, perhaps. But no amount of knowledge would open a heart.

Kokoro, don't be a bookworm! I wanted to tease him like I had when we were kids. Back then, I went by Ako, the milk name I discarded when I came of age and shaved my pate. Once as close as brothers, we had grown apart as we grew older. We're lord and servant, I reminded myself. I held my breath, swallowing the lump forming in my throat.

"My ninja recently observed a peculiar movement in Chifumi's estate," I said, lowering my voice. "She appears to be gathering bushi."

"Don't worry," he said, his eyes still fixed on the page. I fought the urge to yank the book away.

"But my lord," I said. "She has repeatedly turned down your marriage proposals. We have a good reason to distrust her."

"I thought you didn't want me to marry her," he said, looking up for the first time.

I remained silent. There was no incentive for Chifumi to marry Kokoro. If she married him, she'd lose her independence and properties.

"We have gone over this many times before," he said. "Marriage is merely a means to form a military alliance. You have no reason to be jealous."

"I'm not jealous," I said. "What are you reading anyway?"

I stepped closer and saw a woodcut image of naked torsos. It was an illustrated erotic tale featuring two men, but I glimpsed one of them sneaking a kiss from a woman.

"It's none of your business," Kokoro said, turning his body to block my view.

I had stormed out of the library. When I returned to my room, I changed into a green man's kimono, poured myself a large cup of sake, and berated myself for being a lovesick fool.

The past slowly loosened its grip on me, and as my old memories and keen frustrations faded like stale smoke, I felt the hunger pains growing. I placed a hand on my stomach as it groaned.

I looked outside again. Skeletal remains of koi lay scattered in the moat that had been filled with water only a few weeks ago.

Smoke rose in the distance, indicating mealtime. That was how Chifumi tormented us while we starved. Hundreds of bushi surrounded the castle, cutting off all of our supply lines. We were worse off than cornered rats.

I stepped into the kitchen and found Kiyomi, the cook who had been with us since the previous lord's time.

"Any rats?" I asked. She shook her head.

I walked around and checked the traps. They were all empty.

Three weeks had passed since Chifumi's siege began. After running out of food, we resorted to catching rats and roasting them. Now, the rats had run out, as well.

I left the kitchen and found Kokoro in the zashiki where tea was served. Unfortunately, we'd also run out of tea.

"Kokoro-sama," I said.

I fell to my knees and kowtowed, my forehead almost touching the floor. The baked-grass scent of the tatami tickled my nose.

When I was young, Kokoro was the sun to me, too bright for direct contemplation.

"It's only a matter of time before we run out of water."

"What do you suggest?" Kokoro asked, sitting behind the low wooden table.

I glided over to Kokoro, leaning into him. I was close enough to kiss him, but I fought the urge.

"Eat me," I whispered in his ear. "Eat me, and you'll live. You'll figure out a way to survive this."

"Are you serious?" Kokoro asked, raising an eyebrow.

"It's the only way," I said, emboldened. I had nothing to lose. I didn't even need sake to loosen my tongue.

Kokoro kept quiet.

"Trust me," I said. "It will work."

"If you say so," Kokoro said. I tried to hide my trembling lips, devastated by the absence of gratitude in his tone.

"Thank you, Kokoro-sama." I bowed before retiring to my room.

I pulled my wakizashi from my waist and sawed off my right hand. It fell to the floor with a thud. I didn't feel pain or bleed. Perhaps my blood had run dry like the moat below the lattice window.

I picked up my hand, went down to the kitchen, and sought Kiyomi once more.

"Help me roast this," I said.

"It's your hand!" Kiyomi cried, startled. "I cooked a monkey hand years ago to treat Kokoro's father's illness, but never a human hand."

"I'm feeding Kokoro-sama," I said. "I love him."

"I knew that," she said. "But he'll never love you back."

"It doesn't matter," I said. "I was born to serve my lord like my father before me." Unlike me, my father wasn't in love with his lord. However, he committed seppuku on the day of his lord's funeral.

Kokoro and I grew up together. When we were thirteen, I ate a girl who said she was in love with him. She tasted like undercooked chicken. Her sour smell lingered in me for months. After a while, my body rounded with feminine curves.

I watched Kiyomi roast my hand on the kamado. The smell of burned flesh caught in my throat, and I coughed.

I entered Kokoro's room, balancing a wooden ozen on my hip. He sat on the tatami, reading another book.

When I set the ozen in front of Kokoro, he looked up. He became fixed on the plate.

"You've lost yourself in a book again," I said. "I am not jealous of Chifumi, but I'm jealous of the words." He flinched at the mention of our enemy, and it gave me some small satisfaction.

"Don't you need your hand?" he asked, ignoring what I'd said. "You could have chosen some other part." He fidgeted uncomfortably as if a worm was crawling out of his skin.

"But you don't let me touch you anymore," I blurted, surprising myself. I swallowed my tears, knowing my feelings would never be fully reciprocated. "Despite your name, you have no heart."

"Come now, Ako," he said. "Don't be so harsh." Maybe it was my imagination, but his voice trembled. Maybe he was ready to open up again. Hope fluttered in my stomach.

"You've just called me Ako again." Old memories careened back: Kokoro and I had waded through a mountain creek —water caressed our thighs, our fingers brushed, our touches lingered, our tangled bodies rolled down the grassy bank, our lips locked for the first time. When I told him we were bound the same way heaven and earth were bound, he had nodded with a smile.

"Forgive me," Kokoro said, averting his eyes. "I shouldn't have. I know we aren't kids anymore."

You're a servant, my father would have said. *Don't forget your lot in life.* My mind knew he was right, but my heart told me to disobey.

Kokoro's stomach groaned, and he stirred, shifting his weight. I slid behind him, rubbed his tense shoulders, ran my fingers through his hair. I knew he couldn't resist any longer.

"Let me watch you eat," I whispered, nibbling his earlobe. He pulled away, but I pursued him until he surrendered. As he took a bite of my offering, I shivered, and I couldn't stop.

AARON LEBOLD

Two Doors

EMILY APPROACHED THE MCMANSION, Sara at her side. It was the type of place that was copied and pasted throughout the subdivision. Sara could tell that her new friend had money, as the family had sprung for the special garage doors and glass front entrances that few of the otherwise identical houses could boast. Sara was new at Emily's school, and Emily told her she had a nose for picking out popular girls and something about Sara stood out.

They stopped at the gates. Emily pressed a series of buttons and it popped open.

"Such a pain to have to do this every day. The system should know it's me and let me in —like my cell phone."

Sara smiled. "Yeah, but it's good to be protected, right?"

"Yeah, whatever, so what's your house like?"

"We're in an apartment right now. We're still new to the city."

Emily opened the door and both girls stepped inside. "An apartment? Ew, what do your parents do?"

"My parents both passed away. Well, we think they did. They've never been found. Monty is a friend of the family who helped raise me. I kind of look at him like my dad."

Emily didn't respond. They were now in a massive space with what Sara was sure was an original Jean-Michel Basquiat adorned in a steel frame. She recognized the three-pointed crown. There was a television that she guessed was at least eight feet across. "So this is the living room," Emily said. "I told my dad we need a bigger TV but he still hasn't got one. Rude. Come, I'll show you my room."

Sara took a deep breath and followed her new friend up an exceptionally wide staircase with dense wooden handrails and twisted iron spindles. At the top they proceeded down a vast hall. Emily stopped at a door with pink hearts taped to the outside and opened it. "So yeah, this is where I spend most of my time. It's not much but my parents are supposed to be putting in a hot tub. I've already been waiting like, a week, so I don't know what the problem is."

Sara figured the bedroom was as big as the apartment she shared with Monty. "I think it's really nice. You're lucky."

"Lucky? Ahh, no. My friend Lucile is lucky. She got a hot tub in her room the same day she asked for it. It's like my parents don't even care about me."

Sara tried not to roll her eyes. Emily was clearly spoiled and entitled. She would love to give Emily a taste of real problems.

The two girls sat in Emily's room talking. Mostly Emily was showing off her things, and then complaining about them. It wasn't long before a voice could be heard calling up the stairs.

"Emily, honey, we're home."

"Ugh, that's my stupid parents," Emily said before calling back to her mother. "Great, did you get me my hot tub?"

"Not yet sweetie. It needs to be customized for the space —I told you that."

"Bitch," Emily said with frustration. Sara tried to smile but was getting annoyed. Emily could barely sit still. "Let's go downstairs," Emily said. "I need to talk to my father."

Sara nodded and followed her new friend through the hall and down the grand staircase. They were barely at the bottom when Emily called out, "Father?"

Emily's father came out of the kitchen. He wore a sheepish expression, as though he knew he was about to get in trouble. "Yes, Princess?"

"Where is my hot tub? I asked for it a week ago."

Emily's mother joined in. "I told you sweetie —they have to custom-make it. They need measurements and time. We're working on it."

"You're not working very fast."

Her father said, "Princess please, don't get upset. It should be here in three more days."

"Three days? That is so unfair!" Emily began flailing her arms like a toddler. "I hate you both! I wish you were dead!" She stormed back to her room. The door slammed, audible from the bottom of the stairs.

Sara extended a hand to shake. "I'm Sara. I'm new in town. Nice to meet you."

Ignoring her, Emily's parents left the room in a strange sideways embrace, comforting each other in an awkward, dramatic way. Sara pulled out her phone and texted Monty before letting herself out the front door.

Emily awoke in a dark room. The floor was concrete but the atmosphere made identifying other distinguishing features difficult. She couldn't remember how she got here. Sitting up, she rubbed her temples, trying her best to recall anything that could help her figure out where she was. The last thing she remembered was walking home from school. Everything after that was a blur. The more awake and aware she became, the more her reality began to set in. She grew more terrified by the minute.

"Hello? Is anyone here?"

Silence filled the air until a loud noise echoed through the room, followed by a sterile neon light that illuminated her surroundings. She looked around frantically, but the dull glow didn't offer up much new information. "Hello? Who's there? What's going on?"

The room was small and crafted of cement. There were two small, round doors on one of the walls like closed portholes on a ship.

She got up and then froze when she heard a loud distorted voice echoing through the small space.

"Hello, Emily."

"Who's there?"

"In this room, you will see two doors. If you want to live, all you have to do is leave. One door leads to freedom and the other leads to a dead end." There was some distorted chuckling that sent shivers up Emily's spine. The voice added, "Literally."

She squinted, glancing back and forth at the two doors. They were small but she was confident she could fit through either of them.

"That's it? I just have to open the doors and I can leave?"

"If you look on the floor in the corner of the room, you will find all the tools you need to gain access to your freedom."

"What tools?" She padded over to where a Swiss army knife lay on the cement floor. She picked it up and examined it. It was a good one —it had everything: a saw, a screwdriver, and a blade sharpened to an intense edge.

"What am I supposed to do with this?"

No response.

She headed to the first door. It was latched closed with a Philips head screw. The knife had a screwdriver bit that was the perfect shape and size.

"This really isn't that hard you know, whoever you are." She wasn't sure who she was trying to convince, her captor, or herself.

She slid the screwdriver in and began to turn it. The screws came out with ease and the door was free to open.

"Wow, that was hard. See ya, psycho."

She flung the door open and saw her true challenge. The entire interior of the door was blocked with something. It had a pinkish hue and she couldn't tell what it was. She reluctantly pressed her finger against it.

"Hello? Who's there? Help me, please."

Emily jumped back —the obstruction was a living human being. But instead of concern, she felt only annoyance.

"Get out of the way. I need to get through that door. Is there an exit in there?"

"I can't move," said a voice Emily knew. "I'm chained to the wall and I can't see anything. Please, help me."

"Mom?"

"Emily?"

Emily turned around and stared at the ceiling. "What is this? Talk to me! Why is my mother here? How am I supposed to get out?"

Emily pushed her mother's back as hard as she could in an attempt to remove her obstruction from the small porthole. She was determined but made no progress, and could hear her mother rustling trying to free herself on the other side. Emily pushed harder.

"Oww. I can't move. I'm stuck to the wall and my hands are in cuffs or something."

Emily began crying. Panicking, she searched the rest of the room. It was all concrete and there was no other way out. She pulled out the screwdriver and approached the second door. Once the screws were off, it opened with ease. It too was blocked by something that appeared to be flesh.

She poked it. "Hello?"

"Princess? What are we doing here?"

"Daddy?"

The distinct sound of weeping filled the small room. Emily turned, looking for a camera or a speaker.

Something.

She yelled as loudly as she could.

"How am I supposed to get through the doors when my parents are chained to them? What is this? Say something." She was starting to feel helpless.

This wasn't fair.

"Mom! I think he wants me to... go through you..."

Silence.

"What do you mean? Who is he?" Her mother's voice came out shaking and unsteady.

"I don't know," Emily said. "A voice told me that my only way out is through these doors. What do I do?"

Her father spoke. "Try to find another way out."

"I did that. There aren't any."

"Then go through me," he said in a more commanding tone than she was used to. "Save yourself, and your mother."

Crying, Emily sat on the floor, her back against the wall. She closed the screwdriver and pulled out the sharpened blade. She laid it against her wrist but hesitated. She couldn't do it, even if it meant saving herself and her mother. She heard her father from the other side of the wall.

"If you don't do it, we're all going to starve to death. Save yourself. Do what you have to."

Emily wanted to wait it out. She wanted her parents to try harder to get free. Her father insisted he would rather be killed by someone he loved than starve to death and never be found. Emily took a deep breath and perched beside the second window. The knife was locked into place. She had to convince herself she was about to cut into something that wasn't her father —like a pig or a homeless person.

Her father sensed her hesitation. "Just do it."

She closed her eyes and slid the blade into his back. It hit something solid and she could hear him gritting his teeth, screams muted into whines and whispers. She moved the knife around, removing small chunks of flesh. Slowly working her way toward freedom, she could hear him crying on the other side of the wall.

Every time she stopped, he'd say the same thing. "Get it over with. Just do it."

After twenty minutes of digging, she realized his spinal column was too strong to cut through with the small knife. With tears in her eyes, she folded up the blade and replaced it with the saw. She shook as she placed it against the exposed bone, and started at the bottom of the window. Slowly and meticulously she began sliding it back and forth. She could feel the serrated blade chewing through his vertebrae. Her father was still awake, and clearly struggling to control his reactions. Emily could see dangling intestines dancing back and forth as he pushed against his restraints.

Once she made the saw blade through the bottom of the spinal cord she pulled on it hard. She used all of her strength, moving it upward to break it off.

She called out, "I'm so sorry Daddy. Are you all right?"

He didn't respond.

She figured her father had passed out from the pain. She hadn't thought to start at the top, which would have made him lose feeling in his lower half. Her hands were tremorous as she folded up the saw and brought the small knife back into play. With her father unresponsive, the process was less daunting but far from easy.

It took another twenty minutes before she managed to slash and stab her way through his torso. She knew she had to make the hole big enough to fit through. She cut around the inside edge of the round window, shaving the meat and removing the fallen bits with her hands. Eventually, a hole was whittled to a size she thought she could squeeze through. She put both her hands through her father followed by her head. The squeeze was tight, like a newborn baby pushing its way into the world. It was a literal meat tunnel, complete with severed bone and internal organs. She inched her way through, using her hips to push herself forward. Soon her hands touched the floor. She used all her strength to push against the back of the cement wall and drag the rest of her body out of the window.

"Oh my God, Mom. I made it through. I'm on the other side."

From her hands and knees, still dripping with warm bits of her father, she looked up to see a door. It was open but no light shone through. Her eyes had adjusted enough to the light that she could make out the basics of the room. It was small, sterile, with a concrete floor. The only notable feature was the door. She fixed her gaze on it as she slowly climbed to her feet and stepped toward it. The door slammed shut. She froze.

Written on the door in spray paint, mocking her, was, "Sorry, wrong door."

She screamed. Running at the door, she banged on it with all her strength. It wouldn't budge. Exhausted, she dropped to her knees and rotated, facing the room. Her father was shackled to the wall with a large hole bored through his stomach. A pool of blood and bits of flesh gathered on the floor, stretching across the concrete.

"I'm sorry Daddy." It was the first time she felt any sympathy for the man. She had always seen him as a means to getting what she wanted. Now he was gone, and by her hand. The adrenaline coursing through her made it difficult to come to terms with what she had done.

She jumped when her father opened his eyes.

He was still alive.

"I forgive you, Princess. Please, kill me."

"What? Daddy, I can't." Now, she wondered what it would take to save him. Give him back his life after all he had given her.

"Please Emily, kill me. I can't take it." His eyes rolled back and his head slumped down.

Emily walked toward him. She had left the knife on the other side. She poked him and he didn't respond.

"I'm so sorry, Daddy." Tears rolled down her cheeks.

She put her arms back through the hole, pushing her head back through the wound in her father's abdomen and pulling herself as hard as she could. She burst into fresh tears as he screamed in pain and did her best to get through as quickly as possible. She dropped to the floor and picked up the small blade.

"I'll do it, Daddy."

No response —he'd lost a lot of blood.

Emily continued crying as she sat with her back against the cement wall —knife in hand.

"I did it. Let me out of here. What is wrong with you?"

Emily rose to her feet and returned to her mother's window. Her frame was smaller and there were tiny gaps on each side of her waist. She decided that she could cut her mother in half.

"I'm sorry Mom. I need to get out of here."

It was hard for her not to think of herself. She had already killed one of her parents and knew her only option was to repeat the process. She knew her mother had been listening the entire time. She would have known that her husband was already dead and accepted her own fate.

Emily felt she could be far more efficient with her mother. She started at the top and slid the blade into her flesh. Her mother didn't scream. As she sliced away at the muscle tissue, Emily heard only whimpering. Once she got deep enough she could see the white of her mother's vertebrae. She picked up the small saw. Back and forth she dragged it. Small pieces of bone dust fell as she began to gnaw away at the spinal column.

"Motherfucker!" Emily had never heard her mother swear before.

Emily worked faster. Through with the hard part, she switched back to the small knife and began removing flesh. Her mother's back opened up, and her small intestine slipped into the small door, making a squishing sound, snaking its way onto the floor, and landing on Emily's foot. She forced herself to look away and kept working. The gap was widening. The weight of her mother's lower half was helping her see where her body was still connected. She sliced through where she needed as more organs slipped out, staying focused until the bottom half of her mother's body fell to the floor on the other side of the wall. She threw the small knife through the window and climbed her way through. While she squeezed into the bloody opening, she felt warm drops of blood and fluids land on her back. She felt the organs under her feet explode from her weight. She dropped to the floor on the other side and fell onto her mother's legs. Instinctively, she screamed and jumped to her feet.

The door in front of her was open.

She looked back at her mother, who remained silent but her chest was still rising and falling. She was staring wide-eyed and seemed to be in a state of shock. Emily knew she couldn't leave her like that. She picked up the knife and walked slowly toward her bleeding mother.

"I'm so sorry, Mom."

She slid the blade across her mother's throat. Blood gently poured out. It was like a serene fountain on a low setting. It cascaded to the floor, adding to the puddle that had already accumulated. Her mother's eyes rolled back. She looked at peace.

It was over in less than a minute.

Emily turned around and looked at the open door, concerned that it may slam shut like the previous one. She made a run for it. Before she knew it, she was standing in a field in the middle of nowhere.

It took three days for Emily to make it to a town. She was found in a catatonic state and struggled to explain to the police what had happened. When she was finally able to communicate the parts she could recall, the police weren't able to find the building. They asked Emily if anyone else, other than her, had been inside their home the day she was taken captive. She told them that a new girl, Sara, had gone home with her that day. She told them Sara's parents were dead, and she lived in an apartment in town with a guardian whose name, she thought, was Monty.

Sara and Monty sat together at the breakfast table. They were having toast and eggs before Sara headed off to school. Monty took a sip of his orange juice.

"So, has your friend Emily been to school this week?"

"No. I haven't seen her, literally. Funniest thing."

They smiled at each other and Sara gave him a peck on the cheek before heading out of the small apartment.

Emily's parents' bodies were never located.

SHANNON LAWRENCE

Hork

THE RASPY *HORK* ECHOED off the walls, causing my heartbeat to surge. Sweat popped out on my palms and forehead, and I leapt up from my food-encrusted easy chair, stocking feet hitting the carpet. I slid as my socks came into contact with the scuffed kitchen hardwood floor, but caught my balance just in time to glide around the corner, my senses on high alert.

Where had it come from? I paused, trying to hear over my heart pounding in my throat. My entire body pulsed.

Hucka, hucka, wheeeeeze, hork.

Oh, shit.

The sound had come from my left. I ran like I'd never run before, heedless of my safety in the dangerous maze of the dining room, dodging chairs left and right with desperation born of experience. My little toe made contact with a chair leg and bugled pain up the nerves of my foot and ankle.

On soft, padded paws, the culprit walked by me, holding her tail disdainfully in the air. She didn't so much as acknowledge my presence. Instead, she came to a stop by her food dish and preened, tongue rasping through her fur, still ignoring me.

"Real nice, Sasquatch."

I scurried around the room, seeking the offensive pile of hair, vomit, and bile. It had to be here somewhere. The sound she'd produced was not one that left a dry, clean floor in its wake. Any second now, I'd feel the warm, wet, chunky squish of cat vomit between my toes, soaking my sock faster than a sponge in a rain puddle. I steeled my stomach for the inevitable task of soaking up hot bodily fluids with a paltry paper towel. This time I wouldn't gag.

But as I searched, confusion rattled me, and I grew dizzy with panic and puzzlement. No vomit under the chairs or the table, on the cat tree, or on top of the table. The plants appeared safe. Nothing stood out on the stairs. Grimacing, I bent down and felt along the carpeting that lined the steps, waiting for the thick fluidity of the bile to web its way between my fingers.

Still nothing.

Did she swallow it back down?

A whiff of cat-vomit smell, that raw mix of fish and intestines, drifted by, but disappeared before I could follow it to the guilty pile.

I turned and shot a glare at the stupid, majestic beast. Her charcoal-colored fur shone smooth and velvety in the light streaming through the dining room windows. She glanced at me once then proceeded to eat daintily from her dish. The gentle crunch of her teeth sinking through the pellets sent the odor of meat and whatever else cat food contained drifting around the room, gradually replacing the foul stench of her horks and hairball-fueled vomiting.

After looking around one last time, I returned to my chair and restarted my TV show where I'd left off. My heart returned to a normal pace, and my breath calmed.

False alarm.

Damn cat.

From the next room came the delicate lapping of water then her clicking claws on the wood, and she leapt up onto the back of my chair, causing it to shift slightly under her weight. Her purrs vibrated through the thick cloth, and she butted my head with hers, urging me to pet her. I massaged her head and scratched her neck until she'd had enough, at which point she nipped my hand and jumped off the chair, disappearing to nap elsewhere in private. Fed, watered, and petted, she wouldn't show herself again for hours.

Or so I thought.

About twenty minutes later, I heard her approaching. She sounded weird, almost like she was rolling across the floor. And the liquid *sploot* sounding intermittently told me she'd somehow gotten wet. Sometimes she drank from the toilet, but she'd never fallen in. Then again, as graceful as cats were supposed to be, I'd seen this little diva slip and trip in a variety of ways, always standing up immediately and acting like she'd meant to do it.

More concerned about the mess she must be making than her state of wetness, I stood up, but only halfheartedly. My eyes remained on the television screen, where experts discussed a famous serial killer and his methods. Horrified, yet fascinated, I couldn't take my eyes off the crime scene photos that flashed between snippets of talk. The things a person could do with a can opener and a hairbrush were absolutely terrifying and disturbing.

I stepped in something wet and went ass over teakettle, right foot flying into the air, left foot sliding backward. I landed in a split and pain tore up my legs, radiating out along my thighs. Adding insult to injury, the goo on the floor was soaking through my jeans.

I groaned, gripping my groin and rolling to the side to put both legs in front of me. Studying the moisture, I discovered it was a slime trail, grotesque in its viscosity. It looked like something Slimer would have left behind, only yellow and brown instead of green. Mixed into the slime were chunks of what appeared to be cat food, along with elongated rolls of charcoal-gray fur.

No healthy cat could possibly produce this much stomach purge and still be okay. Maybe she'd eaten something bad. I looked around for her, but she wasn't in the room.

My fall must have scared her off, though I'd been too busy shrieking profanity to hear her scamper away.

Wincing, I stood up. The cold air hit my sopping wet crotch, and I shuddered at the unpleasant sensation that dripped down my legs. I limped around the room, peeking under the end tables, but Sasquatch was nowhere to be found. Tracking along the same path I'd followed earlier when seeking the furball, I checked every nook and cranny, careful to avoid the slime trail.

When I got to the cat tree, a muffled *merowp* sounded from within. A peek inside revealed one curious, half-lidded amber eye. She unfurled herself, came partway out of the hidey-hole, and stretched as far as she could, ears pulling back with the intensity of the movement. Then she yawned, turned around, and retreated into the hole, her back to me.

Reaching in, I touched the fur on her back then petted along her spine down to the tip of her tail. A quick scritch of her head and shoulders left her purring, but gave no evidence of slime or vomit. I rubbed her chest and scratched just beneath her chin. The purring stopped when I pushed forward and ran a hand over her belly. The energy she saved from not purring instantly transferred to her tail, which whipped around in irritation. It was amazing how much ire a cat could express with one part of the body, a tail dancing around like an irate cobra.

I straightened. Huh. She seemed fine, and her fur was dry. Not even a trace of dampness on her chin. The cat tree was also dry.

As I stood there, something else dawned on me. The slime trail hadn't even gone to the tree. How had I not noticed that before? Instead, it diverted around the kitchen table and into the bathroom.

I hadn't checked there for the hairball.

Tiptoeing around the sludge path, I approached the bathroom door. It stood slightly ajar. A ray of light fell through the crack, casting a narrow beam of illumination across the sink and cabinet and leaving the rest of the bathroom in shadow. The slime trail disappeared under the door. It wouldn't be the first time Sasquatch shut a door. But for this scenario to happen, she'd have had to vomit on the way in, nudge the door mostly closed, then manage to squeeze out through the crack. Even the most agile of felines —and agile, she wasn't —would have trouble pulling that off. Also her paws should have gotten wet. And in fact, there were no wet pawprints at all, in either direction.

Something had made this trail, and I didn't think it was Sasquatch.

Standing as far back as possible while still within reach of the door, I used two fingers to push at it. The cheap wood caught on a bundle of cat fur dreadlock, so I gave it another shove and the door swung open. This allowed more light in, but I still saw nothing other than the sludge. Once more I reached out, this time to turn on the light. My hand moved out of my sight, groping in the air for the switch. I leaned in farther, shoulder now inside the doorway, arm extended as far as it would go.

Goose bumps crawled up my arm.

As I flipped the switch, something soft and dry touched my skin.

I jerked my arm back, expecting... well, I don't know what I expected.

That was when I looked down and got my first glimpse of the horrid cat sploot on the bathroom floor —if indeed the throw-up had originated from inside a cat. It was the foulest thing I'd ever seen. Oozing across the tiles were half-digested cat food pellets in a thick, slimy bile that looked like squashed jellyfish, only yellow, and a thin bit of red string. Plus what appeared to be blood. Fear for Sasquatch resurged, but the stupid cat had been fine and in her hidey-hole just a moment earlier.

On a whim, I stepped into the bathroom, careful to avoid the gut-splosion, and followed the stream of semi-fluids that disappeared behind the toilet. Furred strands of something lay beside the mostly white porcelain of the toilet pedestal. I squinted to make out what exactly lurked behind the toilet tank, in that shadowy crevice rarely touched by hands or sponges.

I leaned closer.

A gray-furred tendril shot out and wrapped itself around my leg.

Another one came for my face, dripping even as it flew through the air.

I threw myself backward and my head and shoulder slammed into the wall. The appendage just missed my face with a wet splat and rebounded. Bits of caustic stomach juice splashed onto my cheek. At the same time, something wet and heavy landed on the floor, sending out a wave of putrid cat-gut-rot stench in its wake. A large mass emerged from behind the toilet. Multiple furred filaments spidered out from its center. It was using its hold on my leg to pull itself toward me.

I turned to run, yanking at the trapped leg. There was a small amount of give, but not enough. I grabbed the door frame and tried to haul myself out. Disgust filled me as the moisture from the clinging appendage seeped through my jeans to my skin, a sick warmth added to the already cold dampness.

Another tendril snared my thigh. Now both legs were caught. I pulled with all my might, but couldn't breach the doorway. The protrusions continued to seek out my body and limbs, twining around my torso, legs, and arms. The granddaddy of all fur-tendrils reached my throat, and the strong smell of damp cat food and stagnant intestinal juices hit me. The cold, wet strand felt like a thick band of steel wool. I couldn't move my arms to pull at it or try to loosen it.

To my horror, the coils maneuvered my body, turning me against my will, stocking feet easily sliding around on the linoleum. My gaze fell on the mirror, my reflection revealing what looked like a steel wool-encased mummy. Only my face was free.

A loop shot around my forehead. Viscous fluids leaked down into my eyes, causing them to burn. I blinked frantically to clear my vision, but the world only blurred more. The tendril pulled my head forward so that I was forced to look down to the floor and the amorphous blob that awaited me —a matted mess of fur and smooshed-together chunks of cat food, plus what might have been a bit of intestine.

The creature squelched with every movement, a thick, wet sound that made me want to vomit. Only fear of my own puke becoming animated like this glorified hairball kept my gorge at bay.

As I tried to focus on the vomit monster, from the corner of my eye I made out another approaching tendril. This one came for me with slow, dreadful purpose.

It inched forward.

It touched my mouth.

The combination of vomit odor and the sensation of slime against my lips caused my gorge to rise again. I clenched my jaw and squeezed my lips together with all my might.

Unfazed, the creature used the tip of the tendril to pry at my lips. I gagged and murbled out a close-mouthed yell that turned into a scream that vibrated up through my sinuses. It continued to wriggle against my lips, a sensation that defied explanation, like being tickled with a gelatin-coated hair sponge, but grosser. It smelled like cat breath magnified a thousand times. My nasal passages burned.

I fought to keep my mouth closed, but the creature pried its way in. Like a soggy, slimy invading army, its tendril staunchly marched across my tongue and down my throat, suffocating me even as the flavor of rotten cat food and the intense acidic taste of stomach acid coated my taste buds. Tears flooded from my eyes, clearing some of the glutinous muck from my vision.

Fully down my throat now, the appendage expanded inside my intestines. I felt like my guts would explode. By some miracle, I freed a hand from the matted cat fur and grabbed the clammy, mucus-coated tendril, pulling as hard as I could. But my hand kept slipping, lubricated by the abominable goo, and the tendril continued burrowing deeper into my body.

I strained against my binds, struggling to breathe past the thing blocking my airway. It abraded my mouth, lips, and chin. My panic ramped up, causing my heart to pound all the harder. I had no idea how this thing had come to be, but knowing its origin wouldn't matter if it killed me.

My other hand broke free, and I grasped the tendril with both fists now, squeezing as hard as I could to keep my grip. Smaller filaments wrapped around my wrists and yanked, but I resisted their efforts, determined to save my life and pull this putrid thing out of my body.

A *merowp* sounded from somewhere below.

Sasquatch rubbed against my leg, headbutting it. I tried to make a sound of warning, but couldn't. I felt several more rubs, then Sasquatch let out a questioning burr. *Yes, you dumb cat, your hairball is killing me.*

Then came the unmistakable sound of her eating.

Had a tendril not already been feeling around in my digestive system, I surely would have barfed.

Blocking out, to the best of my ability, the sounds of Sasquatch's gobbling —wanting but not wanting to know if she was, oh god, consuming the monster hairball —I made progress, slowly pulling the abomination out of my mouth. I could feel it scratching its way up inside my chest now, free of my stomach. My nose ran with my own mucus mingled with hairball ooze. It felt as if I were breathing through liquid, blowing bubbles through my nostrils. Any second now I would suffocate. All while my cat ate her own sentient vomit.

I fell to my knees, barely feeling the wet squish as I landed on some portion of the creature. I could feel myself weakening. The monstrosity took advantage of my slackening grip and renewed its journey into my intestines.

Closing my eyes, I gathered the last of my strength and pulled, working the tendril, hand over hand. No way in hell would I die this way.

It came all the way up, the tip tickling its way past my tonsils before gliding out of my mouth. I threw it down with a splat and flailed at the abhorrent entity, kicking it aside and writhing to get away. Sasquatch made a disgruntled chirp and scampered off. The cabinet below the sink was just within reach. I flung open the door and pulled out the bleach and enzyme cleaner. Tendrils grabbed for the smooth bottles, but failed to find purchase. I managed to pop the top off of each and douse the hairball with the two liquids.

The protuberances withdrew immediately. Still holding the bottles, I struggled to my feet and drenched every bit of the creature I could get to. It writhed and shook, arching away from me. Emptying first one bottle, then the other, I threw them down and scrambled into the hallway, slamming the door shut and leaving the thing to dissolve in silence on the other side.

Sliding down the wall, I swiped at my eyes, getting the last of the goo out of them. Sasquatch sat in the hallway, grooming herself, her giant eyes fixed on me in silent threat.

"Oh, no you don't." My voice came out in a rasp, throat aching at the effort. I stood up and grabbed her, running to the back door to toss her gently onto the porch. "Go eat some grass and throw up *outside*. Then maybe I'll let you back in."

I limped to the kitchen sink to wash my mouth out with soap, then swallowed down a bunch of vinegar. It stung, which gave me a certain sense of peace. I'd have swallowed bleach if it wouldn't kill me, but vinegar would have to do. Every trace of that thing must be eradicated.

Through the screen door, I heard Sasquatch.

Horka, horka, horka, blap.

NORA B. PEEVY

What's in Her Pimple?

THE PIMPLE ON VERIETTA'S face had doubled in size since the previous evening. About the size of a quarter, it bulged, swollen, an ugly, angry shade of red. But far worse was when she leaned in close to the mirror under the harsh light and saw her flesh wriggling. An alien creature lived inside that gross humongous pimple —she was certain of it. She could feel it with every squirm and every turn, clawing away inside the flesh of her cheek. Verietta's fingers itched to pop that zit and watch the creamy, pale green pus squelch all over the mirror. But her stomach churned at the very thought, because she didn't know *exactly what form* of alien creature squirmed and wriggled inside her body. Was it a spider? A cockroach? A weird parasite as seen on TV. Or worse yet, a monster bug yet unidentified by scientists ready to rip her face off in a feeding frenzy?

What if it clawed its way out from a bloody, gouged-out hole in her cheek and she became a fat, slobbering, flesh-eating monster with horrid pincers?

Squeezing her eyes shut, Verietta pinched her fingers around the fat zit. The alien creature beneath struggled even more, as if aware it was about to perish under her skin or soon be freed from its fleshy prison.

She squeezed.

A giant POP! sent Verietta careening backward. When she opened her eyes hundreds of tiny translucent worms cascaded out of the gaping wound. A few stragglers emerged from the bloody hole and gnawed on the jagged crimson edges of her cheek. Verietta's face erupted in a painful, fiery sting and she opened her mouth to scream. But the tiny worms wriggled their way into her yawning orifice and latched onto her tongue, yanking it out of her mouth with a wet, slurping RIIIP! Blood geysers sprayed from her mouth and splattered the shower, walls, and towels.

The worms, having grown to about an inch long and as thick as a pinky finger, crept down her throat. Under the pressure, her neck bulged and twisted. Verietta's final living thought, upon glimpsing her reflection in the mirror, was that she looked like a contortionist performing for a gleeful audience. She collapsed, dead.

The worms barreled down her trachea, eating their way into her digestive tract, leaving behind a neck of shredded, scarlet holes, like Swiss cheese. Another wave of worms clawed their way up through her nasal cavity. Molting out of their skin into larger, stronger creatures, they sprouted ten sharp clawed legs on either side of their bodies. Thus commenced the munching of hundreds of mandibles, like feet stomping on eggshells. They multiplied as they feasted.

In the next room, Verietta's naked, sweaty parents —in the throes of passion and oblivious to the army of worms that had consumed their daughter —gyrated on the mattress. Now the size of forearms, the invaders vaporized the bathroom door and surged down the hallway. Verietta's father, who lay on top of her mother, had just enough time to look up before the worms burst through the bedroom door and buried themselves in his asshole.

EMMA ROSE DARCY

Cindy

CINDY WAS THE WOMAN of my dreams, delivered in the mail. She was eerily lifelike. With the latest technology in skin, she not only felt like the real deal but even warmed up during physical contact. I spent hours filling in the customisation form. Her height, her weight, the colour of her hair and eyes. There was nothing off limits. If I had wanted her to have a penis and a vagina, they'd have done it. Three tits and translucent purple skin, easy.

I'm a simple creature. In the end, the woman I described was the same one I always made in the life simulation games. The girl-who-lives-next-door type. A little smattering of freckles across the nose. A B-cup. I'm not greedy.

You could pay a little extra to have a chip in her head programmed to say particular phrases and even modulate her voice to sound husky, or sweet and flirty. It took me days to think about what I would want her to say. I didn't even choose particularly sexual things. I mostly chose conversational things, the things I remembered my ex and me saying to each other after sex.

Once I got her out of the box, the odd smell that pervaded the room when I popped the vacuum-sealed bag around her dissipated. I gave her a bath, which felt weird but intimate.

When we went to bed, that first night, I felt shy. Which was crazy —she was a sex doll. I bought her to have something to fuck. It was uncanny, though. She looked too real. Instead, I lay beside her in my bed and stroked her side as my body heat slowly warmed her skin and she felt softer and more inviting.

I woke up in the middle of the night because I thought I heard someone whispering. My apartment was small, but my neighbours worked and were courteous. I wasn't usually bothered by them. It had been in my ear too. I looked down at Cindy and frowned. I must have rolled her onto her back at some point during the night.

I was freaking myself out, telling myself I should have bought a fleshlight and that I had not put enough thought into what it would actually be like having a five-foot-six doll in my bed who never closed her eyes. When I lay back down to sleep, I did so with my back to her.

In the morning, Cindy's hand was in mine. I had rolled over during the night again and somehow pulled her against me so we were practically cheek to cheek. Waking up to see her blue-glass eyes staring right into my soul did direct damage to my morning wood. I'd been hoping to kick-start our relationship, but I was determined to overcome my discomfort and mustered an erection.

Still, I was paranoid. As I positioned myself to enter her, it felt like her gaze was following me. I managed a few perfunctory thrusts before realising I was avoiding eye contact with her. I fondled her breasts, and although they were perfect, they helped less than I hoped. I was on the verge of giving up altogether and going back to my hand and my favourite video previews on RubHub when I felt something *slide over me* —inside her.

I froze.

Again, there was the impossible feeling of her eyes on me as the unmistakable sensation of a hand, a firm hand, slick and rough, jerked me off. It was borderline too rough, something aggressive about it. Domineering. I finished with a perplexed kind of shout and withdrew cringing with shame. There had been nothing in the welcome pack about any kind of automatic weaponised vagina that I remembered reading. I wouldn't have selected anything with an abrasive hand-job setting.

She was sitting up in bed when I came home from work, which was just odd. I honestly couldn't remember what position I'd left her in. I'd planned when I bought her to leave her in a variety of places during the day, like she was a real girlfriend. Pose her reading by the window or whatever. I didn't think I'd started yet. The feeling of her eyes following me was so intense while I was having a shower and making dinner, I eventually laid her back down and put the bed sheet over her face.

There was a note written on the pad I kept by my landline. I was walking from the bathroom back to the kitchen when I saw it.

"Iloveyou"

It was not my handwriting, nor anything I would have written. There was a reason I was lonely enough to be buying an incredibly realistic sex doll. I flipped up the page to tear it off only to see more notes on the next page and the page after that.

"iknowwhereyouroffswitchis"

"sillyboy"

I jumped about a mile high and dropped the pad. The speaker playing my playlist stopped. It does that when I get a phone call. In the second of silence between the music fading out and the phone's ringtone cutting in, I could have sworn I heard some-one's voice in my bedroom.

The phone call was from my friend Dan. Dan is the man —I just ride in his wake. When I answered his query of what was happening in my world with a "nothing much" in completely the wrong pitch, he came back with a skeptical, "uh huh."

I filled him in on my relationship road bumps with Cindy. From where I stood I could see the bed sheet had fallen to her waist. She had somehow gotten her arms up and her hands lodged in the slats of my headboard.

"You bought a real girl doll?" Dan asked. He was enjoying this.

"Yeah man. She is super hot but it is not going well."

"Only you would strike out with a sex doll, dude. Are you cursed? Is your dick cursed?" Dan's laughter over the line mixed with the sounds of a bar in the background. "Come out. I'll get you a *really* real girl."

In a weird way, Dan was making me feel better. I just didn't know how to work the dumb doll. Maybe there was a faulty mechanism or her battery was swollen.

"Nah man. I'm going to see if I can figure out what's going on. Maybe they sent me the wrong model. It'll be a pain if I have to send her back."

I slunk into the bedroom, feeling ridiculous. Her face had turned away from me, and one leg had slipped out of the bed sheet. She was beautiful —the manufacturer had gone all out on the details. I let my hand travel from her ankle up to the soft underside of her knee and to the joint of her hip, then slipped two fingers inside the place that had almost mangled me that morning. I couldn't feel anything inside her now that indicated she had any motorised parts. All I could discern was that she was hot, literally sweltering inside.

I was puzzling it over when her head snapped back and her voice programming activated. Instead of what I'd chosen, the sweet nothings and coupley conversation, she began screaming.

"Help! Someone help me! Oh God, he's killing me! Help!"

She clamped down on my fingers in a vise grip. I yelped and fell backwards, but my fingers remained stuck.

"No! No, Stop! Stop, you can't! You can't! Don't do this!"

There was alarmed shouting out in the hall. A cold sweat broke out across my forehead. I lunged across her, trying to cover her mouth and muffle the sound, but the words weren't coming from her mouth. It was playing from a sound box inside her body. As I flailed around, panicking, her blue-glass eyes stared at me the same way as when she pulled me off that morning. The inertia of the moment felt bizarre.

Someone was knocking, then pounding at my door. Over the sounds of Cindy screaming, I tried shouting to them. "Everything is fine. There is nothing to worry about." But
her voice overpowered mine.

"He has me tied up. Please don't let him kill me!"

I stared at her in disbelief and fear, and an irrational feeling of betrayal surged through
me as my neighbours broke down my front door and I heard the pounding of feet through
the apartment.

I was wrenched backwards as someone hauled me off her, and I bleated as my trapped
fingers snapped. When the EMTs arrived and realised, like my neighbours, the screaming
body in my bed was in fact a sex doll, they were understandably concerned. As the EMTs
that had been called for Cindy attended to my mangled hand, the police concluded that
I had specifically ordered a sex doll that would scream for help.

I was taken in for questioning.

Cindy was confiscated for analysis.

I sat in the police interview room for what felt like hours before anyone came to speak to
me. My broken fingers swelled and ached in the splint the EMTs had rigged for me. I had
been given an aspirin, but the effects had worn off and I was feeling pretty sorry for myself,
wishing I had gone to the pub with Dan the man. The police officer walked in. He had a
coffee cup in hand, but the coffee was for him.

"I'll get you one once we've clarified some things," He said.

"Sure," I agreed, eager to please.

"Can you explain to me why you bought a sex doll with the same name as a recently
missing woman?"

That, I could not explain.

"Can you explain for me why your sex doll shares many physical aspects with the
missing woman?"

I could not explain that either. I was getting more and more nervous. The police officer
did not appreciate my fidgeting.

"I thought I made her up," I blurted out. "I really did. It's the same kind of basic girl
I make in almost all my first-person shooter games. Any computer game where you can
make a woman, that's the woman I make. If I have to make a guy, I usually make them
like —"

"I don't see how that is relevant." The police officer was not impressed with my
computer game explanation, but I had not been arrested —yet.

"When I ordered the doll," I blushed. "The sex doll, you could customise everything,
and I told them what I wanted her to say. Can't you check that?"

"Check what?"

"Check with the manufacturer. What my order details were. You can find that out from them. I didn't ask for her to scream. I wanted her to say nice things, and really, I just asked for a woman with blue eyes and brown hair. Isn't that kind of... isn't that like most of them?"

"Most of whom? Women?" The odds on getting that coffee were diminishing by the second. "We are already in the process of contacting the company and confirming the details of your order."

There was a knock on the door and a young female officer entered, scuttled across the room to whisper into the officer's ear then out again. I didn't think it was wise to comment that she had brown hair and blue eyes.

"Officer Kipley let me know the company responded. Apparently, there was an issue with a disgruntled staff member deliberately sabotaging doll orders as a political stunt. We'll follow up on this, naturally. Take some time and consider your options. If you decide to file charges we'll help with that." He shuffled some papers with a distinct air of finality and stood to leave.

"Well, I do have two broken fingers."

He paused and looked at my hand as if he didn't see the connection. "Your neighbour broke your fingers?"

"Well yes, but —"

"When they thought you had a woman held captive in your apartment?"

"I know but —"

"Maybe you'd be better off seeking relationships with the real people around you, rather than stoking any more ill feeling with legal action?"

They returned Cindy to me wrapped in garbage bags still bearing traces of evidence tape. There were red scuff marks around her wrists where her hands had lodged in my headboard. It looked like she'd been tied up. Her hair was a mess. She stank of cigarettes and drain water. Where had they been keeping her? I gave her another bath, but there was a layer of grime infused in her silicone skin that wouldn't come out.

From my couch, I watched TV with the sound turned way up, but I couldn't relax. I was convinced I could hear sounds in my bedroom —shuffling and crawling. My wardrobe opening and closing repeatedly. A low and monotone voice spoke in a never-ending stream of consciousness. But I couldn't go in to check. I couldn't make my feet go to the door and open it. Wasn't this the classic horror movie setup? I'd walk in and see myself in the mirror, and the terrible truth would be that it had been me the whole time, losing my mind?

There wasn't anything I could do to prove I was watching TV and not a deranged lunatic drooling in my room rattling doors. I got my phone out and scrolled through the numbers. Call it a moment of weakness. Fear and doubt. Loneliness. I don't know what made me select the number I did, but only God or divine providence made her pick up.

"I told you to never call me again."

"Becka?" I whispered into the phone.

"Jesus Chris," she muttered. "What do you want?"

"This is going to sound crazy but you didn't... you didn't put a curse on my cock after we broke up?"

"No —not after we broke up, anyway." I could hear Becka's smirk over the phone. "I've heard some weird stuff about you the last few days."

"What have you heard?"

"That your dick got stuck in a blow-up doll and they had to cut it off."

"It wasn't a blow-up doll —"

"Wait, it's *true?*"

"No, shut up. I still have a dick. It's just a bit... God, it just looks like sausage meat at the moment." I couldn't help but laugh, in spite of both my wounded dick and pride.

Becka was swearing over the phone in a mixture of horror and fascination. I gave her a much more detailed story than I had given Dan, and I could hear her muttering and the click clack of her typing. She was already searching the internet to help me.

"I'm not helping you because we're, like, friends or anything," Becka said, still typing. "This is just the most bizarre thing I have ever heard and I want to know more about these screaming sex dolls. Leave it with me. I'll call you back."

She hung up without saying goodbye, leaving me with the intense memory of the way she used to say "I love you" before the line would go dead.

I cocked my head. Did I say that out loud? Was it in the movie? Someone said *I love you*. I turned down the TV. The apartment was quiet. Completely quiet. The sounds I thought I'd been hearing in the bedroom were gone.

I didn't immediately bring Cindy into bed with me. Instead I sat her up in the armchair in the corner of my room. Unable to get the missing girl thing out of my head, I turned my back on her and tried to sleep.

I awoke nice and slow to the sensation of lips sliding over me. It felt like a nice memory, something that used to happen when I was still with Becka and she would wake me up during the night for some monkey business. I hummed in appreciation. Maybe not quite so smooth as I remembered. Something nicked me. I flinched.

"Hey babe, no teeth," I mumbled.

A low growl brought me closer to consciousness. I fumbled down and felt a mop of tacky and wiglike hair over my stomach.

"Becka?" I sat up on my elbows and squinted down, bleary-eyed, towards the lump hunched over my crotch. "Jesus-fuck what?"

There was another growl and the pleasant pressure around me turned harsh and unyielding as the mouth clamped down and locked. I yowled and thrashed my hips to dislodge Cindy, who had become a deadweight on top of me. It was no use. She would not let go. The pain was excruciating. There was something sharp in her mouth. Every time I moved the sharpness seemed to be in a different place, impossible to avoid. Her mouth was getting wetter and wetter, and I was sure it was my blood. It seemed impossible that I was still erect. I could feel myself growing dizzy and faint. I braced myself. With my hands on her shoulders I prepared to shove her away from me, whatever the cost.

Her voice activation triggered.

She began screaming.

Arriving for the second time in forty-eight hours, the EMTs were less sympathetic. It took them a long time to extricate my mangled penis from Cindy's mouth, at which point I promptly vomited on one of them.

There was no reasonable explanation. From their point of view, after an interview with the police about a missing woman I immediately tried to have sex with a corpse-doll known to have a malfunction that caused it to scream and beg for its life. What could I say to them? That I hadn't touched her? That she had climbed onto me while I was sleeping?

At the ER, the doctor gave me a stern lecture about my penis. I was advised to refrain from arousal for four weeks. I didn't mind, just glad I was in hospital and safe from Cindy. Good-natured and cooperative, I sat while a psychologist talked to me about considering therapy for my *sex addiction and unhealthy sexual thoughts regarding women*. It all sounded great. I didn't even want the doll anymore.

I called Dan. "Can I ask a huge favour?"

"Sure man, shoot."

"I'm in hospital right now, and they're going to let me out in the next couple of days. Can you go to my apartment and get my doll? Can you get rid of her for me?"

"Whoa man, trouble in paradise?"

"I'll tell you all about it over a beer later. For now, can you throw her out for me? Not in the dumpster in the street —you gotta do it properly."

"Don't want the neighbours to see the evidence of your failed tryst? I getcha," Dan said with a chuckle. I laughed along, relieved he wasn't busting my ass about it.

Dan called me back later that night. "What the hell did you do to this doll? She's been through the wringer."

"Oh, yeah." I fidgeted in the hospital bed. "She's pretty messed up. I got...stuck? The EMTs had to cut her mouth open to get me out and she looks kind of ghoulish now."

I could hear Dan's long whistle crackle over the line. He sounded far away, like he was in a tunnel. "Yeah, she looks like she got rode hard and put away wet. Still got great tits though."

"Maybe it would be better if you did this during the day. Dan?" The line buzzed and crackled, and there was no reply for a long time. "Dan?"

"Yeah bud?" He was back. "Sorry, I thought I heard someone talking in the other room."

"I'm just saying you should probably do it during the day."

"I thought you didn't want anyone to see your secret shame." Dan laughed.

"It's not that —it's not safe."

"Not safe?" Dan repeated. "Silly boy."

Silly boy? I remembered the notepad of weird shit by my telephone.

"Please, get out of there," I whispered.

The line went dead.

It was my next-door neighbour, the one who broke my fingers trying to save Cindy, that they found first the next day. His body was arranged on the hallway floor so his feet were at my threshold with his arms outstretched like he was on a crucifix. He looked like he was ecstatically requesting entrance to my apartment, except that he had been eviscerated. His entrails had been arranged into some sort of sigil in my living room. Police would have put more pressure on me to know what it meant, except I was in hospital when it went down.

Dan's body lay in my bedroom, spread out, and violated. The room was baking hot and stank. The police showed me pictures to try to make sense of the writing on the walls.

I didn't understand any of it.

Cindy was on my bed, in her sexy nighttime outfit. She looked rough. There was blood around her mouth and between her thighs.

The conclusion was that Dan and the neighbour had argued, possibly about me. I didn't see how Dan would have it in him to do any of that Satanist bullshit, but the police were convinced from the damage to his hands that he had written on the walls before he died.

The hospital refused to release me with no one to pick me up, especially now that my apartment was an active crime scene. There was only one person I could call. At first, Becka refused. She told me if I was going to use this crisis to rebuild fractured relationships I should give my estranged parents or brother a call. She finally relented and admitted she had found out some interesting information about the sex dolls so at least we had something to talk about in the car.

I was shivering in the pick-up/drop-off zone outside the hospital waiting for Becka, when a police car pulled up in front of me instead.

"Oh, here we go," I muttered to myself. I shuffled over to the passenger window and leaned down to peer into the car.

Inside was a man I had seen at the station while I was being escorted to and from interviews, the captain of the precinct or whatever his rank. He sat behind the wheel, hands at ten and two, his mouth frozen in a rictus of a smile.

"Help you, officer?"

"Good evening, Mr. Watts. We have a few questions for you down at the station." He had not yet blinked. "About your doll. She really is quite remarkable."

I didn't want to get into the car. There was a weird smell and the cop was giving off a peculiar vibe. "Sorry officer. I'm waiting for someone."

"I insist."

"Really, I'd rather not."

"I have a gun."

"Oh, well, if you insist."

He wouldn't stop humming as he drove. It was tuneless and wandering, maddening. Every time I considered saying something, I remembered the gun. When we pulled up at the station, the captain let me out of the back of the cruiser. I recoiled —I couldn't help it —when he leaned over to grip the door, his jacket gaped open. I saw two blooming red discs of blood on the white of his shirt, nipple height, blood dribbling down to pool around his waist.

As I followed him into the precinct, I noticed he was walking funny. His pants were wet with blood from the crotch to the ankle. He left a pattering red trail behind him.

"Sir, are you all right?" I asked.

He stopped to look back at me. He didn't seem aware of the blood he was losing, or didn't care.

"I'm great, son —never better," he said.

My phone rang in my pocket. I checked the screen. It was Becka, no doubt wondering where the hell I was. She'd be so pissed, if she'd driven all the way to the hospital to find me not there. Sure enough, my phone pinged again with a text. The preview displayed a series of curse words cut off at *mother-*. The captain beckoned me to follow him. Reluctantly, I slid the phone into my pocket, feeling the pings continue.

The officer at the front desk was dead. Or I hoped he was. His body hung slack in his chair. His eyes had been gouged out. The computer flickered in a staccato pattern that cast a crazy glare against his washed-out skin. As we passed, he let out a low, tortured moan. So much for him.

The captain led me past the interview rooms to the evidence locker. He opened the door with an excessive amount of ceremony, wielding the key as if conducting an orchestra. There were other people in the small room, other officers, people dragged in from the cells or the waiting room. It was hard to tell how long they'd been dead, but in the evidence room they had been spoilt for choice in terms of weaponry. I assumed the captain had arranged the bodies carefully around Cindy and painstakingly constructed the shrine made out of her.

As I stepped into the room, the captain grabbed me by a fistful of hair and dragged me to the centre of the circle of corpses. He forced me to my knees and unbuckled his dress pants. Ecstatic, the captain arched his back as he unveiled his cock, flayed, adorned with a thatch of nails impaling his deflated and purpled scrotum to his crotch.

"Pray!" he cried joyously, cupping my face as he mashed his mutilated groin against my face. "Pray!" The slick of his red raw meat hit the back of my throat and gave the vomit rising up to meet it nowhere to go but out my nose. I choked on it and him, but if anything my puking gave the captain greater pleasure and he jackknifed into my face. I tore at the nails scratching my chin in desperation, feeling gouts of blood raining down on my hands until finally I hit on one that let out a particularly thick spray and he collapsed to the floor. My mouth full of blood, I let out a ragged breath and locked that memory right in the vault. I slid the phone out of my pocket and saw several texts from Becka.

What the fuck, where are you?

I drove all that way, you could have said if someone else was going to pick you up?

Do not call me again!

That was exactly what I was going to do. There was no reception in the evidence locker, but there was a landline, I suppose for officers working there. I dialed Becka's number and listened to it ring, worried she wouldn't answer.

"Becka Lansbury, who is... oh shit this better not be you, M —"

"It's me. Don't hang up. I'm trapped."

"Trapped?"

"The police locked me in the evidence room with the sex doll. I swear it's cursed or possessed or whatever —they made a fucking shrine for it. Fuck, Becka, they're all dead except for the captain. They're all dead. Except for the captain. Maybe."

"Okay, say I believe you."

"You do?"

"I found out about the doll designer who sabotaged your order. For the others, she used her own voice for the screaming. But she wasn't getting enough attention, so for yours, she got a real recording of a woman who died being tortured, probably from a court or police contact. I never believed in possession or whatever, but if you put something that dark in a sex doll, any doll, I don't know. Maybe it let something in?"

I looked over at the Cindy shrine and shuddered.

"What do I do now?"

"Well, there are manufacturer instructions for how to reset the voice box, but you're not going to like it."

"Tell me."

"The reset switch is inside the doll, and the only access point is...via the *simulated anal ingress* port? Apparently, if you can reach in deep enough there's a second, um, valve you push through, and the voice box is in her chest. You push and hold the reset button for thirty seconds and it will delete all customised data. She'll just be a blank doll again."

"I have to *fist* the possessed doll?"

"Do you think you can do it before the captain comes to? I'm heading there now. You'll be okay?" Becka asked.

"No! Don't come here. It's not safe. I'll call you back if it works, okay? I'll need you to come and let me out."

I eased Cindy down from the shrine, turned her over and bent her legs up so that she was kneeling in a crooked doggy style. She let out a fart of corpse gas right in my face. I gagged at the smell. Her realistic skin felt soft and sticky —it was too loose and sagged on the stiffer framework underneath. I hated touching her. I couldn't even look at the part of her where I was supposed to insert my hand.

"I know where your off switch is," I muttered.

There was a nauseating resistance, then a slip-slide give as I pushed my hand in up to the wrist. I felt bile rise and burn the back of my throat. The smell was stinging my eyes and nose. I pushed again, sinking my arm up to my elbow, but I still couldn't feel anything inside her that was a box, no button I could press, no second valve that I could push through. I groped around, blind and sickened, inside her body. She stiffened, and her head jerked back.

I whispered to myself, "Oh God, no."

She screamed, *"No! Please no, don't do this!"*

"Shut up!" I blurted out of a panicked reflex, as if she would listen. "Oh my God, just shut the fuck up."

"Please don't kill me!" the voice inside Cindy wailed.

I heard heavy footsteps thundering down the hall. Throwing myself on top of her, I rammed my arm deeper inside her, searching as hard as I could for the voice box.

"Come on," I sobbed, my nose running. Shaking and on the verge of wetting myself, I finally felt it. My fingers located a tiny hole in the silicone and I bore in. I forced my hand through and into the cavern of her hollow torso. The tight ring of silicone was cutting off circulation to my forearm. My muscles throbbed and burned. I could feel something rubbing against me in there, scratching me with razor-sharp claws, biting me with pin-sharp teeth, trying to make me let go, withdraw my arm. I could feel myself bleeding. I groped for the voice box and found it in the nebulous space inside her, felt for a button, and pressed it. I had to hold it. I slipped off, had to find it again, and restarted my count. It felt impossible to count to thirty with all of the noise and my own terror, but eventually I had to concede that even I wasn't that terrible at counting to thirty.

The banging at the door was Becka, calling my name. It was morning. I had survived. I was still stuck almost to the shoulder inside a sex doll in a police evidence room, but I was *alive*.

When Becka breached the door and burst in, I whispered, "Oh God, I love you."

SUTTER KANG

Gator Batin' and the Pukwudgie

EARL HADN'T MEANT TO shoot Jake in the face with his sawed-off twelve gauge. He only meant to put a little bit of fear into Jake after hearing he'd been fooling around with Janice, a girl Earl was sweet on. Earl called him over with the false promise they'd have a couple beers. As Jake entered the trailer, Earl grabbed him by the scruff and pressed the barrel of a shotgun under Jake's chin. Earl managed to get out one word, "You," before he accidentally squeezed the trigger and what had been a human face —and a fairly good looking one —became a bouquet of gore resembling raw hamburger meat and cherry Twizzlers.

Such was life. You lived and you learned or, in Jake's case, you didn't.

After a change of underwear and a couple more beers, Earl got to work wrapping what remained of his friend in a blue tarp from Walmart. He scooped the lumps of flesh and bone from the wall and floor into a grocery bag, scrubbed every blood-soaked area until it looked brand new, and stuffed the bag of bits where Jake's face had been. After all that he secured the thing in duct tape and dragged the body outside, laughing as the back of his buddy's head bounced off each of the front porch steps.

Earl loaded Jake into the back of his pickup truck and they were off, destined for the swamplands, where snakes grew as long as the trees were tall, and the alligators made things that needed to be gone disappear.

He parked the truck and left it with the lights on. The woods could be treacherous at night, and he wanted to be able to see his way back, should he get lost.

Jake was heavy. He had gained quite a few pounds over the last year. Beer was more than likely to blame for that. Both of them enjoyed a brew or two —or three. It was what bonded them as friends. They could guzzle gallon after gallon while playing pool, or talking about women. Earl sure would miss that.

He dragged Jake by his boots. The leather was made from ostrich. Earl couldn't remember how much he'd said they cost, but he was sure it had been a small fortune. He would have to remember to keep them for himself before ditching the body.

Reaching the edge of the water, he wiped the sweat from his brow and took a breather. The frogs were ribbeting in unison, and they were loud, so loud he didn't hear the alligator rocketing out of the water until it was on him, snapping its jaws like a set of windup walking teeth.

He dodged as best he could, but as his Dear old Dad would say, he "Weren't no spring chicken, no more." The gator got ahold of his boot at the tip and tore it away. It shook its head violently, sending that Dr. Scholl's insert soaring. The animal rolled away as if it were a bowling ball, and Earl's brain sizzled as he calculated the next step to keep him from becoming the gator shit.

The first thing that came to mind was to punch the thing right square in the nose, which wasn't as good a thought as you'd think. An alligator's mouth has the biting capacity to crush a man's skull, not to mention hand, and if Earl missed his mark by even an inch, he'd be feeling plumb awful. Its eyes studied him with a coldness usually reserved for murderers and children. Earl didn't like that too much. With the speed of a cat he poked that bleak orb dead center. The gator's response was to close the affected eye, hiss, turn tail, and slide back into the water, which was a great relief to Earl.

"Good golly, miss Molly," he said, reaching for the vape he usually kept in his shirt pocket. It was gone. He would have scanned the ground for it but figured it wasn't worth the hassle. He'd dispose of the body, being extra careful this time, then pick up a new vape at the gas station on the way home.

Using his heel, he pushed the corpse, rolling it over. He hoped that would be the end of it. It would fall into the water and sink or the gator would come back and snag it. Either scenario would've been fine with him. Instead, it rolled once and stopped. A vast chasm of grotesqueness greeted him. Various shades of reds, blues, and purples hung in jagged pieces. They reminded him of cookie cutter shapes. Blood thicker than molasses oozed onto the earth, and a stray chunk of bone shifted, revealing another layer to the mound of meat. The tongue lolled out like a gigantic gray worm. How it hadn't been blasted off along with everything else was beyond him.

"Sorry, old buddy," he said as he gave Jake another push, this time sure to use enough force. The body landed in the water like a constipated turd, floated on the surface for what seemed to be a preposterously long time, then sank. The gator's tail swiveled as it swam to observe what had invaded its waters.

"Well, shit," Earl said, hands on his hips as he watched bubbles spring forth along the water's surface. "Forgot the boots."

He gave himself a brief once-over to make sure the gator hadn't snagged him in some unseen way. It would really suck if he was bleeding out and fainted on the way back. All appeared to be in order —ten fingers, ten toes, and no new holes, so he turned and headed for the car.

Earl had heard it was easy to get turned around in the swamp, especially at night, but this was ridiculous. He could see the truck's lights, ergo, if he followed them, he would make it there. That was the problem. He'd been following the lights for a solid thirty-seven minutes —he had checked his watch —and still hadn't gotten there. In fact, it seemed that every time he glanced up, he was the same distance away. If the night continued this way, he'd be watching the sunrise before long.

Laughter erupted around him, causing him to stop dead in his tracks with his sphincter tighter than a hangman's noose. The sound chilled him to the bones. *What was going on? Some teenagers, playing a prank?* No, it was a strange tittering, a cacophonous ringing with a primal undercurrent, as if something was imitating laughter with the intent of unsettling him.

He had already been moving pretty fast but now he broke into a run, which wasn't the smartest of ideas in the swamp. There were too many tree roots to trip over, too many venomous snakes, and most assuredly, too much what-the-fuck-ever was pursuing him.

A shadowy figure lurched from behind a tree a hundred feet or so in front of him. He skidded to a stop. Holding his hands out in a *don't mess with me, I know karate* gesture, Earl said, "Whoever you are, you'll be entering a whole world of hurt if you take one fucking step closer. You hear?"

True, he had taken karate lessons. But that had been before he gained the ability to grow his trademark mustache and sideburn combo, and since then he had forgotten the few things he learned. But this motherfucker didn't know that, so he stood his ground, hoping the threat would be enough.

"Aww, c'mon, buddy. Is that any way to talk to an old friend?"

There was something strikingly familiar about the voice. Earl tried to put a face to it, but couldn't. It wasn't until the figure stepped forward into the moonlight that he recognized who it was.

"Charley?" Earl said, gulping down the fear that constricted his throat.

Charley nodded.

Earl shuddered, unable to believe his eyes and ears on account of Charley being dead for nearly ten years.

Charley's skin was a waterlogged mess of bloat, and when he moved even an inch, he gave off a squishing sound similar to a shoe with a hole in it that's been caught in a bad storm. When he smiled, there were barely enough teeth to call it that. "Been a while, buddy. Was wonderin' when you'd be comin' back for a visit... Gets a mighty lonely out here, it does."

Charley was the reason Earl thought to bring Jake out here. He had disposed of Charley's body in this same location after that accidental overdose, and to be honest about it, had pretty much forgotten about the creep until the dead man appeared in the here and now, standing in front of him. The dead man took a step toward him. Earl leapt back.

"You stay the hell away from me, you sum-bitch!"

The roadrunner itself couldn't have caught up with Earl. He made a mad dash back the way he'd come, hoping he could reach the car before he shit his tighty-whities. The more he moved, the more it seemed that wasn't going to be happening. That was more than likely due to the face that popped out from each tree he passed. It was the same face, he was sure of that. Charley's face. He was being fucked with.

Out of breath, Earl skidded to a stop.

It was tough to talk, but he did his best. "This...Ain't...Funny..." A laugh echoed through the swamp. It seemed to be coming from all directions at once. "Goddammit, what is it you want, Charley?"

Two hands sprung out of the ground at his feet and grabbed him by the ankles. Earl let loose a shriek that would've rivaled any eighties scream queen. The ground loosened as his legs were pulled under. He clawed at the earth, trying to find purchase, but it was too soft. He tried digging in deeper, but that only led to broken nails that dangled off bloodied skin.

"Oh, Lord, please help me! I may be a lowly sinner, but I don't deserve this!"

Once he was waist deep, the hands that gripped him stopped dragging him down. He could feel movement in front of him. Whoever, or whatever it was, was clawing their way up and out. A troll-like face erupted from the dirt. It was about an inch from his crotch, which was bad for it, considering he'd just pissed himself. It licked its lips and winked as though it could read his thoughts.

"Tasty syrup you got there, m'boy. Sweet as can be. I wonder if your blood will be even sweeter."

"Pukwudgie?"

If asked, Earl could not explain how the realization came to him. It was almost like the creature itself had telepathically planted the thought in his head. He hadn't heard about the creature since he was a runt stealing beers from his Daddy's cooler in the garage. He remembered the day he was caught as though it had only happened last week: He had tiptoed down the dark steps, forgoing the light so he would not be caught. He was young; his eyes adjusted to darkness well enough. As he lifted the plastic top to retrieve a can of hoppy goodness, a voice boomed "You shouldn't steal, boy. The Pukwudgie'll find out, and those things don't take kindly to thieves."

Earl had run up those steps two at a time, not stupping until he dove into bed and under the covers. Of course, he hadn't thought about the Pukwudgie since then, but he assumed if it punished someone for the meager act of stealing, then surely it would make a murderer suffer.

Earl closed his eyes and silently prayed.

A hand touched the side of his face. It was as soft as silk and smelled of shea butter and coconut. "It's okay, silly," Janice said in her raspy smoker's voice. Hell, he could smell the menthol. "You're having a bad dream, that's all."

He opened his eyes to find her face staring into his. They were in bed. There was a full bottle of whiskey and half a pack of Marlboros on the nightstand. She ran her fingers through his thinning hair, then tugged his wispy beard. She opened her mouth for a kiss. He wouldn't, no, couldn't keep her waiting. They swapped spit as though the trailer was on fire and they were trying to put out the flames.

The snake entered Earl's mouth and plunged down his throat. The pressure felt akin to puking in reverse. Earl broke free from the hallucination and grabbed its body before it could slither any farther. It was choking him though, and he swore he could feel its tongue flicking the inside of his belly. If it traveled any farther down, it would be well on its way out the other end, assuming it didn't take up residence in his bowels.

Earl yanked hard. Its scales dug into the palms of his hands and his esophagus. They were as sharp as razor wire and planted themselves securely. It wasn't going anywhere if it didn't want to, and what it wanted was to continue down his throat, so it did. His stomach swelled until he looked eight months pregnant. With his throat clear, he could finally scream, and scream he did.

A childish giggling got his eyes to divert from his distended gut. It was the troll thing that had sprung out of the ground. It stood about three feet from him, clapping its hands in glee. The sick monster was getting quite a kick out of the whole situation.

"You —" Whatever Earl was about to say was abruptly ended by the worst pain he'd ever endured. Glancing down, he was greeted by the sight of a forked tongue flicking the air. It appeared that the snake was attempting to bore its way out of his stomach via Earl's belly button. He wanted to look away, yet couldn't. Pure terror had taken hold of him, and it kept his eyes glued to the unfolding horror. Flesh peeled back, and a head emerged. It was not the head of the snake. This was the head of the thing that was laughing at him, the Pukwudgie. The hairs dotting the sides of its head were thick as straw and tickled his insides uncomfortably. It split the seam that ran up to his chest, then erupted from the hole, his organs following its example spilled out at his feet. It shook loose bodily fluids as Earl's vision faded, then winked at him once more before death carried him away.

BASILE LEBRET

You'd Date a Guy

YOU'D DATE A GUY. You say you are ace. He says he understands.

You meet on the commute home, after a movie production briefing. You didn't talk during the meeting —you didn't think he saw you from across the room. He's not your type but he's entertaining. Ultimately, he doesn't get the job.

For your first date, he takes you to see dead babies in formaldehyde. This intrigues you. There's an uncaring attractiveness about him.

You don't really like Paris —not enough trees, wicked dry and hot in the summer. Noisy streets. Bad people. You like Paris even less when Mélanie gets her first job. Still a student, you're left out. When Mélanie finally states she wants to be independent, get her own life, is when you move into Alex's flat.

Alex ain't what you sought in a boyfriend but you feel safe with him. His blabber-mouth prevents you from thinking too much about the mountains or Valenton or Mom. You regret the hikes, the surreal cries of the forest.

You date a guy. You say you're ace. He says he gets it.

Nonetheless, dating Alex implies a sex life. You suck him off from time to time. Not out of desire —this is the protective mechanism you developed around his aggression. Against his, "But you have to understand me too." Against his, "I could fuck other girls, y'know."

Blowjobs enable you to retain control. You're the one giving the rhythm, the one handing out orgasms, the one keeping safe. Even on the 24th of April, when you ask him to facefuck you upside down.

Alex is a nice guy. He yells when he's angry but that's probably because he's an only child. There are no only children in Valenton —you wouldn't know.

He spits out terrible things when furious. Or drunk. You help him work on this. Sometimes, you notice the pause he takes when he's about to insult you. You like this about him, the effort he sometimes indulges in.

He's always there to make you laugh when your job becomes a burden. After the sweaty smell from the commute, the musk of dirt and rats. The flat always smells like panned onions when you get back. For this, you're grateful.

"The hardest thing about a relationship is figuring out what's for dinner," you both often joke.

Being an ace means every time Estelle screams, "Am so wet, right now!" you only nod. You get the need to touch, to kiss, to be hugged. The feeling of belonging. Nothing makes you wet. Not even making Alex come.

Being an ace means your boyfriend lets you go out clubbing since he doesn't think you're fucking other boys.

Or so he says.

Alex says a lot of things, about geopolitics but mostly about horror films.

He's still saying things on this night when he wakes you up by kissing your right cheekbone.

Your dry labia hurts.

You're scared at first because, in the dark, you can't see if it's really him. But you hear the constant drone of his voice permeating the damp obscurity. As if his soothing words could deter you from what's happening.

You feel the thrust from a distance like a medical procedure. You think of bells. He kisses you and you don't kiss him back and you hate yourself for not biting him, and he still goes on as if his childish "sorry" matters. In due time, you'll build a castle around this moment, re-enact it, hate yourself with a passion for every second.

There's this angry you who's jumped out of bed, shrieking like some inflexible Medusa. Only she's screaming at you. The you, lying there awake, unmoving. She screams at you because you do not move.

You take in everything, the scent of dried nettles from his armpits when he gets away from your still body, the tired feel of the fabric of the sheet you both put on that evening, the sad shade of green light that pierces the window and covers his body in spots like a skin disease.

"What're you doing?" you finally ask.

"You know how long I've been waiting for this?" he answers, his breath rotten.

You don't move since you don't exist.

You date a guy. You say you are ace. He says he understands.

When his crotch gets stuck on you, when your vagina finally takes hold of the smooth part that's his pelvis, is when Alex panics.

"The fuck is happening," is his first genuine sentence. "Leave me the fuck alone."

When it doesn't work is when he hits you for the first time. Cloc, cloc, Alex's fists connecting with a cheekbone. It reminds you of your fight with Estelle back in Valenton. Cloc, cloc, tiny fists, tiny knuckles.

When he tires, your eyes are closed and purple. Your face is swollen. You didn't move.

"What's happening?" he asks your limp body, shaking it, searching for an answer he should have sought an hour ago.

Alex doesn't realize it but his feet are gone —they melted like wax onto your calves.

You really are a two-backed beast now.

"Feet are the first to go," you whisper through bloodied teeth. "Otherwise, males could escape."

Pushing on your right arm, you get up. What remains of Alex's body, his torso, folds toward the ground like the upper part of unbuckled overalls.

"Sarah, please," he begs like you ever had a say.

Your index finger slithers upon the sweet skin under your navel that links both your bodies. It is smooth under your digits and your finger now smells like Alex.

You call in sick. People will underestimate how easy it is to knock out your rapist with a remote. You call in sick 'cause you know the process is gonna take some time. Alex hasn't lost his arms yet.

He cries and gulps a lot, probably because he's upside down and saliva is hard to deal with. When he wants your attention, he'll scratch around your navel. Alex never liked the way your skin felt. Never cared for giving you smoochies. It's weird —only now do you get the tactile attention you wanted all along.

When you're bored, you wonder how he's adjusting to the world. The motion sickness now that the world slithers ten inches above his head. You wonder how he feels about having his agency taken away from him.

You date a guy. You say you're ace. He says he gets it.

One day, his arms fall off. You watch the bloody stumps stuffed with shattered bones and hope whatever's doing this will make it rot fast enough so you don't have to deal with the lone limbs.

You feel for him, more so when the assimilation melts his jaw in your belly. With this hole full of teeth in your abdomen, you realize all of this took you away from exercising. You cradle Alex's head, feeling more for him since he can't speak. Since he stopped crying.

One evening while watching some flick, you absentmindedly place your fingers on his scalp, into his hair. You find it a chore to have to think about dinner. Soon it becomes second nature.

When only his face remains as a flat stain across your sternum, you wonder if you should get a tattoo.

Since Alex is invisible now, you get back to work. You realize you won't take the elevator with a lone male anymore. No one notices. Slight details.

Watching *Friday the 13th Part VI: Jason Lives*, Alex's and your favourite, you decide to work on your abs. You realize you never called Estelle through all this. Maybe you should have —maybe you should now.

Sometimes, when the flat smells like fried onions, you cry for no reason. You don't play certain video games anymore.

In due time, you begin to breathe again.

You'd date a guy. You say you're ace. He says he understands.

He leaves his mark inside of you.

THOMAS R CLARK

The Breeders

DRIVING THROUGH THE FOOTHILLS surrounding the Finger Lakes of up-state New York is typically an enviable task. Filled with wineries, farms, and beautiful, rustic homes, it's one of the more enjoyable things to do in the region. Doing so in the middle of the night while a rainstorm rages, however, isn't Gary McCarthy's idea of fun.

The clouds hang low to the ground and the elevation of the hills covers the roadway with a never-ending bank of fog. Gary's inability to use the Ford's high beams is the least of his worries. As it is, any traffic going either way nearly blinds him, reflecting off the road surface and through the windows of the truck's cab. But each swipe of the wipers smears the rain on the windshield, and lights in the oncoming left-hand lane turn this into an obfuscating rainbow.

With it being the middle of summer, and humid, regulating the defroster on the windshield is a chore. It's a pain in the ass, but Gary knows the drive here and back to his hotel in the shitty little city of Cortland will be worth it once he reaches this first destination. He smiles thinking about it. The euphoria lasts until his cell phone rings.

The caller ID on the truck's dashboard tells him his new employer is calling. Gary connects the call but doesn't speak.

"Mac?" the client asks after an uncomfortable silence.

"Yeah."

"How was the flight?"

"Like you'd expect from Dulles to Syracuse in this weather. Why are you calling me for small talk? You only paid for three burners," Gary says.

"Ya think I'd be usin' up a phone just to call and tell ya how pretty yer eyes are?"

"Okay, good point. What's up?"

"The information I gave ya earlier has changed. The, um, package, it's moved an' we can't locate it."

"Are you fucking kidding me? So what's the deal? You know the deposit is nonre-fundable."

"I know. I know. The event isn't off. It's just, well, on hold."

"What happened?"

"She, I mean the package, we lost it yesterday."

"So you're telling me I flew all the way to this shithole, where I'm currently out in the middle of the night driving a rental around in a rainstorm, and —"

"Hey, Mac," the client says, interrupting Gary, who scowls at the act. "Don't forget I'm the banker here. The job wasn't until tomorrow. It's not my fault ya went out in this shit. It ain't supposed to rain tomorrow anyhoot."

"Whatever. If you need to know, I'm getting a new emotional support dog. My old one just died."

"Emotional support dog? Really?"

"Fuck you." Gary wishes this asshole was in front of him right now, with the barrel of a Desert Eagle in his mouth. "You try, um, checking tickets on people for a living. I'm busy. Call me tomorrow when you have an answer. Cycle the phones and don't fucking call me unless you have the location or you're calling it off, got that? And if it's the latter, there's no refunds." Gary doesn't wait for an answer. He ends the call, shaking his head in displeasure. He doesn't like the employer, not one bit. But he doesn't have to.

"There's more natural teeth in a maternity ward than there is in all of Cortland county," the mousey man who went by Dennis told him during their first meet. *A stop at a gas station earlier in the day did nothing to disprove this theory. "Don't ferget yer in the asshole and armpit of the Appalachians. Bring plenty of teepee and deodorant with ya."* The client pronounced it Apple-A-shuns, like the rest of New York's population did, which annoyed this West Virginia native living in Georgetown to no end.

The road swerves as he presses the button for the automated windows to go down. Wind whips rain into the cab, soaking him. Now the truck is on a straightaway with no bends or curves. With one hand on the wheel, Gary fishes a cell phone out of his pocket. He smashes it on the steering wheel and pulls out the SIM card before tossing them both out the window into the stormy darkness.

A few miles later, the GPS tells Gary to turn down an unmarked side road. There's no road on the map, only a waypoint indicated, seemingly in the middle of nowhere. It's quiet, and the rain lets up. The high beams light up the rural setting, revealing a serpentine, pothole-ridden gravel road, if you could call it thus, lined with gigantic oaks. A sign, hidden in the brush and listing to one side, declares this to be BONNEY FARMS. The top of the signpost is decorated with a trio of dog head sculptures.

Nothing bad has ever happened in these situations, he thinks to himself sarcastically as he recalls a night in Afghanistan over a decade ago when everything changed for Gary McCarthy. The night an insurgent's IED gave the Army Ranger a going home gift in the form of a titanium plate covering a majority of his forehead. The resulting PTSD had prompted Gary to adopt an emotional support dog after his recovery. That dog, Rambo, passed away a month ago after a decade at Gary's side.

Now, ahead of him, the brush of the wilderness bordering the gravel road subsides, unveiling the lights of the property. In the back of the F-150, a new dog crate rattles as the Ford hits the superfluous potholes filled with mud and captured water from the storm. The headlights reveal another country road bisecting the property next to a small creek flowing down from the surrounding hills. The stream runs under a wooden footbridge before disappearing into the darkness.

A homestead, or more correctly, a single-wide trailer on a concrete slab, sits on one side of the informal intersection. Following the creek, across the drive sit a half dozen steel and aluminum sheds and an ancient barn. Gary's lights illuminate most of the yard, and he can see half of the barn's roof is listing, with a gaping, black hole near the peak.

Gary finds a gravel drive adjacent to the trailer and parks the Ford next to a shiny, newish black Subaru Forester. The decals with the logos for Lyft and Uber peak his curiosity. *Do these hicks drive rideshare?* he wonders for a moment. Maybe it was how they supplemented their income? He considers the possibility, then disregards the thought. *No, there's something more to this,* he resolves and sits there for a few seconds, pondering the Subaru and mustering the strength to deal with a person and not kill them for the sake of it.

It'll only be long enough to get the dog, Gary mentally reminds himself. *Tomorrow you can take it out on your mark and leave them dead and stinking in the water,* his id adds as a consolation. Gary smiles at the thought. He pulls the card with the details out of his pocket. MELANIE BONNEY, BONNEY FARMS, BOX 2539, HOMER, NY. When he opens the door, the stench of a sulfurous musk immediately assaults him.

"A fuckin' polecat? Really?" He scans the area, making sure the skunk isn't nearby. The last thing he needs is to get sprayed. He walks down the path to the trailer's dilapidated porch. Charms and chimes hang from wires and twine, and the building smells worse than the skunk. It's a sickly sweet, nauseating combination of mildew, piss, and shit. The malodor waters his eyes and makes him wish the skunk would materialize and deodorize the place. *Sweet Jesus.* Gary keeps this thought to himself as he steps up onto the porch.

The shadow of a large dog standing in the corner of the porch catches Gary's eye. He steps back, not wanting to antagonize a mastiff. A curtain inside the trailer moves and light bleeds out, exposing the watchdog as something peculiar. *Is that a stuffed dog?* Gary wonders. Turning on his phone's flashlight, Gary confirms his suspicions. A taxidermized dog, with three poorly stitched together heads and marbles for eyes, silently stares back at him. *That's all sorts of fucked up. What are these people? The welcoming committee for secondhand Hades,* he thinks, shakes his head, and knocks on the door.

The rapping is greeted by a high-pitched barking, followed by a chorus of snarls and howls originating near the proximity of the metal sheds. *At least I'm in the right place,* Gary thinks, as the barking persists. The sounds of someone approaching the door from the interior follow. With each step, the trailer's frame buckles, the metal screaming in distress until he hears the tumblers of the lock fall.

The door opens and Gary is assaulted by a freshness of stench he can't believe possible. A monster of a woman stands before him, as wide as she is tall, dressed in a grease-stained purple housecoat. Her gray hair is thinned by alopecia, and the woman's face is riddled with oozing sores. At first he thinks she's crying, but then he realizes it's pus, not tears, dripping down from her left eyeball. She holds a ring of rusty keys in one swollen hand, and in the other, a coffee cup filled with some steaming liquid.

Behind her, a little ankle biter of a mutt that appears to have combined the worst traits of a pug and chihuahua growls and hisses. It's smaller and thinner than a typical pug, with the lean body of the chihuahua and the familiar anthropomorphic pug face. The dog reminds Gary of David Hedison's infamous last scene in the original version of *The Fly*, where the human-headed insect is trapped by a spider pleading for its life. This poor creature is no better off. A victim of cerebellar hypoplasia, the dog waddles sideways as it runs. Its tilted face is covered with swollen lesions.

Gary stifles a laugh, noting how much the dog and its master mirror each other. He smiles, recollecting how he and Rambo, too, shared similar traits. The correlation nearly kicks off an anxiety attack. He shuts it down with the only coping mechanism he knows to use, outside of killing the old woman outright. Humor.

I guess the commercials are right and shingles don't fucking care who or what you are, poor dog. Gary keeps the joke to his inner monologue. "Melanie Bonney?" he asks.

"Mmmmhmmm, but ya can call me Mamme Mel, it's what da kinfolk roun' here do," the woman replies, nodding.

More like Mamme Nasty Ass, he thinks, ignoring the lady's attempt to teach him her pet name. "Gary McCarthy. We spoke on the phone last week about the puppy."

"Mmmmhmmm. Ya da man who lost his support dog, righty? Y'all din' soun' like no darkie on da phone."

"Beg pardon?" Gary didn't appreciate the woman's verbiage, pointing out his mixed heritage. Gary's father was of Irish-American descent, his mother a dark-skinned Cuban dancer, and their son shared her mocha complexion. *Say one more racist thing and give me an excuse to unload this Desert Eagle in your face, please.*

"T'ain't 'portan'."

"And yes, my emotional support companion passed away. I'm just here for the puppy."

"Mmmmhmmm. Yes ya are, indeed, mmmmhmmm," she says, then shouts out, "emotional support. Hah! Eloy! Get out to da spring house an' get dat pup. Da man is here for it." Gary notes she has one tooth on her bottom jaw and no others. It juts up like a tusk when she closes her mouth. "Eloy's mah boy. He's a little daft, but he's good with da pups. Dis one yer getting, she's a prettyful one. Nice markings. That'ah be sick hunna, carsh."

"That's not a problem." Gary fetches a wad of bills from his pocket and hands it to the woman. Her fingernails are crusted filth and Gary is skeeved by her touch. It sends a shiver up his spine, and it requires all of his willpower to not pull the Desert Eagle out of its holster at the small of his back...

And empty it into her face.

She counts the money then adds, "It's airish tonight. Chillin' me to da bones. Lemme get ya da paperwork for da bloodline." She steps back into the trailer and shuffles through some papers on the kitchen island. The floor is covered in pages from newspapers and magazines, complete with piss stains. A Navy Jack (known to some as the Confederate flag or the flag of the Army of Northern Virginia), stained and torn, hangs on the wall above a sofa. The furniture and flag have seen better days.

Fucking wonderful, Gary thinks when he sees the tattered banner. *The last thing I need to see tonight is that racist piece of shit flag.* Gary knows there are two sorts of people who fly this flag, racists and idiots. He's mostly certain the Bonneys, being in Upstate New York, fall into the latter category. The longer Gary stands here, the more nauseous he gets and less patient. He's about to snap —*and gut the old hag* —when he hears the sniffling and whining of a puppy behind him. The pug-chihuahua's barking resumes.

"Peanut! Quitcher bawlin'!" the woman commands. The yapper doesn't listen. Gary turns around and the puppy comes into view, led by the man called Eloy, who is obviously Melanie Bonney's kin. But unlike Mamme Nasty Ass, the puppy does not resemble Eloy. Eloy's cleft lip was sewn up poorly when he was a child, and now his face appears askew.

The ugly didn't fall too far from the tree, Gary thinks. *Shit, it mighta hit the roots.*

The puppy is excited. Fawn colored, its tail wagging, the wee critter makes eye contact with Gary. As he and the pup stare at one another, he feels the oxytocin course through his body with each second. This is the one, Gary thinks. He bends down at the knees, and the puppy charges to him, jumping into his arms and licking his face.

"Well hello there! Ain't you a sweetheart!" Gary tells the dog. All at once, months of apprehension and stress seem to leave his body. Not since Rambo's last days has Gary felt this good, this emotionally satisfied.

"Her name is Per-Per-Perseffff...Annie." Eloy manages to stutter out of his toothless mouth.

"Persephone?" Gary verifies the name. Eloy answers with an affirming nod.

"I think it's a beautiful name," Gary says, scratching the dog behind the ears. "We'll keep it."

The pup licks and nibbles at Gary's face. He lowers her down and stands up. "Come on Persephone!" He motions to the puppy to follow him to the truck. She obliges. He picks her up, opens the door, and scoops the little dog into the waiting crate where a new bed and toys await her.

"Don'tcha forget dis!" Mamme Mel shouts to him from her spot in the trailer's doorway, the paperwork in her hands.

"Oh, right, can't forget that. Be right there," an elated Gary says as he closes the crate. "I'll be right back, baby girl," he tells Persephone, giving the truck door a gentle slam then returning to the trailer to fetch the dog's papers.

For the first time in weeks Gary doesn't feel the urge to leave anyone dead and stinking —on the land or in the water, for the matter at hand.

He takes three steps and stops when Eloy shouts at him. "Ain't no coon takin' nunna my bitches!" Eloy's words are still hanging in the air when Gary's ears fill with the din of a gong being struck by a mallet. The lights go out for a second as Gary struggles to regain his orientation. This is followed by a wet crunching and an unearthly screech.

It's just like night when the IED went off in Nuristan all those years ago, except those Taliban lunatics were screaming Allahu Akbar at the tops of their lungs, Gary's instincts tell him, but he's about to discover they're wrong. Sweat and salt burn his eyes when he opens them, and he wipes his brow with a free hand. The liquid is sticky, and the coppery scent of blood pulls him from his stupor. *I'm fucking bleeding?* Gary wonders. *That motherfucker hit me in the head with something?*

Then he sees Eloy twitching on the ground in front of him and big Mamme Mel running to her son's aid. The woman is moving faster than Gary thought she could, with the little pus-face dog at her heels, yipping away. The key ring in her hand jingles with each bounding step. *What happened to him?* Gary wonders. His question is answered with a step forward. The barrel of an aluminum baseball bat is embedded in Eloy's face.

"Look at whatcha done to mah boy!" The woman screams. The man's lower jaw is dislocated, the mandible bent and twisted. If he had possessed any teeth, they would've been scattered around him. Instead, a pink froth of snot and blood discerns the seal between flesh and metal.

Bent over on her hands and knees with her housecoat riding up her bare ass, Mamme Mel coddles her son's broken face, still holding her keys. Peanut, the little fucked up dog, stops yipping but the other dogs in the sheds let it out with abandon. It's deafening. Gary slowly steps away from the pair, toward the trailer, while reaching behind his back. A few steps later he withdraws the Desert Eagle, keeping his eyes on the old woman the whole time.

Something he regrets doing almost immediately.

Behind the woman, the little dog is standing on its hind legs. Its front paws are spread out, one to either ass cheek. Her backside is riddled with dripping, pustulant sores. They surround and infest her exposed vulva and labia, swollen with infection. Swabs of toilet tissue are stuck to the inflamed lips.

The image reminds Gary of a spoiled roast beef sub, complete with curdled cheese protruding from between the flaps of meat, that he bought by accident from a vending machine back home in Georgetown.

A thick, matted cake of dried blood, shit, and hair covers where her taint and ass crack should be. Trailing out of a hole in the center of this mass is a lime green, thinned out turd, and Peanut is gobbling it up with glee. The little dog's tongue wipes it clean, before continuing to lap at the blisters and sores surrounding the woman's sagging and flapping vaginal lips.

Gary kicks the dog to the side. "No!" He commands the animal. Peanut ignores him and runs back to its master's exposed genitalia, tongue licking away at the pus-oozing boils.

No no no no no no no no fucking no... the word runs through his brain on repeat at light speed until Gary snaps.

WHAT IN THE EVERLOVING FUCK IS GOING ON HERE?

He aims the giant pistol at Mamme Mel's back around the vicinity of her heart, and squeezes the trigger. The report of the weapon sends gouts of blood squirting out of the exit wound in her chest. The splatter covers Eloy with a second coat of hemoglobin-infused paint. Gary hears the clinking of metal as the woman drops the key ring and slumps to the side, collapsing on her son's ruined face. His body kicks as she smothers him, but it doesn't stop the dog from digging into her ass for more.

Dead and stinking...

Gary has seen enough. He ignores Peanut this time and walks away, but not before grabbing the woman's key ring and taking the papers off the trailer's porch where the Bonney matron dropped them.

Near the sheds, he catches movement from the corner of a blood-covered eye, telling him he's not alone. It's pitch dark without the lights of the trailer and truck illuminating the area. Gary decides it's better to handle this professionally. Unsure if it's a dog or another human, he stuffs the papers into his back pocket and returns to the F-150.

And what is my profession?

He opens the door to the cab and sees little Persephone wagging her tail and whining, happy to see her new human. Gary lets her sniff and lick his fingers. "That's a good girl. I'll be right back," he tells her as he places the paperwork on the seat next to the crate. "Be right back little girl. Daddy's got work to do." He blows her a kiss and shuts the door.

And said work amounts to dealing out death to some redneck motherfuckers who deserve it.

In the truck's bed is a locked case. It's long with no markings indicating what is inside. Gary unlocks the case with a key and opens it. Inside is his weapon of choice for close-up jobs, an SKO-12 semiautomatic shotgun. He loads it with a twenty-five-round drum magazine filled with two dozen shells packed with number four buckshot. At point-blank range the pellets will eat flesh and bone.

He wipes the blood from his brow, grabs a headlamp and slips it onto his head, then closes the case. The glow of the headlamp provides him with a good view of everything around him.

Time to die, motherfuckers.

A quick jog later Gary makes his way across the road and over the little footbridge to the sheds and barn where the other dogs are housed. Or so he believes. What Gary McCarthy is about to discover on this property will change him forever.

Behind the first shed, the headlamp illuminates a trail leading around the metal hovels. The constant barking from the dogs is deafening and emanates from all of the sheds, not any one in particular. Gary notes that the stream runs under the backside of each shed —a practice done to keep salted food cool.

Now why would they need to do this? Gary thinks, not understanding how much he's going to regret asking himself this question. Hearing some commotion from within, he slides open the door to the closest shed and is greeted by a blast of hot air. The sweet stench of rotting meat and the sounds of sex greet him.

Chained to the floor on some sort of support is a large dog, and from the coat markings it looks to be a German Shepherd. The animal squeals in agony. Behind it, a naked man, covered in filth, is busy moaning and humping away at the dog's hind section.

He's fucking a dog? Already nauseous from the surrounding smells and a blow to the head, Gary loses the contents of his stomach and projectile vomits onto the wall. Bile and bits of finely masticated chicken nuggets and fried potatoes splash onto the man's backside. Without missing a hump the naked man turns around, revealing an insane, devilish grin on his face. He has one more tooth than Mamme Mel.

The man raping the dog speaks. "Spota be white? Spota say what? Spota —"

The hitman wipes off his lips and nose. He doesn't talk. Talking is for movies and dead men. There is no hesitation. Gary strikes the freak across the temple with the barrel of the SKO-12, ending the discussion. *There is no discussion,* Gary reminds himself, *only action.* The hillbilly drops to the ground and Gary steps on his neck. A wet crunch resonates from underneath Gary's boot. Blood froths and bubbles out of the freak's mouth and nose as he twitches. After one more convulsion his body evacuates, shitting all over the floor. The Army vet wrinkles his lip in disgust, steps back and kicks the body. A fecal streak marks the path as the dead man rolls off the floor and into the stream. Gary smiles at his work.

Dead and stinking in the water.

The Army vet goes to help the trapped dog. Part of him fears he may have to put the animal down. He looks for the restraints holding the dog in place. He unbuckles a leather strap and quickly steps back, shock and disgust working in tandem to repel him.

"You've got to be fucking kidding," Gary says, throwing a hand to his face and covering his mouth. He grabs the dog's tail and pulls. The head pops back, hollow and empty. The coat tears away from the animal's legs and comes off the body with ease, followed by a wailing screech and a sudden realization for the hitman.

This isn't a dog.

Chained to the floor and mutilated is a mustachioed man with thick, black hair and a bronze complexion. Gary isn't one hundred percent sure of his precise nationality, but he's certain of one thing, the guy is in a world of fucking hurt. His hands are missing, and the bloody stumps of his wrists are duct taped into the front paws of the dog pelt. Whoever had removed his hands, also amputated his legs from the knees down and sewed the stumps into the hindquarters of the pelt. They hadn't done a professional job. Bloody clots encircle the makeshift surgical points and a yellow mucus substance oozes through the fur.

"Help...us...please...help...us," the man manages to say, his words slurred and barely louder than a whisper. But Gary can hear a clear accent. *Is he Afghan?*

"Us?" Gary asks the imprisoned man.

"My...rider...help...Allah...," he manages to say until his words trail off to labored breathing. The man passes out, his head hanging between his shoulders. Drool mixed with blood drips from his mouth. Gary resolves there's nothing he can do for this man.

I can still help someone, all the same. His thoughts are epiphanic as it all becomes clear. The dying man before him owns the rideshare car in the driveway and had a passenger with them. This person is likely somewhere on the property, probably in one of the sheds.

Ain't this a hoot, Gary thinks. After being wounded in the war, he never thought he'd see a day come where he'd be interested in saving a person's life. Yet here he is, putting together a makeshift plan to do just that.

He may not be able to save this man, but his passenger? This remains to be seen. Gary resolves he can only try. This day, or night, it seemed to him, was fast becoming a day of firsts. The hitman backs out of the shed cautiously, keeping the weapon level and his eyes open for any more surprise attacks.

He opens the door to a chorus of snarls, barks, and rattling cages. A first glance through shed number two tells Gary it's filled with a half dozen dogs in crates. They appear to be healthy. The two larger dogs in bigger crates are busy gnawing on bones resembling tibia. He flashes the light at another crate full of puppies, one gnawing on the remnants of a human hand. It's now become obvious, to Gary at least, how the Bonneys are feeding their breeding pack.

They're fucked up, but hey, at least they're not cannibals.

Gary moves on to shed number three.

The fetid stink of rotting meat overpowers the farm's skunky aroma. Other than the stink, at first glance, this one is mostly a bust. It's empty of living things, no barking dogs or people in duress. The origin of the shed's ambient stench is swinging from long hooks attached to the ceiling —pieces of carcasses.

Human parts and pieces.

Gary grimaces at the sight before his headlamp reveals a treasure in the corner, a pile of things. They're personal effects, and judging from their appearance, they aren't things in the Bonney aesthetic. Flip flops, women's clothing, sneakers, men's clothing. On top of the stack are two cell phones. Gary picks them up and notes both are powered down.

"Why the fuck not?" he says, and turns them on. In moments, both phones buzz to life with a cacophony of alerts from missed calls and text messages. He ignores the buzzing and chirping, puts the phones in his pocket, and moves on to shed number four.

As he nears the next building, Gary hears the sounds of a panicked scuffle from within the structure. He checks the SKO-12 to ensure the weapon is ready to rock and roll, and adjusts the headlamp to illuminate as much of his line of sight as possible. Gary aims the SKO-12 and slides the door open.

The Bonney farm does not disappoint, as Gary has learned from more than one instance on this night. The property is fast becoming a smorgasbord of backwoods inbred fuckery.

The hitman had expected something fucked up, and he gets it. A pair of bipedal dog-men are humping away at either end of a bound, naked woman. Gary aims the shotgun at the back of the closest dog-man's head, and squeezes off a single round from the SKO-12. The roar of the shotgun silences the barking dogs, while the blast removes the dog-man's head with a couple dozen pellets of number four buckshot from a 12-gauge shell. Pieces of skull, cartilage, flesh, hair, and brain splatter the ceiling, creating dripping stalactites of crimson goo.

A fountain of blood erupts from the stump of the dog-man's neck and covers the woman and other dog-man in a crimson spray littered with bits and pieces of head. The standing corpse slumps down to the floor and the stream of blood turns into an expanding puddle surrounding the body.

An inhuman screech of rage comes from the other dog-man. He leaps over the woman. The dog-man's dick, an all too human cock, is sticking out of a canine penile sheath, flapping around like a propeller. Through the dog-man-thing's gaping maw, Gary can see human eyes staring back at him from behind the teeth.

These redneck motherfuckers are wearing dog suits? Gary's mind does not want to accept what is going on with the Bonneys. His body shakes, his heart rate rises, his palms sweat. The Army vet's entire being wants to remove them from his presence, delete them from existence.

The shotgun obliges.

The hitman unleashes a barrage of shotgun shells at the man in the dog suit. The kick of the weapon pushes Gary back, out of the shed as the SKO-12 burps out a half dozen shells, creating a moving wall of ball bearings. Fire shoots out a foot from the barrel, lighting up the interior of the shed. Instantly, hundreds of impacts turn the costumed target into a gooey mass resembling a multi-family sized portion of steak tartare.

Then, for the first time since shit went down with the swinging of a baseball bat, the farm is quiet.

The bits and pieces of flesh, bone, and internal organs hover in midair, then fall. With a wet slap the matter covers the prone woman in a sheen of gory goop. Gary stands and stares at the bloody mess, breathing as deep and slow as he can to reduce his heart rate and slow his anxiety. His mind is still trying to rationalize what he has encountered at this farm on this night when his burner phone rings, ruining the moment's peaceful bliss.

This is not the time for this shit, Gary thinks before fishing the phone out of his pocket. He connects the call and doesn't wait for his client to speak. "What did I tell you about using these burners? Right now I'm not in a good place, so this better be important," he says.

"Well hello to you, too, Mac. You'll be happy to know I've regained contact with the mark and everything should be back on for tomorrow."

"Is that so?"

"Yes. It looks like the mark's at one of the ski lodges right now, so you might have to do some wilderness work to get it done."

Ski lodge in the middle of summer? he thinks before replying, "Enough, I'm in the middle of something. Call me tomorrow with the location, I don't care where they are now."

"Copy that."

"What did you say?" Gary's tone turns colder.

"I said copy that, you know, like soldiers say on radios when they're in the field."

"Are you prior service?"

"No. But I thou —"

"Then don't say that again." Gary hangs the up, then crushes the phone with his heel. *Fucking amateurs,* he thinks as he kicks and scatters the phone's pieces and shakes his head. He doesn't have time for this bullshit, and has a victim to save. Gary steps back into the shed and reaches down to the woman lying on the floor. He can hear her labored breathing, confirming she's at least still alive.

"Hey, are you with me?" he asks the woman as he touches her shoulder. She's shivering, shaking. The dogs restart their incessant barking. He speaks louder, so she can hear him over the dogs, but tries to maintain a kind tone. It's difficult for him to do, considering the circumstances. "Hey, it's okay. I'm Gary, I'm going to rescue you." The woman moves, covers her face with her hands and folds herself into a fetal position. "Okay, you stay here, I'm going to get you some clothes and something to clean up with. Nobody's going to hurt you now. They're all —"

A screeching wail erupts from behind Gary, and it drives the barking dogs into a frenzy. He spins around to see Mamme Mel, a giant bloodstain covering the front of her housecoat, charging at him with Eloy's ball bat grasped in both hands, raised over her head.

"Fuck ya, moolie!" she screams. "I'mma gonna hang yer balls on da porch!"

"Oh, would you just fuckin' die already?" Gary says, breaking his silence rule as he raises the SKO-12. He squeezes the trigger and unloads a trio of shells at the Bonney matron before she can reach him. The first burst of buckshot hits her in the chest, erupting into a bloody red flower exposing the bones of her sternum and upper rib cage.

It only slows her down.

The second and third shell loads hit the large woman on her left side. She violently jerks to the side and something black splashes out of the impact points, covering the grass. Hypovolemic shock takes over her body. The baseball bat tumbles out of the woman's hands as she twists and falls from the force of the buckshot. Mamme Mel tumbles and rolls in the rain and blood-soaked grass, sliding to a stop, ass first, at Gary's feet. Sticking out from between her ass cheeks, coated in runny shit, the hindquarters of a little dog lay limp.

"Poor little Peanut," Gary laments for the pug mix before going to the previous shed and gathering the woman's clothes and a blanket. Unsure of which garments are hers, he grabs the whole pile. She's sitting up in a fetal position when he returns, her forehead on her knees. "Here you go. Do you know if there are any more of these hillbillies?" The woman shakes her head. "I think I got them all. Okay, then I'm good with giving you some privacy to get dressed. I'm going back to my truck. Come over when you are ready and we'll, well, we'll get out of here and call the cops. Sound like a plan?" She nods in response. "All right. I think one of these is your phone, too. You need me, holla. I'll be right over there." He points to the truck and leaves her to clean up.

Back at the F-150, Gary stores the SKO-12 before he checks on Persephone. The puppy's eyes light up when she sees her new human. His heart swells at the sight of her. He reaches into the crate and scratches the little dog's head. She licks at his hand and Gary allows himself to laugh for the first time in a month. Their bond is secure.

On the seat next to the crate is the mission briefing for his current job. Gary leans over and grabs it; he can't have the police finding a contract sitting out in the open. The contents spill out onto the truck's floorboards. "Are you fucking shitting me? Goddamnit!" Gary says as the picture of his mark stares back at him. He stands, motionless, gathering his thoughts until the puppy whines and paws at the crate. Gary picks up the papers and stuffs them back into the folder. "It's okay, girl. It's okay," he says to the dog. *No, it's not,* he tells himself, then closes the truck's door.

The woman is walking to him. She's now dressed and has the blanket wrapped around her. Gary stands in front of the truck, his arms crossed.

"I can't tell you how much...oh God, this...all this. I don't know. Who are you?" She shakes her head and starts crying.

"My friends call me Mac."

"I'm... I'm Wendy."

"Of course you are," Gary replies. "What brought you to this shithole if you don't mind me asking? I'm assuming it's for the same reason I came, to get a dog?"

"Yes... I came here to get a dog to protect me from my husband."

"Now why would you want to do that?" Gary asks.

"He's been trying to kill me for over a year. Getting rid of me gives him the free time to fuck his whores without splitting the bill."

"Do you have proof?"

She nods.

"Okay, then if you do, why don't you go to the authorities?"

"It isn't that easy, sir. He owns the police down here. Corruption is rampant in Cortland County. You ain't in Syracuse anymore, honey."

"Thank God I'm not, I'm from Georgetown, so go Hoyas, hah?" They laugh in unison. "It's good to know that after this with witnesses, you have an easy and convenient way to talk to them now, don't you?" She nods. "Hop in and we'll get you to a hospital and call someone who can take care of this for you." He opens the F-150's passenger door wide, almost folding it backward on the hinges before walking to the driver's side. He hops up into the cab and pulls the door shut.

"I can't reach the door handle," Wendy says, reaching out of the cab. Then she notices the folder on the dashboard. The picture of Gary's mark has slid back out. She stops breathing for a moment before asking, "Why do you have a picture of me in your truck?"

"Yeah, I know," Gary says. His right hand slips behind his back and withdraws the Desert Eagle 50AE holstered there. Startled, Wendy moves but it's too late.

He doesn't speak. Speaking is for movie villains and dead men. He is neither. He only squeezes the trigger.

The automatic handgun fires a .50 bullet at just over fifteen hundred feet per second. It strikes Wendy in the face and travels through her cranium before her ears register the roar of the weapon. The woman's head splits in two, well, more like half of it is disintegrated by the impact. The other side still has a stupid fucking "what the fuck is going on" look on its eye and half a lip while cranial fluid and blood slip out the bone cavity. The whole scene resembles a raw oyster in a half-shell, covered with cocktail sauce. Wendy tumbles out of the open door.

Behind him, in her crate, Persephone softly whimpers. "It's okay, girl, we're done here." Gary places the pistol on the seat, starts the truck's engine. He jerks it into reverse, and physics closes the passenger door for him.

The soothing whine of the puppy behind him settles Gary's anxiety ridden nerves. Within a few more moments, he forgets the night's stress. In an hour he knows he'll be in his hotel with Persephone, and tomorrow he'll be getting home early from this job. He waits until he's a few miles from the Bonney farm to make the call. The burner phone rings and the employer answers. Gary doesn't wait for him to speak.

"It's done."

"Whattaya mean it's done? I was just about to call you and tell you we lost contact again."

"Cos I smashed her phone. The news will be all over this, and not on account of me, so you better cover your ass. We'll stay on the line until the transfer comes through."

"Whattaya mean the news will be all over this? Mac? What are you talking about?"

"The transfer, Dennis. Now."

"All right already. But you gotta tell me what is going on." The alert comes across Gary's primary phone for a six-digit deposit in his Bank of the Bahamas account. Gary disconnects the call. He waits until Dennis calls back to smash the burner on the steering wheel, then throws the pieces out the window.

"I don't have to tell you jack or shit, motherfucker," the hitman announces as the window raises back up. Behind him, secure in her crate, Persephone sighs before letting out a little yip, as if to acknowledge her new master's words. Gary reaches behind with his right arm, and scratches the puppy's head. She licks his hand in response and something wet and cold grazes his wrist. Gary turns around and sees a boogery, gray lump on the pup's snout. Realizing it's some of the mark's brains, he freezes in momentary disgust. Before he can act, the dog's tongue snakes out and pulls the cranial matter into her mouth. The dog gobbles down the morsel with glee. Gary snorts a chuckle and feels his muscles relax as the stress of the day leaves his body. "That's right, little girl," Gary McCarthy says to Persephone. "Let's go home."

STEPHANIE SMITH

Legion

THE DEMON SLIPPED OUT of her like an afterbirth, all red and meaty. The pain paralyzed her limbs and sent her into alternating hot and cold shivers. She wanted to bang her skull against the bathroom sink rather than endure the episode.

Pass out. Die. Judith didn't care. No one would find her for days. It's not like she got any calls or visitors, and senile Estelle on the first floor was oblivious to the goings-on above. This pain was her only companion.

The lump beneath her moved. It slithered to a corner of the bathroom and licked itself clean. Clear, gelatinous goo squelched across the linoleum.

A thin film of water-colored haze skewed her vision, while her other senses remained acute. She heard the slick serpent tongue of the demon washing itself, the stink of sulfur and cervical fluid, the reek of contagion.

She struggled to remain still, but the stench was too much to bear. She leaned forward and vomited a colorful array of purples and greens. Within moments she felt better. The film over her eyes dissolved into a delicate sheet of dew and tears. She straightened herself out, took a long hard breath, and used the sleeve of her shirt to wipe her eyes and blow snot out of her nose.

What the hell just happened? Did she miscarry? She wasn't pregnant, was she? It was impossible. She rubbed a hand across her navel, felt the emptiness, the soreness of overworked muscles.

Kidney stones? A ruptured cyst? Christ, there had to be an explanation for the pain.

Refusing to accept the source of her agony, Judith sat panting in the corner by the tub. She made herself believe it was the pain playing tricks on her —until it started gagging on its own excrement and the sickness it licked off itself. The sound echoed off the shower tiles.

Judith screamed and rushed out of the bathroom. The end of the hallway moved farther away as she paced forward. Her head swirled. Her body slammed against the claustrophobic walls. The cold sweats returned. Somehow, she made her way to the kitchen. Grabbing a long steak knife from a drawer, she squeezed inside the tight pantry space by the doorway.

"What the hell was that?" she whispered, sinking into the darkness.

The choking and gagging din filled the apartment like toxic gas.

She remained crouched in the corner on the pantry floor between the wall and lowest shelf, clutching the knife handle, waiting for the noise to wane. The short silence tied her stomach in knots and tightened her chest. There was nothing worse than silence, even after enduring enough trauma to last the rest of her life —which may not be for very long.

A terrible screech pierced the air. The unbearable ripping of bones through flesh. A sound like thick liquid slapping against the wall. The sound permeated the apartment, rattling the windows and sending valuables crashing to the floor.

Somewhere, a voice wailed, deep and guttural, and undoubtedly male.

Judith placed a hand over her mouth, stifling her whimpers.

When the shadow peeked in through the crack below the door, she screamed again. She scooted her toes closer to her body to prevent its shadow from touching her.

It probed a few moments, then retreated.

She waited, counting infinite shallow breaths, until she felt confident the coast was clear. Knife in hand, her joints popped as she stood and opened the pantry door. Just a crack at first. She needed time to breathe. Her heart pounded as she braved the door open enough to slide through.

What she found outside was like the aftermath of a massacre: a murder scene without a body. Blood and black grease painted the walls in macabre abstraction.

The sizzling smells of meat and mucus wafted through the apartment. Unrecognizable gore caked the living room carpet. She bent down to examine it. It was slick in some places, lumpy like cottage cheese in others, and twitched and moved within the plush fibers of the carpeting. As she leaned in closer, she heard hissing and squeaking noises, and felt a tickle arc around her earlobe. Judith bolted to her feet as a colony of black Actaeon beetles rose from the floor and scuttled away into the walls, which rippled in discordant horror.

There was no escaping the sound. It burned her skin in symphonic resonance, becoming one with the chaos, becoming its mother, its queen.

She sensed a presence inside the apartment, messing with her mind and testing her sanity.

Shadow became substance. The figure appeared in the doorway of the living room, naked and streaming with blood, yet glowing with the confidence of an Olympian god. This was no god, however.

That, she was certain of.

His eyes dug deep into her soul, not just with hunger, but lust. They were pitch black, displaying an exquisite labyrinth no mortal was meant to see —let alone walk through. But he welcomed her to its mysteries. He was desperate for her to read the stories off his skin, to taste the succulent familiarity.

She dropped the knife and waltzed toward him. Fear and fascination prompted each anxious step. The balls of her feet sank into the carpet. She felt each prickly burr embedding itself inside her. Yes, there was pleasure in pain. Had she been wrong to resist it? She reached her arms out to her master, her slave. He was both lover and son. Angel and demon.

The cessation of pain in her womb —that great forest of bloody warfare —brought a sense of euphoria. No morphine necessary. There was no Demerol to ward off the inevitable. No knocking on Fat Larry's door begging for the fetty she knew she sold her soul to the Devil for. She's sinned so many times. Perhaps this was the penance, the glorious penance.

What had been gestating inside her —for centuries it seemed —had been born after a long, excruciating labor. It was a miracle. A golden shimmer in the blackest sky. She could walk on water now. She could part the sanguine sea, releasing the creatures imprisoned for so long below the earth.

"Come away with me," were his words. His only words. She wrapped her arms around him, drawing him in close. He pushed her hair away from her face and kissed her lips. She closed her eyes, feeling the journey begin, the heat on her face. The worm, gray and juicy, wriggled inside her mouth as she bit into it. It slid down her throat like a pill. She felt a grip inside her stomach, a vise clamping down, acid bubbling, burning away her insides to make room for something extraordinary.

His hands moved from the side of Judith's head down to her hips. They burned like melted wax. Each body part entered her inch by inch, forming shapes inside her like molten clay: from the fontanelles he still possessed on his skull, to his hot, engorged groin, all the way down to his sharp, pestilent toenails. Each shape was a line spoken in the darkest of poems. Each line became a stanza, which, in turn, became a powerful incantation.

Her brain created thoughts that weren't her own. Diabolical reveries. She was thinking for two now, wasn't she?

What was happening inside her? What was his plan? What was the purpose of longing for freedom, only to imprison yourself over and over like a terrible nightmare?

It wasn't like that. She felt him inside in the same way she felt herself inside. There was a consciousness there. An awareness. She was transcending the pain and sorrow. Her eyes were aflame with secrets —her brain pulsated with the knowledge of the universe's past, present, and future. She ached with yearning. How could one physical body house all this passion? Where was there to go from here?

The answer was *anywhere*. Any damn place she pleased. She would use whatever guise the moment required, take whatever precautions to protect herself and the legion she now housed within her.

She was so euphoric, she barely felt human, as if she was borrowing this body. She wasn't the one responsible for all the shit that had gone down. She was eager to know what it felt like inside the flesh and tear it all apart, to swim inside precious veins only to spill its contents, to live inside the illusion, the joy and pain, then to leave it all behind.

After all, it's not every day the abyss opens up to embrace you.

Without a second thought, Judith outstretched her arms and dove in.

ZOLTÁN KOMOR

Carlo, the Petrified Excrement from the Roman Era Steals My Wife

SINCE A SECURITY GUARD bit me in a Norwegian museum, every full moon I transform into fossilized Viking feces. This is a secret I've been hiding from my wife for a while. I'm afraid she'll think less of me if she finds out sometimes I'm a ninth-century Scandinavian warrior's poop. Fortunately, for a long time she hadn't noticed that she's been sleeping next to a piece of shit.

Eventually, the truth comes to light. On a full-moon night, she rolls over sleeplessly and her fingers wander to my side of the bed. She feels the hard, seven-inch-long stone rod under the blanket and thinks I'm in a mischievous mood. She pulls up her nightgown, squats over the ancient Viking shit in the dark, and slides it into her wet vagina. She quickly realizes the magnificent phallus doesn't belong to anyone. She turns on the light and worries until dawn, wondering where I am, and why a funny-looking brown rock is lying in my place. The first rays of the sun bring the answer when the gnarled stone dildo magically transforms back into her husband.

That's when I reluctantly explain the situation —she can't stop laughing. When she finally speaks, she asks, "So, how much could a more-than-thousand-year-old piece of poop be worth?"

I dismiss the question. Later, I catch her searching online auction sites and studying the fossil market and exchange rates with a furrowed brow.

The following month, my suspicion is confirmed.

"Enjoy your transformation," my wife whispers before bedtime, serving me catnip tea and tucking me in.

The sleepy light of the rising full moon slowly paints our bedroom blue. The next morning, I wake up inside a shattered display case, surrounded by numerous Viking relics: ancient medallions, dragon heads carved from wood, rusty axes... I find myself in a poshly furnished house and have to escape through the window, outrunning two guard Dobermans.

Upon returning home, I realized angrily, "That stupid bitch sold me to a collector last night."

Stepping into our bedroom, ready to yell, I find my wife cramming clothes into a suitcase.

She is trying to run away, but I catch her in time. She looks at me without the slightest sign of surprise and says, "Hurry, I've already packed your stuff, too."

"Uh... where are we going?" I ask, momentarily forgetting her betrayal.

"Away. The guy will soon realize that his recently acquired Viking feces is missing, and he'll definitely call the police. By then, we'll be abroad."

"Abroad? But where? And how? That damn Norwegian vacation already brought us down financially."

That's when my wife opens one of the fat suitcases —it's stuffed with cash. Who would have thought that the fecal fossil business could be so profitable? If anyone asks, a Viking poop is worth roughly thirty-five thousand dollars.

Since then, we've been traveling from country to country, selling shit or more precisely, selling me. Once a month, we manage to fool a collector. The transaction always takes place during a full moon, with me lying as a piece of shit in a lined suitcase. The next morning, I wake up in a display case, and my wife helps me escape from the house. By afternoon, we're in another country. First, we visit airports, then we buy our own plane. We have enough money —it's like we're shitting cash.

"We should slow down a bit. We've already gathered a ton of money," I say, sipping on a blue-colored cocktail on a yacht on the French Riviera.

My wife responds above the little umbrella sticking out of her glass. "As you wish, darling. You're the boss."

Soon it becomes clear that I'm just a little shit in the machine. After the next full moon, I wake up in another private villa.

"We have to stop this," I plead on the Amalfi Coast, sipping on lemon liqueur. "We're insatiable! What if one of those collectors locks me in a safe, and in the morning, I wake up unable to get out? Worse, what if they put me in a tiny safe that I can't fit in? I'd suffocate, my bones breaking while transforming back to my human form... We've been lucky so far, but..."

"Oh, stop whining so much," she scolds. "Let's just make it to Tunisia."

At that moment, I decide it's time for this little shit to stand up for itself. After all, I'm no ordinary piece of fecal matter —I'm the mighty excrement of a Scandinavian hero, a proud Viking warrior who lived on a diet of abundant meat and bran. I'm a hardened shit sausage.

"Okay, I'm done." The words slip out of my lips and hit like a piece of rock-hard excrement falling from a hairy Viking butt on the edge of a frozen marsh.

My wife doesn't respond —her eyeballs are about to burst with anger.

The next month, I awake in a display case. This time, when I return to the hotel where we reside, my wife is not busy packing as usual. Instead, she's lying there between the sheets with a total stranger.

"What's the meaning of this?" I snap.

She giggles, her voice like the clinking sound of coins being tossed together, and points with a lacquered finger at the greasy-haired, chubby Italian man who hasn't even bothered concealing the baby carrot-sized flaccid penis that he just pulled out of my wife.

"This is Carlo, the imperial shit," she says, introducing me to her bacon-scented lover. "Yes, you heard that right, a real Roman emperor's petrified feces, which is worth much more on the market than some dumb barbarian's dried-up dung. And Carlo can transform whenever he wants. Show him, Carlo."

The stocky man instantly transforms into a Roman-era pile of excrement on the expensive hotel sheets.

"As you can see, we don't need you anymore." My wife pulls a black, gleaming revolver from the desk drawer. Pointing it at me, she politely asks me to leave. As a token of her generosity, she throws a small bundle of euros at me, which should last me a few days.

Since then, she and Carlo are probably on the other side of the world. Meanwhile, I wander the Italian alleys selling my body to buy a plane ticket and follow their trail. I've decided to kill them both.

"I'm a real pile of shit, a hundred euros for a night! Just wait another thirteen days, and you can have it..." I encourage people on the street, but no one gets excited about the promise of petrified feces. So, I quickly give up on my murderous plan. Using the last of my euros, I arrange a kind of Viking funeral for myself. I hire a street kid to take me into a public toilet during the full moon and flush me down.

ABOUT THE AUTHORS

Christopher Michael Blake is the author of the horror novel Prey for Dawn and the mystery novella the Cape May Murders. Pyramid of the Parasite is his third book. He lives on the New Jersey shore with his family.

Hannah Brown is a speculative fiction writer who grew up exploring the rocks and crags of Welsh beaches and now lives in Tokyo Bay. By day she teaches writing to teenagers and by night she writes for her audio drama, Englewood After Dark.

J.N.C is a writer and artist who has lived and worked in Thailand, India, and the USA. He draws inspiration from the natural beauty, rich traditions, and mythologies of these cultures. He holds an MFA in creative writing from UNLV and primarily writes horror and science fiction. His horror fiction confronts the many faces of bullying and the culture that enables it. When he's not writing, he expresses his creativity through painting, signing his works with the same initials under which he publishes.

Aisling Campbell is a writer of horror and fantasy from a small seaside town in England, with dodgy genes and murderer's thumbs. She graduated from the University of East Anglia with a degree in English and creative writing, and spent the next four years trying not to die. In 2020 her short story, "Pigpen," was published in the anthology, C is for Cannibals, from Red Cape Publishing. Since then, she has published a variety of short stories in anthologies and webzines.

Claudia Christian began her career on stage as a child in Connecticut. She booked her first television job as a teenager in the hugely popular series Dallas and never stopped working. She has appeared in dozens of films and hundreds of hours of TV, and became a sci-fi icon with her portrayal of Susan Ivanova in the Hugo and Emmy-award-winning series, Babylon 5. She has worked with legends such as Morgan Freeman, Michael Keaton, Kirk Douglas, Burt Lancaster, Faye Dunaway, Bob Hope, Don Ameche, George Clooney, Nicolas Cage, Sharon Stone and more in her thirty-five-plus-year career. She lends her distinctive voice to dozens of the world's most popular games and is a published author of nonfiction and fiction. Claudia runs C Three Foundation and is a TEDx speaker. In 2014 she produced the award-winning documentary, One Little Pill, and is a passionate activist. Along with co-writer Chris McAuley she has created the popular Dark Legacies Universe and has co-authored a popular RPG universe called Musketeers vs. Cthulhu with him as well. Claudia resides in Los Angeles and London.

Speculative fiction author **Thomas R Clark** is a two-time Splatterpunk Award nominee in the categories of best novella 2021 for Bella's Boys and best short story 2022 for "Fireflies & Apple Pies." His most recent release is We Are 13, a collection of splatterpunk and folk horror. His journalism and entertainment critiques have appeared in Memento Mori Ink, where he is a senior columnist, Rue Morgue, Stranger With Friction, House of Stitched Magazine, This Is Infamous, and miscellaneous internet outlets. Tom lives in Central New York with his wife and their canine companions.

J. Rocky Colavito (aka Dr. Damned) writes horror of many types as he transitions into retired life after forty-plus years of college teaching. In addition to short stories appearing in collections and magazines—Grindhouse Resurrection, The Sirens Call, Madame Gray's Poe-Pourri of Terror, The Horror Zine, Carnage House, and a host of others—he is the creator of Buck Neighkyd, former porn star turned occult investigator. Buck's adventures can be followed in serial form in Caveman Magazine, and his origin story, "Creative Control," is available from Quest Omnimedia/The Caveman Adventure Library.

Rebecca Cuthbert is a dark fiction and poetry writer living in Western New York. She loves ghost stories, folklore, witchy women, and anything that involves nature getting revenge. Her debut poetry collection, In Memory of Exoskeletons, won a 2024 Imadjinn Award for Best Poetry Collection; the poems "Still Love" and "Bloodthirsty" were nominated for the Pushcart Prize, and "Still Love" was also nominated for a Best of the Net Award. Creep This Way: How to Become a Horror Writer With 24 Steps to Get You Ghouling was nominated for a Golden Scoop Award. Her hybrid fiction and poetry collection of feminist horrors, Self-Made Monsters, is out from Alien Buddha Press and a literary-speculative story collection, Six O'Clock House & Other Strange Tales, appeared in January 2025 by Watertower Hill Publishing. Her first children's book, Down in the Dark Deep Where the Puddlers Dwell, is out with Malediction and AEA Press. News about a spicy gothic novella, a ghost story collection, and a New Adult urban fantasy trilogy will be out soon.

Emma Rose Darcy emerged, fully formed, five years ago and slithered snakelike down from the mountains. She writes dark fantasy and horror. Emma suffers Basilar Migraine so sometimes real life is weirder than anything she could ever write. She stumbled upon horror, discovering authors like Joe Donnelly and G. M Hague among the Kings and

Rices in charity shop bookcases. It may be why she has a hunger for reading and writing body horror and transformation horror stories, hauntings and huntings.

Douglas Ford's short fiction has appeared in a variety of anthologies, magazines, and podcasts, as well as three collections: Ape in the Ring and Other Tales of the Macabre and Uncanny, The Infection Party and Other Stories of Dis-Ease, and Let's Cut Up Dad! and Other Stories of Transgressive Madness. His longer works include The Beasts of Vissaria County, Little Lugosi (A Love Story), The Trick, and Who Dies First. He lives on the west coast of Florida.

Senior citizen **Michael Fowler** writes humor and horror in Ohio. He has recent work at Little Old Lady Comedy, CommuterLit, Cosmorama, and Altered Reality. Michael spent his career in local government services and recommends a .22 revolver.

Lindsey B. Goddard is an author of dark fiction, poetry, and true crime, whose short stories have been published in e-zines such as Gamut Magazine as well as in anthologies such as Error Code by Riverfolk Books. Her work has been performed on popular podcasts like Creepy Podcast and Chilling Tales for Dark Nights. She is the author of four short story collections, two poetry books, and a novel, Ashes of Another Life. Lindsey lives in Missouri.

Alejandro Gonzales is a writer with stories in Brilliant Flash Fiction, Carnage House, Trembling with Fear, and elsewhere. He attributes the completion and success of this story and all others to the love of his life, current fiancée and soon-to-be wife, Angie.

Galen Gower lives in Memphis, Tennessee, with his infinitely patient and supportive wife, Caroline, and their spoiled rotten dog, Jane. His work has been published by Phobica Books, Undertaker Press, Carnage House, and Broken Antler Monthly, and has been adapted for audio by the Other Stories podcast. His work is meticulously curated from his imagination, nightmares, and mysterious radio transmissions from deep space, where nameless hordes envy our worlds and lust after our women.

Mark F. Grover lives in Des Moines, Iowa, with his husband, two dogs, and four cats. He retired early in 2021 from an office job where he worked twenty years without windows in a cubicle, and doesn't look back or regret that decision. With his new freedom, he enjoys writing and exploring different forms of written expression, and his work has appeared in various mediums over the years. His story, "The Fallen," appears in Dedication: An Anthology Dedicated to all Things Zombie, and his most recent print publication, the story, "It Only Stays Buried So Long," appears in the anthology, The Devil's Playground: A Horror Charity Anthology for Drug Addiction. Mark enjoys classic horror both in writing and movies, and also finding new authors with fresh perspectives. He also discovered he likes drawing, and works each day to find activities that will keep him away from social media, and his days are more pleasant because of this gradual shift. Mark enjoys doing projects with his husband and staying connected, pampering his pets, listening to music on vinyl and electronic devices, Legos, traveling, and living in the moment.

Kay Hanifen was born on a Friday the 13th and once lived for three months in a haunted castle. So, obviously, she had to become a horror writer. Her work has appeared in over one hundred anthologies and magazines. Her first anthology as an editor, Till the Yule Log Burns Out, was published in 2024. Her first novel, The Last Ballard, will debut this year. When she's not consuming pop culture with the voraciousness of a vampire at a twenty-four-hour blood bank, you can usually find her with her black cats.

Alexander Hay is an author who lives in North West England, an area not particularly known for having killer insects. True, wasps will ruin your picnic, but no one has been mercilessly hacked to death by a Cabbage White butterfly or been savagely maimed by a ladybird. Even if they were cosplaying as an aphid at the time. No sleazy eighties horror paperbacks ever covered swarms of man-eating dragonflies either. Pubic lice, meanwhile, remain forever defined by the seventies, disco, and the Atari VCS.

Rob Herzog is a screenwriter who has sold twelve short scripts and won prize money in three small screenwriting competitions. His short screenplay, "Creak and Shriek," was produced in 2019 by Mad Dreamer Entertainment. The other scripts he sold are in various stages of production. Rob received his master's degree in English composition from Northeastern Illinois University and was an English major at Monmouth College in Illinois. His interest in horror stories began during his childhood when he freaked out about spontaneous human combustion, killer bees, and the prospect of a bathtub shark attack. Rob lives in Chicago with his wife, Suzanne, and his daughter, Amy.

Kasey Hill is a critically acclaimed, award-winning writer from Virginia who works across genres, including urban fantasy, horror, thriller, paranormal romance, and metaphysical/New Age topics. She has authored both fiction and nonfiction, with a particular interest in Wicca. She specializes in Trinitarian Wicca as a historical archivist with an upcoming account of the shift from polytheism to monotheism in Abrahamic religions, having already published nonfiction works exploring the subject. Her fiction often dives into the supernatural and macabre, blending mythological elements with modern storytelling. She has published multiple novels, poetry collections, and short stories. Notable works include her Guardians of Light series in the mythology fantasy genre. Her poetry has also received recognition for its depth and emotional resonance. As she grows in the horror genre, she has a particular penchant for Southern Gothic storytelling, such as her adult horror novel, Devil's Claw, and her young adult horror series, The Whispering Spirits, featuring The Haunting at Foxwood Village and Dark Coven.

Ken Hueler teaches kung fu in the San Francisco Bay Area, where he also co-chairs the local Horror Writers Association chapter. His work has appeared in Weirdbook, The Sirens Call, Weekly Mystery Magazine, Andromeda Spaceways, and anthologies such as The Cozy Cosmic and Tales for the Camp Fire. He is an assistant editor at Space and Time magazine and, with Frances Lu-Pai Ippolito, co-edited the game fiction anthology, Winding Paths: A Playable Reading Experience.

Toshiya Kamei (she/they) is a queer Asian writer who takes inspiration from fairy tales, folklore, and mythology. Her short fiction has appeared in Daily Science Fiction, Galaxy's Edge, and elsewhere. Her piece, "Hungry Moon," won the October 2022 Apex Magazine microfiction contest.

Sutter Kang lives deep in the hills of Kentucky. He crawls out of his hole to go to work to make enough money to survive. Bella, the trusty hound, watches and advises in all his writing endeavors —she's a bit of a stickler. He plays guitar on occasion, though most would not call it musical. When not writing, he enjoys watching horror movies, listening to music, and reading.

Benjamin Kardos is a writer and musician from Washington state. His stories have been published by Carnage House, Black Cat Publishing, Wicked Shadow Press and The Sirens Call among others. He hosts the YouTube channel Reading Monstrosities featuring book reviews, author interviews and his musings on horror literature. He's employed as a cemetery groundskeeper where he does his best to put the fun in funeral.

Phil Keeling is a writer and playwright. He is the author of the novella, Juice, along with a smattering of short stories, essays, and plays that have been published, performed, and politely tolerated all over the United States. He is the co-host of Pixel Lit: the best (read: only) podcast dedicated to video game novelizations. He lives somewhere in the woods with his wife and son.

Zoltán Komor lives in Nyiregyhaza, Hungary. He writes surreal short stories and has work in Horror Sleaze and Trash, Drabblecast, The Phantom Drift, Gone Lawn, Bizarro Central, Bizarrocast, Thrice Fiction Magazine, The Missing Slate, The Gap-Toothed Madness, Wilderness House Literary Review, Kafka Review, and more. His first book in English, titled Flamingos in the Ashtray: 25 Bizarro Short Stories, was released by Burning Bulb Publishing in 2014. His second English title, Tumour-djinn, was released by Morbid Books in the same year. His third collection, Turd Mummy, was released by Strangehouse Books in 2016. His latest novel, The Radiator Boy and The Holly Country, was published by Potter's Grove Press in 2021.

Jack Lantey was born in California but was quickly excommunicated to the wastelands of the Midwest. Growing up an asthmatic between the rows of corn, he found safety in movies, comics, and books. A former playwright, comic book writer, and filmmaker, he now works as a commercial producer by day and steals time to write at night when he's not busy with the five dogs he sublets a room from.

Born in Long Island, New York, raised in Queens, and marooned in Germany, **Moaner T. Lawrence** (aka Moaner the Moanarian) was building pumpkins out of his Duplos before he could form complete sentences. Moaner began his career as the face of Rue Morgue Magazine's German branch in 2011. Also a regular contributor to Germany's largest horror magazine, Virus, in 2014, the Pumpkin Knave ascended to assistant editor of Pseudopod from 2015 to 2018. In addition to a collection of cultural and art articles relating to the genre, Moaner has also published short fiction including "Bad Newes from New England," a colorful re-imagining of the first American Thanksgiving, "The Great American Nightmare," a Lovecraftian yarn where C'thulhu is inaugurated as the forty-fifth president of the United States of America, and "Beholden," a short horror sequel to the novel, The Catcher in the Rye, released on Wattpad in commemoration of J.D. Salinger's one hundredth birthday.

A fan of the fantastical and frightening, **Shannon Lawrence** writes horror and fantasy. Her stories appear in over sixty anthologies and magazines in addition to her collections. Her nonfiction work, The Business of Short Stories, and debut urban fantasy novel, Myth Stalker: Wendigo Nights, are available where books are sold. You can get to know her as a co-host of the Mysteries, Monsters, & Mayhem podcast. When not writing, she's hiking through the wilds of Colorado and photographing her magnificent surroundings, where, coincidentally, there's always a place to hide a body or birth a monster.

Aaron Lebold is an author of psychological horror, sometimes dabbling in extreme elements. He came into his love of the genre at an early age with a discovery of slasher films. While always interested in writing, he didn't make any serious attempts at it until 2017. Since then he has completed several novels and novellas. His work can be found with Gloom House Publishing, D&T Publishing, Shadow House Press, and Broken Brain Books, and his short stories appear in various anthologies. Some of his shorts have been narrated for the Cryo Pod Tapes. His novel, Born Sick, took second place at the Godless 666 awards for best novel of 2022.

Basile Lebret is French and lives south of Paris where the cities meet the trees. His work has been published in Monstroddities by SlicedUp, Strange Weeds by Atonic Vision, Step Into the Light by Bag of Bones, Home by Off Topic Publishing, Even Cozier Cosmic from Underland Press, and The Devil's Playground by Dark Moon Rising. In France, his work can be found in Les Feux de la Revolte published by Lufthunger Club.

Chris McAuley is a New York Times best-selling and award-winning writer, known for co-creating the StokerVerse franchise with Dacre Stoker, a continuation of Bram Stoker's legacy spanning graphic novels, books, audio dramas, games, and television. He is also the co-creator of Dark Legacies, a sci-fi franchise with Claudia Christian of Babylon 5. Chris has contributed to iconic franchises like Doctor Who, Star Trek, and Battlestar Galactica. His Three Musketeers vs. Cthulhu RPG earned an ENNIE nomination and became a comic series. Chris co-owns X-G3 Productions and is an executive producer of the award-winning film, The Stranded Warrior. His work has been recognized at film festivals worldwide, including wins at Virgin Spring Cinefest and Sweden Film Awards.

Chris W. McGuinness is a horror writer who lives and works on California's Central Coast. His work has appeared in Chthonic Matter Quarterly, Lovecraftiana Magazine, Fraidy Cat Quarterly, and in Schlock webzine, among many other publications. He is an active member of the Horror Writers Association.

Holly Nicholls has been writing since she could hold a pencil. She lives in the U.K., England, with her husband-to-be, is a mother of one, and has way too many stories in her head that need to escape. She enjoys writing in a variety of genres, from children's books including her book, Curious King Fox, to stomach-churning horror, to poetry. And she will continue to be diverse in what she writes.

Drew Nicks is a writer of horror and weird fiction. His work has been published by the likes of The Ghastling, Gehenna and Hinnom Press, Novel Noctule, Vaughan Street Doubles, and others. He currently resides in Moose Jaw, SK, Canada.

Paul O'Neill is a short story writer with more than fifty published tales. Those works have appeared in the No Sleep Podcast, Scare Street, Sinister Smile Press, Crystal Lake, The Horror Zine, and many other publications and competitions. He runs Short Story Club on Substack where he and over two hundred readers analyse the classics on a regular basis. He lives in Fife, Scotland.

Nora B. Peevy is a cat trapped in a human's body. Please send help or tuna. She toils away for JournalStone-Trepidatio Publishing as a submission reader, writes reviews for Hellnotes, and reads scripts for the H.P. Lovecraft Film Festival. She writes articles for Weird Wide Web, is a syndicate author for Thrill Ride eZine, and works as an editor for Baynam Books Press, also narrating their podcast, the Midnight Manuscripts. Her quirky tales are published by Eighth Tower Press, Carnage House, The Sudden Fictions Podcast, and elsewhere. For the Sake of Brigid, her first novelette, came out in 2024, and her first short story collection debuts from JournalStone-Trepidatio in 2025. She is also a visual artist, and dreams of her turtle painting in watercolor alongside her.

Corinne Pollard is a disabled U.K.-based horror writer and poet, published with Black Hare Press, Three Cousins Publishing, Carnage House, Graveside Press, Inky Bones Press, The Ravens Quoth Press, A Coup of Owls Press, and Raven Tale Publishing. Also, Corinne is co-editor for the Yorkshire anthology Aire Reflections with her dark stories and poetry inside. With a degree in English lit and creative writing, Corinne has always enjoyed the world of dark fantasy. Aside from writing, Corinne enjoys metal music, visiting graveyards, and shopping for books to read.

C. C. Rossi, who also writes under the name Edward R. Rosick, lives in the urban wilds of Michigan. He has published numerous tales of speculative fiction in magazines and anthologies including Pulphouse, DOA, and Monstrous Tales volumes 2 and 3. His short story, "Dead Air," received honorable mention in the 15th annual Year's Best Fantasy and Horror anthology, edited by Ellen Datlow. His horror novel, Deep Roots, was published in 2022. His speculative fiction short story collection, Where the Grass Don't Grow and Vultures Sing, is due out in 2025 by Baynam Books Press.

Matt Scott is the author of more than eighty published horror stories. He has four stand-alone collections with one on the way, as well as a volume of poetry. He lives in southern Colorado with his wife, Heather, and their ever-growing gaggle of furry friends. He loves to hike, play piano, throw knives, and paint, and enjoys spending time outdoors with his family exploring the beautiful state of Colorado.

Stephanie Smith is a writer and poet from Scranton, Pennsylvania. Her work has appeared in such publications as The Horror Zine, Raven Cage, the Chamber, Dark Moon Digest, the Literary Hatchet, Danse Macabre, and Illumen. She cites Clive Barker, John Skipp & Craig Spector, and the late Charlee Jacob as major influences.

Zackary L. Stillings lives in Columbus, Ohio, with his husband and Boston Terrier. He is an attorney by day, but spends his free time growing hot peppers, playing Dungeons & Dragons, and exploring the city's breweries. He is an avid horror fan, and loves uncertain endings and morally ambiguous characters.

Michael Errol Swaim is a horror and fantasy author and proud citizen of the Cherokee Nation of Oklahoma who survived a liver and kidney transplant in 2019. His first horror publication, which also appears in this volume, can be found in Issue 3 of Carnage House, and his stories and poems also appear in several anthologies including Nature Triumphs: A Charity Anthology Of Dark Speculative Fiction from Dark Moon Rising Publications, The Horror Zine, and Dead Girls Walking: The Red Volume from Wicked Shadow Press, with many more on the way. He also writes film and book reviews for the Weird Wide Web. He lives in northeast Oklahoma with his wife Mandy, his kids, and four cats.

Jon Carroll Thomas is a dark fiction writer, event coordinator, and corporate grocery store peon. He lives in a little log house in Raleigh with his beautiful wife, charming son, and six spoiled rescue cats. He leads the Quails from the Crypt book club through Quail Ridge Books and is a founding member of the North Carolina chapter of the Horror Writers Association. His stories appear in Whetstone: Amateur Magazine of Pulp Sword and Sorcery, Cosmic Horror Monthly, and Chthonic Matter Quarterly.

Tamika Thompson is author of The Curse of Hester Gardens (forthcoming, Erewhon). A former journalist and producer, she is also author of Unshod, Cackling, and Naked (Unnerving Books), which is the 2024 Next Generation Indie Book Awards WINNER for Horror, and which Publishers Weekly calls "powerful," "unsettling," and "terrifying," as well as author of Salamander Justice (Madness Heart Press). Her work has appeared in several speculative fiction anthologies as well as in Interzone, Prairie Schooner, The New York Times, and Los Angeles Review of Books, among others. Her long fiction tale, "Bridget Has Disappeared," was translated to Italian for Independent Legions' Molotov Magazine. She received a Bachelor of Arts in Political Science from Columbia University and a Master of Arts in Journalism from the University of Southern California. She lives in the San Francisco Bay area, where she hosts her own blog and newsletter, Tamika Talks Terror.

Tim Tolbert is a Pittsburgh-based writer. His work has appeared in ABSENCE, Junto, and The Sirens Call.

JP Townsend is an American/Australian writer of dark fiction. His work has been published previously in Aurealis and Midnight Echo, and he was the 2023 winner of the AHWA Robert N Stephenson short fiction award. He lives in Brisbane.

Michelle Vizinau spends her days bending to the will of a three-year-old. She's a native San Franciscan who studied creative writing at SFSU, and her work has appeared in Hellbound, Spinetingler Magazine, and Resident Aliens. In her downtime, she writes stories and moderates for a horror film appreciation group.

Valerie B. Williams has short fiction published with Flame Tree Press, Dark Recesses Press, Grendel Press, Death Knell Press, and The Sirens Call e-zine, among others. Her short story, "Red Lipstick," appears in the 2024 Dastardly Damsels anthology from Crystal Lake Publishing, and her debut novel, a supernatural thriller titled The Vanishing Twin, dropped from Crossroad Press in 2024. Valerie spins twisty tales from her home in central Virginia, which she shares with her very patient husband and equally patient golden retriever. When not writing, she can be found reading and drinking either tea or wine, depending on the time of day.

Amanda Worthington is a writer of horror, science fiction, and fantasy, and often finds herself blending them all together to create some new hellscape. Her favorite subgenre is cosmic horror and her least favorite is gothic—her newest work-in-process combines them both. She founded and serves as current chair for Horror in the Heartland, the Heartland chapter of the HWA, or, if you prefer, "The HWA chapter for Midwesterners outside of Chicago." Serving members across eight states, Horror in the Heartland seeks to elevate horror in the rural outposts of the Bible Belt. Amanda has been in several issues of Carnage House because she's deranged that way. She's also had work published in Space and Time and The Sirens Call. When not writing, she's probably playing Zelda or trying to argue with her two recalcitrant black cats, Apollo and Artemis.

The Carnage House Editors

One is the product of twenty years of creative writing teachers' lies. One is a British brat with the attention span of a goldfish. One ate a thesaurus and crapped out a novella. One is the least scary horror writer, possibly ever. We'll leave you to guess which is which, but one thing we all share is a love of horror and splatterpunk. We are also unapologetically left-leaning, pro-LGBTQIA+, pro-BIPOC, pro-women, and anti-Nazi. Nazi punks, fuck off.

Josh Darling, founder and editor-in-chief, fell in love with the works of Clive Barker and the anthologies published by Pocket and Del Books in the nineties. Throughout high school, he wrote gross stuff. Some of it got published. He started abusing words professionally in 2014 as a ghostwriter and book doctor. Under his name, his stories have appeared in anthologies with Richard Chizmar, Elizabeth Massie, Philip Fracassi, and Gwendolyn Kiste. His horror fiction has appeared in The Horror Zine, The Sirens Call, and numerous publications from Hellbound Books. He started Carnage House feeling there are many publishers of splatter/extreme horror books but few for short stories. As an editor, he looks to help writers develop their craft, but primarily, he's famous for being unknown.

Jacque Day is the Carnage House founding co-editor-in-chief, a staff member of Crystal Lake Publishing, and the former longtime managing editor for the New Madrid journal of contemporary literature. She has zigged and zagged as a magazine journalist, book and magazine editor, radio correspondent, TV producer, motion picture crew member, and writer-for-hire. Jacque has an MFA in creative writing (but please don't hold that against her) and has shared tables of contents with many friends —and once, with Louisa May Alcott. She lives in her home state of Pennsylvania with her childhood-sweetheart husband, Art. In the cape cod they share, some doors remain unopened to this day, a peculiarity that inspired the anthology, That Darkened Doorstep, featuring her story, "Seeking a Good Woman."

Holly Nicholls (the British one) has craved truly scary stories for as long as she can remember. Always the odd child growing up, sitting in her bedroom to write or read when everyone was outside playing, she never left that creative phase. She has written a vast range of stories, from the dark romance adult smut novella, Rain of Calm, to flash fiction in exactly 123 words (it isn't as easy as you think!), to a children's picture book. She also writes poems when inspiration hits. But overall, she has a thing for fear and what causes it. She will proudly table herself as a variety author and a proud editor at Carnage House.

Michael Errol Swaim began his career writing fantasy at an early age, but that failed, and he stopped. Twenty five years later he returned to writing and turned to the horror genre. To his surprise, Michael began getting things published. His work can be found in many places such as Carnage House, The Horror Zine, Dark Moon Rising Publications, Hellbound Books, and many other publications, zines, and podcasts. His horror book, Absorbed By Excrement, is forthcoming. He lives in Green Country, Oklahoma, with his wife Mandy, his kids, and four cats.